EDITS

ROSALIE STEVENS

© 2024 Pellen LLC. All rights reserved.

No part of this book may be reproduced, distributed, or transmitted in any form or by any means, including photocopying, recording, or other electronic or mechanical methods, without the prior written permission of the publisher, except in the case of brief quotations embodied in critical reviews and certain other noncommercial uses permitted by copyright law.

ISBN: 979-8-9908261-2-0

First Edition

This is a work of fiction. Names, characters, places, and incidents either are the product of the author's imagination or are used fictitiously. Any resemblance to actual persons, living or dead, events, or locales is entirely coincidental.

For more information, visit rosaliestevens.com

When you're with me, I want your full attention.
Good girl, now I want you between the sheets of my pages.

- Your book boyfriend

For Trigger Warnings please visit
www.rosaliestevens.com/edits-trigger-warnings

To my Fruitbat, *who has been my everything—my support, my love, my friend, and my family. Thank you for always being there for me.*

To my Rootie Toot, *keep dancing my sweet girl*

To my Sunshine girl, *keep smiling, you light up my world.*

To all my readers *who took a chance on my book, thank you for embarking on this journey with me.*

Prologue

The wind kicks up again, billowing past the students and their windbreakers. It gusts through the great land gap between the eastern ocean and the Midwest unit before sweeping through the schoolyard, setting the swings creaking audibly. The schoolyard is a mix of concrete and patches of trampled grass, with a few tired trees swaying in the breeze. The sun is still low, casting a mellow light on the thirty-three students here to test for a scholarship. I stand at the end of the line, scraping my fingernails against my corduroy pants, trying to wedge my fingertips into the grooves, aimlessly stroking the rough velvety texture. A few other children talk in muted tones, their solemnity clear in the way they stand, shoulders hunched against the wind. The pressure of the test and the early hour create a somber atmosphere, the stillness punctuated only by the creaking swings and occasional whispers. I glance at the kid next to me, mumbling facts to himself. He pushes his thick-framed glasses up his face with pudgy fingers, then wipes his sweaty forehead. I look back down at my pants, my mother's voice echoing in my head.

"Don't rub your pants, you'll rub a hole into them," I remember her saying as I dig my fingernails into the thin grooves and scrape harder. "Kira, you're driving me nuts! Stop that nervous behavior," her voice scolds in my mind. I chew on my lip and scrape until it becomes audible, despite Chubster's muttering. An adult walks past, carrying a box. His slacks are militarily pressed, shoes black and polished, shirt starched white with a pristine collar. No tie, I notice. My mother would approve. She is neurotically tidy, insisting on a level of neatness that borders on obsession. Everything in our apartment is meticulously organized, from the color-coded pantry to the perfectly aligned furniture. She often says that appearances matter more than anything else. A wrinkle in clothing or a scuff on shoes would send her into a frenzy of cleaning and straightening. She often forces me to clean for hours until my skin cracks, scrubbing every surface until it gleams, making sure there isn't a speck of dust or a streak left behind. He stops at the classroom door, scans his wrist, and the door opens with a whoosh. The chip implanted in his wrist identifies him, just like the chip we all have. These chips are used for everything: opening doors, purchasing items, and even taking attendance at school. The building is old, with peeling paint and cracked window frames. All the kids straighten up, preparing to follow the proctor inside. I glance at the fence surrounding our city, creating an illusion that instead of a wall the unit extends into the forest. The wall flickers as the forest image briefly fades out and reappears, creating the illusion that there's no barrier at all. There's an urban legend that it flickers when someone runs into it, either trying to escape or end their life. The kids like to sing,

A flicker here, a flicker there, touch the wall if you dare; a zap, a scream, and no one will care.

I SHUFFLE into the room with the rest of the children. By the time I enter, the other kids have grabbed their tablets and taken seats. The room is filled with old metal desks and chairs, from years of use. There is one large window that lets in natural light, but somehow it fails to reach the room. There's a degradation to the space that seems to suck up all light, casting everything in a dull, lifeless hue. The proctor holds out a tablet for me, his serious expression matching his emerald green eyes, eyes almost too green. An Edit.

"Do you need help?" he asks, his voice clear and refined, a product of endless cultivation. I shake my head and take the only seat left, at the front. The metal chair scrapes loudly against the tile floor as I adjust my position. The metallic desks are grooved and etched on their surfaces from years of nervous students. Some have initials or messages scratched into them.

"My name is Magnus Faust. I'm your proctor. You will have two hours to complete the examination. Scan your wrist and you may begin." When he finishes speaking, the kids all look down at their tablets. I center my tablet on the desk and tap the screen, scanning my wrist when prompted. The chip in my wrist identifies me, allowing the test to begin. The screen shifts to the countdown: sixty seconds before the test opens. The proctor leans against the front desk, his long legs crossed at the ankles, arms folded over his well-built chest, eyes flicking around, cataloging each child. The time ticks down to zero, and the first question appears. The room fills with near-silent taps as we work through the test. The timer moves to the top left corner, reminding us of the remaining time. I click through the questions, typing answers or selecting multiple-choice options. Occasionally, I work out a math question. I try to ignore the sniffling nose of the girl next to me, but it distracts me now and then. I look up when I feel the proctor's eyes on me. He's stopped scanning the room and is now watching me solely. I look back down at my tablet and continue to work, but occasionally, my eyes flick up at him. I wonder if he thinks I'm cheating, but I'm not, so I just keep working. The timer begins to flash red as the time ends. I answer my last question before the tablet locks. I look up at the proctor, who finally stops looking at me and glances around at my classmates. Relieved expressions cross some faces, while others look concerned. The tapping on screens ceases. Without prompting, I stand up and place my tablet on the proctor's desk.

"Please take your seat again," he says. I go to take the tablet back, but he places his big palm on top of it. I scratch my pants and walk back to my seat. "Please stay seated if your name is called. The rest of you may leave," the proctor announces.

"Kira Tracer." The classroom waits to see if any other names will be called, but the proctor stops at one name. The children look around in confusion before rising from their seats, placing their tablets on the desk, and filing out. I scratch my pants as I sit and watch the last of the children disappear through the door, leaving me alone with the proctor. He's still looking at me as if assessing me, and I feel my skin prickle with discomfort. "I didn't cheat," I say when I can't stand the silence anymore.

"No one said you did," he replies, still not explaining what he wants with me. I scratch my pants again, and his eyes fly down to watch the gesture. I stop immediately and flatten my palm on top of my thigh. His eyes flick back up to my face.

"Kira, how is your family life?" he asks, his voice carrying such an even cadence that my throat clenches with a need to adjust his speech. No one should sound too perfect. My mouth flicks inside, my tongue hitting the back of my teeth, playing with the words he said, "Kira, pause—how—is—your—family —life?" Unhurried, Edits are famous for how slowly they do things. His eyes follow my mouth's movement, and he tilts his head to the side, watching with interest.

"My family life?" I ask finally. He seems unconcerned with my delayed response.

"Yes, Kira, are you happy at home?"

"It is fine," I say, an automatic response, one I haven't even thought about before answering.

"Please, Kira, take your time before answering," he replies, looking down at his perfectly trimmed nails, polished so well that I can see the glint from where I sit. I am fine, fine with my family life. My mother can be critical, but that's how mothers are.

"It's fine," I say again. He looks up at me, his green eyes narrowing and his lips pursing.

"Very well, good day," he says, standing up from his relaxed position in front of the desk. I am surprised by his quick dismissal but do not argue. I scrape my metal chair against the floor, ensuring maximum sound before standing up. I walk up, and just before I pass the desk, he grabs my wrist and stops me.

"Kira, how is your family life?" he asks again, and I look down at his large hand encircling my thin wrist. I glare up at him.

"Is this part of the test, or are you hoping to become an addition?" I ask, my voice steady but with a hint of defiance. Everyone knows Edits don't have families. His serious face slowly spreads into a large grin.

"Good girl," he says, releasing my wrist and patting me on the back, sending me out of the classroom. "Nice meeting you, Spark," he adds as I walk away, the nickname lingering in the air, leaving me confused and a little annoyed.

Chapter 1

To grow into the person you are meant to be, you must first shed who you were.

- Plymouth Prep Handbook, Page 6.

eight years later

I scrape the wool of my skirt. My fingernail playing with the piling, my sensitive tactile receptors in my fingertips sense each thread, every weave. I scrape so hard I start to experience a burn on my finger pad, friction threatening to light a spark. I am staring straight ahead with the rest of the students who are lined in their dark blue and green plaid uniforms, we are distorted carbon copies. The uniforms are the same, the stance is the same, and only the hair and skin color vary. I am standing at the end of the line vaguely aware that words are being spoken by instructor Belfor. The large gymnasium echoes her voice, each word is a strain on my ears. I try to focus on each syllable uttered, to string the words together but my ears stumble only picking up the cadence and the rise and fall of her tones. The door opens at the far right, opposite end from where I am standing.

"Everyone, here he comes. Welcome our guest. Dr. Faust." Instructor Belfor announces proudly but I barely register her words. I'm too busy scraping my skirt and creating friction to listen. I'm aware in my periphery, that a new entity has entered the assembly, they stop in front of us, in front of the teachers. The girls around me shuffle and straighten but I don't make the same effort. I just want to listen to the rise and fall of my breathing and the breathing of the girl next to me. I want to hear the echo of voices bounce off the walls and then slide into my ears.

"Thank you." I hear a male voice say, *a male voice.* The sound of a man makes my head snap up. The girl next to me starts to lean forward to get a better look, blocking my view. If I wanted to see him I'd have to make a scene. I listen to the deep baritone voice fluctuate and it tickles the insides of my ears traveling up into my eardrum, stroking my brain before lodging itself in my receptors, before it conjures a memory. My spine shivers with familiarity, with recognition, that voice is an echo of a life that once was. It's a voice that has slithered in and out of my dreams, it speaks my name. It calls out to me and beckons. I let the feeling wash over my senses, where is this voice from? I close my eyes listening to the even cadence, words pronounced in simple clear perfection. A face slips into view, a distorted image with blazing eyes, infecting my vision. My scratching continues, the coarse texture of wool is a balm to my nerves, I need to feel the rough texture to drag me into my body. I open my eyes when his words fade and I listen to his deep vibration fill the room as he starts to greet the students in order.

"Nice to meet you, Augusta," he says. "Nice to meet you April " and so on until he reaches the girl next to me. She finally moves out of the way and he steps in front of me. I know those eyes, I know that face. He was the man who had proctored the MD scholarship exam that I failed as a child. My mother had punished me severely for that failure. If I close my eyes I can still feel the pain in my shoulder, I can still feel the pain shake through my bones. His name sits at the tip of my tongue, Maximus? I flick my front tooth with my tongue, trying to flick his name back into my hippocampus. My hippocampus fails to pull his name from the recesses of my mind. I remember his name starts with an M. He is so young and I struggle with the memory I have of him as a child. When I was a little girl, he was an old man, but here he stands in front of me, nearly an adolescent, no older than twenty-five. He stretches out his hand and clasps my hand in his, his long masculine fingers curling around my thin feminine hand. His grip is firm enough that it suppresses my flesh under his closed digits which are dusted with blonde hairs. His forefinger strokes the top of my hand and his blazing eyes stare right into me, through me.

"Nice to meet you," he says. Instead of pulling away as he did with all the girls he lingers. His eyes search my face and his lips part ever so slightly, the plump bordeaux of his Cupid's bow pulling open forming a slot, a perfect place to rest a lazy cigarette, but in its place is a void. He looks at me with those emerald eyes, those haunting eyes that fill my dreams, distorted, some phantasmic aberration that is woven into the tapestry of my mother's death.

"Kira," he says so quietly, only I can hear him. That name feels strange in my ears but my hippocampus recognizes it, conjures it to the forefront of my mind. It's a name I haven't heard since I was a little girl. His hesitation to move on blisters in his eyes as his pupils dilate, dimming the shining green irises. His face is a symmetric masterpiece, nature put to shame as the golden ratio is applied to such a fine detail that god himself would not approve. God prefers to make his people with flaws, asymmetry drawn with an unsteady hand, it's that discord that puts people at ease. The crown of his head hosts a thick swath of blonde hair, not a single strand is in disorder. His tall forehead slopes down to a pair of thick blonde eyebrows that frame his evenly placed eyes. The planes of his face curve over his high cheekbones dipping in the flat hollows of his cheeks and flaring out ever so slightly as his jaw takes its place. He has a small crease between his eyes, the only mark against his flawless skin. His frown is contemplative and I'm drawn to the imperfection. It's the thing that makes him seem real. The pause is the briefest of moments, only an astute observer could know that he is hesitating, but I know, and he knows and that is all that matters. I want to whisper his name back, I want to keep him in front of me, I want to hear his baritone voice resonate, sending a cone of sound wave directly toward me. But I still don't remember his name, I can't bring the name forward so I settle for an unsatisfactory

"Sir". It slips past my lips and lands in his ears, the crease between his eyes deepens, and disappointment momentarily flashes in his eyes before he takes a step back. He pivots and returns to the front of the assembly. As soon as he says farewell, he leaves and I watch his well-muscled back as he walks out. The points of his shoulder blades are bunched up in tension and the sudden urge to reach out to him and soften his mien is strong. It's the same urge I have to scratch at my thigh.

We all stand still, watching him go, and wait for the doors to whoosh closed before the teachers dismiss us. The assembly hall echoes with the shuffle of feet and murmured conversations as students prepare to leave. As soon as we step into the hallways, the girls begin gushing over the newcomer. The corridor, with its pristine white walls and polished floors, amplifies their excited chatter. They don't know what I do, that he is an Edit. They didn't see the unusual reflective surface in his pupils; they saw only the organic nature of his artificial eyes. They don't hear the rise and fall of his voice or the flawless way his words are formed. They don't hear how he takes his time. I listen as they argue over small things, catty things.

One of the girls sneers, "Please, you wouldn't stand a chance with him, even if you somehow could win the mentorship program."

"As if you could," another retorts, and the bickering and competing continues. They attack each other easily, readily. This is one of the many reasons I've failed to make friends at Plymouth, my roommate is the only one whom I tolerate and the only one who seems to tolerate me back. I can almost say we are friends, but it is a friendship designed by the environment. She finds me as the girls scatter into their respective groups. I'm prepared for her to slide up to me because, like me, she isn't well-liked. We walk in silence, listening to the other girls gossip. The hall is filled with chattering females burgeoning on womanhood. Their hormonal drive to pursue this Edit masquerading as a man is a palpable musk in the air. The corridor leading to the cafeteria is lined with plain, identical doors leading to dorm rooms, each one indistinguishable from the next. The scent of institutional cleaner mingles with the faint aroma of food drifting from the cafeteria.

THE CAFETERIA'S tall windows bask the long tables in an afternoon glow, casting long rectangular shadows along the floor. The space buzzes with the noise of clinking cutlery and trays, punctuated by bursts of laughter and conversation. We walk into the line with the rest of the girls, all queuing for their lunch, trays in hand, shuffling past the chicken and kale. I briefly wonder what real chicken tasted like, this 3D-printed chicken is all I've ever known. No one eats real meat anymore, a relic of a "barbaric time" as my history book once called it. We each take a portion and slide the plates onto our trays. I wait while June pours water into a glass and then she looks over at me and decides to pour me one too. She places it on my tray, and we walk companionably over to our usual table. The table is near the windows, allowing us to look out at the meticulously maintained grounds of Plymouth Academy. The greenery outside contrasts sharply with the dreary antiseptic environment inside. As we sit down, the ambient noise of the cafeteria fills the background, but it fades as we focus on our meal. The warmth of the afternoon sun through the windows adds a slight comfort to the otherwise clinical setting. I twist the plastic around the cutlery, peeling it open before sliding the knife and fork free. I wait till June has done the same and then I ask the question I've been wanting to ask since we left the assembly..

"June what was that all about?" I ask and she rolls her eyes at me, but it's a friendly gesture, one that speaks of fondness and not malice.

"You weren't paying attention again?" I never listen to what teachers say, I can't focus on their words. My brain sifts the words like sand through a sieve. My attention if they can get it, circles around their tones, phrasing, and cadence. I shrug my shoulders at June and she explains what I missed.

"An examination series is coming up, and the person who performs the best will receive mentoring from Dr. Faust," June shares.

"Oh. What does that mean, mentored?" I ask because I have no idea what that implies. This is my last year at Plymouth and I don't know what I'll do after, I don't like to think about it. The state will no longer be responsible for me, which means I'll have to fend for myself. I have applied for college scholarships. I'm unsure about my life's direction, but education is the only certainty I have.

"I don't know, they didn't go into details. I hope it's me though, God can you imagine being in close proximity to him?" she asks while dreamily, tilting her head to the side. I ignore the comment because I can imagine it because my hand still feels the depressions from where he touched me, the top of my hand clings to the ghost of his gentle stroke. I cut a piece of chicken with a plastic knife that has been made from some kind of biodegradable food. The faux-plastic cutlery is meant to be dissolvable in water, which is a good thing for the planet but they fail to do a good job of working as cutlery. The warm chicken warps the grooved teeth of my knife, it's already dissolving into my meal.

"I hope it is me," June says unconcerned by my lack of response, and takes a crunchy bite of her kale chip.

"I don't see why it couldn't be," I respond and take a bite of my chicken.

"What about you, it could be you," she says, but there is a look in her eye that says, "I hope it's not you because I don't want you to win.

"Yes, it could, I'll try as hard as anyone," I say because I'd also like to be mentored. I want to see those emerald eyes that hold a glint of elusive blue.

"Oh my god, really?" June whines and I look up from my chicken.

"What?" did she expect me to stand aside and not try? Why would she ask that of me? I am entitled to try as much as anyone.

"Well, we both know it's going to be you." June stabs her chicken, breaking the flimsy knife in the process.

"That's not true, I don't understand why you think that."

"It is, you always get top placement." June throws her fork and knife down on the table and scoots her chair back intending to stand up. She gives the table one final shove before stomping out of the cafeteria, leaving her unfinished lunch tray on the table in front of me. I sit at the table with my fork filled with chicken. I'm stunned because I always thought we were at least allies if not friends. Can it be that June is jealous of me? She has never acted this way.

JUNE ISN'T in the dorm when I get back from my last class. The small indent of her mattress, the depression she has made over the years is the only evidence that she occupies this room with me. I am frustrated because I want to address what happened at lunch. I don't want to walk around with this knot in my chest, the unease of alienating my only person around here. I change into my leotard and tights because it's a free period and I've been eager to practice in the dance studio. The dance studio is dark and empty because while other girls dance ballet, no one loves it the way I do. No one else craves the movement in their limbs outside of class hours. The studio lights up as soon as I pass the sensor. I ask RITA, our school's automated assistant to play some music. Prokofiev from the ballet Romeo and Juliet. It's one of my favorite ballets because music has a way of driving into my soul. I stretch before the song I want comes on. I pull my leg up and place it on the top of the ballet barre, until my hamstrings ache, pulling against me as I lean over my leg.

Chapter 2

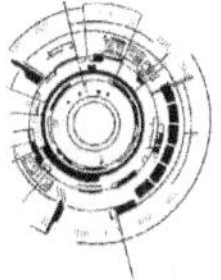

Talent can emerge from any quadrant. The challenge lies in its identification and cultivation

-Magnus Compendium, Section 12.7

Magnus

I'm wandering the halls, not aimlessly, never aimlessly, but with a singular purpose. A purpose that I'm still trying to deny, trying to pretend is something else. I want to see her again, I am hoping to catch glimpses of her. I need to confirm something, and the only way to do that is to see her eyes again. The lights to the dance studio are on, spilling through the cracks and space in the door frame. I hear the dark melancholy of Prokofiev and I'm drawn in, aware that Kira likes to dance. Fate has decided to intervene on my behalf because instead of catching a glimpse of her passing in the hallway, I find her stationary and alone. Her body is folded over an outstretched leg resting on the ballet barre, her back an effortless arch, her head resting on her foot. The room's mirrors reflect her elegant pose from multiple angles, creating a mesmerizing illusion of endless grace. The polished wooden floor gleams beneath her, and the soft light filtering through the windows casts delicate shadows, accentuating the curves of her body. Her hair is pulled back in a bun at the back of her head, a donut of silvery blonde strands. I examine the loose strands at the back of her neck, delicately hanging, drawing my attention to the enticing cove where her head meets her neck. She's a vision in pallor pink, a matching trio of leotard, stockings, and pointe shoes. My eyes travel the curve of her body down to the leg that still rests on the ground, her flatfoot pointing outward. The woven ribbon around her ankles climbs up her calves into precious little bows. A glorious sunset streams in through the window, painting the sky with a Saturday night kind of pink, streaking across the golden hue and blending with the cerulean. This light bathes her in an unworldly glow, she's dreamily absorbing the sunset and doesn't detect me. This suits me fine because I want to look at her without any interruption. A song she must have been waiting for comes on. She quickly gets into first position and begins dancing to some choreography that looks well-rehearsed. The way her body moves to this music suggests that she has spent hours honing her craft. The magic hour continues to wash her in light as she moves across the floor. I experience a floating sensation in my body as I watch her. Her muscles strain against her tights, displaying their limber strength while her hands and her finger-tips are dainty points. Her neck arches, stretching and contracting, and I watch each delicate flick of her wrist, each flex of her foot, each balance on the tips of her pointe shoes. The move-ments are purposeful, but an amateur spectator would not see the effort or the difficulty, they would assume she was born to dance across a stage, like an ethereal being gliding across the sea with ease. She spins and spins until she should become dizzy, but she has a singular focus that spares her from dizziness or missing a step. She comes to a stop, her right leg landing behind her while her left leg comes forward with a slightly bent knee, both feet planted, pointing away from her center. She straightens, shakes out her limbs, and grabs a towel that is hanging loosely from the ballet barre. Her face glistens with sweat, and I watch as she drags the towel down her long neck to her chest and dabs at the perspiration. When she opens her eyes, they lock with mine. An almost imperceptible suspended moment ensues as her face registers my presence behind her. They widen with surprise, and then with the grace of movement, she spins on her toes, her pointe shoes facilitating a perfect twist. I'm leaning against the doorframe with my arms crossed, watching her.

"That was lovely, Kir," I begin to say her real name but I stop myself and finish with "May." It's not her name, it's a placeholder for her until she leaves school and can pick a new one. It is unusual for me to be so imprecise in speech. Yet, something about her has always been this disarming.

"What are you doing here?" she asks, with a hint of acknowledgment that she finds me supercilious. I'm not one of her peers and while I dislike the conflation, that as her mentor, she has to treat me differently. She throws her hand over her mouth before deciding she doesn't want me to know that she thinks that, that she sees me as a superior. She drops her hand and slides it down to her tights, and she scrapes. I can't help but follow the movement. She has always done that, scrape her thigh. I'm wondering if her thigh is marred underneath those tights, as a consequence of the constant scraping. It is hard to imagine her skin as anything but perfection. My fingers itch to split the tights and have a look to slake my curiosity.

"Don't you know?" I ask instead. I step closer to her, leaving my perch from the doorway. She instinctively moves back, but the ballet barre is right behind and she has nowhere to go. I stop in my tracks; I don't want to scare her.

"You were at the assembly this morning," I continue, as I attempt to distract her from her distress.

"I don't mean in the school; I mean what are you doing

here?" Kira gestures around the room to indicate the dance studio.

"I heard the music, I was curious," I say and take another step toward her. "Prokofiev is very beautiful but dark."

"I don't think it's dark, I think it's powerful, earth-shattering. My skin tingles when I hear it." She brings her hand up again to her mouth like she's worried she has overshared, or maybe she is worried she shouldn't contradict me. I want her to overshare. I want to dig into that large brain and see all the layers, dips, and turns that have formed the woman standing in front of me. Woman. It's the answer to the question that has been sitting in my cerebellum, forcing its way up and out. She's not a little girl anymore, she is a woman.

"I like that, but darkness can be powerful, it can especially be earth-shattering." I am only a couple of feet away from her now, my body moves of its own volition, somehow all my careful practiced demeanor is shattering near her. Kira cranes her neck to look up at me, she is much taller than when she was a young girl, yet still, I tower over her. Goosebumps are beading up on her flesh, sprinkling her lean muscular arms with little mounds of nervous energy.

"It isn't so much darkness I am seeking when I pour my heart out in dance, but a sense of control, purpose, strength. I have never once considered it dark, not until this moment." Her navy eyes look through me in contemplation. They refocus when her thought has fully formed and petered out. Her nervous energy returns. Her fear makes her eyes glitter in an alluring way. I stem the impulse to lick her pupils and taste her inner light. If I did, would it be like licking a battery or would I get hit by an electric shock capable of stopping my heart? I'm worried it's the latter and if that's true I'm in big trouble.

"Not many people understand that," I say after a moment of silence.

"What?" She doesn't remember what we were talking about because we've been staring at each other. It's not the kind of staring you do with just anyone. It's the stare of someone digging into an oddity, drawn in by sheer curiosity.

"Tingles from hearing music. It's called frisson, it means your brain has more pathways than others. That you are attuned to beauty and are open to new experiences." She moves closer to me, and it takes me by surprise because suddenly her reticence is gone. I inch closer, enjoying the clean musky scent of her sweat.

"They say people who experience frisson also have an easier time communicating and have a deeper emotional range."

"They do?"

"mmhmm," I say, and somehow, she moves even closer to me. It's invigorating.

"You've grown up to be very talented." I compliment and I can't help but sweep my eyes down over her body to admire the woman she has become. She starts to shrink back as she sees what my unruly eyes are doing. No more are the gangling long limbs of youth present or the awkward gait of an amorphous body. Her long, lean figure is pillowed in all the right places, with generous flesh that denotes womanhood.

"I'm surprised to see you here," she says, and my fears abate because she remembers me. To forget me was to claim that my worth was less than, placing us on an uneven keel. She has stayed in my thoughts all these years and despite her disadvantage, realizing she stored the memory of me, fires something inside me.

"So, you remember me?" I ask, needing her to say the words, to alleviate my doubts.

"I never forget a voice," she bites her lip but adds "or a face."

I nod slowly and watch as her eyes flit around the room as if looking for escape.

"Something else we have in common." I lean in further, unable to stop myself and her breath hitches at my nearness. Her throat swells and shrinks with a swill of saliva.

"What else?" she asks, and I tilt my head slightly, inches from her face. It's my turn to be too distracted to follow the conversation and while I could pull up the memory with my interface, I'm enjoying this purely organic exchange.

"What else?" I mimic, my voice softening, my eyes searching hers.

"What else do we have in common?"

I can feel a small smile begin to spread out on my face, my lips stretching and my cheeks lifting. The tension between us crackles like electricity, and I watch as a blush creeps up her neck, coloring her cheeks.

"Frisson," I say and her soft, warm little breath wafts over my lips. We are both lost in this moment, this immersive moment. I should leave. I should step back and put a large distance between us. But I'm caged, struck dumb. A moment passes and then another until my neurons finally fire, kicking my stagnant brain and sending a message out to my extremities and I drag myself away.

"Well, I'll see you around, Spark," I say and I turn around and leave before I do something I can't take back.

Chapter 3

An organized life is a peaceful life. Keep your surroundings and mind tidy.
    -Plymouth Prep Handbook, Page 72

May

It's not that I'm afraid of him, it's not. I think. I just have to run straight back to my dorm because I don't know what to think. I don't know how to process it. I walk in out of breath and June is sitting on her bed reading something off her school tablet. Her eyes flick up to me and she looks back down at her tablet. Then she shoves it aside, before taking a deep breath, steeling herself. She looks up at me with contrition in her eyes and even though I feel a little raw and insecure, I'm sure I'll forgive her. The room is stark and utilitarian, with identical narrow beds on either side, each made with crisp, white linens pulled tight. The overhead lighting casts a harsh, bright glow, eliminating any shadows and making the room feel even more impersonal. The window is merely a digital rendering, displaying a changing scenery of serene landscapes that cycle periodically to mimic the passage of time. The current scene shows a calm, sunlit meadow, but it does nothing to break the clinical atmosphere of the room. I slump down on my bed, the mattress firm beneath me, offering little comfort. June watches me carefully, the tension between us hanging in the air.

"I'm sorry," she says at once. Her willingness to apologize when we disagree is one of the reasons we are friends. She is always willing to own up to her mistakes and claim them. I respect that, because so few people can admit when they are wrong, and face the consequences.

"It's okay," I say before I drop my ballet bag on the floor. I want to ask her why she is so upset with me, but I'm waiting to see if she will just tell me. I slump down on my bed and June groans. She digs the palms of her hands into her eye sockets and keeps them there.

"Look, it's not that I'm not super proud of you, or proud to be the best friend of the most brilliant girl at this school, just sometimes…" she trails off and drops her hands in her lap. "Sometimes it's hard to exist in your shadow." Never in all my life have I considered June less than, certainly not my shadow. Nor do I think I cast a long enough shadow to cover her in shade. My canopy is a spindly little thing hardly worth noting.

"I don't even have the words," I say, crossing the small space between our beds and kneeling in front of her. "June, you are anything but my shadow. I've never seen you that way."

"I know you don't, it's not what you think, it's what everyone else thinks. It kind of stinks knowing that I have no shot at being mentored by him." June is not academically minded, she isn't disciplined in her studies. She is in remedial math and all the times I've tried to help her with her homework were met with angry outbursts that threatened to permanently bruise our relationship. We decided that it was best if she sought tutoring from the teachers to avoid harming the only friendship we both have here. She spends most of her free time in the hydroponics gardens. She loves to tend the plants, but I'm not sure she's told anyone else. Strictly speaking, we haven't spoken about it, but sometimes I see her going in there and her fingernails often have dirt under them.

"Since when do you care what everyone else thinks?" I ask because she has never once looked over at a group of girls with longing, she has never sat at the outskirts dreaming of joining another tribe. At least I never saw her do that.

"Since always."

"No, you've always been yourself."

"Well sure, but within a certain framework."

"What does that mean?"

"I mean everyone limits themselves a little bit, we filter ourselves, and guard our responses, but I suppose I'm as genuine as possible in this world." June looks up into the ceiling. She is just now coming to this conclusion, and I try to process this strange bit of self-revelation and observation of the human plight. Homo Sapiens, by design, requires some integration, because without a tribe you die.

"I didn't realize that's how you felt. If you want, I can just not compete." I say the words without really thinking about the consequences. I realize that maybe June doesn't have a lot of options, because when all is said and done, she doesn't have the grades to go to college. I have more choices.

"Really?" she chirps up in a high-pitched voice.

"No, I can't ask you to do that," she adds, but I can hear how disingenuous it sounds.

"Yeah, really, I don't really want to be mentored by him anyway." After my strange encounter with him today I don't know how I feel about spending more time with him. There is an inexorable draw to him, but on the other hand his intensity is intimidating and confusing.

"What, why?" June jumps on the news and she can't hide her surprise.

"He's just a bit too intense for me."

"Intense? You can't possibly assess that from the brief encounter we had today." I debate telling June about my strange history with him and my encounter in the ballet studio. But maybe if she hears a good excuse for dropping out she won't see it as an act of charity. June's pride is one of the things that holds her back, because she can't handle failure. She would rather tell herself that she failed because she didn't try, then admit it's because she didn't apply herself enough.

"Umm, it's not my first time meeting him," I admit and she stares at me with a slack jaw. Her eyes are flicking around trying to piece together how it's possible. Because we've spent the last eight years together in the same place. Summer holidays or sojourns on the coast were nonexistent. Quarantine and our circumstances have kept us in this school, locked inside.

"I met him from, you know, before," I say before I scrape my hands down my tights, I pull myself up to stand and put some distance between us.

"What, no way, how, where, when?" June knows that I can't talk about my past, because not only is it too hard for me, but we've been told that we shouldn't. That we should move on and worry more about who we want to be than who we were. It is an unwritten rule, but it's etched deeply in the culture. Despite her deep curiosity, the culture drives her decision to take back her question.

"No, wait, you better not tell me." The pale skin on her cheeks stretches as she sucks them into her mouth. Her lips pucker like a fish before she blows out a sputtering breath.

"No, tell me," she says after an indecisive second, and quickly adds, "No, don't." She chews on her thumb and flops down onto her bed. I sit on my bed and watch as she works something out. I can see her eyes staring at the ceiling, barely blinking. After several minutes pass in silence and I remember that I'm still wearing my sweaty ballet uniform. I need a shower, so I get up and go to my closet and take out the shower caddy that sits at the bottom. I lift the caddy and look at the well-worn spot where it rests, water has been stripping away the laminate surface of the faux wood closet. I grab the towel on the hook and my pajamas that I've thrown into a drawer without folding. June doesn't notice my preparation.

"In what way is he intense?" she asks, chewing on her thumb, her teeth lightly grazing the nail. "Surely you can tell me without breaking any rules."

"I don't know how to tell you without telling you about before, but I guess I could tell you about what happened in the now." June sits up abruptly, her eyes widening and her brows shooting up, wrinkling her forehead.

"What does that mean?" she leans forward, curiosity evident in her posture.

"He watched me dance in the dance studio," I admit, ducking my head to hide how awkward I felt about the whole encounter, my cheeks warming with the memory.

"What? Just now?" she asks, her voice rising slightly with surprise.

"Yeah, I didn't sense he was present until I stopped."

"You do get very caught up in what you're doing. What did he do?" June's eyes narrow slightly, her fingers stilling in their nervous chewing.

"He just talked about the music." I shrug, trying to downplay the significance of the moment.

"What about that was intense?" She tilts her head, confusion knitting her brows together.

"It's not so much what he said." I struggle to find the right words, my hands fidgeting in my lap, fingers twisting together.

"What then?" She leans in closer, her gaze fixed on me, waiting for an explanation.

"I don't know, it's hard to put into words, anyways I just don't want to be mentored by him, that's all." It's all I can force past my lips, I can't bring myself to say what really happened. Because it feels private, it feels like something I have to keep inside. If I utter how he had shaken me to my core and how he stirred something inside me. How he drew up a foreign entity in my psyche that before today didn't exist. It feels like it will slip away, slither out of my lips and slink into the dark. I'm not ready for it to hide, because I want to ruminate on it, chew it to pieces, until I understand. I want to peel at the layers husking and hulling until the kernel is naked and exposed.

"That's a shitty explanation," she says, her eyebrows knitting together in frustration.

"Well, I'm sorry, that's all I got. Okay? I don't know how to explain it." I throw my hands up, feeling exasperated.

"Okay, fine, fine," she says, leaning back and crossing her arms, her expression softening slightly. "So, you'll drop out and maybe I have an actual shot at winning top place for a change."

"Yeah, exactly." I agree, managing a small, tight smile as I nod, feeling the tension between us start to dissolve. June goes back to staring at a spot on the ceiling with a blank look on her face, the way she always does when she is in deep thought and I take it as my chance to go and take a quick shower before dinner.

MORNING ARRIVES NOT by sunlight streaming in through the window, because it is still too dark out for that, but with the automatic lighting system designed to wake us through a gentle increment of light. I wake up slick between my legs and it is to some alarm. I try to recall my dreams but there is only this feeling of longing and want. Green eyes flash before my mind's eye and suddenly a picture of Faust appears before me; he's leaning into me and instead of walking out of the dance studio, his lips skate over mine. It's a strong sensation that I suck in a lung full of air and pull the covers over my head, to try and hide my shame and the throb between my legs. I'd never had a wet dream before, and until now I had assumed it was only something boys experienced. What little exposure I've had to sex came from novels and they were pg-rated. The hulling is nearly complete and the kernel is desire, one that I didn't know my body was ready for. Faust is the catalyst, but I decide quickly that he isn't the object. I stem the angsty feeling and I pull down the covers and take a deep breath; homeostasis returns gradually. June groans and covers her face with a blanket. Fighting June in the morning is a fruitless battle. I roll over to my side and watch her throw her milky leg over the sheets. She rolls into a fetal position in an attempt to burrow back to sleep. It often amazes me that after all these years she still fights the inevitable. She groans and protests, making a grand show of not wanting to wake up, before finally succumbing to reality. It's like this every morning, and I watch her each morning waiting for the one day that she will just jump out of bed and say, "I've overcome my programming and changed." That day will signify that humanity is no longer doomed. It will signify that we are capable of growth and change. The pessimist in me says, don't hold your breath, because June will never do that. She will never just wake up and get out of bed the way I do. But the optimist in me still looks over every morning, hoping that she does it. I leave her to her morning procedure. I pull out my uniform from the closet, and my toiletries, and get ready in the bathroom.

I'M LEAVING the bathroom when June stumbles in. Her tawny hair is sticking up in disarray and her eyes are still half-closed.

"Hurry up, June, being late will get you docked points. You don't want to hurt your chances of being mentored." She waves me off.

"Fine!" She nearly yells. She has dark circles under her eyes and rheum lingering at the creases of her eyes. I can't help but chuckle at my friend's inability to cope with the mornings.

Despite her protests, we manage to get to the gym in time.

"You know it's actual bullshit that they want us to do this first thing in the morning," June grumbles right before we open the gym doors. The students are all lining up, waiting for class to start, and we split up to join them in our respective spots. Belfor walks in with her clipboard, her whistle hanging around her neck. Her long blue shorts end below her knee, accentuating her thick calves. The blue veining looks prepared to force its way out of her bluish-pale skin. The gymnasium is expansive, with tumbling mats arranged neatly on one side and a running track encircling the space. Various pieces of gym equipment are clustered in a corner, including weight benches and a set of parallel bars. I stop looking at her when the doors swoosh open and Faust walks in. He has his signature crease between his eyes as he scans the room. When his eyes land on me, they stop. Belfor goes up to him, and while they are conversing, his eyes stay on me. I feel my cheeks flush and my heart starts to race. The intensity in his eyes brings me back to my childhood, the last time he stared at me with equal intensity. I begin to feel small and helpless; I half expect my mother to come storming into the gym to grab at me or pinch me. His jaw ticks and then he looks away, and I can't help but wonder if he ascertains how I am beginning to shrink into myself. He isn't looking at me anymore, but he isn't looking at the other students either; he focuses on some distant point. The girl next to me leans over and whispers something to the girl on the other side of her. I don't hear what they say, but it's the thing that drags my own eyes off him. I look down at my gym shorts to see that I'm scratching at my thigh. I still my hand and close my eyes. Belfor starts speaking, and I try to listen to the words and not the cadence. Her voice feels garbled. I hear her voice but not the words. I go back to scratching my thigh, trying to drag my mind back down into my body. The gym smells of sweat and disinfectant, a familiar mix that usually grounds me, but today it feels distant, almost surreal.

"You all met Faust yesterday. He is here to observe the class today." I hear those words and this strange feeling of being exposed and watched comes over me. I look up and his eyes are back on me. Something about the way he looks at me is unsettling. I'm a fish in an aquarium and he hasn't moved from his spot for hours. That's what it feels like. I'm worried he might tap on the glass and shake up my environment. The glass will crack, and then he will tap it again until it shatters. I'll spill out of my safe space and flop on the floor fighting for breath, and all the while he will just stand still and watch with that strange intense gaze of his, the one that thrills me and paralyzes me all at once. I'm vaguely aware that the group of girls step forward, but I don't follow suit. I stay put until I hear the whistle, which means it's time to start the morning warmup. I start jogging along the perimeter with the other girls. June catches up to me, and we jog in silence for a minute. June has athletic abilities, where she fails in academia she makes up for in physical stamina. I can hear her breathing next to me, but it isn't labored; it's even and soothing. If I was in bad shape it would probably annoy me, while I struggled for breath, but we are well matched.

"Thanks for opting out," she tells me, and I nod at her because of course, I'm happy to not do the mentorship program if it helps her with her future. I shrug a shoulder and keep running. June picks up her pace and leaves me behind. I watch as she starts to do laps around some of the stragglers. I sense him before I look over; Faust is jogging next to me, but he isn't breathing heavy like the rest of us.

"Kira," he greets me.

"Faust." I greet him back and try to ignore him while I keep running. Of course, it's impossible because his presence is undeniable. He's a splinter wedged under my skin, and even when I try to not notice it, it stings and draws my attention back. It demands to be paid attention to; it demands to be removed before it festers and infects.

"Were you paying attention this morning?" he asks me. There is a lot implied with that question. One is that he knows I have an attention problem, which brings up a lot of other questions like how he knows that and why he cares.

"Sure," I say because I don't want him to know he is right.

He spins around and starts running backward so I can see his face while he is talking to me.

"Funny, because you looked distracted." He looks utterly at ease, without a single indication that he is feeling the efforts from the physical activity. He has a small smile on his face, and although I'm in good shape, it rankles that it's still more of an effort for me than it is for him. The sweat drips down my neck, slides into my shirt, and traces my spine. For a human, I'm in excellent shape, but Edits have their own metrics, and the discordant difference is what sets my teeth on edge. How is anyone expected to compete against them?

"Is there a point to this?" I ask because one, I am uncomfortable with his constant assessment of me, and secondly, I don't want unwanted attention from the other girls.

"I am just confirming that you didn't plan on opting out of the mentorship program." I come to a stop and girls are forced to run around me. I can see their confused expressions as Faust stops in front of me.

"Actually, I did," I say, and I cross my arms over my chest. His eyes flicker with some emotion, and then his smile fades into a hard line.

"Kira, you are not allowed to skip out on this opportunity. I am sorry, but your request to opt out has been denied."

"You can't tell me what to do." I retort. It's a weak argument, and I feel like a child shouting back to a parent. It's an interesting moment because I've never shouted at a parent or talked back to any authoritative figure before. Sometimes life gives you opportunities to make up for the things you missed out on as a child. They are formative in the sense they fill a bone-deep void.

"Actually, I can." He crosses his arms over his broad chest. This instinct to push him overwhelms my system and I dig my fingernails into my palm. I start preparing some equally weak retorts. I don't know what to say. He might be right; I'm still a student here, and as far as I know, I have no rights while I'm here. Someone calls my name, and I look up at Belfor, who is pointing toward the tumbling mat. Now that my attention has been drawn away, I refuse to look at him again. I scrape my pants as I walk up to one of the large tumbling mats. Two of my classmates are already sparring on the mat, and I stand there on the sidelines, watching and waiting for my turn. Augusta and Septa are red and sweaty from the effort of trying to take each other down. Their unfeminine grunts and growls echo through the large space. Faust slides up next to me, and I refuse to turn and look at him. He leans down and whispers in my ear.

"Do you have any particular reason you don't want to participate?" he whispers. I focus solely on the sparring in front of me and ignore him. I ignore the shiver his breath causes coursing down my spine. I ignore the way his voice caresses my senses. When I was younger, his slow even cadence bothered me, but now it's a balm. Now I enjoy the ease with which I can follow what he says to me. The strain is absent, and the need to figure out why some people talk the way they do is gone. I turn my attention back to the match. Augusta brings up her elbow to strike Septa in the face, but Septa blocks, forcing Augusta to stumble backward. Septa follows it by doing a roundhouse kick, striking Augusta on the side of the head. Augusta goes down hard, and Septa is awarded winning points. Augusta slams her fist against the mat in anger before she pulls herself up and goes off to the side to get some water. Septa is grinning wildly, and there is that streak of hers, that competitive streak that is so revolting. I read a Chinese proverb once that said you should be a warrior tending a garden instead of a gardener in a war. I understand the basis behind that, but this is a friendly match. A time and a place exist for being vicious. Besides, I'm not convinced you need to be a dick to be a warrior. I believe skill is all that you need, skill with a good heart.

"You're up," Belfor calls from across the mat, and I step up in front of Septa. Septa drinks several gulps from her bottle.

When she looks up and sees me, her eyes narrow. I get into my fighting stance and wait for Belfor to blow her whistle.

"This might be the day I finally beat you." Septa taunts with some bravado after defeating Augusta.

"Let's find out," I say, and ball my fists in front of me. As soon as the whistle blows, Septa lunges toward me with a right hook. I instinctively dodge out of the way and strike Septa in the gut with an undercut. Septa stumbles backward and sucks in a deep breath, the wind is knocked out of her. When she regains her equilibrium, her eyes narrow again, and she begins to seethe with rage. She lunges toward me again and this time lands a blow on my shoulder and knocks me to the ground. I have to physically restrain my instincts to let her land the blow. It hurts, but it is worth it to get out of this stupid mentorship track. I tap out on the ground and Belfor's mouth hangs open, but after a long moment, she blows her whistle before Septa has a chance to strike at me again.

"Points to Septa," Belfor announces. Belfor doesn't say anything at first, but her eyes follow me as I get off the mat. I stand to the side and rub my arm.

"Is that arm bothering you?" Belfor asks with some concern.

"I'm fine," I say, and it is true, but I keep rubbing my arm, making it a big deal.

"Go to the nurse," Belfor tells me. I nod my head and head for the door. I look at Faust by the mat, his narrowed gaze tracking my departure. I half expect him to come bounding after me.

Chapter 4

Memories are like roadmaps to our personalities and we often don't see the paths that shape us.
— **Kira's Journal, Third Book, Page 2**

Kira

8 years earlier

The MD exam results came two weeks later. My mother clicks open the email with her pink fingernails, delicately scrolling down to read the results. I watch as she scans the letter, her eyes flicking left to right, mouth slightly ajar. She reaches the end of the page, her lips pursing and face hardening. I take a deep breath, waiting for what she will say.

"You failed. You failed," my mother says with shock and anger. She scrolls up and down the page to see if she missed anything, then rereads it, as if the contents might change.

"How did you fail, Kira?" her voice turns sour and bitter.

"You didn't even try, did you?" she accuses, slamming the tablet down on the kitchen table. The weight of her flat palm makes the silverware shake and tinkle, plates rising enough to make an audible thunk, but nothing breaks. I instinctually jump at the sound and stiffen.

"Go to your room. Dinner is not for failures," she commands, schooling her features and straightening her blonde hair as if preparing to be photographed. I get up from the ground where I had been playing and dutifully walk toward the hall that leads to my room. After I turn my back, her hand clamps down on my shoulder, her long pink nails digging into my flesh.

"You will regret this," she hisses in my ear. I already regret it, but I have no doubt she will add to the regret. She releases her hand, but not before squeezing as hard as her skinny fingers can manage. I want to whimper from the pain but know that will only make her angrier. I bite my lip, scratch my pants, and suck in my breath to stop from crying. I walk to the hall slowly, while she watches. Once I am out of sight, I run into my room and silently close the door. I sit on the bed, take the nearest pillow, and cover my face before letting my tears flow.

THE NEXT DAY, my mind drifts aimlessly during class, barely registering the teacher's words. They are discussing fractions. My teacher's voice sounds underwater as she scribbles furiously on her tablet, displaying the fractions on the screen behind her. I look forward, but I am not looking at the classroom or my teacher, whose oversized figure strains the buttons on her shirt. If someone asked me what I was looking at, I would say nothing. Yet, the images flashing through my head are of my mother brushing my hair. I sit down in front of the mirror as instructed, her long nails digging into my scalp as she fluffs my hair and combs it back with her fingers.

"Kira, your hair is always a mess," she says critically. I don't think my hair is a mess; my scalp hurts from the constant grooming. She scrapes my scalp with her fingernails, and I know she has drawn blood. She lets the hair flop and goes for the wide-toothed comb, pulling at my hair from top to bottom. I try to keep my head still as she tugs; my neck aches from resisting each pull. After she is satisfied, she pulls out the boar's bristle brush and smooths my hair more gently. I relax as the gentle bristles make my white, blonde hair shine. She smiles at me through the mirror, and I manage a small smile back.

"I've decided to forgive you," she says magnanimously. "I know exactly how you can make it up to me," she says, and she digs her fingernails back into my shoulders. I flinch, but she ignores the movement.

"I've decided you will do all the housework for a month," she says with a serene smile. "That should teach you the value of responsibility." I look at her and nod. This is a common punishment when I fail.

"Good girl," she says, pulling out the braid rope, winding my hair around it, and fastening the ends. "Goodnight, my dear, sleep, for you have a full day's work tomorrow after school," she says. I hear my name being called and readjust my eyes to focus on my teacher.

"Kira, please complete the problem on the board," she says, and I tap my tablet, filling in the answers. She watches expectantly until I look up to indicate I am done. Her mouth purses as she reads my answer. "That's right," she says, sounding surprised. The door whooshes open, and the class turns to look at the source; the principal walks in. Her gray hair is up in a French twist, and she scans the room with shrewd eyes.

"I need to speak with Kira Tracer," she says, looking up. The class makes "ohhh" sounds like I am in trouble, and I scratch my jeans, scraping the thick coarse texture.

"Well, stand up, girl," my teacher says, and I obediently rise. The principal spots me and waves me over.

"Come with me," she says, and I follow her out of the classroom; the students now animatedly talking. The hallway is empty, and as soon as the door closes behind us, it is silent except for the principal's heeled footsteps. I walk behind her, eyes cast down, watching her uneven gait. Her left foot doesn't lift as high as her right, creating an almost glide every third step. I begin to count each slide, confirming my assessment. Clack clack scrape clack, clack clack, scrape clack. Uneven but rhythmic. When we reach her office, she scans her wrist, and the door whooshes open. We both step inside; I take a seat facing the desk. An officer and a woman wearing a poorly fitted green pantsuit are already in the room. The woman sits next to me; the officer stands off to the side with folded arms. He has a five o'clock shadow at ten am, a sizable gut, but well-defined arms, remnants of a fit past. The woman in the green pantsuit has cornrows pulled into a tight bun atop her head, slanted slightly to the right. She turns to me, wearing a somber, practiced expression.

"Kira, we have some bad news," she says, pausing for emphasis. I fist my fingers, digging my nails into my palm, trying not to scrape my pants.

"Your mother was in a hit and run, dear," she says, touching my shoulder sympathetically. I flinch and pull away.

"She is dead?" I ask, my voice flat.

"Yes, I'm sorry," she responds, pouting slightly as she pats my hand. Her caramel black hand covers my pale white one, dry and cold. I slowly withdraw my hand, dragging it closer to my body.

"What now?" I ask, the adults exchanging concerned glances.

"I am with Child Protective Services; you will come with us until we locate your relatives," the woman says, and I nod.

"Very well," I say, standing and walking toward the door.

• • •

THE WHITE-WALLED ROOM IS BLUE; someone has turned the smart lights to blue, meant to calm me, but I don't feel calm. I have been here a long time alone. Someone gave me a coloring book with crayons and promised to return soon. My mother is dead, and I feel an icky feeling inside, like walking through a dark cave without knowing when or if it will end. I break "Dreams come blue" in half, chips of the blue crayon sprinkling the surface, the paper now reading "dream" on one end and "blue" on the other, "come" lost in the tear. I snap yellow-green this time, splintering "yellow gr" and "en". The door whooshes open, and I look up from the broken crayons. A man I have never seen walks in; he wears black pleated pants and a light blue shirt with stiff cuffs and collar. He takes the seat opposite me, looking at the pile of broken crayons and the untouched coloring book. He has piercing violet eyes. He assesses me, taking his time.

"Kira," he finally says after coming to some internal conclusion. "I'm your new case worker. We couldn't locate any living relatives," he pauses, looking up from his hands folded on the desk. I look him straight in the eye, silent. The silence stretches before he takes a deep breath.

"The good news is, we found a situation for you."

"Situation?" I ask, the stone in my stomach floating up to my throat, making it hard to breathe. My face feels wet, and I wipe my cheek to discover tears streaming down unbidden.

"No tears, little one, you will go to a boarding school until you are of legal age," he says, the words practiced. We sit that way until my tears stop.

"Kira, my name is Dalton; I'm here to take you to a new home," he says. I wipe the tears from my eyes.

"It will be a big change, but one I'm sure you will thrive in," he says in that slow manner that reminds me of the proctor from my exam. I scratch my jeans.

"Why isn't there a foster care situation?" I ask, looking at the Edit with new eyes.

"This is a much more stable environment, I assure you; better than jumping from foster family to foster family," he licks his upper lip, a nervous tick.

"Come, Kira, I will show you," he says, standing and extending his hand. I look at his proffered hand. If I take it, I accept the home he has in mind. I hesitate, then look up at the Edit and his violet eyes. He licks his lips, waiting for me to accept his help. I stretch out my hand and take his; I don't see another choice. Perhaps a good school is a better option. We drive together in the back seat of a self-driving car, him staring straight ahead, legs stretched out. He doesn't look down at me once. Life in my unit is all I have ever known. When AI launched a full-scale attack on the human population it released a plethora of bacterial and viral infections. The world became isolated and fragmented. Everyone is separated into quarantine units, small self-contained communities designed to prevent the spread of diseases and maintain control. To pass from one unit to another, you must undergo a two-week quarantine, a precaution that has made travel nearly nonexistent. The once bustling world has come to a standstill. The aftermath of the AI wars left deep scars. Banning AI technology was just the beginning. Economic collapse followed, grinding progress to a near halt. The dream of a future where no one had to toil endlessly was shattered. As the units filled beyond capacity, harsh birth limitations were imposed to control the overcrowded, suffocating spaces. The world has become a place where survival trumps ambition, and every day is a struggle to maintain even the most basic of comforts. I have never left my unit before. The Edit has permission to travel freely between units since he is immune to our human diseases. As we drive through one unit into the next, I can't help but stare at the changing landscape. Each checkpoint is a stark reminder of the boundaries I've never crossed, guarded heavily and scrutinizing everyone who passes. The cities we pass are crowded and worn, a continuous sprawl of metropolises that seem to merge into one another. People flood the streets, their faces weary, their clothes a patchwork of repairs. The buildings loom overhead, their facades cracked and grime-covered, telling tales of a time when maintenance and care were possible luxuries. I watch the endless sea of humanity, realizing for the first time how dense and inescapable it all is. The landscape changes subtly, but the sense of overcrowding and decay remains constant. There is no empty space, no respite from the press of civilization. My unit suddenly feels like a small, controlled haven in a world that's spiraled out of control. After several hours, I fall asleep, the monotonous hum of the vehicle lulling me into slumber.

WHEN I WAKE UP, we have arrived at Plymouth Academy. The gates loom overhead, their imposing presence sending a cramp through my stomach. I try to quell the strange feeling of doom that is slithering into my stomach. The school is set apart from the world, not by spatial separation, for there is none on a planet hosting billions. The separation comes from high walls. The gates open after confirming his identity, and we drive into the school drive. There is a small outbuilding at the edge of the school, almost resembling a gamekeeper's hut. The first thing I observe about Plymouth Academy is its lack of visible decay. It's the first building I've seen in my life that looks new. The main building is built with ornately carved stones, reminiscent of an old castle picture, something more ostentatious than I've ever seen before. The outbuilding, in contrast, is a little cement structure that sits right next to the flickering wall. A sense of foreboding washes over me as we step out of the car and he leads me over to it. The door whooshes open after he scans it, revealing nothing but darkness inside. As we approach, I take in the details. The walls of the main building are adorned with intricate carvings and ivy creeping up, giving it an ancient yet well-maintained appearance. Large windows reflect the overcast sky, and the sheer size of the building is imposing. It feels like stepping into another world, one where decay and neglect have been kept at bay. "This is where I leave you," he says, and I gulp. "You will do well here," he adds, standing there, looking at me with a mix of assessment and something I can't quite place, licking his lips. He takes me into the building, and inside is a partition with the principal on the other side. I turn back to look at him before the doors close, but he is already out of sight.

The small space looks like a little jail cell. The walls are stark white, almost blinding under the harsh fluorescent lights. There's a narrow bed pushed against one wall, covered with a thin, gray blanket and a flat pillow. Across from the bed, a small desk and chair are bolted to the floor, both made of cold, uninviting metal. In one corner of the room, a toilet and sink are situated with no partitions, offering no privacy. The only window is small, high up on the wall, and barred, allowing just a sliver of light to penetrate the room. The principal, a stern-looking woman with sharp features and blonde hair pinned in a tight bun, looks at me through the partition.

"Welcome, Kira," she says, her voice formal. "It is our custom at Plymouth to shed our names and focus on the new life ahead of us. Therefore, you will now be called May." I stare at her, unsure of what to ask, even though my questions are many.

"You will undergo a two-week quarantine," she continues, "and afterward, you will be integrated into the school. Here, you will remain until you reach the legal age." The weight of the new name, the new life, presses down on me. I nod slowly, not trusting myself to speak. The principal's expression softens slightly. "You will be safe here, May. Follow the rules, and you will do well." I nod again, my throat tight with emotion. The doors close behind me, sealing my fate.

Chapter 5

Neglecting your academic duties shadows your future, casting a long and inescapable darkness over your future success.

— Plymouth Academy Handbook, Chapter 7, Section 3

May

Present Time

The charming sound of the school bell rings, echoing like distant church bells, as Mrs. Lilton finishes her announcement about returning the graded exams to our tablets. The classroom is orderly, with rows of desks arranged in precise lines, each equipped with a sleek tablet holder. Digital chalkboards line the front wall, displaying various mathematical equations and notes that fluctuate slightly as they update. The walls are adorned with educational posters, their bright colors slightly faded, and the large windows let in soft, natural light, casting long shadows on the polished floor. I get up from my desk, taking my tablet along with me, without checking on the results. I know exactly what I got. Just like all my other classes, I get an exact 50. The hum of students gathering their things and murmuring about their grades fills the room. Mrs. Lilton, standing by her desk with a stack of papers in her hands, stops me before I make it out of the classroom.

"May, stay a minute." The rest of the classroom files out, and I walk up to Mrs. Lilton's desk and wait to hear what she has to say. I know she is going to ask me about the exam, but I don't want to stay here and let her drill me. Mrs. Lilton is a small woman, much smaller than me, maybe only five feet tall. Her rosy cheeks have been overly painted with rouge, but somehow it flatters her dark skin and curly hair.

"May, what happened?" she asks, popping a hip up on her desk corner. I shrug, opting for the illusion of ignorance, keeping my expression neutral and avoiding her eyes.

"The exam, you've never had a low grade before, what happened?" she presses, her eyes narrowing with concern.

"It just caught me by surprise," I lie and shrug again, trying to appear nonchalant.

"Really? That's never happened before, you always remember everything," she calls me out, but I am not ready to surrender the truth.

"Well, I guess I forgot, I dunno." I grip my tablet tighter, my knuckles whitening, and try to hide my internal distress at being caught. I knew it would happen, but it still doesn't make it easier. The way her eyes look at me with concern and how she is pursing her lips in dismay makes me hot and unfocused. I feel like a real failure, even though I did it on purpose. This is how June must feel every time she does poorly, and a wave of sympathy hits me because if I was failing for real, this would hurt. This would dig into my backbone and shrink me, pulling out discs until I became deformed and handicapped.

"Really?" Her voice is laced with incredulity. I see her eyebrows raise, but I just shrug again. It takes all my willpower to not own up to it, to continue allowing this shame to surround my aura.

"Yeah, I mean it was bound to happen someday." I force a weak smile, trying to play it off.

"That's not true, and usually not how it works. Top students don't start failing exams. So, you want to tell me what's going on?" Her voice softens, but her gaze remains intense, searching my face for answers.

"Geez, you're making a big deal out of nothing. I'm just a little tired, okay? Don't worry about it. I'm sure I'll do better next time." I manage to keep my voice steady, but I scratch at my thigh and I look away, unable to bear the weight of her scrutiny any longer. Lilton purses her lips again and looks unhappy with my response, but she nods and gestures for me to move along. I don't hesitate and quickly leave the classroom before I am forced to listen to any more scolding. If I was any other student, she wouldn't have stopped me. She would have ignored my failure. I think it speaks volumes about humanity that we hold people to different standards. If anything, because I'm a top student, she should have let it go and focused on the students who actually need her attention. It's just not how the world works; we train people with our behavior. Suddenly they have expectations, and if we fail to meet those expectations, they become concerned.

THE CAFETERIA IS ALREADY full of students when I finally arrive. The room buzzes with the hum of conversation and the clatter of cutlery against plates. Long tables stretch across the space, each filled with students engaged in animated discussions. The overhead lights cast a warm, even glow, illuminating the rows of identical chairs and tables. I walk up to the counter and pick up a tray, my eyes scanning the options laid out in neat, stainless steel containers. My neck begins to tingle with awareness—someone is behind me. I glance over to see Faust standing right next to me, sliding a tray along beside me. He doesn't even look over at me as he collects a plate of boiled potatoes and steak. His movements are precise, almost mechanical, as he selects his food I try to ignore him as I make my way down to the drink section, where rows of drinks are lined up, their colorful labels facing out. Faust follows me with his tray and looks at the selection of drinks, his eyes moving methodically from one option to the next. He is absorbed and completely unaware that another human being is nearby. I honestly thought I would be relieved that he is no longer paying attention to me, but somehow it niggles at me. As soon as I start failing, he just dismisses me out of hand. It's what I wanted, I tell myself, but still, it grates me in a way I can't explain. I stride over to my table where June is already eating and plop down across from her. The table is in a quieter corner of the cafeteria, away from the main throng of students. June looks up from her plate, her eyes reflecting a mixture of curiosity and concern. The tray in my hands feels heavier than usual as I set it down, the dull thud lost in the ambient noise of the room.

"Hey, Sugar bum, what did Mrs. Lilton want?" June asks, a playful glint in her eyes.

"It's a good thing you're not a boy trying to hit on me because that was terrible." I retort, rolling my eyes before unwrapping my cutlery. I push down my irritation, or at least try to.

"Aww, if I was a boy, you'd be obsessed with me. We would be lovers before you could say crackalackin," June jeers with a cheeky grin, winking at me.

"Where do you find these strange phrases?" I ask, raising an eyebrow, because she is always using slang I've never heard before.

"It was in the library in a book called *Slang from the 20th*

Century," June answers before popping a cherry tomato in her mouth, her eyes twinkling with mischief.

"And you read it, why?" I ask, shaking my head slightly in disbelief.

"Because what if there were some good phrases that have been lost to the sands of time? I think it's our duty to resurrect them," she says with a dramatic flourish, leaning back in her chair.

"Well, if crackalackin is any indicator, I'd say it's better lost," I reply, a small smile tugging at my lips despite myself.

"That is such a bummer attitude," June sighs, theatrically slumping her shoulders. I just roll my eyes and dig into my small, boiled potatoes. We both eat in silence for a minute before June speaks again.

"Hey, look, Faust is here," June points out, nudging me with her elbow. I don't even bother to look up from my plate.

"Yup." I stab my steak with more force than necessary. It's nearly impossible to cut with the flimsy cutlery. The table shifts from my violent stabbing. June stops mid-chew to look over at me, her brow furrowed in concern. I am aware of her eyes on me, but I zero in on my steak like it's my mission in life, my jaw tightening with frustration.

"Woah, what's wrong?" June asks, her voice softer, a hint of worry creeping in.

"Nothing. I just hate these forks and knives. How do they actually expect us to eat this?" I say, viciously sawing at the meat with my pathetic excuse for a knife, my knuckles white from the grip.

"Right!" June exclaims, her face lighting up as if I've finally come on to something important.

"I mean, would it kill them to just give us, like, a real knife and fork, honestly?" I continue, my tone edging on exasperation.

"Exactly," June agrees, nodding enthusiastically. I shove an overly large piece of steak in my mouth. It's tough, and I end up chewing through it akin to a cow ruminating on some grass. June watches me, her eyes flicking between my face and my hands, before finally giving a small, understanding smile.

"Woah, May, Faust is full-on staring at you," June announces, and I look up at June with a dubious expression. I know he is staring at me; I can feel it, but I refuse to look over or even consider why. He is hot and cold, and I'm not prepared to keep getting burned by the extreme temperatures. He was super happy to ignore me five minutes ago, and I'm happy to return the favor.

"I doubt it. He's probably looking at you. After all, you are killing it on the scoreboard."

"You think?" June asks gleefully, her eyes lighting up with excitement.

"Yeah, I mean I'm sure he is just scouting out potential winners," I say and keep working on my difficult-to-eat meal. My flimsy plastic knife and fork bend slightly as I try to cut through the tough steak. I try to fight the urge to look over at Faust, but my neck keeps tingling the entire time I am eating, and after a while, my resistance breaks down. I turn my head and see that he is, in fact, staring right at me. He is sitting at a table with a group of girls who are animatedly talking to him about something, but he only nods or gives small responses because he is too busy staring at me.

"Do you think I should go up to him and introduce myself?" June asks, smoothing her hair in a self-conscious gesture. Her hair is undeniably lovely. It has its own natural shine, like well-polished leather. I sometimes have the urge to run my fingers through her straight hair, but I never do. I never reach over and test if it feels as soft and silky as it looks.

"Knock yourself out," I say, forcing a smile as I turn back to my meal. This time the glasses rattle from the effort of stabbing my food. June gets up from the table, and it takes all my willpower to not look over at the exchange. But I hear June giggling, and my head snaps up. I look at Faust, who is smiling widely at June. She is standing at the end of the table next to him. She giggles at something he says, and I get a sour feeling in my stomach like I ate too many rotten eggs. I push my tray aside and decide the steak must be rancid. I get up from the table, bus my tray, and head for the exit, my footsteps heavy and my heart hammering in my chest. The hallways are brightly lit as I walk to the bathroom before my next class begins.

THE BATHROOM IS EMPTY, with everyone still at lunch. The stalls are all closed, and the only sound is the faint hum of the ventilation system. I finish up my business and go up to the sink. The counter is spotless, and the mirrors above it reflect the bright lights, making the space seem even larger. I am standing by the sink washing my hands, the cool water running over my fingers, when the door flies open. My eyes flick up from my hands, and I expect to see another student, but instead, Faust saunters in like he owns the place. I spin on my toes, my heart racing, and I am about to yell at him for coming into the girl's bathroom. "What are you?" it's all I manage to get out before he is eerily close to my face.

"You don't want to be mentored by me?" he seethes angrily at me, and I am so stunned that I swallow the sudden lump in my throat. My complaints about him entering the bathroom all but vanish.

"What do you mean?" The sink edge is digging into my thighs as he crowds me in. I can smell him, he is so close, he smells like leather and something citrusy, maybe lemon or grapefruit. I'm surprised he is surprised because we already discussed this in the gym, but I guess he didn't expect me to tank my results, eliminating any chance I had.

"Because you deliberately try to opt-out, and now you are intentionally failing all your assignments." He declares matter-of-factly, and the facts as they are, are hard to deny.

"Maybe I'm just a terrible student." I offer.

"We both know that's bullshit. I've seen your marks. May, you've had straight A's since the day you came here, top marks on everything. So, why is it that you're trying to avoid me?"

"I'm not," I say defensively, but I know it's a lie. I'm simultaneously drawn to and terrified of Faust. He is like a spider in the corner of the room—you're unsure if he is going to strike, but you can't stop looking for it, making sure it stays in one place. A very pretty, dangerous spider, one with a green mark on its abdomen, terrible and lovely.

"Don't lie to me again." he nearly shouts it at me, his eyes blazing, and my mouth goes dry.

"Well, if you recall, I did fail that scholarship exam as a child, so you know, sometimes I'm not perfect." I manage to say through my cottonmouth. My voice trembling slightly. His eyes flicker with some unknown emotion as he looks me up and down.

"Right," he says and takes a step back. "Right, that," he repeats, and he runs his hands through his blonde hair as he paces in front of me like a caged animal.

"You are way more emotional than I thought Edits were supposed to be," I blurt out before I can stop myself. I clamp a hand over my mouth. His head jerks up and he looks at me in surprise.

"You know I'm an Edit?" he asks and completely ignores the quip about him being over-emotional. Maybe he would have addressed it if I called him a drama queen instead.

"Yes, it's obvious," I say and look down at my nails like my heart isn't racing in my chest.

"Obvious? How?" he asks, and I look back at him and those unreal green eyes. His pink lips are parted in surprise, and for a second my mind flashes with an image of what it would be like to drag my tongue across his pouty lower lip. I gulp at the strange unfamiliar feeling and look down at my nails again.

"It's the cadence of your voice for one. It's slower, more

precise, well, usually. Right now, I'd say you sound like a hysterical drama queen."

"Excuse me?" he retorts with shock. I ignore him and keep going. I don't know what else to do. I'm internally torn between the memory of him and the person standing before me. In my memory, he is an old man, an authority, someone I had to pay heed to. Now he is this young attractive male who has some fixation on me. I try to shuck away the confusing thoughts because I don't have time to parse them.

"It's also how you dress, how you carry yourself. Too perfect, too pristine."

"This, right here," he does a wide arc with his wrist, waving his hand in the air. "This is how I know that you're failing your classes on purpose."

"Whatever do you mean?" I ask, keeping up the pretense that this hasn't been my plan all along. I hear the scraping sound before I realize that my hand is down on my thigh, scraping the fabric of my skirt. He just shakes his head in dismay and takes a deep breath.

"Kira," he whispers with a sad sigh. I look up from my scraping fingers.

"You keep calling me that." I protest because it's no longer who I am. Not that May is who I am either; it's just the month I was born in.

"I know," he agrees but doesn't explain. I look at that lower lip again, and a visceral reaction enters my body. I want to taste him. I can't help it; it's an itch on my tongue, this need to swipe out, to lick and drag his lip into my own mouth. I become unsteady and flushed because I've never had this feeling before. It's new and unprecedented, and I don't know what it means, or what it says about me. Meanwhile, the fight has left him, at least that is what I think, but he takes several steps toward me and closes the distance. He is so near, the heat from his body envelops me, and I am forced to crane my neck to look up at his face.

"Kira." He whispers my name, a prayer or chant on his lips. He takes a deep inhale, breathing me in. I lean as far back as I can, but my head hits the mirror. His hands come up to fist my hair, his fingertips gently massaging my scalp. The last time someone touched my hair was when my mother used to painfully brush my hair, often intentionally scraping her fingernails through my scalp, making me bleed. My first instinct is to pull away, but the soothing circles tickle my scalp and make me tingle all over.

"Kira, you beautiful thing, why are you making this so hard?" He places his forehead on mine, and I am oddly subdued, I don't move. His deep breath wafts over my face as he slowly inhales and exhales, and another shiver runs down my spine at his familiar contact. Warmth spreads up and down my arms. I feel gelatinous—warm and pliable. My knees begin to shake, and he opens his eyes to look at me.

"Kira," he whispers, and this time I am certain that he is going to kiss me. The door to the bathroom swishes open, and Faust takes an abrupt step backward. A girl exclaims "Woah" and backs out, slamming the door shut. I brace against the sink, preventing my shaky limbs from dropping me like a rock on the bathroom floor. I am breathing harder than I realized. Faust isn't breathing heavily, but he looks like the world unraveled, a loose thread on a garment being pulled by invisible hands. His eyes look wild, and we both stand there staring at each other in a shocked stupor.

"I didn't mean—" Faust begins.

"Sorry," he says, and he quickly turns and walks out of the bathroom, leaving me on my own.

Chapter 6

Obedience is the hallmark of a good student; it is through discipline that we achieve greatness.

— **Plymouth Academy Handbook, Chapter 4, Section 2**

The morning quickly shifts to the evening. The halls are bustling with other girls, even the younger ones who have come to the academy this year. The little girls look wide-eyed and afraid, and I can't help but think of the days when I wandered these now-familiar halls scared and confused. The contrast is dramatic because I can hardly imagine life outside these walls. The outside world is a vague memory, a mist swirling around in my brain. The strongest memories are of my mother and the random cruelty she would dole out. I didn't mourn my mother's death as much as I mourned the idea of having a mother. I sometimes imagine my mother baking cookies and reading bedtime stories, instead of tapping her long apple-red fingernails on the counter and counting every calorie we ate. As I walk down the hallway, dodging students, I can't help but search every nook and cranny for Faust. The floors are polished but worn, with scuff marks from years of footsteps crossing them. The faint scent of cleaning supplies lingers in the air, mingling with the remnants of dinner from the cafeteria. I haven't seen him since our encounter in the bathroom four days ago. I round a corner heading for my dorm when Principal Kilroy steps in front of me, blocking my path. Her tall frame casts a long shadow in the dimming light, and her stern expression makes my heart skip a beat.

"Come with me," she tells me without any explanation. Principal Kilroy has a sing-songy voice, with a hint of an accent. She is tall, with tan glowing skin. Her nose is pert, and her cheeks are high; she always reminds me of my mother, but instead of flowy perfectly coiffed hair, her blonde hair is always severely tied back in a bun. I walk behind the principal, following her down the halls leading to the principal's office. An office I have only been in once when I first came to the school as a child. Kilroy scans her wrist and we both step inside. Kilroy takes a seat at her large glass desk, tents her fingertips together on the spotless surface. She purses her lips and twists them slightly to the side before taking a deep breath.

"Your academic record has been flagged by several teachers." I listen more to the cadence of her words than the meaning of the words as is my habit. *your academIC record HAS beeeen flagged by SEveral teachersss.* The pattern is too random for her to be an Edit. I can barely track a pattern at all. She emphasizes the strangest parts of her sentences.

"What do you have to say for yourself?" *whaT do You have to Say for Yourself?* I stare past Kilroy's shoulder, looking at the cherry tree that fills half the floor-length glass window behind Kilroy's desk. I often think of what it would be like to live inside a tree. I haven't seen many trees in my life, but I can imagine that they are a wonderful place to dwell. It isn't until Kilroy snaps her fingers that I look back at the principal.

"I require an explanation, May." Her eyes narrow, and she

leans forward slightly, her fingers tapping rhythmically on the desk. How do I explain that I am failing on purpose? At first, it was because Faust freaked me out so much, and it was because June was so determined to win. Part of me can't help but be curious about Faust and what a mentorship would mean with him. Ever since the bathroom encounter, my brain has been filled with him, like balloons crowding a small room, preventing anything else from coming in.

"I don't want it as much as some of the girls, and since the mentorship isn't compulsory..." I trail off, unable to finish my sentence, my gaze dropping to my hands nervously fidgeting in my lap. Kilroy narrows her eyes.

"Who said it was mandatory?" Her voice sharpens, and she tilts her head slightly.

"Faust." I meet her gaze briefly before looking away again, feeling a knot tighten in my stomach.

"I see." She leans back in her chair, rubbing her temples and taking a deep breath. Her shoulders sag slightly, and she exhales slowly.

"Can you tell me why you don't want to be considered for such an advantageous opportunity?" she asks, her voice softer but laced with frustration.

"Can you explain what the mentorship program is?" I retort with more sass than is strictly allowed in this school, crossing my arms over my chest. Kilroy purses her lips again, her expression hardening.

"It's an opportunity to learn some vital skills from a renowned doctor," she replies, her tone measured and controlled.

"Renowned because he's an Edit?" I shoot back, unable to hide the edge in my voice. Kilroy's eyes freeze, her body stiffening. The silence stretches, heavy and uncomfortable. Then she blinks, her face smoothing into a neutral mask.

"Here is what I am going to do," she says, her tone clipped, her eyes narrowing slightly. "If you agree to retake your exams and make up the homework assignments, I'll have you removed from the mentorship track."

"I can agree to that," I respond, my voice steady, even though my hands are nervously scraping my thigh through the fabric of my wool skirt.

"Good." Kilroy leans back in her chair, her posture relaxing a bit, though her eyes remain sharp. "Now, go back to your dorm. I will speak with your teachers."

"Thank you," I say, and Kilroy nods curtly, her lips pressing into a thin line. She gestures toward the door with a tilt of her head, her gaze already shifting back to her desk. I stand up, smoothing my skirt, and head for the door, feeling the tension slowly drain from my shoulders as I leave her office. The hallway is empty by the time I am done with the impromptu meeting with Kilroy. I wander back to my dorm, my eyes flitting around, aimlessly searching for a glimpse of Faust. The dorms are all quiet on the outside, all the girls have filed into their rooms as curfew dictates, and I'm the only one breaking the curfew. I quickly duck into my dorm before I get docked more points by the automatic monitoring system. June is listening to some song that I've never heard before and looks up from whatever she is working on.

"Hey, where have you been?" she asks, flopping onto her side to face me.

"Kilroy pulled me into her office," I say, closing the door softly behind me.

"Shit, really? What did Killjoy want?" June's eyes widen, and she sits up, concern etched on her face. Killjoy is the students' pet name for her, because whenever she walks into a room, she, well, kills the joy. Luckily, Killjoy is pretty hands-off; besides the random announcements and assemblies, the only time you see Killjoy is when you're in trouble.

"Yeah, she is making me retake my failed exams and redo my homework, in exchange for excluding me from the mentorship track."

"Wow! That's great news. You can still be a top student without having to deal with intense Faust." June says, tossing her tablet aside. "Although, I thought he was super charming when I spoke to him at lunch. I think he liked me." June says and her porcelain cheeks start turning red.

"Oh yeah?" I say, ignoring the strange irritation that creeps over my skin, an unwelcome caterpillar scattering along its surface. I duck my head and fuss with my bed; it's already perfectly made, military points and all.

"He's so, ugh, perfect, dreamy," June says, ignoring me and my unproductive avoidance. "Our babies would be something."

"I don't think Edits can have babies." I say, plopping down on my bed, and reject the thoughts that scream, "But our babies would be even more perfect." My skin feels raw. What if he does like June? Does it matter? I'm out of the mentorship program; dwelling on it serves no purpose. Besides, he's all but vanished. Whatever happened in that bathroom was a fluke, a fleeting aberration.

"What? Really? What a waste, I mean he is like primo DNA stock."

"Who knows what his DNA stock looked like before he became an Edit? He could have been a five-foot weirdo with crooked teeth and a comb-over."

"And a micro penis." June wiggles her pinkie finger to illustrate her point.

"A what!?" I nearly squeal, my eyes widening with shock and amusement.

"An itty-bitty little dick," June says, barely suppressing a laugh, her eyes sparkling with mischief.

"Is that a thing?" I ask curiosity piqued despite myself.

"I think so. I read it in a book once," she replies, shrugging her shoulders.

"Have you ever, you know, seen one?" I lean in slightly, my voice dropping to a conspiratorial whisper.

"What, a micro penis?" she asks, still grinning.

"No, I mean yeah, that too, but just like any penis?"

"No. When and where would that have happened exactly?" June raises an eyebrow, her lips still quivering with a smile.

"Point well made, but who knows with you."I chuckle, shaking my head.

"How about you? You're so private, the fact that you've met two Edits in your life is insane. I've heard the odds of meeting an Edit is like winning the lottery." I shrug, leaning back on my bed. I don't know what to make of it either, but some people get struck by lightning more than once.

"I've never seen one either," I say, and she shrugs and rolls over onto her stomach, flipping her legs up behind her. She changes her mind, immediately scoots off her bed, goes over to the floor-length mirror, and does her routine breakdown of her body. She flashes her teeth and pivots to the side so she can see the shape and size of her butt.

"Some of the girls are talking about meeting up with some of the boys from the west wing." June shares and leans in to check her skin for blackheads.

"Okay," I say and pull off my uniform to get into my pajamas.

"You should come. Maybe you can see a penis." June grins wildly at me.

"Ugh!" I throw my sock at June, and June dodges it with a laugh.

"First of all, I don't want to see anyone's penis. Secondly, there is no way anyone is getting past the automatic monitoring system. So, you guys might as well just stay in your dorms and forget it.

"Jan said she knows how to hack the monitoring system, and then we can all sneak to the unmonitored classrooms."

"Jan?" I scoff, and June laughs.

"Oh, come on. She isn't that." June searches for the right word and taps her finger to her chin. "Laggard?"

"I'm just saying, the fact that anyone thinks that Jan has a legitimate plan to sneak out with boys is laughable," I say, rolling my eyes.

"Harsh." June crosses her arms, her expression turning serious.

"Hardly, just a fact. Do yourself a favor and stay put." I grab my bathroom caddy and head to the bathroom to clean my face and brush my teeth.

WHEN I GET THERE, several other girls are getting ready for bed. The bathroom has several shower stalls and toilets, with simple sinks and almost no counter space. Each girl wears flip-flops that squish against the wet tile floor. Juli, Septa, and April are standing by the sink talking. Septa is filing her nails, while the other two are just standing by, watching. Their reflections shift and blur in the mirrors as they move.

"I'm just saying, I know what I saw," Septa says and pauses when she sees me walk in. She flips one of the loose strands of her brown hair over her shoulder to clear her vision.

"Speak of the devil," Juli announces, and Septa and April pivot their heads to look at me.

"Good evening, ladies," I say, trying to keep my tone neutral as I go to the far sink to set up my things. I try to ignore their odd looks as I pull out my toothbrush, toothpaste, face soap, and facial scrubbing pad. The fluorescent lights cast a stark glare, making the white porcelain of the sink almost blinding.

"Is it true?" Septa asks, and I ignore her because I assume that she isn't talking to me but rather one of her cohorts.

"I asked you a question!" Septa shouts, and I look up from the sink to see that she is staring directly at me, her eyes narrowed with suspicion. I pull the toothbrush from my mouth and speak with a toothpaste-filled mouth, trying to keep my composure.

"Is what true?"

"That you had sex with Faust in the bathroom," Septa asks,

and I nearly choke on the toothpaste in surprise. I bend over to spit out the toothpaste and wash my mouth out with water. After I wipe off my chin, I turn back to Septa, my heart racing.

"I'm sorry, what?"

"Did you, or did you not have sex with Faust in the bathroom?"

"Are you kidding?" I raise an eyebrow, disbelief coloring my voice.

The three girls are all lined up to stare at me. I look between all their sour expressions, waiting for the punchline. Septa is a Latina girl with freckles across the bridge of her nose. Her brown hair is cut short, a straight bob angled at her chin. She crosses her arms over her chest, while April, the tallest girl at school, looks down from her high vantage point at the gesture and decides to mimic Septa's stance. April is a little gruff on the outside, but before this moment, I had always considered her sweet.

"I am a virgin," I answer at last when it's clear that they believe whatever rumor they heard or started. I try to keep my voice steady, but my hands tremble slightly as I pack my things back into my caddy.

"You were seen!" Juli insists, her eyes narrowing in accusation. I can't help but wonder who walked in on us when we were in the bathroom, and what in the world she thought she saw.

"Okay, well, we were just talking in the bathroom, fully dressed. I have no idea who told you that bit of nonsense, but I can assure you, I have never had sex, kissed, or had any other variety of sexual contact with Faust."

"Why were you talking to Faust in the bathroom?" April asks, her voice dripping with suspicion.

"I don't know that it's any of your business," I grate out, feeling cornered and annoyed by the entire situation.

"Tell us, or we will tell the whole school that you spread your legs for him, so you can get ahead of the competition. Everyone knows you're failing horribly." Septa's eyes flash with a malicious glee. I pack up my pink bathroom caddy and attempt to storm past the trio of girls, but they push me in the shoulder when I try to leave.

"Tell us," one of them demands again, placing their hands on their hips like they are trying to intimidate me. I smirk at their pathetic attempt to bully me.

"How about you move, and I'll leave you all in one piece." I square my shoulders, meeting their glares with my own. Juli and April look nervously at each other, but Septa just sneers at me.

"There are three of us, and besides, I've won three out of four of our matches in the last two weeks." Of course, there's no way for them to know that I let her win, so I just shrug.

"Well, I guess if you want to find out how good I am when I care, we can always try right now."

"You are so full of shit, May, always so stuck up and full of yourself. You're just orphan trash, just like the rest of us, so don't think you're any better." Septa spits on the ground, and I take a giant step back to avoid getting hit by the spray.

"This is your last chance to move." I put my caddy on the sink to free my hands. It is starting to look like I am not getting out of this one without a fight. Septa balls her fists, and we both get into a fighting stance. A gaggle of girls enters the bathroom, led by Jan.

"Oh! Ladies!" Jan says, bouncing into the room with a cheery expression, one that she almost always wears. Her strawberry blonde curls spring as she moves, and her petite frame hosts a surprisingly generous bosom and bottom that look almost comical in the extreme dichotomy.

"We are going to meet boys!" Jan announces, with no regard for the fact that someone might tell on her. The tension in the room is palpable, but Jan is too oblivious in her own magical world to notice.

"You four should totally come!" Jan chirps, her enthusiasm undeterred.

"Yeah, May, you should go with her. Maybe you can get

some experience for your next rendezvous with Faust." Septa cajoles with a malicious grin on her face. "I'm told men like some experience." Septa brings her fist up to her head and moves it back and forth while poking her tongue inside her cheek on one side. I don't understand what it means, but I am guessing it's some crude sexual gesture.

"I'll pass." I push past the group of girls, who finally part formation and let me through.

Chapter 7

Peer pressure feels like you'll turn into a diamond, but it's the inverse; your spark goes out and you become a lump of coal instead.

— Kira's Journal, Book 3, Page 17

I'm on my way out the bathroom when June walks in and prevents me from leaving.

"Hey, we are going to go meet boys," she announces, and her eyes look over at Jan's group. She gives Jan a small excited wave.

"You're not going too, are you?" I whine, unable to hide my annoyance at my friend.

"Don't be sooooooo uptight, let's live a little." June urges and starts pushing me back into the bathroom.

"The last time we saw the boys was easily three years ago, aren't you curious?" I'm not curious. I mean sure, it's weird seeing only girls all the time, but on the other hand, Faust has sort of replaced all my curiosity. Despite being MIA recently, he's like a constant shadow in my mind.

"No, not really," I admit and move to leave when I hear Septa speak up.

"That's because she is already getting some vitamin D from Faust." her voice is bitter and unpleasant and a big part of me just wants to ignore her, but call it ego, or pride, or stupidity, I just can't stop myself from responding.

"Sounds like you are jealous Septa, are you worried that my charms are more powerful than all your effort to beat me?"

"So, you admit it, you're fucking him?" Septa rejoinders without skipping a beat. I should have seen that coming, and part of me did, but I can't keep my mouth shut.

"I've never even seen a penis, Septa, but you certainly know some crude gestures that would indicate that you have been sneaking into the boy's dorm for years." her face turns red and a collective ooooo rings out in the bathroom as the girls all stop what they are doing to witness the exchange.

"Oh my gosh, Drama! I love it!" Jan squeals and makes a gesture of eating popcorn.

"What is she talking about May?" June questions me and I am too focused on Septa to respond.

"If you're not into Faust, why don't you go with the group?" Septa asks, daring me, the last refuge of someone who has no evidence to back up her bold claims.

"Because I don't want to get into trouble, and the rest of you would be smart to just stay in your dorms."

"Likely story, why do you care? You're at the bottom of the class right now, one more demerit is hardly going to make a difference."

"May is failing on purpose you nitwits," June announces before I have a chance to stop her. Everyone stops looking at me and looks at June. I stretch my arms wide and look at June with irritation. I don't want anyone to know that. It comes with too many questions, questions I don't even know how to answer.

"What? Why would she do that?"

"Because she is a good friend, and I wanted to win, but we

all had no chance of winning if she was in the running, admit it." June challenges and eyes everyone down, daring them to challenge her. I look around at the girls in the bathroom, each of them coming to a verdict about the revelation. Resignation appears on everyone's faces except Septa's, of course.

"That doesn't explain what she and Faust were doing in the bathroom together." Septa points out and renewed interest forms on everyone's faces including June. So much for my staunchest supporter. It's becoming clear I have to say something, or this will just explode into something that isn't true.

"He was just asking me why I was doing so poorly; he has seen my academic record," I tell them and hope it's enough of an explanation.

"Why does he care?"

"I don't know, if anyone else was failing as poorly as me, I'm sure that he would have asked them too."

"Well, I'm not gonna say who, but the person who saw you said he was close to you like you were kissing," Septa reveals and the way she said it, makes it clear to me that she was the one who saw us.

"He's not great about personal space, he's always been that way." I retort before I think better of it.

"Always?" at least four other girls reply at the same time.

"Yeah, I mean, I've met him before, okay? Like, before before, and I can't talk about it as you all know."

"I've had several chats with him, and he never got that close to me," Jan says and I sigh heavily.

"Look, it doesn't even matter, Kilroy took me out of the running, he is not going to mentor me, I have not had any kind of physical relations with him, okay?" I utter with severe annoyance. I don't understand his interest in me. How many girls is he bothering? Is it just me?

"Has he gotten close to anyone here?" I query, unable to hide my curiosity. I look around at the girls who also are looking around, seeing if anyone else will speak up. No one says anything for a full minute.

"Well, it's clear that something is going on between you guys." Septa decides and her sneer returns. "Prove it."

"Prove what?" I am unable to follow her line of thinking.

"Prove you're not into him, or fucking your way up, go with Jan and make out with one of the boys."

"What? No way!"

"Do it, or we will tell the whole school what you've been up to with him."

"I just told you, I haven't done anything!" I am starting to hate Septa, we have never been friends, but we have never been real enemies before.

"Do it!" several of the girls squeal and I feel this sudden sense of dread flooding into my skin. Most people believe that peer pressure is something they would never be influenced by, but when it comes down to it, we are all subject to its whim. It's a simple by-product of being a homo sapien. Survival has always meant fitting in or risking being ejected from the tribe. How do you fight millions of years of programming without strong conviction or unwavering inner voice? The answer is you don't, you step out on the ledge while holding hands with your tribe.

"Okay, fine. I'll go. But I can't force anyone to make out with me if they aren't interested." I am hoping to god that if I am standoffish no one will bother trying to kiss me.

"Oh, I'm sure there is at least one boy who wouldn't mind slumming it." Septa jeers and my fists involuntarily ball, and my fingernails dig into my palms. It takes all my willpower to stem the urge to hit her in her smug face.

JAN LEADS us all to one of the empty classrooms. I keep expecting the alarms to sound and the monitoring system to kick in. Every hallway we go down I hold my breath, waiting for the shoe to drop. The Sword of Damocles is dangling above our heads but I'm the only one who can see it. I have no idea how Jan was able to get us all here without triggering the alarm. The monitoring system alerts teachers 60 seconds after a violation. I try not to think about getting caught. All I have to do is stand off to the side and not draw any attention as the rest of the girls flirt with the boys. We walk in, and a group of seven guys is sitting on top of the desks. They all turn to look at us as we walk in. The guys smile but none of them move. The girls all stop at the entrance, and for a long second nothing happens. Maybe we will just stand here forever, unable to break the awkward tension that fills the air with humid reticence. One of the boys scoots off his desk and Jan breaks away from the group and they get closer to each other.

"Hey! I'm Jan." she greets bubbly, and the boy stretches out his lanky arm toward her.

"I'm Martius." he greets back and they both shake hands, in one of the most awkward greetings I've ever seen in my life. The rest of the people start following their lead, inching forward to say hi. I stand back and just do an awkward unenthusiastic wave with my hand, a semi-circle in front of my body. Some pleasantries are exchanged, and the group starts talking about things that they can all relate to. How strict the teachers are, how long they have been here, how they think the world has changed since we all got locked up in this school. Despite my best efforts to fade into the background, I can't help but notice one guy staring at me, letting the rest of his friends do the talking. I keep looking away from him, he's easier to ignore than Faust, but it's hard not to look up when someone is staring at you. Septa is still standing by my side, a prison guard, making sure I meet her demands.

"He's cute," she whispers to me. As long as I am cooperating, she is happy to forget that only minutes ago she was very eager to fight me. The cattiness is gone from her voice and I rub my arm uncomfortable by the shift in her behavior.

"This is your chance, go up to him." He is cute, he has dark black hair and he is tall, not as tall as Faust, but taller than the rest of the boys. His hair is unruly, but somehow it works on his face, making him look roguish and mysterious. I have this impulse to flip his hair to see if it flops back the same way, draping over his forehead nearly covering one eye. I hesitate of course. After all, I have no intention of making out with a total stranger because someone dares me to. Septa pushes past me and walks right up to him. I am relieved because maybe she's decided to let it go and go after him herself. There are more girls than guys here, so her choices are limited. She starts talking to him, and he bends down to listen to her, but then she points to me and he looks up at me and a large grin spreads across his face. What the hell did she say to him? He nods something and they both approach me.

"Hey May, this is Maius, he wants to go make out with you." I cannot see my face and maybe it is too dark for everyone else to tell, but my skin gets hot and red, and I want to die on the spot.

"I'm sorry, what?" I ask, could I have heard her right?

"Yes, I told him about your goal to lose your virginity tonight, and so he was more than happy to oblige."

"What!?" I shout, and the whole room shushes me in unison.

"Look, she's obviously been pulling your leg," I tell Maius who is now silently laughing so hard he looks ready to double over. After a minute he reigns it in.

"Don't worry, I didn't think you wanted to do that, but I did want to meet you." he expounds after regaining his composure. He has an affable smile and something about his demeanor that puts me at ease. He puts one hand in his uniform pocket and leans against one of the desks as he speaks to me. He has a surprising amount of confidence talking to girls, considering he grew up isolated from the opposite sex, just like me.

"Oh." is all I can think of to say. He smiles at me and Septa crosses her arms and tilts her chin toward him. Egging me on to kiss him already. I decide to ignore her. I am not going to be bullied into making out with anyone.

"I'll leave you two to it," she says and winks at him. He shakes his head and smiles big, almost breaking out into laughter again.

"What's her deal anyway? She seemed pretty keen on us hooking up."

"She's just got some weird ideas, is all." I don't want to explain Faust and all the strangeness that comes with it.

"Like what?"

"Oh, like I somehow need to prove myself by hooking up with a boy."

"Yeah? Well, if that's what it takes, I'm happy to volunteer," he says, his lips pursing together, keeping a laugh from bubbling out again.

"Nice try. I think we should at least know something about each other before embarking on that adventure, don't you agree?"

"Yes, absolutely, I agree."

"You do? Good."

"Yeah, what's your favorite color?"

"Umm, I guess I like blue. What about you?"

"Red, definitely red," he says, and he grins. "Alright, so now that we know each other better, wanna go to another classroom?"

"God, you're incorrigible." I chastise, but we both burst into laughter. We get shushed again and we cover our mouths trying not to make any sound as our shoulders shake. Whenever I'm laughing big enough to rack my whole body, I think of old cartoons where the characters' shoulders move up and down in an exaggerated motion. I almost want to drag my shoulders up and down on purpose to act it out. The ease with which we fall into conversation is surprising. He tells me about his classes where he excels and where he struggles. He tells me what he wants to do once he graduates. It surprises me; I have never heard anyone in school talk about what they would do after. He has some ideas about going out in the world and traveling until he finds a good spot to build his own house. He wants to live so far away from people that it will take them weeks to reach him. I don't think it is possible, I remember enough about the world to know that that kind of distance no longer exists. We live on top of each other and traveling between units is nearly impossible, but if he isn't worried about being stuck in quarantine endlessly, who am I to tell him that his dreams are untenable? Despite knowing the pitfalls of his future life, I can't help getting drawn into his dream, and the feeling of endless, open, freedom. His eyes light up when he describes his future plot of land and the imaginary house. He has worked it all out, it seems. What will I do after this? After the government is no longer responsible for me? I don't have an answer and for the first time in my life, it scares me.

Chapter 8

Plymouth Academy prioritizes collective success over individual autonomy. Always remember how fortunate you are to be here.

— **Plymouth Academy Handbook, Chapter 1, Section 5**

The next morning, June and I are dead on our feet. We don't sleep when we get back; we are too keyed up to close our eyes. She tells me all about the guy she talked to. She says she doesn't like him, but he is as good as anyone to have a first kiss with. I can't understand that logic, but she says she would rather get it out of the way with someone she doesn't care about so that when she finally kisses someone she likes, she will know what she is doing. I can't help but admire her twisted logic, even if I would never want to do it that way. I want my first kiss to be with someone who stirs something inside me, someone who turns my insides to gelatin. My thoughts flash to Faust and his pink pouty lips and the scent of his nearness. I immediately tamp down the thought and instead try to think about Maius. Maius would probably be a good kisser. It is unlikely that he has any more experience than me, but maybe chemistry and friendliness would make up for it. I have no idea what a good kiss is. I always assume that it would be obvious, that you just know when it's good or bad, but maybe that's not how it works at all. Maybe you don't know what you're missing until you experience it. I have never thought about kissing so much in my life, and foreign feelings are creeping into my bones, reshaping and shifting my consciousness. Every time I see a pair of lips, my mind fills with kissing. It doesn't even matter who the lips belong to. Every person who speaks to me sets me off, and I imagine Faust's lips. Instead of focusing on only their voices, I focus on the movement of their lips, and the way people shape their lips as they speak. The strange way some people don't seem to form the right shapes to accommodate the sounds they are making. Their curious speech is becoming clearer to me with each pair of lips memorized and cataloged. I am discovering the missing puzzle pieces to explain the cadences and the mispronounced words—slightly slurred, garbled, and sometimes too precise. It is the precise words that always bring my thoughts back to Faust, who has all but vanished. I retake all my exams, getting 100% on each one. If I had been in the running, I would have easily outpaced the rest of the girls. Academically, I have one rival, Octavia, but she is a meek girl, and she can't keep up with me in the physical courses. Septa comes close, doing her best to beat every girl in the class. She is livid when we are forced to spar again, erasing her top score.

"I swear to god, May, if I hadn't seen you flirting with Maius last week, I would have said the only reason you got to redo all your work is because you fucked your way up to it," she spits at me after losing our final match. She says it loud enough that some of the girls look up from what they are doing, and my eyes shoot over to the instructor, who is luckily talking to another girl and doesn't hear her.

"What's wrong with you, Septa? If you say something like that again, you'll get both of us in trouble."

"So?" she says, but her eyes cast around the room, looking at the instructor, and some relief washes over her features before she schools them into indifference.

"So? So, you still have a chance of winning, if that's what you want." She does, as much as I had stepped aside for June, her chances aren't good. She doesn't compete academically, and she keeps getting demerits for tardiness. Her eyes flicker about, and she does a slow nod. It is the first time she hasn't argued with me in a long time. Octavia and Septa are in the top place. If either one of them could get up their score in their weaker categories, they could win. June is number ten on the list, and all the enthusiasm she poured in the first week has slowly dwindled until she is completely unmotivated. I kind of regret dropping out. Okay, I really regret it. I want to see Faust again and maybe get some answers. I have stopped looking for him because he obviously isn't coming back anytime soon, and since I am out, for all I know, I'll never see him again. I am stretching in the gym after the morning session when Killjoy marches into the classroom. She says something to Instructor Belfor, and Belfor nods and points in my direction. I watch as Killjoy walks over to me. She carries herself stiffly, and I can't help but wonder if she is trying to imitate Edits. If she is, she is doing a poor imitation, but maybe she can trick some people who have never seen one before.

"May, there you are," Killjoy says, and I get up from my spot on the floor and stand to attention.

"At ease," Killjoy says, her lips forming the words. Her mouth is flat for "At," and her lips pull back for "ease," revealing her perfectly white, straight teeth. I switch to a wide stance with my arms clasped behind me as I look ahead, waiting for her to address me.

"Well, I've got some good news," Killjoy says and doesn't wait for me to respond.

"You've been reinstated into the mentorship track." I want to protest, and my mouth opens up, but she holds up her hands to silence me.

"No, don't thank me. Your academic record has vastly improved. You should be proud of your hard work. It would be shame if a student of your caliber missed out." My mouth hangs open, unsure of what to say or how to react. Do I want to be in it? Yes, but now nothing is stopping Septa from thinking I somehow manipulated my way into it, or as she so often puts it, fucked my way up. She leaves me standing there, and I hope to God that no one finds out anytime soon. I need time to plan what to say, and how to handle it. That night, we gathered in the gym for an announcement. The girls all line up, curiosity etched on their features, but they try to school them and look out at the far wall. The room is silent as we wait. Killjoy and the rest of the instructors are lined up before us. Killjoy stands smack dab in the center, and occasionally her eyes flick over to the time on the wall, but she doesn't speak. Some of the girls start to lose their perfect posture, their shoulders begin to slump. My neck starts to ache, and I wonder why we are still standing here. I want to yell at Killjoy to just get it over with, which is not a real option. Finally, the door to the gym whooshes open, and Faust saunters in. He is slow and precise in his movements. He doesn't act hurried, even though he has kept a room of seventy women waiting for him. Something that I would describe as dread starts to come over me. I know what is going to happen before it happens. I want to run from the room and take cover in the nearest dark corner. Killjoy smiles at him, and Faust simply nods and stands in front of her, facing the girls.

"It is my pleasure to announce the winner of the mentorship program," he says, and his green eyes immediately land on me, a lion in the savannah spotting his prey.

"After several weeks of watching all of you work so hard, I am pleased to say that May is the winner." I can feel the shock from the girls next to me, and if they could turn on me and attack me, they would.

"May," he says, and he holds out his hand to me. I don't know what to do; I just stand there, lead encasing my feet.

"Come now, don't be shy, you've earned it," he says, and he walks up to me and reaches for my hand that is hanging limply at my side. He takes it in his and shakes it. He stands a few feet from me, an appropriate distance. No one would think anything was amiss. I am the only one who is aware of the way he strokes my hand with his thumb and the way his eyes look at me. He's able to penetrate my mental shield. I am a volcano pouring out lava, emptying its contents. I am a stoic mountain whose soul is hidden from the world, but it is on display for Faust.

"Congratulations, May," he says, and he strokes my hand one last time before stepping back to the line with the rest of the teachers.

Killjoy waits for Faust to take a spot next to her before she speaks.

"It is a great honor, May, and we are all very proud of you. You will stay behind, and we will tell you the particulars of the mentorship program. The rest of you girls are dismissed," Killjoy announces, and the girls all file out, but not before a few of them give me some nasty looks. In particular, Septa, looks ready to kill me.

She mouths, "I knew it," as she passes me. The only people who remain are Killjoy, Faust, and me. I stand still, waiting for them to address me. Faust and Killjoy exchange a few words, and I catch "Thanks again, Kilroy," before she leaves. Faust waits until Killjoy crosses the large gymnasium and closes the door behind her before he approaches me.

"Spark, congratulations," he says again. Using that nickname he has for me, one that feels far too personal, and one I'm unable to interpret the meaning of, it grates at me.

"Please address me as May," I respond, feeling disjointed and slightly angry. The whole thing is strange, and I can't put my finger on why. I feel I was always meant to win, but why even have a competition in the first place? Why put all the girls through all this effort if I was always going to get chosen?

"No, I think not. Why don't you pick your new designation? It's time." He steps in front of me and stops a few inches short. Whenever he has me alone, personal space has no meaning. I crane my neck to look up at him. We aren't supposed to choose a designation until we leave the school. I don't even have a name in mind; I've been putting it off, waiting for something that feels right. There is a disjointed sense of myself when I think of my rotating names, in my rotating life. A spinning door of endless doubts and unknowns always pushing me out before I'm ready.

"I will choose my designation when I graduate," I say, looking off to the side, fixing my eyes on a blue tumbling mat.

"You're done here, Kira; you're leaving with me tomorrow." He takes a stray hair that has gotten loose from my ponytail and twirls it around his finger. I pull my head away and take a large step back. My hair slips from his finger, and he stands there with his hand in the air, one finger pointing toward the ceiling. He slowly retracts his finger into his fist and drops his hand. He steps toward me, erasing the distance I had just made.

"Don't run from me, Spark." His voice softens, but there's an edge to it, a warning. His eyes, usually inscrutable, now flash with an intensity that sends a shiver down my spine.

"What does a mentorship program entail, sir?" I ask, ignoring his comment, trying to keep my voice steady.

"It means you will take your place in the world, and I will make sure you become the person you were always meant to be," he says vaguely, picking up the strand of hair again and rubbing the tip between his fingers.

"Where are we going?" I wasn't ready to go. What about June? No one has prepared me for this. I had just started to think about life beyond these walls, and now it was here, without any warning.

"To your new home. Don't bother packing; you don't need

anything from your life here. Pick a new designation, or I will pick one for you."

"I am not ready; I don't understand any of this." My throat feels tight, and I swallow painfully. Am I getting sick?

"You will understand in time." He takes a step back and starts walking toward the exit.

"I'll see you tomorrow, Spark," he announces before exiting through the door, leaving me alone in the gymnasium.

It seems my life will always be this way, abrupt changes without any chance to prepare. Never being able to look back or take anything with me. Would I ever see June or any of the girls again?

Chapter 9

Rebellion is the spark that ignites individuality.
— Kira's Journal, Book 3, Page 20

When I get back to the dorm, June is pacing back and forth, her feet making soft thuds on the worn carpet. She stops mid-stride when the door closes behind me.

"Oh my gosh! May, this is huge!" she shouts, her eyes wide with excitement. She practically bounces on the balls of her feet, unusually excited for me.

"You're not mad at me?" I ask, still reeling from the whirlwind of events.

"Are you kidding? No way, I'm so happy and proud of you. I wasn't going to win anyway; I shouldn't even have asked you to not compete." June says and swoops in to hug me, her arms wrapping around me tightly. She is a ball of happy nervous energy, her body vibrating with it. It takes her a minute to realize I'm sobbing. She stops hugging and pulls back to look at my face, her hands resting on my shoulders.

"What is going on, May? Aren't you excited?" Her brow furrows in concern, her eyes searching mine for answers. I shrug, unable to find the words, and pull her in for another hug, my tears soaking into her shirt. "I'm leaving," I tell her, my voice muffled as I press my face into her shoulder.

"What?!" she shouts in surprise and pulls back from the hug again, her eyes wide with shock.

"I'm going with Faust tomorrow," I repeat, my voice trembling.

"What?" she echoes, her voice barely above a whisper as she slumps onto her bed, processing the news. She runs a hand through her hair, her expression shifting from confusion to worry.

"Yes, he just told me. I'm going tomorrow morning, and I'm not even supposed to take anything with me." I look around the small dorm room. I don't need anything—no keepsakes or personal items. There are only my uniforms, pajamas, bathroom kit, ballet clothing, and my sheets, which have all been assigned to me along with every girl here.

"Wow, going with Faust." June's eyes light up, and she grins. "He is sooo gonna fall in love with you!" She apparently thought this was an exciting prospect, but I was worried he already had. At least he seems to have some fixation on me that makes no sense.

"Don't say that," I scold, falling face-first into my pillow, sucking in shallow breaths through the cotton fabric.

"Why? Every girl here wants Faust to fall in love with them. Why do you think they are acting so crazy about this whole mentorship?" June sits on her bed, her fingers fiddling with the edge of her blanket. I flip over to my side and look at her, groaning, and then fall back into my pillow again.

"I don't..." An idea takes hold. If Faust is going to take me away tomorrow, I have nothing to lose. I shoot up into a seated position.

"Let's go meet the boys one more time before I leave!"

June bursts out laughing, clutching her stomach.

"Of course, now that you have the hottest man alive taking you away, you want to flirt with boys." The room feels smaller with the sudden burst of excitement. I jump off my bed, the worn carpet soft under my feet, and start pacing. The fluorescent lights above cast a harsh glow on the sparse furnishings, making the moment feel surreal. June's laughter fills the room, and for a moment, it feels like everything is normal again.

"Come on, June. Let's make tonight memorable," I say, a hint of mischief in my voice as I stop pacing and face her. She shakes her head, still laughing, but the sparkle in her eyes shows she's considering it. "Alright, May. Let's go have some fun."

"I'm gonna make out with Maius!" I declare that if I am going to be dragged around this life as a puppet on a string, I am at least going to make some choices in my life and I decide in the moment that Maius is going to be my first kiss. June is all for the plan and she sends a PM to Jan's tablet. A few minutes later the tablet dinges and tells us it is on and to be ready to go after lights out. The group of girls has expanded since the last outing, and I am immediately disappointed to see that Septa is one of them. She spots me in the dark hallway, her face barely illuminated by the faint glow of our tablets. She looks ready to jump me, her eyes glinting with anger. She is about to spew at me when the other girls see it coming and shush her, pointing to the monitoring system that somehow is not setting off alarms. I never did figure out how Jan managed to rig this setup. I thank the gods that at least I am safe for now; no one wants to get into trouble, so Septa has no chance to start anything tonight.

THE HALLWAY IS DARK, with only the occasional flicker of tablet lights turning on when needed, casting eerie, shifting shadows on the walls. I don't want to fight anyone tonight, and I don't want to hurt Septa. I wish she would just understand that these circumstances are entirely out of my control. We enter the same classroom as last time, and the boys are sitting on the desks again, talking about something. When we come in, their heads snap up, and instead of the awkward silence that had occurred the first time, the girls and boys immediately go up to the person they had flirted with the night before. Maius spots me at once, and I meet him halfway. "Hey!" he greets me and gives me an unexpected bear hug. It feels nice and warm, like a security blanket, and I sink into him, absorbing the feeling. He doesn't mind at all, and when he finally breaks the hug, he doesn't let go of my waist.

"Hey, you good?" he asks. Maius is evidently a keen observer because he can tell I am not myself.

"Yeah, I'm fine. Can we go to another classroom?" I don't see the point of beating around the bush; my time is limited, and I will never see him again anyway. His readily available smile bursts forth, and he takes my hand, leading me out of the classroom. He occasionally looks back at me as we make our way to the next room, his eyes holding a glint that I can see even in the dark. His hand feels warm in mine, maybe a little bit sweaty. When he pulls me inside, he is breathing more heavily than is strictly necessary from going from one room to another.

"Hey," he says in the dark. I step forward, closing the distance between us. I look at his friendly face.

"Hey yourself," I retort. I can't tell you where my boldness comes from, except I feel I have nothing to lose. I can hear him gulp, but he smiles at me and leans forward. I close my eyes, and just when I think our lips are going to meet, I fall forward and meet air. I open my eyes, and instead of Maius standing in front of me, an intimidating Faust is holding Maius in a neck hold. I am so stunned that for a moment, I just stand there, but then I see Maius's face turning red, and I shake my head and lunge forward at Faust.

"Let him go!" I shout, pulling on his arm, which doesn't budge at all. The dim light casts ominous shadows on Faust's face, his jaw clenched with determination.

"Stop this, Kira," Faust chides, annoyance lacing his voice. He pushes me away with his free hand and speaks to Maius. "You don't get to touch her. I will let you go, but this is going to be reported. Your group's dalliances have come to an end."

"Faust! Let him go! He can't breathe!" I cry out and try to grab at him again, but his hand keeps me firmly in place. I didn't realize Edits were this strong. He is a brick wall for all the effort it takes.

Faust lets go of Maius, who collapses to the floor, grabbing his neck and gasping for air. I try to drop to the floor to help him, but Faust picks me up around the waist and throws me over his shoulder.

"You always have to make things so hard, Kira," he says with his practiced cadence. He is so calm; you would never believe he had just choked a teenager. I bang on his back and shout profanities as he strolls out of the classroom with me. When we reach the hallway, the teenagers from the other classes come out to see what the sudden commotion is about.

"Put me down, Goddamnit, Faust, you son of a bitch!" I shout, not caring who hears me at this point. He just ignores me and keeps walking. What was his first name, God-damnit? Mason, Max, Ma… Magnus? "Magnus!" I shout, hoping it is the right one. He stops for a second, which can only mean I had the right one.

"Magnus, put me down," I ask him again, this time in a nicer voice. He puts me down and instead takes my hand.

"We are going tonight before you come up with any more bright ideas," he tells me. I try to pull free, digging in my feet, and the group of delinquents stand there watching the whole show. Maius comes scrambling out of the classroom we have just left and charges Faust. Maius throws his shoulder into Faust's stomach, and had it been a normal man, he would have knocked him off his feet. Faust doesn't budge; his reaction would have been the same if a mosquito had bitten him.

"Are you done, boy? I don't want to hurt you," he sounds

exasperated like he's dealing with unruly children. Maius steps back, confusion etching his features.

"He's an Edit," I tell Maius in explanation. Maius looks between the two of us, trying to work out what is happening.

"Who is he to you?" he asks me, but before I can answer, Faust speaks.

"Don't address her," he tells Maius. "Kira, pick up your feet and start moving, or I'm going to pick you up again."

"I don't know," I say to Maius, ignoring Faust altogether.

"If you don't want to go with him," Maius offers, but before he can finish his sentence, Faust just picks me up and slings me over his shoulder. I am just a bag of potatoes. Maius looks ready to attack him, but I can't let him do that. He will lose, and what would be the point? Faust will take me anyway.

"Don't, Maius. I want to go, okay?" I say and speak to Faust. "Magnus put me down and I'll behave." Faust puts me on my feet and I follow him out of the hallway. The alarms finally start going off, and I can hear the group of kids scattering behind us as we go. I don't see June in the crowd, and I wonder if she knows what has happened. I also can't help but wonder where she has gone, and I will probably never know because I will probably never see her again. He leads me down a corridor I'd never been down before, which is weird since I thought I knew every inch of this school. The walls seem to close in, making it feel like a twilight zone or a dream. Things aren't exactly as they are in real life; in dreams, the ceilings aren't quite at the same height, or the distance from one end of the room to the other doesn't add up. We reach a door, and he scans his wrist. He holds out his hand to me, and I reluctantly take it as we step through. It is still dark outside, but we are outside at night. I can't even remember the last time I saw the night sky. There are no stars to see, but the chill of the air is invigorating. I almost forget for a minute that I am going against my will to some unknown location with some Edit. There is a car waiting just outside the door, and just as quickly as we had come outside, we are back inside again. He lets me sit down first and then scoots in next to me. The car starts moving on its own accord. He sits back and stretches out his long legs in front of him.

"Well, this is not how I wanted this to go," he says after several minutes of silence have passed. I ignore him and look out the window. Why does he always talk so weirdly?

"You could have left in daylight and said goodbye to your classmates and your instructors." I still could, I think bitterly.

"Instead, you run off and try to do God knows what, with some boy." I just keep staring out the window. I have nothing to say to him.

"What were you planning on doing with that boy Kira?" When I don't turn to look at him, he grabs me by the neck and turns me toward him. His face is right in front of mine.

"Were you going to kiss him?" he asks, and his eyes fly down to my lips. His tongue darts out and traces my bottom lip and my entire body stills with surprise.

"These lips are not meant for others," he murmurs and sucks my lower lip into his mouth and claims my mouth. His kiss is soft at first, tentative, but when I don't pull away mostly from surprise, he deepens his kiss. He pulls me closer, and his tongue invades my mouth. It flicks in and out, exploring every crevice of my mouth. I eventually dare to dart my own tongue into his mouth when my body begins to respond to him, in a way I don't want to. My body starts to tingle and heat, and a sensation of warmth floods into my core. I make a sound in my throat, and he pulls back from the kiss and just stares at me. This time he is breathing as hard as me.

"It wasn't meant to happen that way, Kira."

"What do you mean?" I cry out, confused, and disjointed. I want to kiss him again, but I also want nothing to do with him. I'm being ripped apart internally. My body is warring with my brain. I feel like I'm about to enter the battle of Verdun, an endless siege until someone is forced to surrender or retreat. It remains to be seen if my brain is French or German. I'm worried, my brain is the Germans and my body will win out in the end. Fury clouded my brain, but I am not going to let him kiss me again.

"Shhh," he says in response and strokes my hair gently, I feel no different than a child. I push his hand away and pull away from him.

Chapter 10

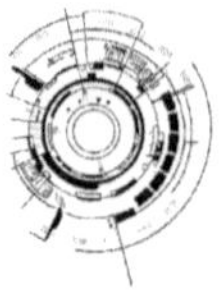

If a ship is steering off course, sometimes the only way to correct it is with firm guidance, ensuring it reaches its intended destination.

— Magnus Compendium, Section 3.4

Magnus

I hate that she pushes me away, I hate that she fights me, and I hate that she almost kissed that boy. It is a good thing that I couldn't relax from excitement and decided to check up on my little mentee. If I hadn't, who knows what she would have done with that boy? As soon as I saw her sneak through the corridors with her girlfriends, I followed her, curiosity being something of an addiction with me. After all, curiosity is sometimes the only thing worth living for. When I saw her with that boy, I almost lost it. I felt the same as I had when I was human, with no control over my emotions. I scan the video logs as soon as I sit in the car. The interior is sleek and modern, with dark leather seats and a softly glowing dashboard.

The hum of the electric engine is barely audible as we glide through the streets. What if she had done something else with that boy? My eyes used to flicker when I watched digital content inside my mind, but with the recent upgrade, it no longer alerts people that I'm doing it. I am pleased to find that the video footage shows they had only met once before, and nothing had happened. I don't like the way she smiled at him; I want her to smile at me that way. I just have to be patient, I tell myself, and I have plenty of time. I do have plenty of time, but some things are hard to wait for. I let her stay on her side of the car and tamp down the need to pull her onto my lap and hold her. I shouldn't have kissed her so soon; that was another mistake, a mistake my human self would have made. Every time I've interacted with her, I've barely been able to restrain myself. It's a good thing that being upgraded to an Edit comes with an emotional filter, because a human with my strength would have killed that boy. Kira is scratching her thigh again; the gesture should be annoying, but I find it soothing. It is so her; it is a little piece of her that I know so well, and it feels comfortable hearing the scrape scrape scrape of her nails. That uniform has to go. As soon as we get home, she will take it off and it will go straight in the unraveller. I make a note to do a self-diagnosis after we get home. My emotional filter might be malfunctioning. She falls asleep halfway through the drive before we get to the terminal that will take us the rest of the way home. I pick her up and carry her to the next vehicle that will fly us up to the house. She nestles into my chest, and I feel my heart rate increasing. It feels magical to see her peaceful, sleeping body cradled in my arms. I tell my heart to slow its tempo and resume regular beats. I sit down and keep her in my arms as she sleeps. I can't resist the urge to stroke her long blonde hair, filled with an array of platinum blonde shades, the moon and stars streaking through her strands. It's a pool of starlight flowing out of her scalp. It amazes me sometimes that I found her, after all this time. The ride up to the house is quick. After we land, I carry her to her room and place her on the bed. If she knew she was mine, I would have bathed her and dressed her, but I need her to come to me on her terms. I need her to need me as much as I need her. She will have one more night in that uniform, and tomorrow her life will change.

IN THE MORNING, after a self-diagnostic, I discovered one of my filters had a bug, and I was forced to do an upgrade, which took longer than I would have liked. I don't want her to wake up alone and confused. Luckily, she is still asleep when I am done. I sometimes forget how much humans sleep, what a waste of hours. I want to wake her up and start the day, but she needs sleep. I sit at the piano and work on my latest composition. It is incomplete, and despite my musical proclivities, I can't quite figure out the end. It is there somewhere in the corner of my brain, in a place that feels inaccessible. The melody fills the vaulted ceilings and bounces off the glass windows that stretch floor to ceiling, illuminating the room in a stunning morning sunrise. Up here above the world, it is magical to see the sun rise above the clouds. The clouds' white puffy shapes become outlined in a rainbow of colors, sunlight peeking through the cracks. Even after all the years I've lived, the sunrise always has a way of making me stop what I am doing to watch the splendor. My hands are on the keys, resting in position, but my neck is craned toward the window, watching as each strand of light bursts through, making the room brighter and brighter with each passing moment. I hear a noise and turn to find Kira standing there at the entrance of the living room. She looks mesmerized by the sight of the clouds and the sunrise, and she doesn't even seem to detect me at all. I watch her watch the sunrise, completely engrossed in the sight of her. She is more compelling than the sunrise. Her eyes light up, magic filling her senses, and it is a pang of pride that I can bring her this moment. When the sun seems to settle firmly in place, her eyes scan the room and land on me. I can see the blues of her eyes even from here, and she looks glorious, despite the horrendous uniform. Her hair is a mess, but her skin is glowing as it always does.

"Come here," I say on impulse, but she doesn't budge. I want to pull her to me, but my emotional filter is balanced this morning. Instead, I begin to play the piano. I play Tchaikovsky's Swan Lake theme, and after a moment or two, she slowly approaches the piano. She runs a tentative hand over my satin black Steinway concert grand piano, one of the few possessions I value. The only relic of my human life. She strokes the piano with reverence as I play and then drops a hand, embarrassed for overstepping. If she only knew how much that was impossible for her to do. I play through till the end, and by then she has inched closer to me, standing at my side and watching my hands at work.

"You play beautifully," she says with some awe in her voice. I smile at her and start playing another song. This is a good way to make her feel at ease. It is one of my compositions, and she has a confused look on her face as she tries to place the unknown piece. She rounds the piano, leaving my side, and I watch her delicate fingers stretch out as if wanting to touch the beautiful instrument again. Her graceful movements remind me of how she danced. Had there been room for her to dance, I think she would. I make a mental note to make room. I finish the song and sit there, unsure of how to address her next. I want her to come to me, so I decide to say nothing. She slowly comes around back to the piano bench, but this time she stays a good two feet away from me. The music had bewitched her before, and she had forgotten her fear of me, but now that the music is over, she is wary of me again.

"So, what now?" she asks after a long silence. She rocks on the heels of her feet and shoves her hands into her skirt pocket, which reminds me, that outfit has to go.

"Now you shower, and change," I say, and perhaps it was the

wrong way to say it because her eyes widen, and she instinctively crosses her arms.

I ignore it. "There are towels and clothes in your room," I instruct her and turn back to the piano, beginning to play another piece.

Chapter 11

While the true extent of their capabilities remains largely speculative due to their secretive nature, Edits are believed to possess lifespans extending several centuries, thanks to their advanced genetic modifications and cybernetic enhancements. Their exact composition—whether predominantly biological or mechanical—remains a topic of debate among scholars.

- Advanced Studies in Post-Human Societies, Chapter 8, Page 157

Kira

I don't know where we are, but all I can see are clouds. We must be somewhere high indeed, perhaps a mountain top. His music is unsettling, beautiful, and flawless. I hadn't expected his smile to be so beautiful; he had never looked so at ease and peaceful before. It takes me by surprise, and despite his perfect playing, his eyes never leave me. They trace my every movement. I wonder what kind of upgrades give you the ability to have such a deep focus on multiple things. Everyone knows that I could use that upgrade. I have never been good at focusing on more than one thing at a time. I did well in my classes not because I paid attention to them, but because I was an excellent self-learner and I always read through the textbooks before classes even began. I have almost an eidetic memory for texts. I leave the giant living room, with its open floor plan and massive floor-to-ceiling windows that showcase the endless sky. The walls are adorned with intricate wood inlays, and the floors are a gleaming marble that reflects the morning light. I trace my footsteps back to the room I awoke in. It is unsettling to find myself in a completely new place with no memory of getting here. The piano music had woken me up, and I followed the sound out to the living room, only to be met with the most glorious display of a sunrise I'd ever seen. The room is brightly lit now with the sun filtering in through the large windows. The only thing outside is clouds, and I can't help but wonder how far up we are. I don't understand how we are avoiding altitude sickness. Although maybe the signs haven't come yet. There is no way for me to know how long I've been here, but it can't have been too long since the sun has just come up. I try the only other door in the room, and it whooshes open and reveals a long walk-in closet that is filled with clothes my size. I can't help but feel creeped out at the gesture. How did he fill a closet full of my clothes this quickly? It only adds to my theory that somehow I was meant to win the mentorship. Something doesn't sit right with me, a centipede creeping up my spine telling me something is dreadfully wrong. It's tickling my neck, and the more I pay attention to it, the more it tickles. The walk-in closet leads into a modest bathroom with a separate shower and bathtub, a luxury from a bygone era. Bathtubs were outlawed long before I was born to stem the water crisis. The sink is attached to a vanity with a soft-looking chair that slides under the counter. Above it is a mirror with lights framing it. There is an assortment of beauty products I don't know anything about and makeup, which I have never worn before. I don't think I want to use it; it reminds me too much of my mother. I strip off my clothes and turn on the shower. I don't dare use the bathtub in case it isn't allowed. It is an enticing prospect to take my first bath. The bathroom is covered in white marble floor-to-ceiling tiles. The tiles look handmade and expensive. The entire place looks more extravagant than anything I could have imagined in my small world. I don't know much about Edits, but everyone knows you have to be dreadfully rich to become an Edit. The shower is hot, and the water feels silky. I don't understand how the water can feel different here, but it does. I wash my hair with the shampoo and conditioner that is already in the shower. I pick up the bottle to read it, and I am surprised when it says Kira on the label. I turn it and read the back. It is a specialized formula designed for me. I drop the bottle. It makes a loud sound, and I quickly bend down to pick it up. I half expect Faust to show up and ask me not to make such a loud racket. I clutch the bottle to me for a minute before feeling silly and placing the shampoo back on the shelf. When I am done, I grab one of the fluffy white towels and dry myself off. With dripping hair, I grab another and wrap it around my head in a turban twist. I wander into the closet to see what I'm going to wear. The materials are all natural fibers: cotton, silk, and wool. One of the silk dresses is almost too soft to feel, and I desperately want to put it on, but it is so tight and revealing I don't want to send Faust the wrong message. I love the buttery white color of it, but I hang it back in the closet and choose a pair of soft cotton tights and a slouchy wool sweater instead. The underwear drawer is almost too embarrassing to look at. I have to wonder if Faust has picked everything out himself. Each pair is silky or lacy, and I am positive I'd never worn underwear so extravagant in my life. I chose a pair of silky underwear; it has a bit more coverage than the lace. I go back into the bathroom, find a comb, and comb out my hair. I look around for a hair tie, but I can't find anything, so I am forced to leave it down. I can feel my still-wet hair dripping down my back, making my sweater wet, but I don't want to do anything about it. It will dry eventually. Something is soothing about how the water makes the wool itchy. It's a reminder to stay in my body and not float out into space. My brain is its own galaxy, and if the world didn't force the issue, I'd probably just continue floating around looking at all the constellations. When I finally feel brave enough to leave the room, my hair has mostly dried. The aroma of bacon leads me to open the door and follow it to the source. The long, pristine hallway with its high ceilings and spotless surfaces reminds me a little bit of the academy, but it is much more decadent. The marble and wood detailing are so beautiful that I sometimes stop to just look at a particular piece of inlay. When I find the kitchen, Faust is standing by the stove stirring something in a pan. He looks up when I enter the room, smiles at me with a closed mouth, and turns back to what he was doing. I don't know what to do with the new Faust. He isn't crowding me or being possessive; he is completely at ease. I stand in the doorway, feeling out of place. I scratch my cotton tights, bunching the fabric with my fingertips.

"Are you hungry?" he asks over his shoulder and gestures toward the kitchen table, which is already set. There is coffee and juice and bacon and toast, with real butter. I take one of the two seats, and he comes up behind me with a plate of scrambled eggs made from real eggs. I can feel his breath on the top of my head before he takes a seat across from me. He takes the cloth napkin from one of the plates and folds it over his lap. I look at the flower-shaped napkin on my plate, tentatively pick it up

"Did you fold this?" I hear myself asking, my voice barely above a whisper as I touch the delicate flower-shaped napkin. I hesitantly stretch it out over my lap. It feels a shame to destroy the flower.

"Yes," he admits without further explanation and starts pouring me some coffee from the French press, his movements smooth and precise. The aroma of freshly brewed coffee fills the air, mingling with the aroma of bacon and toast.

"I hope you like coffee," he says, looking at me with a small smile. "Cream?" he asks, holding the pitcher poised above the cup, his eyes locking onto mine.

The truth is I've never had coffee before, and I thought he would know, but it is a relief that he doesn't. I fidget with the napkin, twisting it in my lap, avoiding his gaze.

"Umm, I'm not sure," I say and take a tentative sip of the dark hot beverage. It is bitter and I nearly spit it out from surprise. I guess I had expected coffee to taste like chocolate. I tried real chocolate once, it was a birthday gift when I was a little girl. Faust chuckles, "It's an acquired taste, one you don't need to indulge." he says, and he pours me some juice instead. He takes my cup of coffee instead of pouring himself a new one and when he turns the cup to drink from where I had. It feels too intimate, I feel exposed. I have to avert my eyes from his and I focus on the bacon instead and take a piece from the pile.

"It's probably hard for you to believe, but this is very good coffee." he takes another deep pull of the coffee before putting it down on the table.

"You see, in many ways, coffee is like wine, it is difficult to grow, harvest, roast, and brew. Every single step of the way is crucial, if one mistake is made the coffee is ruined. Wine and Coffee both have notes of flavor that an educated tongue can taste. If you like, I can teach you someday to appreciate these things, the way I do. He takes a piece of toast and butter it for me and places it on my plate without asking if I want it.

"I'm not sure I have much call for knowing the finer things in life, after all, I'm just a lowly orphan, and when our time here is done, I'm sure I'll go back to my meager beginnings." He takes a deep breath through his nose and sits back in his chair.

"Kira, there is something that we have to get straight right now," he says and for a moment he is back to being the old Faust, the one who was intimidating and unsettling and *sometimes* even exciting.

"You belong here; you will never go back to that life, so you might as well get used to it."

"I belong here?" I can't help but ask. What the hell does that mean?

"Yes, Kira, you belong here. This is your home now." He gestures around the room as if to illustrate what's mine is yours, and I feel that tight lump in my throat again.

"I don't understand." I don't, I don't understand anything. He sighs and leans forward, taking my hand.

"You belong with me," he says, and there is an intensity in his eyes that makes me feel like I can't breathe.

"I still don't understand. Do you mean I belong to you?" His eyes do something strange, like a flicker, before refocusing on me.

"No. Not exactly." He pulls me over to him, and my legs are Jell-O as I move without volition. He pulls me into his lap and turns my head to look me in the eyes.

"I'm going to tell you something because I think the truth is always a good place to start." He nuzzles his nose into my neck for a second and takes a deep breath. He is steeling himself or breathing me in, or steeling himself by breathing me in. It makes my skin feel hot and strange. My skin doesn't feel like it belongs on my body.

"I want you to try to be calm about it, but I'll understand if you can't be. I just hope you will at least think it through and understand over time." It is hard to focus on his words when he is close with his arms wrapped around my waist.

"Kira, your mother didn't die, she sold you." of all the things I thought he might have said, that was the last one I could have imagined. I can hear my own heartbeat in my ears as if someone has shoved fingers inside muffling the outside world. "She sold you to me." he continues and the more he speaks the more the world seems to spin. I vaguely feel the picture slip from my hand, it floats down on the ground in a zig-zag landing face down. My stomach starts to flip flop and bile starts to travel up through my esophagus. It's burning a way through my insides and demanding to be released before it engulfs my body leaving me a singed heap.

"You bought me?!" I screech before trying to jump off his lap to reach the sink in time to vomit. He holds me tight, misunderstanding the gesture. He thinks I am only trying to escape him and before I can protest the bile flies out of my mouth and lands on his chest. Strangely he doesn't seem revolted, and he picks me up and carries me to the bedroom ignoring the vomit that now coats his own shirt. When we get to the bathroom, he puts me down on the vanity chair and strips off his shirt. He takes a white hand towel and soaks it in water and rings it out. I watch his arms and back muscles flexing with each movement. He comes up to me and squats in front of me and wipes off my face gently.

"That's an understandable reaction." He speaks as if no time has elapsed since he carried me in from the living room.

"I knew she was abusing you, little one and I couldn't stand to see such a beautifully brilliant girl suffer like that. You see, you never failed that exam, Kira." I don't dare to speak because I want to hear what he has to say. "No, in fact, you did so well that you beat the highest score by a long shot. If we had given your mother that scholarship money, she would have squandered it on something for herself and you wouldn't have gotten anything out of it." He strokes my cheek gets up picks up my toothbrush and spreads toothpaste over it.

"It was an easy decision to make, I had a lawyer approach your mother and made a generous offer, not too generous, but one I was sure she would take; the truth is I would have offered an innumerable sum." He brings me a toothbrush and hands it to me. I get off the seat and brush my teeth, keeping my eyes on him through the mirror as he reveals the most heartbreaking thing I've ever heard. I shake my head, trying to process his words. He continues, his tone measured and calm,

"She took the first offer, Kira. She didn't even hesitate, nor did she ask what I wanted with you." His eyes meet mine steadily, his expression serene but resolute. I spit out the toothpaste and rinse my mouth, the vile taste of vomit is gone, but the feeling of bile in my throat remains.

"I enrolled you in the school, a place I knew you would be safe until you were old enough for me to get you," he explains.

"This next bit might be the hardest part for you to accept," he says, and I spin around to look at him. He is behind me, close as he tends to be, and I look up at him, my eyes wide with anxiety.

"What could possibly be worse than that?" I am surprised at how raw my voice sounds, my throat tight with emotion.

"Well, I personally think it's wonderful, but you might not see it that way, yet." He leans down and whispers in my ear, his breath warm against my skin.

"Before I tell you, I'd very much like to kiss you," he says, and I can't believe the gall of him.

"Are you kidding?" I push him aside, my palms pressing against his chest, and stomp over to my room. He follows me, and I cross my arms, hoping he gets the message to keep his distance. He stops a few feet short of me, his eyes searching mine.

"I wasn't looking for you, but life brought you to me," he tells me, his voice gentle but unwavering. If I had felt confused, scared, or angry before, it is nothing compared to how I feel in this moment. My hands tremble slightly, and I clench them tighter, trying to steady myself.

"You see, I'm old. I've been alone for a long time. Everyone I've ever known or loved has died. I have been looking for my soulmate for ages. When I found you, I had a flash of recognition, somehow you matched my soul. It wasn't love, not like it is now. I simply wanted to keep you safe. When I saw you at the assembly, I knew you were the one for me. I knew you were my soulmate, the person who fit perfectly into my polygon. You were also someone I could shape, someone who could be mine forever, someone who was intrinsically smart and beautiful, someone who could one day give me a child and eventually become an Edit herself."

"Polygon?" I ask. For some reason, that is the question that comes out of my mouth, unbidden.

"I have this polygon theory for friendship. Each person has several sides to their personality, and if you're lucky, one or more of those sides will align with another person's. These alignment points are what enable friendship to develop. A good friend will connect with you on multiple sides, while a soulmate will link up with every single one. It's like finding a perfect puzzle piece, laser-cut to fit without any gaps. When you meet these people, sometimes you just know they belong in your polygon," he explains. "You're a perfect match. I just know it."

"I don't understand," I whisper, but in truth, it's probably the only time in my life I've had the truth, the only time I should understand. My world is unraveling and reshaping itself all in the span of ten minutes. Every confusion I've ever felt vanishes, everything makes sense. The reason why I had met two Edits, why I was sent to such an isolated all-girls school, why he had been so possessive with me from the first minute we met. I have never made a single decision in my life; he was behind everything I've done since I left home. Before that, my controlling mother had made all my decisions for me. In short, he is a madman and my life is not mine. He bought me on a whim, and now he thinks he owns me. Now he thinks I'll just fall into his arms, and give him babies.

"You're insane!" I shout at him. His eyes flicker momentarily but he doesn't move from his spot.

"You can't just pull people out of their lives and just decide that they are the one! It doesn't work that way." I approach him and poke him hard in the chest, but he doesn't budge.

"You will never have me; I will never give you children! You let me go, you let me go!" I start pacing when he still doesn't move a muscle.

"I didn't even think Edits could have children!" I snap and I slap him across the face. His head turns but he seems unharmed. I think it hurts me more than it hurts him. I clutch my hand trying to soothe the sting.

"See what you've done, Spark," he says, and he tries to take my hand to soothe it, I pull my wrist free and stomp out of the room.

"Don't call me that!" I bellow as I make my way through the large house. I have no idea where I am going. I just can't stand to look at him.

"Kira, your reaction is very understandable."

"You think!?" I round a corner and stumble into an atrium. Birds are chirping and plants are growing everywhere. It is gorgeous; I can hardly take in the variety of flowers and colors that spring forth in every direction. Vines creep up the sides of the glass walls, reaching toward a glass roof that allows the light to pour in, creating a surreal, ethereal glow. Exotic plants and vibrant blooms fill every nook and cranny, their scents mingling in the air, intoxicating and overwhelming. Damn him for having such an incredible place. Damn him for stealing me from my home. Damn him for thinking he can just own me. The lush greenery and cascading flowers create a stark contrast to the clinical environment of the academy. I see butterflies flitting from flower to flower, their delicate wings adding to the enchanting atmosphere. The air feels fresh and clean, filled with the sounds of rustling leaves and the occasional flutter of wings. I take a hesitant step forward, my feet sinking into the soft, moss-covered ground. A small pond in the center of the atrium catches my eye, its surface shimmering with reflections of the plants and sky above. Koi fish glide gracefully through the water, their vibrant colors are mesmerizing. The beauty of this place is almost too much to bear. It feels like a dream, a cruel trick of the senses designed to lull me into complacency. I clench my fists, my nails digging into my palms as I fight the urge to lose myself in the tranquility. This place may be beautiful, but it is still a cage. And no matter how gilded, a prison is still a prison.

"I'm just a child!" I yell at no one in particular, but of course, he is still right behind me. My voice echoes slightly in the expansive space, mixing with the chirping of the birds.

"Technically, you're not a child anymore, Kira," he says calmly, his voice a constant presence. "And anyways, your age was initially a downside, but I thought about it. Being young will help you to be molded; it will make us perfect for each other. As if by design."

"You can't just buy people! You can't just raise someone and try to mate them. It's sick!" My fists clench at my sides, and I turn to face him, my eyes blazing with fury. How does he justify it?

"I didn't raise you. It's one reason I put you in that school! I didn't want you to see me as your father. I'm not! I may be significantly older, but I will always look young and be healthy. I didn't set out to mate you." His face is earnest, but his logic is twisted.

"You're mincing the details to suit your sick needs," I snap, my voice shaking with anger. I can feel the heat rising in my cheeks.

"God, you're smart. Do you know that? I love your brain." He steps closer, his eyes filled with a strange admiration.

"No, I'm not. I'm a moron because I've been tricked my entire life!" I step back, trying to put more distance between us, but the lush plants and vines make it difficult to navigate.

"I hardly think a top-tier education and being taken from your appalling mother as trickery," he retorts, his voice still maddeningly calm.

"No? What do you call it?" I demand, crossing my arms over my chest defensively.

"I'd say, I saved you and gave you a rare opportunity," he replies, his eyes locked on mine.

"You saved me for yourself! Not exactly the act of a selfless human being." Those words stop him dead in his tracks. He looks into the distance as if contemplating my accusation. I groan in frustration and stomp further into the atrium. The vibrant flowers and greenery blur in my vision, and I stop abruptly when I see a giant pool in the center. My mouth falls open in disbelief. How rich is this guy? Owning a pool? Then again, he also owns me. Owning a person trumps owning a pool. I glare at the sparkling water, my thoughts a chaotic whirlwind. He moves closer, and I can feel his presence behind me again.

"Spark, please try to understand," he says softly, but I can't bring myself to look at him. My mind is too tangled with anger and confusion, and the serene beauty of the atrium feels like a cruel mockery of my situation. On impulse, I spin around and I'm going to yell at him when, but instead of words flying out of my mouth, I feel myself falling backward. I reach out my hands trying to grab something but I only catch air before I am engulfed in wetness. I can't breathe as I submerge deeper and deeper into the pool. It is a big mistake on my part because I can't swim and I've never even been underwater before. I start thrashing in the water trying to find something to grab onto to pull myself up. My lungs burn and panic sets in quickly. I hear the splash before I feel his arms wrap around my waist and he pulls me up to the surface. I suck in a greedy lungful of air as he carries me out of the pool and puts me on the ground on my side and encourages me to take deep breaths. I sputter up some water and he gently pats me on the back.

"How could you be so careless?" he shouts at me. He pulls me into his lap and he rocks me back and forth.

"Don't ever risk your life that way again," he demands as he peppers my head with kisses. I honestly don't know what to do, I weakly push on his chest, but I am still catching my breath and in this singular moment, it feels nice to be held.

"You're so emotional," I tell him through coughing fits. I feel his body shake and at first, I think he is crying but when I look up at him, his face is lit up and he is laughing with a giant smile on his face. The silent laughter turns into real laughter, and I feel more confused than ever.

"And you are wonderful." he finally says when he reigns it in. He leans in and kisses me on my face and my lips, dragging my lower lip into his mouth. I know I should resist and push him away, after all, he's my master or something. Owner? I am a show horse or a dog. Something pretty that he owns. His hand starts to make gentle circles on my back, and he slides the other hand down back to my waist. The vines creeping up the glass walls and the chirping of the birds are such a stark dichotomy to my situation. It feels like heaven but I'm pretty sure I've ended up in hell with a powerful madman. No, not even a man, some kind of part man, part machine, immortal being with twisted morality that I'm supposed to capitulate to. His touch is gentle, yet possessive, and the conflicting emotions inside of me make it hard to think clearly. He continues to hold me, his fingers tracing soothing patterns on my back, I can't help but feel a mix of anger and confusion and something even worse, desire. All this opulence seems to mock my predicament. Who would balk at such a place, such a life? If they had been given the chance, most people would take it at any price, but I'm not sure my freedom is worth it. A hefty toll. I push against his chest, trying to create some distance between us.

"You can't just buy people," I repeat, my voice trembling with a mix of defiance and desperation. "You can't own someone and expect them to love you." He stops laughing, his face softening as he looks into my eyes.

"I don't expect you to love me, Spark, not at first," he says quietly. "I just want to protect you, to give you the life you deserve. I can love enough for the both of us, for now." He wedges my chin with his nose and brings his lips back to mine. He squeezes my hip and makes a noise in his throat as he devours my mouth. He lowers me to the ground and climbs over me, hovering with one arm as support, while the other one explores my body. He strokes my arm with the back of his hand, and he circles my waist with his large hand. He slides up my sweater revealing my breasts which are covered in a wet white silky bra that is probably transparent now. When I don't resist, he gently squeezes one of my breasts and he makes another sound in the back of his throat. He pulls away from my mouth long enough to swear, but kisses me again, lowering more of his weight over my body. I can feel his bare chest pressed against mine, the heat of his body flooding warmth into my cold wet body. I am sinking into the feeling of him when he stands up and carries me with him. He doesn't break the kiss as he carries me out of the atrium. We end up in the bathroom again. He sets me down at the edge of the tub and squats in front of me.

"I want to make love to you, but not until you are ready. It will be up to you," he whispers in my ear, and he leans over and turns on the water behind me. Intellectually I know this situation is wrong, I know I should be repulsed by him and what he's done, but when he touches me, a firecracker is set off inside my chest and it spreads out reaching all my extremities until my brain feels cloudy. When he's happy with the temperature of the water he squats back down in front of me and slides a finger underneath my bra strap.

"May I?" he asks and when I don't say anything he slides his finger down the back and unsnaps the clasp. I bring a hand up to cover myself, but the bra is see-through and he has seen everything already. He waits patiently in front of me and after a moment I drop my arm and the bra slides off. He inhales deeply, it sounds almost painful the way he sucks in the air like *he* was the one drowning only to emerge at the last minute before succumbing to death.

"So lovely," he murmurs, and his fingertips delicately touch the tips of my nipples and a shiver runs up my body.

"Let's get you in the warm water," he says, and he slides his hands down my waist to unpeel my tights. I let him, and when I'm left in my underwear he pauses. He leaves his hands on my hips and squeezes my hip bones.

"You better take these off," he says. But he's so singularly focused on the spot between my legs that the urge to clamp my legs shut is overwhelming.

"I don't trust myself to do it." he shudders, stands up abruptly and turns around. The clouds in my brain start to lift, and his spell over me is dwindling. The minute he breaks eye contact with me, my brain reignites and reason takes hold again. I don't hesitate to slide off my underwear and sink into the hot water underneath the bubbles. The hot water stings; the contrast between my cold body and the heat of the water creates an almost burning sensation as my body tries to find equilibrium. The Second Law of Thermodynamics violently forces my body to respond. After a minute the sting dissipates and it starts to feel delicious against my cold skin. Despite my urge to run, I can't help but enjoy the new sensation of being surrounded by warm soft water. I look up at Faust who stands there watching me, some mental debate going on in his large Edit brain.

"I'd like to wash you." it's a statement, not a question.

"No." I say firmly, "In fact, if you could please give me some space. I have a lot to think about." Instead of getting mad, like I expected, he nods his head and leaves the bathroom without a word. The clouds have only parted enough for me to speak up, but not enough to be glad to see him go. Part of me wants to call him back and let him do whatever he wants to me. To play his little doll and be petted and loved. Is it a product of never having felt loved in my whole life? The draw to him is real and dangerous. I sink until my hair is underwater. I can hear my heartbeat in my ears underwater, it's slow and perfectly rhythmic. Thump, thump, thump, thump. If this was his plan all along, why did he even bother with the pretense of some kind of mentorship program? I have more questions than I have answers. The biggest one is, should I be grateful for what he did? He wasn't wrong about my mother, she was horrible. Nevertheless, he isn't going around saving all abused children, just the one that met his needs. When the water starts to get cold, I step out of the bath and take the bathrobe that is hanging in the closet. I don't want to see Faust, so I curl myself into a ball in bed and eventually fall asleep.

Chapter 12

Dreams tell us things we don't want to listen to, reluctant viewers.

—The Journal of Kira, Book 4, page 3

Small hands bathed in soapy bubbles, raw and cracking. The scalding heat of the water sears into the raw cracks. I sob silently as I scrub the floor. I dunk the brush back into the bucket and scrape the bristles over the hardwood floor once more. This is the third time I have to clean the floor today. My mother deemed the first two attempts sloppy. She looms over me in her stilettos, white wine in one hand, sneering at the floor. The robot mop sits idly by in the corner, unused while I continue to scrub.

"This is what comes of being unfocused, Kira. If you could just spend some time applying yourself, this could all be avoided," my mother says, stepping over my fingers, the heel of her shoe scraping the hardwood. The heel leaves a black mark on the spot I just scrubbed.

"Look at that, you missed a spot," my mother hisses, pivoting to look down at me. "Stop crying; ladies don't cry!" she whisper-yells in my ear.

My chest aches, and I try to stop the silent tears from forming. I wipe at my face, spreading soapy water onto my cheeks.

"Stop that, you'll make a mess of yourself." I look down at my cracked hands and sodden clothing and hardly think it matters. "You'll never amount to anything if you have such a lousy attitude about hard work!"

I WAKE UP WITH A START. It has been a long time since I dreamt about my mother. Every time I have a dream about her my stomach fills with cramps and it takes an entire day before I can eat again. I feel like that small child, the one who can't breathe through her tears, the one who has no one to turn to, no one who will lift the burden and tell her she is loved. It can sometimes take days before I start to feel like myself again. It's like being hungover, but instead of alcohol, it's abuse that drowns me. The sun has set, and the room is dark. I climb out of the low bed and I sit there with my feet planted on the hardwood for a minute before deciding what to do. The hardwood floor sends my thoughts back into my dreams and I feel the knot in my stomach tighten further. I don't want to think about her. I get up and walk to the door. Upon opening the door, the bright lights in the hallway blind me, I shield my eyes until they adjust. The whole house is lit except my dark room. I stop to listen, hoping I can hear him, so I know where to go. There aren't any obvious sounds to direct me, so I choose to go in the direction of the living room. I peek inside every room as I pass. There are a surprising number of bedrooms for someone who claims to have been alone for so long. I open the last door before the landing to the living room and there in front of a large canvas is Faust. He is still shirtless, but now he is covered in paint. It is so unlike his pristine self that I can't help but stare as he works. His arms make large arcs as he paints in various shades of blues and whites. His muscles ripple and contract, and his powerful torso twists extenuating his perfectly muscular sides, displaying his ribs underneath his corded muscles. I must make a sound because he turns to look at me. His face has small smudges of paint on it and his arms are streaked. There is a hand mark on his abs. He has dragged his fingers across the hard surface in an attempt to clean off the paint. It is the most boyish and charming I have ever seen him, even more charming than when he played the piano. Which is saying something. He doesn't smile at me, he just observes me from his spot in front of the canvas. His paint-brush is hanging loosely from his fingers and is dripping paint on the floor. I step forward toward him and he doesn't move, just continues to watch as I near. I stop in front of him and slowly raise my arm to touch the blue paint that coats his cheek. I wipe it off with a fingertip and he leans into my hand and closes his eyes. I withdraw my hand and he opens up those blazing green eyes and he refocuses on me.

"Kira," he whispers, and the way he says it makes it feel like a question. It means many things, where do we stand? Can I touch you? I need you. I can almost feel his soul reaching out to me, begging me to let him have me. It's tempting, it's so tempting. He's so beautiful in this light, so beautiful that even covered in paint it's daunting. He might be the most beautiful creature alive and he might stay that way for eternity. Mirror mirror on the wall, who is the most beautiful of all, but the mirror would never change its answer, it would always answer, "You are, Faust." It's almost sad, the way he will never change, stagnant like a rock in a mountain, beautiful but unchanging as the world moves past him.

"I have questions," I say in response. He does a slight nod that indicates that I can ask.

"Why the pretense of the mentorship program?"

"It wasn't a pretense; we are supposed to go to work together. This wasn't the plan. It was meant to ease you into the situation. You were never supposed to find out about your mother, but you made things so difficult. First trying to opt out and then failing and then you told Kilroy you wanted out entirely. She was clever enough to have you bring up your grades and then slide you back into the program. Then when you saw that timeline, well it all just sort of unraveled."

"She knows about this?" I gesture between the two of us. How could she be a principal and be involved in human trafficking?

"That school is a school made by Edits for their progeny."

"Are you telling me that everyone in that school has been chosen as some kind of child bride?" The knot in my stomach feels heavier than ever. How can people be this way?

"No, not necessarily, everyone's needs are unique."

"What does that mean?"

"Truthfully, I don't know what all those kids are there for, it's up to the Edit that sponsors them."

"So, Human trafficking is just an accepted thing amongst Edits?"

"You make it sound so vulgar," he says, he closes his eyes, sighs, and drops the paintbrush in a jar that has an acrid scent of turpentine.

"It is vulgar and awful. Did you all forget what it's like to be a human being and want choices?"

"Human beings make shitty choices," he announces, and I take a big step back. "Look at what they have done to this planet, we gave them the rights, voting, and freedom and they destroyed it. They are children, always wanting more, always demanding more, never willing to change or fix anything. Never taking responsibility, passing the buck on." He takes a deep breath and takes a step toward me, and I take another step back.

"You're lucky that I found you, you're lucky I pulled you out of that unit and that abusive sociopathic mother. Yes, I made the choice for you, but everyone knows children are not equipped to make life choices for themselves."

"I'm not a child anymore!" I yell at him, and he stops.

"Compared to me, you are very much a child, you have no idea what the real world is like."

"Yes, and who is responsible for that!?" I sidestep him and it is the first time I see what is on the canvas. It is a portrait of me, and it is so lifelike, I am looking in a distorted blue mirror. I fold my arms and stare at the painting. He comes up behind me, looking over my shoulder.

"I will make you a deal, Spark." His voice is soft, and it tickles my ear but I refuse to respond to his nearness.

"Give me six months of your time, and after that time, if you don't love me, burn for me, the way I burn for you. I will give you enough money to go live your own life in any manner you see fit." I turn around, I need to see his face to understand if he is sincere or not.

"You would do that?" I ask him, stunned by the offer. His face looks sincere, and I wonder if Edits can lie better than humans.

"Yes, however, if you do fall in love with me, you will agree to marry me," he demands and he holds up his hand, his finger-tips reaching out to touch my face. He sees the paint on his hands, and he slowly folds his fingers back into his palm.

"After a few years, you will give me a child and after that, you will become an Edit. We have to preserve the perfection that you are." It is probably the best offer I'll ever get and well it is only the offer on the table. Six months of my life to see if I can share eternity with him. My mind instantly starts to race with possibilities, maybe I'll go to a dance academy somewhere or I'd find a plot of land like Maius and live so far away from everyone it would take weeks to get to me. Six months is no time at all, and I will be free to make my own life choices, free to be me, without anyone else dictating the terms. It dawns on me that Maius will never get that plot of land, some Edit would swoop in and take him to whatever life they had set out for him. I hope it is someone kind and will make Maius happy. June will never go for what someone else has set out for her, and whoever her Edit is they have their hands full. I'll find both of them one day, and if they need it, I will do what I can to help them.

"Okay, it's a deal," I say. A smile spreads out over his face, he forgets about his paint-splattered body, and he wraps himself around me and kisses my face, first my eyelids and then my nose.

"I'll make you happy." He promises and kisses my lips, slipping his warm tongue into my mouth. I can hardly breathe from how tight he is holding me. He is so certain I'll fall in love with him, but I could never fall in love with someone who trades in human lives. The white bathrobe I am still wearing is now covered in blue paint and I can feel that my face is smeared in it, the tacky texture slowly drying on my skin. The strong stench of oil paint fills my nostrils and mingles with the leathery citrus scent that belongs to Faust. His fingertips dig into my sides as he holds me. His grip slowly lessens, and his hands slip out from my waist loosening the bathrobe ribbon, and exposing my front to him. I have nothing underneath and he sucks in a breath when he sees my naked body.

"You're perfect," he whispers in awe, delicately tracing his fingertips down the front of my body starting at my neck and sliding all the way down to my collarbone. His hand continues traveling in-between my breasts, sliding down to my belly button, and stopping when he reaches my pubic bone. Streaks of blue paint follow the path his finger takes, marking me.

"I don't think I've ever seen anyone more lovely," he tells me, and his fingers play with the hair that I have down there.

"Even Edits with all their upgrades, can't match this." He is worshiping me, and I don't dare move. I don't know what to do, my body feels on fire, but I also feel deep shame. I am under his microscope. I shift on my feet and my hand finds my thigh, the need to scrape a texture is strong, but there are no pants, just skin.

"I wondered if your legs would be scratched up, but they are flawless." he follows the gesture, he never misses anything I do. He drops to his knees and kisses my belly.

"To think one day, my child could be growing in here," he says, and he licks a circle around my belly button and my legs begin to shake. He grips the back of my thighs to keep me still.

"Relax, I won't do anything you don't like," he murmurs and he nuzzles his face against my stomach, scraping his five o'clock shadow on the soft skin on my belly. He is branding me and when he withdraws his face, my skin is red, raw, and hot. His hands wrap around my thigh, and he forces my legs apart.

"I'm going to taste you now," he says. I want to slam my legs closed, but his grip is firm.

"If you don't like it, I will stop," he adds. His fingertips spread me open to him and his tongue darts out and swipes me. I can feel his hot wet tongue in my most private place. The sensation is so alarming and new that I almost fall. I grab onto his head to have something to keep me steady.

"Perfect," he murmurs between my legs. I can feel his voice's vibration on my flesh and blood pools in my core. His tongue swipes out again, but instead of retracting again, he massages me, exploring every fold, and sliding it along the seam. He flicks something and the shame I feel gets replaced with a strange pleasure. My knees buckle and I make an involuntary sound. I can feel his mouth smile, his lips stretching against me, and he flicks the same spot again. I grip his hair, tugging at him. He pulls back and looks up at me and he pulls me down onto the paint-splattered ground. He lays himself down and slides down on his stomach and pushes my legs apart. My feet are planted on the ground with his head planted between my legs. I can feel my cheeks reddening and I can't look at him. I can feel his eyes on it, looking and I want to die. I push on his head, but he resists my attempts. His tongue darts out again and he slides it along the entire seam from bottom to top. I moan when he reaches that same spot. He makes a sound in the back of his throat like he is getting the same amount of pleasure from it that I am.

"You're very responsive," he says before assaulting me with his tongue again. He sucks the sensitive spot into his mouth and my body involuntarily arches off the ground. He keeps licking and sucking until my body starts to shake and my vision starts to turn black. I can't stop the moans that are coming out of my mouth, I can't breathe. The pleasure is so intense, my hips try to lift off the ground as the pleasure turns into a dizzy feeling and I close my eyes and all I see is white, my brain turning to mush, he places a palm on my pelvis to keep me in place as he lavishes me. The sensation starts to pass but he continues his assault, my legs close around his head, I feel too sensitive to let him continue. He gives one final suck that makes me spasm and he pulls his head away from in-between my knees. He crawls up along my body, looks down at me and places a delicate kiss on my nose.

"That was your first orgasm," he declares. "Of many," he promises. I just lay there, a limp sack of potatoes. I had no idea it could feel that way. I feel embarrassed for not even fully understanding what he has done to me.

"Come, another shower for us," he says, and he carries me into the bathroom.

Chapter 13

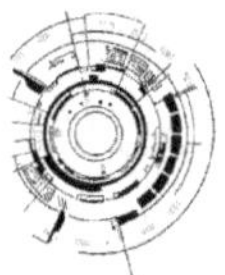

Love is the essence of life. Without it, emptiness reigns, leaving a void that no achievement or possession can ever fill.

-Magnus Compendium, Section 15.5

Magnus

The days are filled with little moments of connection. She gets angry at me at random intervals and lashes out. I have to turn up my emotional filter to withstand her rage. The rest of the time she is jelly in my arms. I will pet her and hold her, pleasure her with my tongue and fingers. I want her to be ready for me, I want to ease her into it before I finally take her virginity. My cock aches constantly, a self-imposed chastity belt, a vice restraining me. I ignore the sensations as best I can. When I am not worshiping her body, I try to teach her things. She has a curious mind, and she is a quick learner. It is easy to convey complex concepts, things that I had struggled with until I became an Edit. She struggles with the swimming lessons, and I made her promise never to go in the pool alone until she is a stronger swimmer. I am clearing out the living room when she finally wakes up. It is hard to wait for her to wake up sometimes. It's hard to remember that humans sleep for at least eight hours every day. She comes traipsing into the room with a sleepy expression, but she smiles when she sees me. It is the first time she has done that. She normally looks unsure of me, and it always takes her a little while to warm up. I can't stop the smile that bursts forth on my face and I put down the table I am carrying and go over to kiss her.

"Good morning Spark," I say after withdrawing from the deep kiss she gives me. I take this as the first real sign that she is capable of falling in love with me. She kisses me again and wraps her arms around my neck pulling me closer. My cock stirs at the close contact of her body. It is the first time in my life, I wish I had a filter for my dick. She makes a needy sound, and I slip my hand under her dress. She isn't wearing any underwear; I am so surprised I pause. I don't want to make her feel self-conscious about it, so I continue to check if she is wet. I can smell her arousal, and I skim a finger between her folds. She is drenched and my cock strains against my pants. I can't wait to stretch that tight little pussy and finally claim her as mine. I am determined to keep my promise and wait till she tells me she is ready. Her thighs are coated in her wetness, and I have to suck in some air to restrain myself.

"God, baby, you are so perfect." I praise her, and I inhale the scent of her neck and hair. I bite her shoulder gently and she stretches out her neck giving me access. "You woke up this way?" I ask before dragging my tongue along the long column of her neck, stopping at the earlobe. I suck her earlobe into my mouth, and she shivers.

"I want you," I whisper to her, and she moans when I scrape my teeth down the same path I had just licked.

"Yes," she says in a breathy voice, and I am not sure what

she was saying yes to. Yes, she woke up this way, or yes, I could take her.

"Yes, what Spark?"

"Yes, I woke up this way," she answers and turns back to kiss me. I feel a momentary pang of disappointment. Still, she hasn't said no and the fact that she is so willing and open with me right now is a victory in itself. I lift my fingers to my mouth and suck her wetness off them and her eyes widen but there is a gleam of intrigue and lust whenever I do that. I slip my finger back into her folds and this time I bring my fingers up to her. "taste." I tell her and she hesitates before she darts out her tongue and tentatively licks my fingertip. My dick jumps in my pants at the filthiness of it.

"Come, Spark," I tell her and I lead her into my room. She follows dutifully and when we get inside, I place her on the bed before climbing behind her. I spread my legs out and she nestles in between them. I gently coax her legs open, a task that has become easier and easier with each passing day. She is still shy, but this morning she is eager to have me touch her.

"I'm going to try something new today." I murmur in her ear, "Do you trust me?" She hesitates for a brief second before nodding her consent.

"Good, I'm going to do something called edging. I will bring you close to an orgasm but pull away before you cum. It will feel frustrating for you, but when I finally let you cum, it will be even more intense than your normal orgasms." She likes it when I explain what I am doing. It turns out that she didn't know the word for clit or what it was. Ever since that astounding revelation, she has asked me to explain every detail as they come up.

"I'm also going to give your clit a little smack, it will sting for a second, but I'll rub it out and it will feel very good." she looks up at me in surprise, "It draws the blood down, making you more swollen and sensitive," I add. She looks mildly apprehensive, but she nods and doesn't close her legs to me. She is already so wet that I don't need to use any lubricant as I start to rub her clit in small circles with my thumb. She immediately throws her head back onto my shoulder and squirms. She is so beautiful when she opens up to me. She is a Cereus flower only blooming at night, once a year, a rare sight and perfect in its unfolding. I withdraw my thumb almost immediately in fear that she will cum. Her sweet little cunt follows my hand, seeking contact. I couldn't have made a more perfect woman in a laboratory and believe me I briefly considered it. I reward her with a swipe of my thumb down her wet pussy ending at her tight hole. I have never penetrated her, not even with my tongue. It is an act of self-discipline to not explore her sweet entrance. She turns her head to face me, and she starts to nibble on my neck as I play with her. She whimpers whenever I withdraw my thumb. I bring my other hand around to spread her open for me.

"I'm going to smack you now," I tell her, she tenses a little and I flatten my fingertips and give her a swift tight smack. She yelps at the contact, and I follow it up with a gentle rubbing, mixing her wetness into her clit relieving the sting. I can see her pussy already looks plumper and she feels even juicier than she was. When she starts to writhe again, I withdraw my thumb again.

"One more smack, you're doing so good," I tell her and this time she spreads her legs further for me, practically begging me to slap her little pussy. My dick starts weeping inside my pants, I can feel the wetness of my precum against the fabric. I spread her lips again and I give her another swift smack, calculated to be ever so slightly harder than the last one. She yells again and draws her legs together. I pull them apart and rub out the sting. She moans loudly and her eyes close. She is so deep pink and plump now, the slightest touch by me, makes her jump and whimper. The sheets are soaked underneath us, and I decide it is time to let her cum. I rub her gently and don't stop until her back arches off of me. I hold her in place as she comes, her pussy quivers and my penis leaks precum inside my pants. The sight of her coming all over my fingers while she arches off me is easily the most beautiful thing I have ever seen in my life. I can't believe my luck, finding a woman who is so perfect. She isn't breathing and her orgasm goes on for ages. Her whole body quivers, and I watch as all her muscles strain in the effort. She finally slumps back down on me, and I remove my drenched hand away from her sensitive flesh. She sucks in a lungful of air, and then she sucks in another. She breathes heavily on me, and I can feel the heat of her as she sinks into me. She is trusting me; I'm making real progress. I slap her pussy one more time, it's a delicate smack but she pulls her legs together and squeaks and giggles. After a minute she regains her composure and turns to me.

"What is sex like, when will we..?"

"Darling one day, hopefully soon, I will enter here". My finger finds her little hole to illustrate, and she is still sensitive, so she jumps at my touch. "My penis will stretch you and fill you. It will feel different than this, in some ways better. At first, it will hurt, because you are so very tight, but I'll be gentle and let you stretch around me. Once I can freely move inside of you, you will learn to love the way I feel there. It will get to the point where when I'm not inside you, you will be longing for me to fill you up."

"Oh," she says and pauses before she says "Oh!" with emphasis.

"You haven't been enjoying this, have you?" she asks me, and she looks deeply ashamed. I can't help the chuckle that comes out of my mouth, her crimson cheeks deepen, and she looks away from me and closes her legs.

"Sweetheart, pleasuring you, brings me great pleasure, but it is true that I haven't had orgasms yet."

"Oh," she repeats, sounding disappointed with herself. "When, when are you going to do that?" she asks

"I told you, I wouldn't do it until you asked me to remember?"

She is silent for a minute, and she looks up at me with tear-filled eyes.

"I'm sorry, I thought." she wipes her eyes and sucks in a breath.

"What's wrong, my Spark?" I kiss her tear-stained face and taste her salty tears.

"You can, now if you need to," she says and she schools her features putting on a tough face. She isn't ready, and that's okay, sex is a new thing to her and I have time, even though sometimes, waiting can feel painful. My desire and longing for her is so strong it's almost become a singular focus.

"Oh little Spark, you're far too sensitive for me to do that right now. I want to, I want to be inside you very much, but it has to wait. You don't owe me anything. I've given you pleasure for your sake, as much as my own. The feeling of you is pleasure in itself. My tongue loves the way you taste, and how your folds feel, sliding against me. My fingertips tingle to touch you. Touching you is its own pleasure. I love to snuggle your sweet warm pussy with my face." She looks dubious.

"Watching you respond to my touch is the loveliest thing I've ever seen. If you never touched me back it would still have been worth every second." I kiss her pert little nose and she sucks in a shuddering breath of air.

"Okay?" I ask her and she nods and rests her head on my shoulder.

Chapter 14

When information is withheld, society crumbles because knowledge is sacred, and it is up to the individual to filter its value.

— The Journal of Kira, Book 4, Page 15

Kira

I am sitting there in his lap, coming down from the most intense feeling I've ever had in my life. He knows how to make my body respond in ways I didn't even know were possible. He is stroking my hair as I lean on his shoulder, I look up at him and his eyes are closed, and he looks serene.

"Can I see it?" I ask, needing to understand what he meant by stretching me, mainly what he intended to use. Plus, I have never seen a penis, despite the many mock discussions June and I had about genitalia when we were in school. My ignorance is palpable, and I am so deeply embarrassed by my lack of skill and knowledge. We have just skimmed the surface. I can hardly imagine sex getting much better than this. He has awoken a deep-seated sex monster in me; I am needy all the time. I wake up with a deep ache between my legs, and I want him to touch me and bring me to orgasm. I have become shameless in my pursuit of pleasure. The more he gives, the more I crave him, and the more he seems to approve. He always whispers words of encouragement whenever I take pleasure from him, whispering to my ego that I am a precious gem, infallible and perfect. My ego is a dangerous thing that needs to be stroked and loved, and despite knowing this, I'm eager to have it petted and inflated.

He opens one eye and looks at me. "It?" he says with a small grin on his face. He knows what I mean but it is clear he wants me to use the word.

"Can I see your penis?" I force myself to say. His grin spreads into a smile but then he purses his lips.

"I don't know." he contemplates and rubs his chin with his free hand.

"Why, not?" it hardly seems possible for him to be shy.

"Because I'm not sure I'll be able to stop myself from cumming if you look at it or touch it"

"You could cum just from that?" I ask, surprised by all the things I don't know about sex. It is becoming clear to me I have a lifetime's worth of things to learn about sex.

"I want to see." I do, he has seen me cum so many times now. I am ashamed to think of all the countless times I have taken my pleasure without reciprocating, mainly through ignorance, partly through willful ignorance. He raises one dubious eyebrow at me and when I don't falter, he nods.

"Turn around and take it out," he instructs and looks down at his pants. There is an obvious bulge inside his pants that I have ignored up until now. I don't hesitate to unzip his pants, his underwear is in the way so I slide them down and out springs his penis before I have a chance to prepare myself. I jump a little and he chuckles.

"Don't worry, it won't bite," he assures me, and I stare at the large phallus. It looks red at the tip and wet and it has deep purple veins running along the shaft.

"It looks mad," I say, forgetting my filter.

He laughs outright at that and shakes his head.

"It just very much wants to be inside you."

"I don't think that's possible," I say, taking a finger and running it along the thick shaft. "That will never work," I add. His penis jumps at my touch, and I pull my hand back in surprise.

"God your sweet." he says, "it will work, I promise you." I stretch out my hand again and wrap my fingers around it, my pinky finger isn't able to span the distance in my grip around his girth. His dick jumps again, but this time I expect it and hold on. He sucks in a lungful of air and closes his eyes.

"That feels so good," he says through a groan, and his penis begins to release some liquid from the tiny hole at his tip.

"What's that?" I ask and point to his wetness.

"That's called precum," he says

"Can you get me a book?" I hate being so blindsided by all of this.

"If you like, but I don't mind teaching you," he tells me and he takes my hand that is still wrapped around his dick and moves it up and down his shaft.

"Loosen your grip a little," he tells me and when I do, he slides it over his wet tip and back down. He groans and grits his teeth, closes his eyes.

"Did I hurt you?" I ask and pull my hand away.

"No." He takes my hand and puts it back on his shaft.

"It felt very good." I follow his lead and move my hand up and down, gliding over the tip with my palm and sliding back down spreading his precum making the glide easier with each pull. His legs spread out more and his pelvis tilts slightly toward me. He closes his eyes again; he begins to move his hips in rhythm with my hands and I can't keep my eyes off the entire thing. It is startling in some ways, to have this heavy dick in my hand. It does seem impossible that he will fit that inside me somehow. Conversely, it is exhilarating watching him respond to me the way I have responded to him. He is making small sounds in the back of his throat and breathing erratically, sometimes making hissing sounds when I touch his tip. His eyes are closed, and he has let me take over entirely. On impulse, I bend down and lick his tip. His eyes open in alarm and I wonder if I did something wrong, but his dick seeps a large amount of precum. I lick his tip again, tasting him. It is bitter but not unpleasant, it is almost sweet in a way.

He grits his teeth again, "Do that again." he exhales out the words and I oblige by licking his tip clean of the precum.

"Fuck" He groans and I do it again and he grabs my hair. He must think better of it because he pulls his hands back and puts them behind his head.

"Tell me what to do," I tell him and he is watching me carefully, he hesitates a moment before he says.

"Put it in your mouth." I put the tip into my mouth, the large tip filling it up easily. "Suck on it." He says, I suck in, and his dick jumps, and he pushes me off for a second.

"Not like that, flatten your tongue and slide it in and out of your mouth," he says and holding his dick in one hand and offering it to me. I slide it into my mouth and out again like he instructed.

"Good girl. Keep going," he says, and I do, I take his dick in my mouth, tasting his bitter, sweet wetness. I keep my eyes on him, so I can see if he is enjoying it or if I am doing something wrong. His eyes are fixed on me like he can't look away even if someone were to burn him.

"Can you take it deeper?" he asks me after I have been sucking on his tip for a couple of minutes.

"I don't know, where would it go?" I ask after pulling off his dick.

"Relax your throat and let it slide back," he says, and I raise an eyebrow at him. He chuckles at me.

"Alright, don't worry about it, that will be a lesson for another time." I am no quitter though, so I take him back in my mouth and let him glide back into my throat. I try to relax but despite my preparation, I gag on him. His eyes flare with something new, but he doesn't move. He likes that a lot, but he doesn't ask me to do it again. I discover something new about myself at this moment, pleasing him brings me a deep sense of accomplishment. I like it, I like it a lot. I can feel my clit beginning to throb with new need. It is surprising since I came so hard only moments ago. I take him in the back of my throat, this time intentionally gagging a little on his dick. He swears under his breath and his hands come out like he wants to grab my head, but he folds his fingers in and holds them up in the air, he doesn't know what to do with himself. I take his hands and put them on my head and give him a look that says please do what you want with me. This causes him to swear some more.

"Tap my thigh if you want me to stop," he commands. I arch my eyebrow but nod slightly while still sliding his dick in and out of my mouth. When I pull him in again and gag on his dick, he holds me there and I sputter for air around him. He pulls me off for a lungful of air and he waits a second to see if I am going to protest and he does it again. We get into a rhythm of me gagging and sucking in air and gagging again. He is cursing and groaning and I feel his cock swell even more inside my throat. He pulls me off him and he pushes my head away, his dick starts spraying out white liquid, thick ropes, it looks different from the precum that seeped out before. He is pumping his dick with his hand as the ropes of semen cover his fist. I take some deep breaths trying to catch my breath from the intensity of how he had taken his pleasure in my mouth. I can't keep my eyes off him, and I watch as the last of his semen leaks out around his fingertips. He is breathing heavily, and he leans his head against the headboard and closes his eyes. I sit back on my heels and wait for him to come back to me. A full minute passes before he opens his eyes. He zeroes in on me and a lazy smile spreads across his gorgeous face.

"That was incredible." he praises me, and he strokes my arm with his free hand.

"I need to go clean up," he says looking down at his dick and sticky hand. I smile back at him, and we both get off the bed and go into the bathroom. He washes his hands in the sink before stripping off the rest of his clothes. I have never seen him fully nude before, but he is gorgeous. His legs are thick and long, and his butt is beautifully shaped. He is so powerful looking, every sinew of his muscles on display as he works to turn on the shower. I watch him in the center of the bathroom, unsure of what to do with myself. He comes back and pulls off my silk dress and pulls me into his arms for a kiss.

"You're perfect," he tells me and he leads me into the shower. He washes my hair and my body, and when he gets near my pussy I whimper involuntarily. He grins at me from his crouched position in front of me.

"You're insatiable," he says, and his smile tells me he thinks that's a good thing. I am not sure it is. It makes it hard to think straight. He slides his fingers up and around my pussy, but he never touches it. I grab his hands and place him where I want him. "You're not too sore?" he asks me, he looks like the cat who ate the cream when I shake my head no.

"We take a break for now," he tells me, and I groan, pushing his hands away. He chuckles and kisses my stomach, ignoring the water streaming over his face as he does so. He stands up, kisses my nose, and proceeds to wash himself. I feel grumpy, but I lean my head against his back after he finishes washing his hair, wrapping my arms around his narrow, muscular waist. He holds both my hands in one of his. His other arm is stretched out, his large palm spread on the tile next to the showerhead, supporting both of our weights. We stand there for a couple of minutes, the hot water streaming over both of our bodies.

Chapter 15

The heart can be both enchanted and ensnared, leaving us to wonder if we are in love or simply captivated by the illusion.

-The Journal of Kira, Book Four, Page 16

Kira

When I come out the next morning after getting dressed, the living room is almost empty except for the grand piano. I stop and look at Faust, who is sitting at the piano bench, scribbling something on a piece of paper. It's one of his weird quirks; he still uses paper. The school has a few real books in the library, but most of the content is digital. The library is mostly a place to read, with plush chairs in cozy corners, some with a view over the wall. It's still too hard to make out the people, but sometimes I used to imagine what their lives were like. My life has been a series of cages, and this is the kind of cage that will be hard to leave. He is trying to tame me, and he is succeeding. Despite my initial protests, I can't stop touching him. It doesn't matter that he bought me; it doesn't matter that he wants to mold me, as he calls it. I'm addicted to his scent, the way his eyes light up when they see me, and how good he makes me feel. My body responds to him like a live wire, and I have no way to stop it. I'm worried there's a hill over the horizon strapped with dynamite, and one of these days he's going to blow it sky-high until there's no more resolve left. Until I'm broken and brittle, and the only thing I can think of is how I need him, how I want him, endlessly. There is no protection against it; I have no off switch, no sharp object to sever the tie. I'm a helpless little bird, and every day I burn deeper for him. He looks up from what he's doing, and that smile he keeps for me spreads across his face.

"Come here," he says, opening his arms for me. I go willingly, a glutton for his love. He holds me for a long moment, stroking my back. He pulls back but keeps one arm around my waist.

"Look," he says, pointing to the page on the piano. It's music; I don't know how to read it, but I can still recognize it. Unsure of what I'm looking for, I bite my lower lip and look at him for guidance. He nuzzles my shoulder and speaks quietly.

"I finished my composition." He takes his pen and scribbles something at the top of one of the pages. I think he's signing his name, but it doesn't say Magnus. It says "Zoriya."

"What does that mean?" I ask him.

"Zoriya is your new name; it means golden dawn. It suits you. You don't need to hold on to the name you were born with. Especially considering who gave it to you," he says, looking at me and waiting for me to protest. Part of me wants to protest, but I'm surprised to discover I like how it sounds. It's better than May, and Kira feels strange in my ears after eight years without using it. Spark certainly isn't a real name and he still hasn't explained why he calls me that.

"We'll call you Zori, for short," he says. "Zoriya Faust," he murmurs, and I go still in his arms. It hasn't been long, and he is already so sure I am going to marry him. I step away from him and go to the window.

"Zori?" he asks but doesn't move from his spot on the piano bench. He starts playing something on the piano, presumably the composition he has just finished. My throat feels tight as I listen to the haunting music. My body begins to respond, goosebumps spread across my skin, and a shiver runs down my spine. His music has given me frisson, and I suck in a deep breath, trying not to cry. How can this man, who bartered in people, write something with such deep soul? I can hardly begin to understand his mind. He has been nothing but wonderful toward me, but the resentment from being bought, I was certain would always be there. I look out the tall window at the idle clouds floating by and wonder where in the world we are. If I wanted to leave, how could I? We are on top of the world. What if he doesn't hold up his end of the bargain? What if I give myself to him and he can't bear to part with me? I will have no say; I will have to stay. The music comes to a gentle close, and I hear him stand up from the piano bench before I see his reflection behind me. He wraps his arms around my waist and just holds me there, without words. He always knows how to put me at ease; he never pushes me. I have expected him to push and prod at me, an animal tamer, but he has always waited for me to come to him. I let my head lean against his chest, close my eyes, and revel in his warmth around me.

"If you don't like it, you can pick something else," he says after a long minute has passed. I open my eyes and see his haunting emerald eyes staring at me through the window.

"I like the name," I say, but I'm uncertain about the last part. I want to say it, but I'm a coward. In my twisted way, I don't want to hurt his feelings. He kisses the top of my head and releases my waist, stepping back.

"I've made space so you can practice," he says, and I turn to look at the empty living room.

"Practice? Practice what?"

"Yes, you are a beautiful dancer, Zori. It would be a shame if you didn't keep it up."

"I don't have any ballet clothing," I say as I scan the vast living room. It's probably bigger than the school studio.

"Ah, that," he says, and he goes over to a box sitting in the corner. It's white and wrapped in a large pink bow. He hands it to me, and I gingerly take the box from him. I put the box down on the piano bench and undo the beautiful pink bow, the delicate silk fabric falling open effortlessly, draping down around the black piano bench. I slip open the box, and inside is an assortment of leotards, tights, and ballet slippers in my size. At the bottom of the box, there is an extravagant tutu, something that I have always dreamed of wearing. It is white throughout, and the bodice is encrusted with pearls and gems. The white tutu is short, the kind that points straight outwards, and I feel the stiff mesh fabric between my fingers. I wonder if they use starch to make this fabric so stiff. There is a pair of matching white pointe shoes and white tights. I am admiring the tutu, hardly daring to put it on, when he taps me.

"There is one more thing," he says. He pulls a black box from behind his back. This one has a navy ribbon on it. It is much smaller than the first box, and the velvet casing gives me pause. I don't take it from his hands, and I give him a look, telling him there's no way I'm opening that. He laughs, "want me to open it for you?" he asks, and I shake my head no, which causes his shoulders to shake with laughter. He slips the blue ribbon off and flips open the lid, revealing a tiara. It is covered with white diamonds in a platinum frame, with delicate little points. The diamonds catch the light from the windows, sparkling brilliantly.

"No prima ballerina is complete without a tiara," he remarks. I don't move, frozen with the white tutu clutched in my hand. That tiara could have changed my life as a child. It can change my life now. It is the security I need if he decides to keep me against my will. I drop the tutu back into the box and stretch out my hand, delicately stroking the diamonds with my finger-tips. The cold metal and gems feel delicate and unbreakable all at once. I half expect him to snap the box shut on my fingers, but he just watches me as I admire the piece.

"Put it on," he says, thrusting the box at me. "Put the whole outfit on and come out and dance for me." I take the box, and he picks up the white box of outfits and carries it in the direction of my room. I trail after him, holding the velvet box far away from my body. It feels deeply disconcerting to have this type of monetary value in my hands.

FORTY MINUTES LATER, I am dressed and laced up in the white tutu with all its trimmings. The only thing remaining is the tiara that sits on my bed, taunting me. Part of me screams, "Take it and run". I don't know how to get off this mountain, but if he is able to get things up here, there has to be a viable way down. Instead of doing that, I take the delicate tiara out of the case and go over to the mirror, affixing it to my head. My hair is in a chignon, and I am, for a brief moment, the ballerina I have always wanted to be. The only thing missing is the scenery and the audience. Even gifts come at a price. I leave the room feeling the weight.

Chapter 16

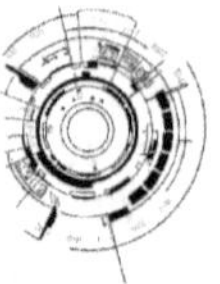

Beauty in motion is the purest form of art; it captivates
the soul and ignites the deepest passions within.
-Magnus Compendium, Section 23.2

Magnus

Zori steps out of her room. Her body moves differently now that she is wearing her pointe shoes. Her feet are pointed outward as she glides into the room, a living sprite brought to life. I sit at the piano bench and watch her; my eyes glued to her beauty. She is intoxicating and my hormones oscillate from their normal homeostasis. Instead of telling my body to regulate, I allow myself to feel the sensation flood me. I feel possessive as my testosterone increases and I feel compelled to grab at her and hold her. At the same time, I don't want to disrupt her. I want to see her move. When she stops at the center of the floor. I start to play the same song she has danced to before. She moves effortlessly, the same rehearsed choreography and I watch her glide across the floor as my fingers glide along the keys. The music reaches its penultimate ending and instead of finishing the way she had before she leaps into the air, and I almost stop playing. Her arms and legs spread out in a long split and her back arches in a perfect arc at the top of the jump. My brain pulls up the ballet leap name as a grand jeté. She lands with a muffled thump from her pointe shoes, slides into a split on the floor, and then folds forward, draping herself over her extended leg. The tutu spreads out around her and for a moment she is an exotic graceful bird, Odette from Swan Lake herself has materialized on my living room floor. I slide from the piano bench, crawl over to her and pull her up from her splits into my arms. I feel possessed and I shower her with kisses. My hands roam her body feeling every curve and sinew, every muscle that moments ago strained against the soft material. I can't get close enough to her. My fingers ache to feel her skin and I hear the rip before I make a conscious decision to do it. The tutu splits into two and she looks stunned. All my patience has vanished, I need her with every atom of my being. I rip the rest of the bodice leaving her in her tights and pointe shoes. I tear the tights in half too. If I regulated my hormones like I should have I would see the alarm on her face. I don't care, I spread her open, a feast, and sink my tongue into her pussy. She responds to me immediately, her body arching off the floor and moans leaving her delicate throat. I will have her now, I will finally take her, claim her, as she was always meant to be claimed by me. I lick her like a starved man, her sweet juice filling my mouth, her musky scent filling my nostrils. It is like a drug to me, and my hormones grow even wilder. I slip a pinky finger into her entrance to test her out and she is so tight I can hardly get in. It will hurt, it will hurt a great deal, but there is no other way but through. I continue to eat her out as I pull off my shirt and slip out of my pants and underwear, only pausing when I have to. She is wet now and I can see the wetness pool on the hardwood below her bottom. It will help that she is so easily aroused by me, but I can't wait any longer, her next orgasm will have to be on my cock or not at all. I crawl over her and drag her red lips into my mouth, the only time I have ever seen her wear makeup is right now. My face is covered in her wetness, but she doesn't care, she kisses me back hungrily. I line my cock up with her entrance and only then does she pause her frenzied kisses. I swirl my dick around in her wetness, coating my tip and making her moan from the contact.

"Spark, I'm going to make love to you now. If I don't sink into you immediately, I'll lose my mind." She smiles at me and closes her eyes, focusing on the feeling of me "It will hurt, I'm sorry." she bravely nods, and I notch my dick in ever so slightly. She stiffens immediately. "Relax baby, try to relax." she nods her head, but her eyes are closed, she is biting down a scream. I ease out and she looks calm again, I slide back in, this time going deeper, and she bites her lip but doesn't cry out. I let her stretch around me before pulling out and sliding in deeper.

"It hurts," she tells me, and I kiss her brow and her eyes and her lips.

"I know, I'm almost in. just a little bit more." Her tight vagina is gripping my dick so hard it is difficult not to cum instantly. I pull out one last time before sinking all the way into her. I still and just lay there, feeling her. She is stretched so tightly around me but after a moment her body's stiffness slackens and the grip loosens ever so slightly. "Does it still hurt?" I ask her, certain that the hard part is over.

"No," she says but she has a strange expression on her face.

"How does it feel?"

"I feel so full," she says and she moves her hips testing the feel of me and my head drops into the nape of her neck. It feels so heavenly to be inside her at long last. It feels like returning home after roaming the desert for an eon.

"Are you ready for more?" I ask her and she nods her head thoughtfully.

"I think so."

"Tell me to stop if you need it," I say and I tentatively slide out of her and slide back in. She doesn't look like she is in pain, so I do it again. I slowly increase my tempo and her legs wrap around my waist as I drag my cock along her slick wall. Her body language changes from curiosity and pain to something I have begun to recognize, as desire. She is starting to enjoy it and when she moans after I hit her clit with my pubic bone, she loses herself in the rhythm. She starts to move with me, and I sink into her faster and faster until I am slamming into her hard enough for both of us to slide up along the hardwood. I have to brace my arms to counteract the movement. She cries out, her entire body begins to shake, and I feel her tightening around me. Her breathing becomes ragged and seeing her cum on my cock is all it takes for my own body to begin its release. Her back is arched, and her long neck muscles strain as she stops breathing altogether. Her small tits brush against my chest. Her brows are creased, and her mouth hangs open. I drive into her with everything I have and feel my orgasm crest deep and hard. I explode inside of her wave after wave of semen filling her up, coating her insides, it even begins to slide out around our union. When my balls feel empty, I slow down and come to a stop inside of her. Her back comes back to the floor and we both lay there coated in sweat and fluids. When our breathing slows down and the high begins to dwindle, I slowly slide out of her causing more of our joined fluids to drip out onto the floor. I look down at the mess, there is blood, semen, and her juices coalescing around her entrance and on the floor directly below her. A small streak of blood trailed after us as we slid up on the floor. I can't help but admire the evidence of our lovemaking and the surrender of her maidenhood. I pick her up and carry her in my arms into my bathroom. I sit her down on the edge of the tub and I turn on the hot water. I grab a towel to clean her up. There are fluids coating her legs and what remains of her white stockings. I start to remove her pointe shoes, undoing the lovely little knots she has tied and unwinding each sash. I remove each shoe and lay them aside. I slide off the rest of the ruined stockings.

"I'll replace these" I promise, she gives a slight nod as she watches me. Her tiara is still on her head, but her makeup is smeared, and her hair is coming loose in messy strands. To me, she is utterly perfect. I pick her up, lower her into the bath, and climb in behind her. I pour in some magnesium, and arnica and add some bubbles. She relaxes into my chest, and I delicately wash her raw flesh. I was rougher with her than I had planned.

"You did so beautifully," I tell her, she likes it when I say soothing things to her, but it helps that they are always true and easy to say. She leans her head over so she can look up at me.

"It was okay?" she asks, always so eager to please.

"Darling, there are no words." it was everything I'd ever imagined and so much more. "How are you feeling?"

She hesitates before answering and her hands trail down to her pussy and feels her entrance. "Sore."

"I'm sorry," I say and I am, sort of, but I would do it again in a heartbeat.

"It's okay, it hurt at first but then it felt very good," she says and she smiles up at me so proudly that my mouth glues onto her smeared lips of their own volition, magnets being pulled together.

Chapter 17

Zoriya

He left the next day, saying something had come up and he would be back soon. It's been two days, and I wish I had asked what "soon" meant. Soon to an Edit could be a year for all I knew. I take the opportunity to explore the vast compound that makes up his home. The house is a marvel of modern architecture, a blend of sleek metal, glass, and natural elements that seem to merge seamlessly with the sky outside. Every room is bathed in natural light, with floor-to-ceiling windows offering breathtaking views of the clouds below. The furniture is minimalist yet luxurious, with plush couches, intricately designed coffee tables, and art pieces that look like they belong in a museum. The walls are adorned with abstract paintings and sculptures that add a touch of elegance and mystery to the space. I discover a hydroponics garden in the far wing of the house, which explains why we have fresh fruit and vegetables every day. The garden is a vibrant oasis of green, with rows of lush plants growing in nutrient-rich water. The air is humid and filled with the scent of fresh herbs and flowers. The school had a hydroponics garden, and the students all had to take turns tending to it. June loved spending her free time there. Her fingernails often had dirt underneath them. She never talked about it, but it was clear she had a passion for plants. Taking care of plants is surprisingly relaxing. I look around to see if there's something I can do, but all his plants look healthy and well-tended. I give up on the garden and continue my exploration. I try every door in the house, hoping to find the entrance or exit, depending on if you are coming or going. Several doors are locked, and despite many attempts to scan my wrist and even pry open one of the panels, the doors don't budge. The technology here is advanced, and I can see various control panels and touchscreens embedded in the walls. The sleek design of the doors and the seamless integration of technology make it clear that this house is a fortress. There isn't much for me to do. I can't swim yet, so the pool is out. He has given me one lesson, but I haven't taken to water like a fish at all. The pool itself is a stunning infinity pool, with water that seems to blend into the sky. The edge of the pool is made of glass, giving the illusion that you could swim right off the edge of the world. The surrounding area is beautifully landscaped with tropical plants and comfortable lounge chairs. The bedrooms hold little interest, with empty closets and unused beds. Each bedroom is elegantly decorated, with large beds covered in soft, luxurious linens and pillows. The windows in the bedrooms offer the same breathtaking views as the rest of the house, and The closets are spacious and empty, waiting to be filled with personal belongings. The bathrooms are equally luxurious, with marble countertops, deep soaking tubs, and rainfall showerheads. I spend some of my time stretching and dancing in the expansive living room. The high ceilings and open space are perfect for practicing my routines, but I can't figure out if there's a music system in the house, so I am forced to dance in silence. The floor-to-ceiling windows let in an abundance of natural light, making the room feel even more vast and airy. Sometimes, I sit down at the grand piano, stroking the keys and trying to make music, but whenever I play, it sounds like a cat sitting down on the keys. The notes clash and jar, a stark contrast to the effortless melodies he creates. I'm starting to miss the sound of his playing, the way his fingers dance over the keys, producing hauntingly beautiful music.

HE LEFT ME A TABLET, and on it, he put a book on sexual anatomy. I read it one day, and it explained a lot of things that my school had somehow decided to skip. My biggest concern is that he came inside me; does it mean that I am pregnant now? I always thought Edits couldn't have children, but he has been clear he wants me to have his children. Is this another way he plans on trapping me here? The biggest discovery so far is that he has no filters on the internet, unlike at school, where you could only look at approved sites. I spend endless hours looking up all sorts of things. The freedom to explore is exhilarating and overwhelming. I debated looking up my mother's name, but I am not brave enough to find out if she is out there or worse if she is out there and doing well. The thought of her thriving after she sold me makes my stomach turn. I also look up information about the Units, wondering if anything has changed since I was a kid. I find some articles detailing that the Units have become even more isolated. Resources are scarce, and the population is still struggling, the would-be Restoration Era has been a failure. The Units remain walled off to prevent the spread of lingering infections. I read about the ongoing distrust between humans and Edits. Many humans believe that the Edits are hoarding resources and technology. There's a mention of attempts to introduce an immunity booster to embryos during early pregnancy stages, a project spearheaded by a tech trillionaire Memphis Penigren in collaboration with a leading research institute. Despite some successes, distrust has limited the number of people willing to participate. It's still a work in progress. As I read, I can't help but think about the stark contrast between my current life and the one people in the Units lead. Here, surrounded by luxury and abundance, it feels like another world entirely. The opulence of this place is almost surreal compared to the cramped, deteriorating conditions I remember from my childhood. The disparity is jarring, making me question the ethics of such a divided society. I do spend a great deal of time on sexual discussion sites, and I discover that it is popular for women to remove all hair down there. This revelation is intriguing and intimidating. The vastness of the internet, with its unfiltered access, provides me with a wealth of information. The house's sleek, modern design contrasts sharply with the utilitarian confines of Plymouth. The absence of strict oversight is a stark reminder of how different my life is now. Since soreness in my vagina has finally abated, I go into the bathroom and find my epilator. It takes a great deal of crying, yelling, and grit, but I manage to epilate my cooch, which is now my favorite way to say vagina. Coooooch. He better like it, because otherwise, I'm not sure it was worth the effort. His bedroom is left open, and I go through every single drawer and cabinet. I even check underneath the mattresses, but if he has something interesting, he doesn't keep it there. His room is as meticulously organized as the rest of the house, with sleek, modern furniture and minimalist decor. The large bed, with its pristine white sheets and large frame, dominates the space. It's been three days, and now I'm really starting to feel alone. I'm also a little worried because what if he never comes back? I'm trapped in his fortress with no way out. I can survive a long time with the hydroponics garden. Given time, I can figure out the wiring underneath the panels, but mostly, I just miss him. I crawl into his bed, desperate for some connection with him. The cool sheets feel soothing against my skin, but they lack the warmth I crave. I want to smell him, and luckily, it does have that citrusy, musky scent that belongs to Faust. The only thing missing is that leather scent that follows him around. I feel this deep pang of longing and homesickness that is so foreign to me; I don't even know how to fully process it. I've never been homesick in my life, and I've never had anyone or anything to long for. Maybe just the idea of something, but not a real tangible thing, a person who has become ingrained into my skin like a tattoo. I go into his closet to find something made of leather. The closet is as orderly as the rest of his room, with perfectly aligned shoes and neatly hung suits. There is a pair of boots at the bottom of the closet; they are freshly polished, and I pick them up and sniff them. It's definitely one of the sources of his smell. I carry the shoes to the bed and lie down next to them. I close my eyes and pretend he is lying next to me. Although he never sleeps next to me. He never sleeps, period, as far as I know. The bed feels vast and empty without him. I fall asleep this way, snuggling his boots, the leather cool and comforting against my skin.

SOMETIME LATER I feel the bed dip and I open my eyes to see Faust looking down at me with a peculiar expression on his face. His eyes are warm but curious, a small smile playing on his lips.

"Hello, Spark," he says and he leans down, brushing a strand of hair from my face, and kisses me on my mouth with a delicate peck. He pulls away and I wrap my arms around his neck, pulling him down and demanding more kisses from him. He smiles and chuckles through the kiss, his breath mingling with mine, and finally breaks away, releasing my grip on his neck.

"I missed you too," he says softly, his eyes searching mine. He picks up his boots, hooking his finger under the laces, and arches his eyebrow at me. I forgot about them entirely. I don't know what to say. If I tell him the real reason, he might think it means something more than it does. After all, I was just lonely. There is no reason to draw any conclusions about love so early on. Love? Could I love him? I shake my head unconsciously and he raises his eyebrow again at me.

"You must have left them in the bed." I lie, my voice barely steady.

"Really? What a strange place for me to store them." He sarcastically jibes, a smirk forming on his lips. I shrug a shoulder and look away, my face heating up. "I'm not one to judge; you manage your closet space the way you see fit."

"You're a terrible liar, you know." He chides me gently, and I sit up and cross my arms over my chest defensively, avoiding his gaze.

"Prove it, prove that I'm lying," I challenge him, my chin jutting out defiantly.

"Very well," he says, his eyes narrowing slightly. "Your eyes dilate when you lie and you can't look me in the eye, your body language becomes closed off, and you often cross your arms over your chest. The tone of your voice changes as well." It is easy for me to forget that he is an Edit. "Your body temperature changes and I can smell it."

"You can smell a lie?" I am horrified. If he can smell lies, there is no way I can ever escape here if he decides to keep me against my will.

"Yes, human emotions have a scent, little one."

"All of them?" I ask, my voice tinged with disbelief.

"Yes, but it's a personal signature. You still have to know the person well to know what they mean."

"Do you know all of mine?"

"Not yet, but I'm cataloging each and every one of them carefully," he says with a smile, his eyes twinkling with amusement. He brings my attention back to the boots, by dangling them in front of me.

.   .   .

"FINE, I missed you and your bed smelled like you, but it was missing the leather scent that you always have." I huff out air and look away, too embarrassed to look him in the eye. He tilts my head back gently with his hand, forcing me to look at him. He is smiling so broadly, it looks like his teeth might break. His eyes are shining with happiness.

"You have no idea how happy that makes me," he says cheerfully and leans over, pressing a deep, lingering kiss to my lips. His touch is warm and reassuring, and despite my embarrassment, I can't help but respond to him. He is wearing a suit, something I haven't seen him in before. I am used to him being neat, all of his clothing is always well-ironed, and I'd wager even his socks are pressed. This suit still manages to put all of his other clothes to shame in terms of neatness. He crawls up on the bed and mounts me on his hands and knees. He is kissing me with desperate longing, and I mimic his need in a returned frenzy.

"What do I smell like?" he asks, abruptly breaking our kiss.

"What?" I say somewhat dazed.

"What else do I smell like, besides boots?" he asks, chuckling at the thought of smelling like a pair of shoes. I admit it isn't the most flattering comparison.

"Citrus and your personal musky scent," I say quickly and try to kiss him again. He pulls back again.

"Citrus must be the laundry detergent," he looks off thoughtfully.

"Shhhh." I shush him and try to pull his neck down and he laughs at me again. I throw my arms around my head and look away and sigh.

"Hmm, you really did miss me," he says, and he nibbles on my ear which tickles and I giggle and try to roll away but his body prevents me from escaping. I push at his face with my hands and so he traps both of my hands over my head with one of his hands. He rubs my neck and ear with the scruff on his face and I laugh until I can't breathe. His other hand starts to roam down my body. He tickles my sides and I start to screech and thrash. My cotton nightgown has starts to ride up from the effort of trying to escape . When his hand reaches my bare belly, he finds his way down to my newly bald cooch. His fingers still when he feels the new state of affairs. "What's this?" he asks, and he looks down at my handiwork.

"I read some stuff on the internet," I confess. He is so quiet as he sits back on his heels. He spreads open my thighs and sends me knees up to my shoulders. I try to close my legs feeling self-conscious, but his grip is firm, and he shakes his head no. I twist my nightgown in tight bundles in my fists. He doesn't say anything for a long time, he is just looking at it and I try to close my legs again.

"Don't move," he commands, and his body slides down so he is lying on his stomach with his head between my legs. He smells me, a deep inhale and I can feel myself turning red.

"Are you still sore?" he asks. I shake my head, but he can't see, due to his singular focus.

"Zori?" he asks again and he blows on my pussy and my entire body shakes.

"It's not sore," I mumble through an inhale of breath. His tongue lashes out and strokes me from bottom to top and the wet heat of his tongue feels so good I can feel my legs falling open more. He does it several more times, dragging his tongue up, similar to licking a dripping popsicle. He swirls his tongue around my clit and a deep moan breaks out of my throat. He circles his tongue several more times over the tight bundle of nerves directly under my clit until my body starts to convulse with an orgasm. It happens so fast it is almost embarrassing. As I am shaking through the orgasm, he slides one of his large fingers into my pussy and rubs something in there and it has the effect of making the orgasm stretch out. He holds me down as my body tries to fly out of the bed.

"Fuck your perfect," he swears, and he keeps pumping a finger inside of me as he sits up on his knees and starts to unbutton his shirt. When he is forced to use both hands, he withdraws his finger and brings it up to his mouth and licks it clean, like he thinks my fluid is too precious to waste. He makes short work of removing his suit and it ends up in a rumbled heap on the ground. I am so wet I can feel it dripping down my thighs and my bottom. He mounts me again and lines up his dick and he rubs the tip through my folds, coating himself in my wetness and mixing it with his own precum. He pushes his cock inside of me slowly, sinking into me like quicksand. My internet search revealed to me that he is considered larger than average and despite no longer being a virgin, it takes quite a bit of effort to stretch around his girth and length. When he is fully seated, he slowly withdraws and slides back languidly. He does this several times and after a while the uncomfortable tightness disappears, and it feels so good. Part of my brain yells, deeper, but he is already hitting the end of my vagina. He doesn't need to ask, somehow, he just knows that it no longer hurts and I watch as his beautiful muscular pelvis starts to move with a quicker tempo. His pubic bone hits my clit perfectly as he strokes in. When he strokes out, he slides past that spot inside that he rubbed earlier. His ab muscles contract with each stroke, and I am in awe of his beautiful body as much as I am in awe of the sensation flooding my body. It doesn't take long for my second orgasm to crest, my pussy starts squeezing his shaft as my vision goes white and my limbs shake. He picks up his pace and slams into me so hard the bed starts to shake and groan. I expect him to cum but after I come down from my orgasm he still hasn't. He slides out and flips me around and puts me on my hands and knees. He slides in again from behind and the angle feels different, deeper. He kneads my butt cheeks with his hand as he starts to move again. He spreads my cheeks open and slaps my butt cheek with a hard swift smack. I yelp in surprise. He rubs the spot he slapped with his palm and squeezes it. The sting disappears and is replaced with a soothing warmth. His cock is hitting me so deep inside it almost hurts.

He grabs both of my hips, one hand on each side and he begins to thrust quicker. I can barely hold myself up as he rams into me, I am forced up to brace against the headboard. His balls are hitting my clit now, each deep thrust hitting the end of my vagina. He is practically in my womb and the orgasm that hits me feels different. It feels almost violent in nature, it is ripped out of my body just as if my soul is being ripped from my body. I scream out and throw my head down between my shoulders as I hold onto the headboard. My fingers dig into the wood, my fingernails scraping into the rough texture. I don't think it is possible for him to fuck me harder but then he starts coming and his pace hastens and deepens and I slide down onto my face as he pummels me. I feel his cock start to spray into my womb, coating every inch of me as he roars. His orgasm seems to mimic mine in violence and intensity. When he is empty, he folds his body over mine and his movements slow but he continues to pump into me. He pulls my hair and forces my head back and kisses me so hard and deep that the breath I just managed to draw in evaporates. I gasp for air as he breaks the kiss. I suck in a lungful of air and he kisses me again and stills inside of me. His free arm wraps around my waist, and he pulls me with him as he sits down on his heels. He is still inside me, and he is still gripping my hair with one hand. The hand that is wrapped around my waist slides down and plays with my clit again. I don't think I can possibly handle anymore, and I try to move but he squeezes his arm around my waist and tightens his grip on my hair.

"Shhh," he whispers and sticks his tongue into my mouth again, licking the inside of my mouth and sliding in and around my lips. His fingers are gently stroking my clit in a circular motion. It is painful because I have come so many times, but despite the discomfort, he manages to coax another orgasm out of me. It is short and hard, my core tightens around his hard cock. I make a deep guttural sound into his mouth as he kisses me and my pussy convulses. My body slumps while he wraps his arms around me to hold me up. He kisses the side of my head and begins whispering words of love and encouragement.

"You did so good, my love." His voice is tender, a soothing balm.

"You're a work of art." His fingers trace gentle patterns on my stomach, sending shivers down my spine, even though my back is pressed against his warm, hard abdomen.

"Thank you." His eyes lock onto mine, filled with a depth of emotion that takes my breath away. On and on he goes, and I just sit there, a rag doll, unable to move. He lifts me off his dick and lays me down on the side of the bed that isn't wet with our fluids. He gets off the bed and goes into the bathroom. He comes back with a damp warm towel, and he cleans between my legs while peppering my body with kisses and whispering words of reverence.

Chapter 18

Dolls are best left unplayed with, for they never quite do what you expect.

-The Journal of Kira, Book Five, Page 35

I must have fallen asleep because when I wake up, it is dark, and I am alone. I feel sore in a well-used way, but emotionally raw. I want him to hold me, and I hate waking up alone. I climb out of bed and walk through the house; it is dark in the hallways, which is unusual. Whenever Faust is roaming the halls like a ghost who never sleeps, the house is usually lit up. I wonder if he has left me again, this time without saying anything. There is a green flickering light in one room that I have never been in before. The door is open, and I enter. It's a sitting room, featuring an oversized French-style marble fireplace. The room looks like it belongs to a different era. The large overstuffed sofas and chairs are upholstered in rich, red damask fabrics, inviting anyone to sink into them. The walls are paneled in dark wood. Art covers the walls. Heavy blue drapes frame the windows, casting the room in a dim light. An opulent chandelier hangs from the ceiling, its crystal facets catching and reflecting the flickering green light from an unknown source. One entire wall is lined with shelves filled with books, their spines colorful with metallic lettering. Each one looks like a collector's edition, lovingly preserved. This is the kind of space I could sit and read in for hours, lost in another world. Faust is sitting on the couch facing the fireplace. There is no fire in the fireplace, but there is a green flickering light coming from Faust's direction.

"Faust," I say, still having a hard time calling him Magnus, even though he hates it when I call him Faust. I wonder if he doesn't respond because he wants me to call him by his first name.

"Magnus," I say louder, but he still doesn't move. I round the couch, expecting him to look mad, maybe I have done something. When I stop in front of him, his face is completely passive, and his eyes are flickering. It's the first time I have seen him so fully inhuman. I stumble back from surprise.

"Magnus?" I ask again with a softer voice, but he still doesn't move. Has he been shut off? I wave a hand in front of his face, but I get no reaction whatsoever. I stretch my arm to touch him, but I curl my fingers in hesitation. Somehow he feels too alien to touch. I close my eyes and muster up the courage to tap him on the shoulder. I tap a fleshy statue; he doesn't budge.

"Magnus!" I shout close to his face, but still, he doesn't move. This is starting to freak me out. I know next to nothing about Edits; there is a lot of mystery and secrecy about them, and most of what people say is probably just conjecture. I don't know what is real, what is still human, and what is a computer. Do they just shut down sometimes? Is this their way of sleeping? I sit in one of the empty chairs adjacent to the couch and watch him. Maybe it is some kind of update? His back is ramrod straight, his hands rest on his lap, and his legs are bent at a perfect ninety-degree angle over the couch end. I keep expecting him to move or do something, snap out of it. Time ticks by, and I fold my legs underneath me, leaning my head back on the chair. I watch those emerald eyes flicker for a long time before I fall asleep.

WHEN I WAKE UP, my neck hurts, and there is an unusual strain running up along one tendon. I tilt my neck and try to shake out the shooting sensation. I forgot I was sitting in one of Faust's office chairs, and I blink my eyes, clearing the rheum from my eyes before I spot Faust still sitting across from me, with flickering eyes. The sun is high in the sky, streaming in through the window behind his desk. The antique clock on the fireplace mantle catches my eye, its intricate gears and wooden craftsmanship. Seeing clocks like this in books is one thing, but witnessing it in real life fills me with curiosity. I can't help but wonder if it's an authentic piece or a replica carefully preserved by Magnus. As I rise from the chair, my knees protest against their long period of confinement during the night. Stretching them out, I shuffle towards the clock to examine its delicate details further. But before I reach it, my attention is captured by an old picture resting next to the clock in a silver frame. The scenery depicted in the photograph suggests that it was taken several hundred years ago. In the image stands Magnus, recognizable yet somehow different from how I know him now. His appearance seems less refined, dressed simply in a white t-shirt paired with dark jeans. He leans casually against a car with his legs crossed and his wind-blown hair dancing freely around his face. A genuine smile graces his features as he gazes at someone behind the camera lens. Is this him, before he became an Edit? I make my way to my immortal doll and snap my fingers in front of his face, hoping he will finally come back, but unfortunately, he's still a wax figurine, perfect and immobile. What if something is wrong with him? What if he is malfunctioning, dying?

Maybe Edits can die from hardware failure. The sudden thought freaks me out, and I start pacing in front of him. What will I do if he just stops working and never wakes up again? I have no way of getting out of here. I can probably figure out the panels, but then would I have to hike down this mountain? I'm still not even sure that it is a mountain; every window I've looked out of shows nothing but clouds. Maybe I can contact someone on the internet, and they can send help, but who would I even ask? Logistics aside, the thought of him being gone freaks me out more than being stuck up here alone. A world without him seems impossible, akin to the sun just vanishing from the sky. He's become so integral to my existence. I didn't even realize how much until this moment. There is always this deep ache to see him and touch him, but I had chalked it up to desire. Now I'm starting to see his imprint upon my soul; he wedged himself in with a pickaxe, and now there is a void where he should be.

"Magnus," I cry, and I crawl into his lap, wrapping my arms around his neck and crying into his shoulder.

"Wake up," I beg. I cry until my tears dry out and a spot on his shirt is soaked through. I feel like a child, and all the tears I should have cried for the loss of my mother are the tears I now cry for him. In a twisted world where my lover is also my keeper. He still doesn't move; my stomach grumbles, and I have other needs to tend to. I am forced to get up from his lap and leave him to use the bathroom.

EVERY TIME I COME BACK, I expect him to be back to normal, but he is stuck. I start to bring my meals into the office; I sit across from him and tell him things. It doesn't matter what I say, but for some reason, it feels important to keep talking to him. I search the internet for an answer, but I'm unable to find anything helpful, mostly just conjecture. I even go as far as to search for an Edit database, some sort of list of names or contact information, which of course there is nothing. I think maybe some other Edits could help. There is no hotline on how to troubleshoot your malfunctioning Edit.

ONE DAY, when I'm out of ideas, I decide to do a visual inspection of him; maybe there is some kind of reset button somewhere. I search his scalp, under his ears, behind his earlobe; I even try to remove all his clothes to see if there is something on his body. Lifting his limbs is impossible though, and my attempts to strip him are pitiful. He is completely stiff and heavy, and I am forced to give up. I put him back in order and sit down next to him, with my head on his shoulder.

"Magnus. Don't leave me," I whisper, nuzzling his arm, and rubbing my cheek against the rough texture of his linen shirt.

Chapter 19

"Freedom is not just the absence of walls, but the presence of choices."
—The Journal of Kira, Book Four, Page 156

I am asleep on his lap when I hear a sound. I sit up and look over at Magnus, hoping he has finally woken up. He is still sitting there, and I hear the sound again from another room. Someone is moving around. I get up from the couch and creep toward the door. How can anyone else be here, and further to the point, who? My pulse quickens as I clutch a fire poker from the mantle, holding it like a bat and silently go out of the office toward the source of the noise. I don't have to go far. In the hallway is a man, one I have never seen before. He is walking toward the office when he stops in his tracks. He takes in the sight of me with my fire poker held up like a bat in my arms, ready to swing at him. He is tall with dark brown hair and lilac eyes, an Edit. His skin is darker than Magnus's, more olive in tone. His surprise vanishes, and he breaks into a smile. On second thought, he looks familiar, but I can't place him.

"Well, hello there," he says. I scan him up and down and don't loosen my grip on the poker. His eyes flick to the fire poker, then back to my face.

"Who are you? What are you doing here?" My voice is steady, but my grip on the poker tightens.

He raises his hands in surrender. "I'm Dalton. I'm Magnus's, uh, shall we say friend?" he grins at me and takes a step forward. I stiffen my arms, and he stops.

"You must be his new little pet," he says, glancing past me toward the office. "Where is he?" I don't know if I can trust him, but conversely, if he is an Edit, maybe he can help Magnus. I don't like him, though, and I certainly don't like being called a pet. Although it might not be an entirely unfair description. I wait another minute to see what he will do, but he just stands there, waiting for me to put down the poker, with his hands raised, showing me he means no harm. That remains to be seen, but since I am so desperate for Magnus to wake up, I decide to trust him, for now.

"He's in the office, something's wrong with him," I say and lower the poker but keep a firm grip on it in my hand. Dalton strides past me into the office with casual confidence, and I follow him, my steps hesitant. He squats down in front of Magnus, and he grins.

"Oh, he's just doing his annual update," he says and stands up, looking around at the mess I have made in the office. There are plates and cups stacked on the coffee table.

"How long has he been like this?" he asks, picking up a half-empty cup of water and inspecting the contents. Why? Maybe he expects that it will somehow reveal the answer to his question or explain why I am such a pig.

"A few days now," I say, ignoring his judgmental looks.

"I'm surprised he didn't warn you," he says, putting the cup down. He raises an eyebrow at the scattered dishes.

"I was wondering why he wasn't responding, so I came for a visit," he adds, sitting down in one of the chairs and making himself at home. He stretches out his legs and puts his arms behind his head like he has been in this office dozens of times, which he probably has. He crosses his outstretched legs at his ankles and rocks his legs back and forth, staring at me. I don't like how he's looking at me; I'm not sure if he is checking me out or sizing me up, but I feel judged and exposed. My skin prickles under his penetrating gaze. His lilac eyes are penetrating, but there is something lazy about him, something I can't put my finger on. He isn't as put together or functional as Magnus. He exudes cockiness out of his pores; it's different from Magnus. With Magnus, it's effortless, like he is oblivious to how he affects the people around him, but Dalton, he knows. It's obvious he thinks highly of himself. I shift uncomfortably under his scrutiny. For all I know, Dalton knows more about Magnus than I do. I am relieved that nothing is wrong with Magnus, but it gets replaced with annoyance and some anger. How could he not warn me that he would go zombie on me? Some of the annoyance is directed at Dalton; his smugness digs into my bones like a toothpick, wedged into my skin like a splinter. I pick up the pile of dishes and leave the office without looking back at his stupid smug face. I can hear his footsteps trailing after me, and something else occurs to me. He said "new pet"; did that mean that Magnus has had other pets before? I want to ask him, but at the same time, I don't want to know. I don't want him to hear the insecurity in my voice. What if I am just a temporary toy for his amusement? I don't feel emotionally equipped to deal with that revelation at this moment. The last few days have been an emotional roller-coaster.

"Well, now I know he's fine, feel free to go," I say, I am surprised by how bitter I sound but he is trailing after me and the last thing I want is this guy's company.

"Tut tut tut, that's no way to be a good hostess." he chides and when I dump the dishes in the sink, he leans against the counter facing me.

"I'm not a hostess, as you said I'm just a pet." I counter and leave the kitchen, he continues to follow me into the living room which is still empty except for the grand piano.

"Is that why you're so prickly?" he asks, "you don't like being called a pet?" he stops mid-stride when he takes in the empty space.

"What happened here? Redecorating?" I just ignore him and keep walking toward the Atrium, hoping he'll take the hint and stop following me.

"If it makes you feel better, he's never been quite so obsessed with any of his pets before," he announces behind me and that doesn't make me feel better at all. It confirms my suspicion that I am just another toy in a long line of toys. I want to cry but I refuse to put on a show for this guy. I spin on my heels and he is right behind me. Maybe it is an Edit quality, a lack of respect for personal space. I poke him in the chest.

"Do you mind just leaving me alone?" I bark.

"Oh, you are a feisty one," he says slowly and he grins down at me, completely unperturbed by my unfriendliness.

"He's really done a number on you huh?"

"What does that mean?"

"I mean you're in love with him." I don't know if that is true, I am not even sure I know what love is, I have never experienced it in my life. I have never had love growing up. It is fair to say that I have become attached to him and I crave his attention and his encouraging words. Now I have to wonder how much of what he says to me is true. If he is just saying words he thinks I want to hear. When I hesitate to respond he smiles knowingly as if my silence is confirmation.

"Don't worry, he's easy to love, nothing to be ashamed of," he says, picking up a piece of my hair, mirroring something Magnus had done in one of our earlier meetings.

"I didn't say I was in love with him."

"You don't have to. It's written all over you, etched like a tattoo on your face." I tug my hair free and take a big step back from him, which he regards with some amusement.

"Is there some kind of Edit rule where you invade people's personal space and touch them without permission?" I ask.

"Ah, you see, we don't think of humans as people, more like toys or pets. It's hard to not want to pet a pretty one or a cute one. Just like you humans like to touch strangers' dogs when they pass on the street," he says, stretching out his arm to stroke my shoulder.

"You are very pretty; I can see why he picked you," he adds, licking his upper lip. My brain immediately flashes to an image of him doing that. It's then that I remember who he is and why I've met him. He is the other Edit I've met, the one from my childhood, the one who took me to that school. I shrug off his touch and fold my arms. He laughs and drops his hand. If Magnus trusted him to take me to that school, this man must know him enough for everything he's said to be true. I'm just a plaything for a bored immortal, and I was dumb enough to fall in love with him. Shit. Love? This is the last thing I had planned for. The sooner I get out of here, the better, before I ruin my life.

"Feisty indeed," Dalton remarks, glancing around the atrium before putting his hands in his pockets. "I like them feisty. When Magnus is done with you, if you want another benefactor, I'll be happy to take you on. I'll be in touch," he says, spinning on his heels and walking out. I stand there watching him leave, shaking with anger. I'm so mad that I almost don't think about the fact that this guy has somehow managed to get in here and now he is going to leave. I decide to follow him and see how he is getting in and out. I tiptoe behind him, knowing that Edits have great hearing, so either I am doing a good job, or he is ignoring me and he just doesn't care. He goes down the hall to the end and opens one of the doors that I haven't been in before. I still have the fire poker in my hand and before the door slams shut, I wedge it in at the bottom, preventing the door from closing all the way. I wait by the door, listening to various sounds he is making, and hear a car door opening and closing. When it has been silent for a long time, I run back to my room, throw on some different clothes, and grab my tiara. I don't know where to put it, so I shove it into the pocket of my oversized sweater. I return to the door and start to pry it open. The door slides open almost immediately. It startles me, and I think maybe Dalton hasn't left, but when I peek inside, the space is empty. There must be some type of safety mechanism. It's some kind of garage with strange vehicles I don't recognize. I step inside and get into one of the cars. It isn't a car in the traditional sense; it is sleek and shaped like a car but there are no wheels. It just rests on the ground. A display lights up when I sit down, but there are no knobs or buttons. It is as sleek inside as it is outside, black inside and out. I wonder if you have to be an Edit to control this thing, which will do me little to no good.

"Car, turn on," I say, and nothing happens. It was worth a shot.

"Up, up, and away!" I shout, and a robotic voice responds, "I'm not familiar with that command, please state a valid destination." The vehicle has some kind of onboard computer with audio commands. I don't know any destinations, so I sit there for a minute unsure of what to do.

"Take me to the nearest town," I say, hoping that will work, and to my utter surprise, the vehicle starts hovering off the ground and slowly glides to the center of the garage. A large hole in the center of the ground starts opening, revealing a large circle. A seat belt comes around me automatically, securing me in my seat, and the vehicle drops out of the hole.

I SCREAM from surprise as it goes straight down. I have no idea if I'm plummeting to my death, but abruptly the freefall stops. The vehicle starts moving horizontally. I reopen my eyes, and the earth below us is filled with greenery, rolling gentle hills that are cut off by man-made structures. I gasp at the sight; it's so open, so vast. I was always told there was no room left, but here, it feels like there's endless space. A cityscape appears; one I don't recognize. I have no memory of going through it, and I wonder how far away the unit I was born in is. The vehicle flies over it, a slow glide, so I'm able to take in the sights. There are some tall skyscrapers, but it is green everywhere. Plants cover almost every surface. There don't seem to be many people out, but I do see a few groups walking down one sidewalk as the vehicle gets closer to the ground. It finally lands in what has to be some kind of terminal, with several other similar vehicles parked in nearby marked spots. I gingerly get out of the car, half expecting someone to jump out at me and tell me I am doing something wrong. There is no one at the terminal; it's completely empty. So I just make my way through the other vehicles to the exit, walking out into the empty street, feeling like I have somehow wandered into some kind of ghost town. I have never seen such an empty place in my life. The unit I grew up in was crowded, and people just learned to live on top of each other. The school was different, of course, but never empty. I know there have to be some people, despite the varied plant life. It's overgrown but mani-cured, so I know that it can't be completely abandoned. The streets are pristine, not a speck of dirt anywhere. There are some storefronts, but there is no one inside and nothing on display. I keep walking; I don't know what else to do. I come across a vehicle, some sort of bus, with a menu on the side. There is no one inside, but it is the first thing that I can interact with. I go up to it and try to peek inside. A voice star-tles me, and I jump.

"Please make your selection," it says, and it is the bus talking to me. I look at the menu. I am not hungry, but I am curious.

"I'll take a vanilla shake," I say and wait for something to happen. I'm about to leave when a cup appears at the window with a shake inside. I don't have any money, all I have is the tiara, so I am not sure if I should take it.

"How much?" I ask on impulse, and nothing happens. I take the shake and get tapped on the shoulder, nearly dropping it from surprise. It is a young guy, maybe a few years older than me. He looks friendly enough, so I relax a little.

"New?" he asks, and I wonder how he knows.

"Um, yes?" I reply, unsure.

"Cool, I'm Pete," he says, stretching out his hand to greet me. It's a little unusual, but apparently, they don't get new people around here too often.

"Hi, I'm May," I start to say May but I remember my new name. "Zoriya."

"Oh, you went to the academy?" he concludes as if it is the most natural thing in the world. "Yeah, I used to be Aprilis, back in the day."

"Oh?" I am unsure of what to do next. I scrape my jeans, and he doesn't notice the gesture. Magnus would have spotted it right away. Are there a lot of kids in this town who went to the academy? Is this an extension of that place?

"Yeah, so anyways, all the food carts are free, I mean everything is free around here," Pete says and orders himself a drink.

"Everything?" I am unable to hide the surprise in my voice.

"Yeah, I mean, I kind of assume our Edits pay for it all, but yeah, we don't need to shell anything out."

"You have an Edit?"

"Man, you really are new, wow. Yes, of course I do. I'm surprised your Edit didn't explain this stuff to you," he shrugs, implying my Edit is careless.

"Hey, if you want, I can show you around," Pete offers.

"Okay, yes, that would be great," I reply, following him as he points stuff out. He is keen on showing all the places you get stuff for free. There are endless storefronts without merchandise; apparently, they are there so you can pick stuff out and it is either made right away or shipped to your house. Pete encourages me to get myself something, but since I am just trying to get out of here, it doesn't seem the best way to draw attention to myself. There are little robots everywhere constantly cleaning the streets and tidying everything up. There are also flying robots that seem to be tending to the plant life. The air down here is surprisingly good compared to anywhere else I've been. I take a deep breath, which draws a comment from Pete.

"Oh yeah, you'd think it was the plant life alone, but there are carbon scrubbers everywhere," he says and points to something that I can't quite make out. "The entire city is green, literally and figuratively." He tells me and he explains how all the food is grown in hydroponics gardens and the water is recycled; there is zero waste. Clothing is made to order, and once people are done with them, they are unraveled and remade. The city's power comes from underground nuclear power. The city belongs to Edits, and you aren't allowed in unless you belong to one. Pete doesn't appear to have qualms about belonging to someone, a piece of property. Eventually, when we don't run into anyone for a long time, my curiosity gets the better of me.

"Where are all the people?"

"Oh, people don't come down too often; they like to stay up in their houses and fuck," Pete says with a laugh, observing my horrified face.

"I'm just kidding, mostly. They do other things too."

Chapter 20

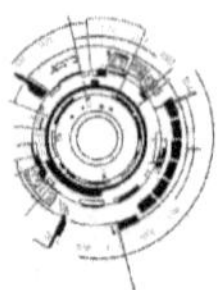

An Edit's power lies in a delicate balance of control. Misuse can unravel the very fabric of what we strive to protect.

— Magnus Compendium, Section 43.2

Magnus

My update came to an end, it had started unexpectedly. I had meant to select delay but hit the wrong option. I was going to tell Zori about it, I hope she isn't too concerned. The room smells of her and I look around wondering if she was still in here. The office is empty and I stand up and walk down the hallway, expecting to find her in one of the rooms. I go into her room but it is empty. There is some clothing on the ground and her tiara box is on the bed, open and empty. I wonder if she was walking around the house wearing it. The idea is cute and I want to find her in the act. It is always fun to tease her a little, she is so sweet. When I can't find her in the living room or the kitchen I get concerned. In the kitchen, I pick up another scent, one that doesn't belong to either of us. Dalton, shit, what was he doing here? I run to the end of the hall to the hangar. It is open and one of the vehicles is missing. Did he take her with him? That son of bitch would do that to mess with me. His anger towards me better not mess things up with Zori. I jump in the nearest vehicle, the red one, and scan the logs for an activity from Zori. There was an order for a Vanilla shake at one of the food carts. The vehicle descends into the town and I keep my eyes peeled for her. There is no footage to look at, the Edit's decided they preferred their privacy, and activity logs are enough to keep tabs on things. Right now, I'd kill for a video log since the last activity was more than six hours ago and God knows where she is now. It is starting to get dark and the sun is setting on the horizon. As soon as I land, I jump out of the vehicle. I don't know where else to start so I run over to the food cart where she ordered her shake. She isn't here of course. I dial Dalton.

"Dalton, what the fuck, where is she?"

"Who?" he replies in his most innocent voice.

"You know who, where is she?"

"Oh, don't tell me that little minx escaped?" he doesn't sound surprised and I can't help but wonder if he helped her on purpose.

"I honestly don't know, I left her up at your place in one untouched piece. I must admit it was quite a challenge to keep my hands to myself. Nice job finding that one." he says and I have a deep urge to strangle him.

"I told her, I'd take her on when you're done with her, I am normally not a fan of sloppy seconds, but I'd make an exception for her."

"Keep your fucking hands off her, in fact, don't even think about her, okay?"

"Touchy, tut tut tut," he says with mock shock. Dalton used to be a nice guy, or so I thought, right now he is quickly descending onto my shit list.

"You never used to be so selfish," he says and chuckles. "Good luck on your hunt for your little pet." he hangs up the call without another word.

"Fuck!" I yell, I have to regain my emotional control. I turn up my filters to suppress panic and anger. It's been a very long time since I've felt so unmoored. She has shaken me up and what used to be a stable compound is now explosive and volatile. Testosterone is high in my subcortical areas. I start flooding in cortisol and serotonin to get a grip. It takes a few minutes for my system to regulate, my brain feels foggy and disoriented. When my mind starts to clear I catch a whiff of her, it's subtle. I start following the scent. I follow it and as I go I pick up another scent that accompanies hers, it is a male and what is worse he smells aroused. My heightened senses require constant regulation to prevent me from being overwhelmed. I have to modulate the intensity of my hearing, sight, and smell. If I don't, the cacophony of sounds, the flood of visual details, and the barrage of scents could easily incapacitate me. My augmented eyes can see for miles, picking up minute details, but I often dial back their sensitivity to focus on immediate surroundings. My enhanced sense of smell can detect the faintest odors, which means I can track Zori's scent, but I must carefully filter out the myriad of other smells. My auditory system can catch whispers from a great distance, yet I have to temper this ability, or the collective noise of the world would be deafening. The constant adjustments are second nature now, a symphony of control that allows me to function without sensory overload. I run as fast as I can, I lose the scent a couple of times and I have to stop and double back until I pick it up again. I'm a bloodhound hunting my prey, but when I capture her, I want to keep her safe. I yearn to envelop her in my arms like a tentacle clinging to hope. It's a rare and marvelous sensation, this hope, fleeting and ephemeral, like a delicate veil that flutters and evaporates in the wind. He is easier to smell than her, his precum is nauseating and my fear for her increases. I catch the faint trace of her lavender and vanilla scent, mixed with a hint of the citrusy detergent we both use. It's soft and comforting, lingering gently in the air, subtle yet distinct. When she's been dancing, there's also a faint undertone of sweat, mingling with her natural fragrance to create something uniquely hers, something that soothes and intoxicates me all at once. There can come no good from anyone in this town lusting after her. It's a powder keg and she has no idea she's stepped into the blast radius. I run into the city park and finally spot her talking to some sniffly-looking teenager on a bench. They are talking animatedly and he is sitting closer to her than he should. The words mine come to mind, a raging inferno of possession, mine, mine, fucking mine. I march over to them, pick him up by the collar and remove him from the bench and her nearness. I hold him by the scruff of the neck, just like a puppy. Zori jumps to her feet and looks prepared to run away from me.

"Hey, man! I didn't touch her I swear," he says and holds his hands up in surrender.

"Fuck, your Edit is Faust? Fuck. Please sir, please, forgive me, I swear I didn't do anything."I drop the pathetic little punk and he runs off in the other direction. Zori backs away from me when I take a step toward her.

"Spark, tell me what happened," I say, stopping in my tracks so she doesn't try to run away.

"Stay away from me," she says and takes another big step away from me.

"What happened, my love?" I repeat calmly with my hands at my side trying not to just grab her and hold her.

Her eyes flit around, looking for a way to escape. I take a small step toward her and this time she does pick up her feet and runs away from me. Fucking shit, I can only imagine what she has been told and what she thinks now, and it's not true, at least not in her case. It is easy enough to catch up to her and I pick her up from behind wrapping my arms around her. She kicks out with her legs and yells for me to let her go.

"Fucking put me down!" she screams in my ears. I'm not sure I've ever heard her curse before, she is very angry at me.

"I will, but only if you promise not to run away from me and tell me what happened."

"Fuck you!" she yells again and she stomps on my foot. I won't admit it to her but it actually hurts, I turn down my pain levels and keep ahold of her. I start to shush her as she thrashes in my arm, trying to calm her down.

"Shh Zori, shh, calm down, it's me, baby, it's me." her wild movements stop and she hangs in my arms shaking with tears. I drop to the ground and gather her in my arms, onto my lap. My legs are splayed out in front of me and she is on me, a babe weeping. I let her cry, her sobs wracking her body and when she clutches onto my shirt and buries her face in my chest I start to relax. She still trusts me enough to cling to me at least. When her tears slow down, I tilt her chin up to me and wipe some of her tears off her face. Her hair is plastered onto her skin and I smooth the delicate strands away. I want to look at her beautiful tear-stained face. Even like this, even covered in snot and tears she's lovely. So vulnerable and precious. God, I adore her.

"Now, tell me what happened." she shakes her head and buries her face back into my chest.

"Ok, I'm going to tell you what I think happened?" she nods but doesn't come out from hiding.

"My update started accidentally, you found me in my office, and I was unresponsive. I bet it scared you?" she nods in agreement, her cute little nose rubs against my chest.

"I was out for four days and Dalton showed up and said something to you." she nods again.

"He probably said some things that didn't sound good, like how you were a pet and how when I was done with you, he'd take you?"I happen to know that particular bit of information is true. She nods, but this time she pulls away from my chest and looks up at me with a heartbreaking expression. I smooth her face again and look her in the eye.

"Edits do take on pets. But Spark, you are not my pet, you are my love. I am going to marry you if you'll have me. One day you'll be an Edit, so we can be equals," I reassure her. "I would never have a pet give birth to my children, which I very much hope someday you'll be willing to do." She takes a deep inhale and closes her eyes. When she opens them, she looks calmer, but she still appears unsure and confused.

"Have you already impregnated me?" she asks. Of course, she thinks that. I should have explained it to her.

"Spark, I'm sterile," I confess. The confusion that crosses her face is amusing. "You're wondering how you can have my children if I'm sterile?"

"Yes?" she asks, her tone sounding confused and a little annoyed.

"Edits can't have children the traditional way, but we can make new sperm or eggs in a lab, with our cellular material." Some relief crosses her face, and I'm not sure if I should be offended or not. Is the idea of being pregnant with my young so terrible?

"Is it that bad, the idea of mothering my offspring?" I can't help but ask, my pride feeling wounded. The ego is a fragile thing, and no time can allay its brittleness. I care for her so deeply it is hard to take the rejection.

"It's not that exactly," she says, chewing on her lower lip and starting to scrape her pants. She notices me watching the movement and stills her hand. She takes a deep breath and looks away when she speaks.

"I just thought maybe you were trying to trap me, so I had to stay."

I have a deep unsettling realization, one that probably should have been obvious. She can never love me until she feels free, and maybe not even then. My heart feels tight, and my throat closes as I try to suck in some air. I realize I have to let her go. I am drowning in my sorrow, being held underwater. I gently scoot her off and put her on the ground. I stand up and look away from her. I can't handle her seeing how much this hurts me.

She begins to speak, confusion laces her voice, and she says, "Magnus?" I cut her off before she can say anything else.

"You're free to go where you like. I'll give you access to your account with the money I promise. Go to First Tech Bank to access it. Take one of the hovercrafts to the terminal outside the city. There, you will have to take a car, and you can go wherever you want." I get up and start numbly walking away from the park. I don't head to the terminal right away because I know that's where she will run to, and watching her leave would be more than I could bear.

SHE DOESN'T FOLLOW ME. My hope that she would try to stop me quickly dwindles and dries up. I'm left as a husk of sadness. I start walking aimlessly ensconced in a growing cloud of despair, increasingly blind to anything besides my hurt. My chest feels tight and my throat constricts as I continue walking down the empty streets. The cityscape around me is eerily silent. The futuristic buildings with their sleek lines and reflective surfaces seem almost mocking in their perfection. This stupid Edit town that no one uses. I had hoped this would be a metropolis of the future. I spared no expense in its design but Edits don't want to build a better world, they just want to build their own worlds. I look at the little robots tending the trellises that run up alongside the building. We were meant to be an inspiration for humanity, but I feel ashamed for my kind. I try to take a deep breath, my sorrow seeping out of my pores. I look up into the sky in time to see my black hovercraft fly overhead, heading out of the city. If a person could die from heartbreak, I think I might just fall on the spot. I drop to my knees and watch as it flies away, eventually leaving my extra-long visual range, my heart disappearing into the horizon. The veil of hope evaporates into the gloaming.

Chapter 21

Truth and logic are not always synonymous.
-The Journal of Zoriya, Book Five, Page 64

Zoriya

I don't even think about it; I just run toward the terminal as soon as Magnus starts walking away. I don't want to be someone's pet or property. I'm not sure I want to be an Edit either. Their world is bizarre, and I don't understand how they get away with it all. They are an authority all to themselves. They pluck people out of their lives as if shopping for a puppy at a pet store. I jump into the hovercraft and ask to go to the terminal outside the city. I don't know where I am going; I just go because what else can I do? I'm sitting in the hovercraft, and my heartbeat is finally slowing. It's been kicked up into high gear since I met Dalton. I suddenly feel tired, confused, and mildly panicked. I can hear my fingernails scratching my pants, but I don't stop. It's the only thing that feels real. Am I making the wrong choice? The thought of never seeing Magnus again is overwhelming. Everything he has done feels wrong, and everything they all are doing is wrong. Do they replace their humans every decade or two? I have to question why everyone at Plymouth is young, why Pete was so young. Why I'm so young. What do they do with us when they are done? I'm worried we are just entertainment to amuse the Edits, who have been alive for far too long. Novelty must be a currency for them. Money must not be a big deal after having accumulated so much of it over their long lifetime. If I lived forever, would I forget my humanity? If I became a new type of being, with augmentations and gene editing, would it make me feel different, superior? Is that where this ends? I become so disconnected from the human race that one day I'll go into the Units and select my own child to play with? If I am just a plaything, does Magnus even love me? Is it like unwrapping a new toy and for a moment it's the most wonderful thing in the world? Eventually, even the shiniest toy gets forgotten in a corner, accumulating dust. Unloved, and unwanted. Yet somehow, it doesn't matter. Somehow, I think living wrongly with him is better than living right without him. I'd rather be a twisted knot in his arms than out in the world all alone. It occurs to me that sometimes the heart wants what it wants, even if the heart is wrong. My thigh begins to burn from how hard I'm scratching. I scream into the void of the hovercraft. I want to be free but I don't know if I can leave. It's not entirely fair to say everything he did was wrong; he did save me from my mother. He did give me a good education. He also let me go. It is his final act, his final gift that somehow transforms or allows me to feel what I now know I feel for him. Right or wrong, I love Magnus. I love him so much the idea of never seeing him again is a bitter ache in my heart. I'm a puppy who has bonded with its Master. I feel shame, but I also feel the need to trudge through miles of forest to find home. To be that dog that conquers all odds to get back to its owner, redefining how the world thinks of pets. They aren't just mindless entertainment, but deeply loyal and clever enough to find their way back.

Perhaps they represent the fact that animals and humans aren't so different after all. Perhaps Edits and humans can coexist. After all a pet is treated differently than a toy. Humans love their animals, spend a fortune on them, and treat them like their babies. Maybe that's the difference, maybe I can live a long happy life at my master's side.

I LAND at the terminal outside the city. I sit there in the dark, contemplating what to do. Where would I go? I could return home to find my mother. If I did that, would I like the person I became? I don't know if I'm a good enough person to not want some kind of revenge on her. I don't want to find out if I'm capable of violence. She might be the worst mother alive, but she is still my mother. I wouldn't be in this world without her, for whatever little that's worth. I don't know a soul outside Plymouth. I never knew who my dad was; I don't even think my mother knew who he was. I sit inside the hovercraft until the sun is long gone. I don't know what to do. The logical side of my brain tells me to get out, get in a car, and drive away. Go, build your own life. The part of my brain, or heart, that belongs to Magnus says, "What are you doing sitting here? Go home and tell him how you feel. Run to him with your tail wagging in the air and crawl into his lap. There is also a third part of my brain that thinks he sent me away because he doesn't want me anymore, it's a virus injected into my brain, and the hacker is my insecurities. I shove the thought aside and think of home. Is Magnus sitting there alone in that giant house, playing the piano? Will I never hear his music again? It suddenly strikes me that his house feels like home. It isn't just Magnus's house; it is mine, and the only reason it is home is because Magnus is there. He is my home.

. . .

IT'S PITCH BLACK OUTSIDE, but I finally make a decision. I give directions to the hovercraft, and I can hardly sit still. I can see the landscape underneath the hovercraft, but just barely. The landscape is shrouded in darkness, and I can just make out the shape of the hills. I close my eyes and breathe because I hope I'm not making a mistake. This is a decision I know I can't take back. I look up and I see now that his house is built into the side of a cliffside. Jutting out from the side of the rock, defying gravity. The bottom of the house is lit up with little lights, allowing vision in the dark for the hanger doors. I see dozens of these lights dotted along the cliffside, Edit homes; compounds, and now I understand why I only see clouds when I'm in Magnus's house. I don't understand what keeps them suspended up there in the air, but all the other lights must be Edit homes that are littering the skyline. The lights get nearer and I see the hatch for the garage open up in slivers, four pizza slices sliding away to make a circle, and the hovercraft glides in and parks in the garage. I run out of the hovercraft. I dash down the hallway with my proverbial tail wagging behind me. The house is dark, and I don't know how to turn the lights on. I search through the office, his room, the living room, and the kitchen. Maybe he never came back? I head back to my old room when I lose hope of finding him. I will just have to wait for him until he comes home. I stop when I walk in and find Magnus lying on my bed, with an arm draped over his eyes.

"Magnus!" I shout joyfully, and he shoots up to sit when he hears me. He pauses, staring at me with those green, emerald eyes which illuminate the room. He looks like he doesn't believe what he is seeing. I don't wait for him to respond; I jump up on the bed and crawl onto his lap, straddling him.

"Zoriya, you came back?" he asks me, starting to look me over and touches me everywhere as if he's making sure it isn't just his brain playing tricks on him. For all I know, Edit Brains can do that. He places his hands on the sides of my face, pausing.

"Why are you back?" Magnus's voice is filled with uncertainty and for a moment I feel like I've made a mistake. Maybe he doesn't want me back at all. I start to crawl out of his lap, but he holds me firmly in place.

"Zori?" His voice matches my hesitation, and I realize he doesn't know if I came back to stay or not. "Did you encounter some problem leaving?"

"Yes, I did." His eyes flash with disappointment, but he quickly composes himself and restores his stoic facade, a skill Edits seem to have mastered.

"Okay, what went wrong?" Suddenly, he sounds all business, and his hands drop from my face. I pick up his hands and place them back. His facade crumbles, leaving him looking confused and hurt for the first time since I met him as if he has no idea what to say.

"What went wrong? Well, I ran into this big problem." I know I should put him out of his misery, but watching his heartache helps assure me of his affection.

"Okay, I'll see what I can do to help if you tell me," he says, withdrawing his hands again and looking past my shoulder. I take his chin and force him to look at me, just as he has done to me so many times.

"The problem is that I'm in love with you, and having come to that realization, leaving you was impossible." It takes a moment for him to register what I've said because my tone of voice doesn't match that of someone declaring their love.

"Spark!" he bursts out suddenly, hugging me tightly against his body. I can hardly breathe from how tight he holds me. He withdraws slightly so he can kiss me deeply, covering my face with kisses. "Zoriya," he chants, "my little spark."

He pulls back to look me in the eye. "Does this mean you'll stay with me?" he asks, his eyes scanning me carefully.

"Yes, I'm staying. If you'll have me," I add, just in case my third option was right.

"Spark, do you know why I call you that?" he asks me, and I

shake my head. "Because you're the spark of my life. I felt empty and numb, and then I saw your eyes and my derelict heart thudded alive. You dazzled me with your test scores. You continued to shine with every encounter, leaving me in awe. You are the spark that reignited my heart, my purpose. If I stop wanting you, it's because my heart has permanently ceased beating." I look at his perfect Edit face, I notice it's not so perfect right now. Tear streaks have dried on his face, and new ones bead up in the corners of his eyes, making them glisten even more than they normally do. My dramatic Edit, my heart swells, and I lean in to kiss him with everything I have. I knock him backward, and he lets me. I'm on my knees, straddling him, and he wraps his arms around me as I hold onto his face and the back of his head with my other hand. His fingers dig into the back of my thighs, scraping my jeans with his fingertips.

"These need to come off," he says, breaking our passionate kiss. We both strip naked and he lays down next to me. I am on my back and he is on his side and looking down at me, his fingers lazily tracing circles over my skin. The frenzy has passed and instead, he appears to be lingering in the moment. Trying to create a core memory and lock this moment away forever. I can feel his naked body pressed against mine and I feel wholly in my body and in my soul and my brain is at rest, for the first time in my life. There is no need to scratch at myself to feel present. He memorizes my body with his fingertips, tracing little circles as he goes and my body shivers with each delicate swirl. I wonder how much of his real brain is left, and how much has been replaced by a computer.

"What's you?" I ask when he is thoughtfully circling my belly button. He looks up at me with an arched eyebrow asking for clarification.

"What is left of the original you?" I ask again and his eyebrows crease for a minute.

"You mean when I was still a human?" he stills his finger and purses his lips in thought.

"I don't know if anything is original anymore." he must see the surprise on my face and he smiles at me.

"It's not like I'm all machine. I'm still about 99% flesh and bone. I have a processing chip in my brain and some fluid regulators running through my body that help me adjust certain hormones, emotions, and other things. These are all made from genetic materials, not hardware. I can control my nerve endings, which helps me control my senses." He kisses my belly tenderly, sticking his tongue into my belly button. I can't help but giggle, and I push his head away.

"That tickles," he just grins at me and sticks out his tongue toward my belly button like he's going to do it again. I push his face away again and he laughs heartily. He's at ease with himself, and I find that I like Magnus best like this, when he's languid, boyish, and thoughtful.

"So, what, do you get new body parts from time to time?" I ask, slightly horrified by the idea. Frankenstein's monster comes to mind, and I have to shake my head clear of the thought.

He laughs, "No, it's not like that. It's a regeneration process that I do every ten years. It's difficult and it's painful."

"How painful?"

"Like being burned alive, but it's a small price to pay for immortality." That doesn't sound quite worth it to me. I'm not sure I want to be burned alive every ten years.

"That sounds awful. I don't see why you would want to live forever," he stops his ministrations and looks up at me sharply.

"Everyone wants to live forever," he says like it's a fact.

"No, I don't."He sits up and looks at me like I stung him.

"What?"

"I don't want to live forever; I don't want to be an Edit."

"But you said you came back, you said you'll stay!?" He is staring at me intensely, and I throw my hand over my eyes and take a deep breath.

"Yes, I came back to be with you, but I never agreed to become an Edit."

He pries my arm off my face. "Do you have any idea how many people would literally kill to get this opportunity? I am handing it to you and you're declining?" His voice has almost become shrill, and it is one of those weird moments where his voice sounds just human.

"Why can't we just be together? Why do I have to become an Edit?" I ask and scoot back, resting my head on the headboard.

"Because you would die, and I'd have to live an eternity without you!" he is angry now, and his eyes flash at me like I am insane and heartless.

"Maybe it's time to use some of those regulators," I snap at him, and he sits back on his heels, just looking at me with contempt.

"It suppresses some emotions but it doesn't stop them, and you have a funny way of making my internal systems go out of whack," he says, running a frustrated hand through his thick golden hair. He closes his eyes and takes a deep breath through his nose, expelling the air and taking a deep breath in. I regret my outburst, but his tone got to me, and I feel cornered. I crawl over to him and touch his face with my hand, cupping his cheek, and he leans into my hand, accepting my peace offering.

"I don't want to live without you," he says into my palm.

"Then don't," I say, and his eyes spring open with hope.

"So, you will become an Edit?"

"That's not what I meant. I meant you could stop being an Edit too," he pushes my hand away and sinks further back on the bed. He looks at me up and down, his eyes working something out.

"You want me to die?"

"I want to grow old with you," I correct him. "How long have you been alive?" He doesn't say anything for a full minute. His eyes move away from me and he closes them. He looks so human with his eyes closed. It's easy to become accustomed to his Edit eyes, they are beautiful and they are incredibly dupes but I can still see that they aren't like other human eyes.

"I've been alive for four hundred years." My jaw drops; that is way longer than I had guessed. I didn't even know they had Edits that long ago. The timeline doesn't add up and this sinking feeling floods me as I try to process that revelation.

"Four hundred? And you're not tired of life yet?"

"No, especially since I found you."

"I didn't know they had Edits four hundred years ago."

"I was the first," he says, and that fact slaps me in the face. "I invented the process." It becomes clear to me that arguing against immortality with the man who invented it is laughable. The truth is, that immortality is too big of a responsibility for anyone to bear. It is through renewal that we move forward. If we lived for eternity, the world would stand still, unable to shift. It is the changing of the guard that allows generations to redefine their predecessor's trajectory and hopefully move the needle toward better and greater things.

"I feel like we are at an impasse," I say and sling my legs over the side of the bed. Coming back is starting to look like a big mistake. I get up and start lifting my clothes off the floor. I'm about to pull my shirt over my head when he comes up from behind, grabs my wrists, and wraps my shirt around them to restrain me. His other hand runs down my body and he slides a finger into my folds. I'm not wet, and I think it is the first time he has ever touched me when I haven't been ready for him. He spins me around and keeps my arms restrained in the shirt. He pulls my arms down forcing my breasts forward and up. He takes one nipple in his mouth and flicks his tongue. He fills his mouth with as much breast as he can fit. My boobs are small so it is a fair amount. When he pulls off with a pop, he bites the nipple hard. I yelp but he just glares up at me. He does the same to the other, before he falls to his knees, while he keeps my arms restrained with one of his hands. My back is still arched and my breasts are still elevated. I can't see what he is doing but I feel his tongue lick my slit.

"That's better," he says and swipes his tongue up my slit one more time.

"So wet. Do you like me a little rough?" His tone sharpens, but I'm too engrossed in how he makes me feel to fully parse it. His assault on my tits has made me wet instantly. I don't know what that says about me, but instead of rejecting his mean tone, I open my legs wider for him.

"Fuck." he swears and he drives his tongue into me and I throw my head back and moan. His tongue swirls around my bud and my head falls back and I can feel my hair cascading down my back. He pauses his assault and he drags me over to the bed and he takes the shirt and wraps it tightly around the base of the footboard. I am on the ground with my arms over-head and he pulls my body out in front of me. He goes into the closet and I move my knees to the side to see what he is doing, when he comes back with another shirt he rips it in half. Then he kneels back down on the ground and he holds my legs with one hand and I watch wide-eyed as he wraps my ankle in one and secures it to the footboard next to my hands and he does the same to the other ankle. My knees are by my head and I am completely open to him and helpless. I pull on the straps to test how tight they are, they don't even budge. I won't get out of this position until he wills it.

"They are secure," he says, as he watches me pull on the makeshift ropes.

"Magnus?" I ask because the way he is looking at me scares me. He is on his knees above me. His dick is rock hard and weeping, he runs a finger down my slit. He adds his second hand and stretches open my folds even more than they are. He slaps my clit hard, I scream out and pull on the restraints. He drives his tongue down and sucks on my clit and flicks it with his tongue. He slaps it again, this time even harder and I scream again but he immediately covers the pain with his wet adept tongue.

"You're so fucking wet." he sounds angry still and I feel

confused. He slaps my pussy three more times in quick succession and I kick at the restraints. He sucks my clit into his mouth soothing me. My pussy is throbbing and swollen, it also feels so needy, and desperate to be satisfied. I'm on edge with this intense need, it makes my brain feel foggy and splintered.

"Magnus." I wail, it is part plea and partly because I need reassurance. He doesn't respond to me, he pulls himself up and he runs his dick along my pussy, and he quickly drives into me without warning. It feels slightly painful but I am so wet that he glides in easily enough. He slowly pulls out and he drives into me quickly again, and I cum. It is like a band inside me snaps and I yell out with a violent shake, squeezing his dick.

"You do like it," he says and I can't tell if he is ashamed of me or proud of me.

"Is this what you want?" he asks me and the meanness is back in his voice.

"You want to remain human, and be my little Edit toy? Just like the rest of them?" His voice sounds dangerous and my fear reignites. He isn't the Magnus that is kind and loving, he is the intimidating, enigmatic version of himself, the one that keeps me at bay and on my toes. The one who bought me and forgot to consider that I was a human being, one with autonomy, and a future in mind.

"No, I don't want that," I yell at him. That is the last thing I want. "It's the one reason I don't want to be an Edit at all. Your lifestyle is sick!" He slides out of me and sits back on his ass like I've slapped him in the face. Ironic since he was the only one here who had done any real slapping.

"Untie me" I yell at him and he just sits there staring straight ahead. Immobile and confused. I yell his name and after a little while he shakes his head and crawls over to me and unties me. My wrists and ankles are sore and I take my wrist in my hand and scoot away from him.

"I'm sorry," he says, reaching out to touch me, but I pull away.

"Don't," I snap, and he sits back, his hands raised in front of him, a gesture of surrender. Despite his four hundred years, he looks as clueless and helpless as a twenty-five-year-old. I get up and run out of my room, slamming the door behind me.

Chapter 22

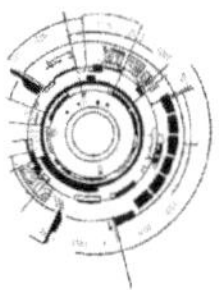

Despite their upgrades and longevity, Edits remain bound by their human origins—and their human flaws.
-Magnus Compendium, Section 54.3

Magnus

Mistakes were made. It often surprises me that after such a long life, I keep making mistakes again and again. I always think I've learned from them and overcome my foibles, but I manage to mess things up again. When she told me she didn't want to live forever, my brain had some kind of meltdown. The thought of her dying was so devastating to me. To top it off, she asked me to stop being what I am. She wanted me to die too. The truth is, I forget that some people don't believe in what I am. I am surrounded by other Edits. What happens when you are around like-minded people, you create an echo chamber. It doesn't even matter if you know there is such a thing as an echo chamber or that you are in one. If you're in the chamber long enough, you stop noticing the echo. She runs away from me, and I chase after her, but she slams the door to my room. I slide down on the other side and plead with her.

"Zori, please, open the door." I can easily open the door, but I want her to want me to come in. After what I just did to her, she needs to see that I can respect her space. That kind of sex had a place in my life for a long time, and I slipped back into it when I got upset. I had promised myself that I wouldn't be like that with her, that I would be different. If she never wanted to see me again, I'm not sure I could blame her. How stupid can one person be? She came back to me, and I immediately ruined it.

"Fuck off!" she shouts from the other side of the door, and I can hear the tears in her voice, each sob a knife to my heart.

"I'm sorry, Zori. I messed up. I love you, Spark," I say, pressing my head against the door, focusing on the sounds inside. My enhanced hearing picks up every movement: the rustle of the sheets as she shifts on the bed, the catch in her breath as she tries to calm herself. My mind maps her actions, painting a vivid image of her curled up, tear-streaked, and trembling. My words sound hollow even in my ears, but it's all I have. I made a mistake. I do love her. She is sniffling, on my bed, and I want to go in there and wrap my arms around her.

"I didn't mean it," I add, but there's no response.

"My lovely little golden dawn, please let me in," I continue. I hear some rustling on the bed, and I hold my breath, hoping she is coming to the door. Instead, something hits the door; she threw something at it.

"Go away!" she yells, and I hear her throw herself back down on the bed again. The bed creaks slightly under her weight, the sound amplified in my mind, adding to the detailed image of her distress. I hit my head against the door and sigh.

"Baby, I know I deserve your anger, but please forgive me. At least let me come in so we can talk about it." It is quiet for a while, and I sit there in my nakedness on the cold ground and think, I deserve this and worse. It is frankly a miracle that I got her to love me in the first place.

"If you don't want to be an Edit, you don't have to. I'll still love you your whole life. Even when you're a little old lady and I have to carry you around because you can't walk anymore," I add, reminiscing about my first wife, my first life. She didn't want to be an Edit either; it was new, and no one knew anything about it. She told me she couldn't stand the thought of going into the regeneration chamber. I always thought she would change her mind, but she never did. We had a couple of kids and they grew up and died and then their kids grew up and died. None of them wanted any part of it. After that, I stopped following the family tree. I couldn't stand watching my offspring die over and over again. I have great, great, great grandkids that I've never met and I hope it stays that way. Zori opens the door and I fall into the room backward, hitting my head on the hardwood. She stands there looking down on me with zero sympathy and walks back to the bed with arms crossed. She is wearing one of my shirts and she climbs up and crosses her legs at the center of the bed. I flip over and do a push-up to get off the ground, the cold floor pressing against my palms. There is something appropriate about being naked while she is dressed. After all, I am trying to humble myself before her. She has never seen my dick soft before and I can't help but notice that her eyes keep sliding down to look at it. I am a grower, not a shower and it is a good thing she saw me hard first otherwise she might get the wrong idea. My boots are on the ground next to the door, which explains what she threw at the door.

"Zori, If I had a choice, I'd keep you young and alive forever, but if you don't want it, I can accept that. Under one condition."

"What condition is that?" she says looking feisty and ready to fight whatever I have to say.

"If you change your mind, you tell me right away. It's always on the table." She nods her head like she can agree to that but she looks dubious like it can't be that easy.

"There is one more thing."

"I knew it," she says and leans back on her hands. Her shirt is white and thin cotton and I can see her nipples poking through. I drag my eyes away from her perfect form and focus on what I have to say.

"If we have kids, I want them to decide for themselves, I don't want you to tell them they can't do it."

"Then you can't tell them to do it, we both have to be completely impartial." she retorts. It is a blessing and curse how smart she is. It is going to be an interesting life, short but interesting. I nod in agreement.

"One more tiny thing," I say and she arches her eyebrow and stretches out her hand, gesturing for me to go on.

"I want us to get married," I say. She sits up straight at that. "You call that a tiny thing?"

"I've already dedicated my life to you, what does a piece of paper matter?" I ask her.

"Exactly, why does it matter?" she questions. I suppose I have to just tell her; that she won't ever be an equal citizen here as a mere human. She will never garner the respect she deserves. The only thing I can do is give her my name as protection. I take a deep breath, knowing I have to be honest.

"It matters because if you don't have my name and my ring on your finger, I can't guarantee your safety here," I explain, nervous about her response.

"What the hell does that mean?" she demands, her tone sharp. I wonder what happened to the shy little schoolgirl I had once brought home. She is no longer so willing to meekly go into the night.

"It means that other Edits will see you as sport, not all of them, but enough. It is the safest I can make you if you decide not to become an Edit," I clarify.

"Revolting," she sneers, her eyes flashing with anger and

disgust. I have nothing to say to that. I am not entirely innocent in the fabric of Edit society. I've had to make deals—deals that tie me to them, ones that keep them tied to me. It's their leverage and it's my leverage. If she knew, I don't know if she would approve. I can't tell her, not until I know she can accept the realities and still stay with me. After the death of my family members, I disconnected myself entirely from my emotions. It was an experimental addition then. I left some on, like lust, mainly because I'm a man, and even with a chip in our brains to make us smarter, we still think with our dicks. Star Trek is to blame; I stand by that. I thought if the Vulcans were superior for their emotionless logic, surely that would be the ideal. No more wasteful human emotions, the cause of all suffering, the cause of all mistakes. It turns out, that was entirely wrong. Human emotions are challenging to cope with but they also ground us. They enable us to understand compassion, an essential component in building a functional society. I had endless amounts of sex with Edits and humans alike, never connecting with anyone. It was too easy to find willing partners, I never once considered their feelings or needs and, in the end, I was using them like toys to slake my lust. I ended up being lucky because I had a malfunction in my chip and the emotional filter disconnected. It was the most hellish thing I had ever experienced. Every horrible thing I had done in the name of science and lust flooded back to me. I remember laying on the floor for days just crying and screaming. One day I picked myself off the ground and I was still weeping but I fixed the chip's connection. I never turned the emotions off completely again. All I can do is regulate them and I try to keep them balanced. I added a safeguard in the programming and updated all the Edits. There was a major outcry from the Edit community, some chose to lower their emotions to the minimum threshold, and there have even been a few who have tried to hack the program to delete the safeguard.

"Zori, you would be wise to keep that opinion between the

two of us, okay?" I say gently, noticing the way she throws her hands up in the air and falls back on the bed in a huff.

"I don't get it, if you're like the father of Edits why can't you just make them change?" I sit down on the bed, take her ankle in my hand, and start to soothe the red marks from tying her up. "Because once you release the beast into the wild, you can't cage it again. These are powerful people, even more so now that they are Edits."

"I'm sorry about this," I say, and she shrugs, looking up at the ceiling.

"I didn't mind that. It's how you spoke to me, how mean you were, and hurtful," she replies. Her eyes flicker with a mixture of anger and hurt. I don't need to hear that she liked being tied up, because it's a particular beast I don't need to feed.

"I'm sorry about that, Zori. I just snapped. I don't like the idea of you dying," I apologize, reaching out to her.

"Everyone dies," she says, looking at me. "Well, almost everyone dies."

"Remember I told you I've been alone for a long time?" I slide up beside her and pull her into my arms. I can't stand not touching her; my fingers itch with the need to feel her skin as if her presence is the only thing that can calm the restless energy within me. Every moment without her touch feels unbearable, a reminder of how deeply I crave her and how much I want to possess her entirely.

"Yes," she says quietly, snuggling into my chest. Her warmth and closeness make me feel like I am floating on air. I have never met anyone like Zoriya in my life; even my first wife, God rest her soul, didn't compare.

"I was married before I became an Edit," I confess, waiting for a reaction. She remains silent and still, trying not to miss anything.

"She didn't want to become one. I stayed with her until she died at the age of 82," I continue, noting her lack of movement. "She told our children that I was messing with God's plans and that even though she loved me, we couldn't follow in my foot-steps because it was the work of the devil. All they could do was pray for my soul. My children didn't follow in my footsteps, and neither did their children. It's funny, Zoriya, when we got married, she was a scientist, just like me." I glance at Zoriya, seeing the curiosity in her eyes. "We met working in the same lab. After making the chamber with a group of engineers, she became religious. She quit her job and joined the church. I still loved her, and she still loved me, but we were like two ships passing in the night, unable to see eye to eye," I recount with a deep sigh. It has been a long time since I thought about my first wife. If I had been a regular human who had lived this long, I probably would have forgotten all about her. She would be like a weird childhood memory that I could vaguely recall, but each one of my memories is stored forever. I can remember every detail about her and our life together, though I choose to access those memories only rarely.

"I'm sorry," she whispers into my chest. Her breath warm against my skin. "And I'm sorry you fell in love with another woman who doesn't believe in being an Edit."

"It looks like I have a type," I jibe, trying to lighten the mood and failing. I brush a stray hair from her face, but she doesn't smile.

"What did she look like?" she asks, patting my chest.

"She had nut-brown hair, pale skin, small pink little lips, and the biggest green eyes. They were framed by these lashes that looked fake; they were so thick and long. I was crazy about her the minute I saw her. You know, I designed my eyes after hers. I used to have blue eyes before I replaced them with the chip interface."

"Oh?" She looks up at me, and I wonder if it's disturbing, the idea of looking into my dead wife's eyes. I stopped thinking of them in those terms long ago. I used to walk by mirrors and jump whenever I saw myself. I'd have this cognitive disconnect, unable to process who was looking back at me.

"Do you still miss her?" Zori sounds jealous, and I can't help but smile at her being jealous of my dead wife who has been long gone for hundreds of years. I cup her cheek, my thumb brushing against her soft skin, Zoriyas skin is so soft that sometimes my calloused fingers can't even feel how delicate it is.

"I don't really think about her much anymore. I remember everything about her, but it's just not the same feelings I had when we were both young and alive. It's almost like remembering a movie you were once fond of but have since grown out of it." She yawns big and I remember how late it is and how this little human needs to sleep. I stroke her hair, watching her eyes droop with exhaustion.

"Maybe one day, you'll replace a body part with something that reminds you of me," she says in a joking voice but my entire body stills and that horrible feeling in my stomach returns.

"Don't talk about you being dead so casually, I can't take it."

"I'm sorry, I don't mean to." She crawls on top of me and looks me in the eye. Her gaze is intense, filled with remorse. "I'm sorry," she reaffirms. I slide my hand up her thigh and I'm reminded that she is nude under that thin shirt. My stupid cock gets hard instantly at the realization. I half expect her to giggle or roll her eyes but she does the most unexpected thing. She lifts herself up, takes my cock in her hand, and slides down on it. I throw my head back and groan.

"Zori." I shake my head back and forth, unable to believe I lucked into such an incredibly sexual, smart, beautiful soul. We make love slowly, she rides me up and down. She is unpracticed but she makes up for it with enthusiasm. She feels every inch of me with the tilt of her hips, she's languorously exploring the feel of me. I watch her lips part and I feel small quivers that go through her body when she hits a particularly good spot. I wish I could be inside her head, just so I could feel everything she is feeling. If she became an Edit, I could. She could grant me access to her and I could live for a moment as her. I shove the thoughts aside, I haven't given up the idea that someday she will become one. All she has seen is the ugliness, but there is beauty too. I flip us over, taking the reins. It is slow and unhurried, we look into each other's eyes the entire time. I can feel her tightening around me and her breathing becomes erratic. She starts to cum and I follow her. Watching that pure pleasure on her face is enough to make me jump over the edge with her. It is an explosion that is wrought out more from love than physical sensation. When we are done, I wrap myself tightly around her and she falls asleep. I lay there beside her the whole night and watch, and think. I can't bring myself to be away from her, even for a minute.

Chapter 23

It leaches in slowly, obsession.
-The journal of Kira, Book five, Page 34

Zoriya

He is still there when I wake up, I stretch out and turn to find him looking at me.

"Uh, good morning." I am surprised by his presence. He smiles at me and pulls me in for a languorous kiss.

"Finally. I missed you," he murmurs into my neck, and I raise both my eyebrows in confusion.

"Have you been here all night?"

"Mmhmm," he says, and I hope he goes back to leaving me when I sleep. It is weird having someone watch me all night, even the person I am in love with. I can feel his skin pressed against mine. The hairs on his legs tickle mine, and the blanket feels too hot and heavy with his warmth seeping into my skin. I kick off the blanket.

"That must have been very boring for you," I say and stretch out some more before sitting up. He pushes me back and rolls on top of me. His forearms trap my head in, and he picks at my hair and runs his cheek along the side of my face.

"Not really, I did some work," he mumbles, and I look around the room for some evidence of that work. He notices and points to his head. "I don't need anything. I can do all my work here." I have to admit, that's a pretty useful feature, but it does me little good. It also isn't good enough motivation to become an Edit. I slide out from under him and out of bed, feeling his gaze on me as I make my way through the closet and into the bathroom. After using the toilet, I go to the sink to brush my teeth. When I look up from applying toothpaste to the bristles, he is standing right behind me, and I jump. He ignores my surprise and wraps his arm around my waist, using his own body to bend me over the sink. He uses his right hand to slide down my back and he spreads my buttcheeks and slides in between them finding my pussy.

"I need to be inside you," he murmurs in my ear. I can feel his hard cock pressed against my back. He kisses my neck and shoulder. His right hand starts to play with my clit and I drop the toothbrush in the sink and brace against the cold marble surface. Blood immediately rushes down to my core and I spread my legs for him, giving him full access. He rewards me by scraping his teeth along the side of my neck and licking a trail up the same path he came. It sends shivers down my spine. He pushes one of his long fingers inside of me and slowly removes it. He adds a second one and starts to pump my pussy a couple of times before withdrawing both of his long digits. He releases me a little and backs up. The angle is all wrong for him to enter me, our height difference is significant so he hoists me up onto the counter next to the sink, my body is partly laid out, my breasts pressed against the cool surface. He picks up my legs and wraps me around his waist and he lines himself and slides in, in one long stroke. His legs are bent as he holds me in place. He starts to move slowly, I can feel each slide of his large cock inside my walls, scraping and slipping, drawing more blood down to my pussy. His tempo increases with each slide, the sound of him fucking me echos in the fully tiled bathroom, his flesh meeting mine. Slap, slap, slap, my head starts to make contact with the wall, so I bring my hands up and brace against the tiled surface to avoid a head injury. Halfway through the fucking I am at an acute angle, my legs and torso are higher than my upper body. He is fucking me so hard that my breasts are sliding back and forth on the marble. He says he is still mostly flesh and bone, but it doesn't explain what makes him so much stronger than everyone else. His balls are hitting my clit in rhythm and I feel an orgasm crest.

"Yes baby, fucking cum on my dick," he commands and his tempo increases turning my brain into mush as he assaults my pussy. When I am gasping for breath at the top of my orgasm, he does something I don't expect. He slides a finger into my anus and if I wasn't cumming so hard I would turn around in shock or ask him to stop. He leaves his finger there for the entire duration and when I come down from it, he still leaves it there.

"I'm going to fuck you here someday," he announces and wiggles his finger a little, I turn around and give him a look he pulls out, finger and cock. He flips me around like a rag doll, dragging me off the counter and spinning me at my waist. He picks me up again and slides me onto his dick, but this time I am facing him with my legs wrapped around his torso. Without any external support he holds me there and fucks me so hard I think I might actually break into pieces. My pussy feels swollen and each assault of his dick is bringing me closer to another orgasm. His powerful legs hold us there and his hands are on my butt bouncing me up and down on him. I am just about to cum again when he makes a deep sound of pleasure in his throat and I feel him spray his cum inside me, his pumping becomes more erratic and frenzied and it is that movement that brings me over the top and I start to cum with him. I clench around him, my entire core tightening, I throw my head onto his shoulder as I lose the ability to breathe or think. My mind goes blank and it feels like a full minute before the fog lifts and I open my eyes again. He is still holding me, but his movements have ceased. I look up at his face and he is smiling at me like I am the most precious thing in the world and he is so proud of me. I wish I wasn't so gluttonous for that look, for that need to have someone approve of me. I feel like clay and I want to be molded and shaped as long as the shape is something that pleases him. How can anyone respect themselves knowing that? How can I live with myself? But then I feel his cock still inside me, his cum dripping down my thigh and I think, this is why. This is why I would do anything for him, the way he makes me feel. I am so deeply connected to my body that all the anxiety and the floating is gone. I have found an anchor and it's him.

"I lost you there for a second, where did you go?" he asks me and kisses my nose.

"To the abyss, I guess." I reach up and kiss his mouth, dragging his beautiful plump lip into my mouth. He kisses me back with those pink lips and slips his tongue into my mouth with a slow delicious tempo. He doesn't even appear tired of holding me up on him and another full minute passes before he breaks our kiss. He lifts me off his dick and puts me down on the ground. I feel so empty without him inside of me, and I remember the words he had once told me.

"It will get to the point where you are longing for me to fill you up." I can feel his cum dripping out of me and all I want in this moment is for him to be inside me again. The sex monster is coming out again and I feel insatiable, like no matter how many times he takes me it won't be enough. I drop to my knees and he gives me a quizzical look. I take his dick and slip it into my mouth. It is still semi-hard, I can taste the saltiness of his cum and myself and I lick him clean. I let him slide to the back of my throat until I can't take it anymore and gag. His hands come to my head and I feel his dick harden inside my mouth.

"Shit," he mumbles and he pulls me off his dick and forces

me to look up at him. The angle is too steep and I can't see his face, only his perfectly sculpted abs, so he bends his torso to look at me.

"What are you doing spark?"

"I want you hard and inside me," I tell him bluntly and his eyes dilate before closing them and mumbling something. He bends down and picks me off the tile floor, the hard stone is digging into my flesh and even this young body feels the ache. He carries me out of the bathroom and back into the bed. He dumps me on the bed and crawls over to me; his dick pressed into my bottom.

"Are you sure you can handle more?" he asks and I wiggle my ass in response.

"Fuck, you're perfect. You're so fucking perfect," he murmurs in my ear. I am lying flat on my stomach and he nestles in between my legs.

"This angle will be very tight, tell me if it's too much." he slides into me again it is tight, so tight he has to pull back and slide back in a few times to get fully seated. I can feel him so deeply inside of me it is like he is inside my organs. I relish it, my twisted brain wants to be joined to him, be a part of him. I want him to live inside me. It isn't even so much about the incredible orgasms, it is this need to be one with him.

"Fuck you're so tight, is it too much?" he asks after struggling to move with ease.

"I love it, I want you so deep inside of me I break," I mumble into the bedspread, and he curses under his breath and flattens his body over mine. He slowly moves in and out of me, a faster pace is probably impossible at this angle, each stroke feels like he is hitting my uterus and I moan with dizzy joy.

Chapter 24

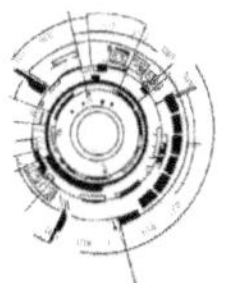

Preservation is the act of honoring the best that the world has ever offered

—Magnus Compendium, Section 2.2

Magnus

She is incredible, so tight, and so needy. I am sliding into her tight pussy, dragging my cock in and out slowly, afraid I might hurt her. It must hurt a little but she seems to be enjoying it. A part of me is scared of the demons she is dragging out of me. I could never have anticipated that she would enjoy the pain. Every time I reach the end she moans a deep sound that comes from some place in the base of her core. It is a long-drawn-out sound, almost painful in nature.

"Do you want me to change the angle?" I ask her again and she shakes her head tilts her pelvis a little and takes me even deeper. It feels so good and part of me is on the verge of stopping because I am enjoying hurting her. I don't like that part of my personality. I have spent the last half-century trying not to be that person anymore.

"Just, fuck me hard," she commands, and my self-control that is already on a tight string snaps. I start to move faster and deeper, hitting her so deep I know it is hurting her. I don't care anymore, I want her to feel me deeply, I want to imprint on her. Mark her so completely that she will never be able to forget me. She will walk around and there will be an ache and constant reminder of me. It's so twisted and wrong and I fucking love it. I fuck her until sweat starts to break out in beads all over my body. She goes utterly still under me as I assault her little pussy, but I don't stop to check on her well-being. I think part of it is a punishment because I am so mad at her for not wanting to be an Edit, for wanting to die someday. I reach the point of no return, my orgasm is advancing. My penis swells, engorging, a moment passes before it starts in my toes and travels up to my spine and back down into my torso. My muscles tighten and strain around my pelvis, and my balls draw up tight before it shoots out into her like a long-dormant volcano spewing its insides. I pump inside her until I feel completely empty but she still isn't moving. When I come to a stop, she takes a giant deep inhale of breath. It sounds like the kind of breath someone takes after being rescued from drowning. I roll off of her and flip her over so I can look at her to see if something is wrong. The little minx is smiling widely; she doesn't even open her eyes to look at me. She looks blissfully well-used. I lie down next to her and throw my arms over my eyes. She is going to be my undoing. She suddenly starts laughing and I can't stop the grin that spreads out over my face.

"You're insane." I exhale and she crawls over to me.

"Insane for you," she says and she bites me on the nipple, I shoot up to a seated position. She giggles and jumps off the bed when she sees my expression. I jump out of the bed after her and chase her out of the room. She is laughing hysterically, occasionally looking back at me as she tries to escape. Her long curtain of blonde hair is flying behind her and whips her in the face whenever she turns to see if I am gaining on her. She runs into the living room and takes refuge behind the grand piano. I stop my pursuit and slowly circle the piano and she moves to counteract my movements. I can easily catch her, but it is too fun to let her feel like she can outrun me. "Don't make me throw this piano out of the way." I threaten.

"You wouldn't dare." she counters and her happy face is worth more than anything to me.

"I'm rich, I can buy another one." I bluff.

"Yes, but you love that piano," she says. I don't know how she knows that, but she has a way of seeing straight into me. That piano belonged to my youngest son; he was a brilliant pianist. When he died and his music stopped, a part of me died with him. His children didn't want the piano, so I took it. When I play, it's his hands I see running across the keys, it's his spirit that fills my body and demands musical perfection. I strive to live true to that spirit. His soul reaching past the grave and using me as a vessel to fill the world with music the way he did. I didn't even know how to play a note back then or read a single line of music. My dedication to music came from him, and it's my small way of keeping him alive.

"It's just a piano and I love you more." I lie and her smile fades a little, like she is either wrong about the sentimental value of the piano, or she thinks that I might actually be capable of tossing a grand piano to the side. I am strong enough, but I am only marginally stronger than the record-high deadlift for a regular human.

"You wouldn't dare." she declares and she rounds the piano and runs in the direction of the kitchen. She reaches the center island and uses it like she had the piano, as a barrier between us. It is time for our little game to come to an end, so I jump up on the island and snatch her off the ground. Her face is stunned, I don't think she knew I could move that quickly. We are both still completely naked and I pull her up so she is at eye level with me.

"Are you ready for the consequences?" I ask her and she bites her lip stifling a laugh. I arch my eyebrow in challenge, does she no longer find me intimidating? Her warm little body is pressed completely against me as I hold her up, standing on top of the island. I can feel her nipples that are erect from either arousal or the thrill of the chase. I put her dangling feet down on the granite surface, and she is still holding back a laugh, shaking. I bend down so we are at eye level again.

"You asked for it," I say and I bend even further and I bite her nipple just like she had bit me earlier. She yelps but sticks her chest out for me, offering herself. Does she have it in her for another round, after how rough I had been with her, or is she just being a good girl? I decide to not look a gift horse in the mouth and I suck in her breast, relishing the feel of her taut nipple in my mouth, it elicits a moan from her. My sperm is still drying on her legs and she still wants more. I can hardly believe it. She takes my hand and places it between her legs and I still because she is still so wet.

"Baby, we can't. You'll be too sore." I admonish her, as much as I want to be inside her all the time, there are limits and she is still so new to sex. She ignores me and uses my fingers to rub herself. I pull my hand free. She smirks at me and slips her own fingers into her labia and starts massaging her breast with her other hand. I think I've created a monster, my dick responds going from semi-erect to erect again.

"You're killing me."

"I would have thought an immortal could keep up." She taunts.

"I'm trying to be responsible here." She keeps rubbing herself and starts moaning, it is a fake moan, I can tell, but it is still sexy as hell.

"I think it's up to *me* to tell you when I've had enough." she challenges and then she adds, "unless, of course, *you've* had enough." That is hardly the case, I have an intense stamina for sex. It is one of my many failings, as I see it. There was a time when I needed multiple partners to satisfy my desires. Sex without love has a funny way of turning to ashes in your mouth. It feels amazing at first, even exciting, but enough of it without ever connecting on a deeper level and it becomes almost robotic. It's addictive, and just like drugs, the need to up the ante is real. It has a way of pulling you into seedy things, things you didn't think you'd ever try at the outset. I lay down on the island, my knees dangling over the edge and I pull her on top of me. I fold my arms underneath my head.

"If you need to use up some energy, be my guest." She doesn't hesitate to slide me inside her, she sits up and sinks all the way down. She is lovely this way, the sun is filtering in through the kitchen windows, and her naturally sunkissed skin looks golden in the streaks of sunlight. Her moonlight hair hangs loosely over her shoulders and down her back. Her pink nipples peek through the strands and her tight stomach stretches as she arches herself backward and deepens the position. She moves slowly at first, just circling her hips, feeling every inch of me along her walls. Her pubic bone is perfectly bald and as she lifts herself slightly off, I can see my cock sliding out of her, when she goes back down it disappears. I wonder if there will come a time when I'm no longer in awe just looking at her. The long column of her neck stretches back as she throws her head back and moans. Her pink plump lips part slightly, revealing her two front teeth. Her brows pinch inward and her eyes close, fanning her blonde eyelashes along her high cheekbones. She is a work of art, completely natural in her beauty. No enhancements, no make-up, and she doesn't even fuss with her hair. In short, perfection. It would be like destroying a priceless masterpiece to let her age and die. I know I can't let it go without a fight. She just has to get used to the idea and meet some of the Edits who aren't repulsive. She will come around, it won't be like my first family, it can't be.

Chapter 25

Zoriya

My need for him never abates. We reluctantly participate in life. We eat fresh delicious meals that he cooks. I sleep while he wanders around the house. He takes me to his home lab and he teaches me things. He gives me books that I devour. The instigator will oscillate between us, but somehow, we always end up having sex. I ask him about his life and he will tell me details, like they had just happened. Some things he won't talk about, and that bothers me greatly. He says he doesn't feel like discussing them that they don't matter, or that some things are better left in the past. I know Faust has secrets but it feels somehow unfair that he knows almost everything about me and I know only a fragment of him. Of course, to be fair, I've had a much smaller life, a much shorter one. He has four hundred years of experience and I have eighteen. Most of my life has been cloistered, by his design, but nonetheless, I have less to share. He had gotten regular reports on me during my time in school so there is little he doesn't know already. I also found out how he knew about my mother abusing me. It turns out that he hadn't known the first time he met me. He was scouting for potential talent, and when he spotted me, he paid attention to me. There were some tell-tale signs, I flinched a lot and I had some scratches on my scalp, and bruises that he noticed, which no one else had paid attention to. He followed up by listening in on the personal home assistant my mother had, which kept recordings outside of the command periods. As a result, he was able to collect enough evidence of her abuse. He knew that rescuing me was a civil service, his words not mine. Someone with my beauty and brains would have been destroyed by my mother and it would be like destroying a priceless work of art. I'm not sure I agree with him entirely. It's not about humility, but because rescuing someone from abuse should matter regardless of whether they are deemed 'worthwhile' or not. He doesn't like it when I say things like that. I think it makes him feel bad, and so I keep it up because he should feel bad. I tell him that he should rescue more abused children and not just because he wants to mold a person to suit his needs. I also point out that molding me hasn't worked out for him as he had hoped, because I refuse to become an Edit. Whenever I mention my desire to die one day, he looks away from me, focuses on something in the distance, and quickly changes the topic. I finally learned how to swim, I'm not good in water. I can't float at all; I just sink to the bottom like a rock. Faust on the other hand is buoyant and floats without any real effort. I can do laps but as soon as I'm tired, I have to hang on to the edge or get out.

. . .

I AM LYING in the atrium eating strawberries when Magnus comes in dressed in a suit. We have more or less given up clothes the last couple of weeks so I sit up to look at him.

"Get dressed, something nice, we have to go out," he says, he looks unhappy about something.

"Where?" It is the first time he has taken me out of this house.

"I have a problem with someone and it can't wait, I don't want to leave you alone here, last time it didn't go so well." I cross my arms over my chest.

"I'm not gonna run off this time," I grumble but I start walking to my bedroom anyway because I want to go with him.

"I don't want you to come, but it's not optional at the moment." he begins but I hold my hand to silence him.

"I want to come along."

"It's not going to be enjoyable," he says vaguely. "It's not an ideal situation." he huffs out a big breath and goes into my closet to pull out the buttery white silk dress. I grab it from him, take a quick shower, and get dressed. He looks dressed to the nines, so I briefly consider putting on some makeup but decide against it. I do blow dry my hair since time is short and I can't let it air dry on the silk. He is pacing my bedroom when I come out, I've never seen him look so uncomfortable before. He takes my hand and leads me to the garage. We get into the black hovercraft and he gives directions to someone's house by the name of Henrik Dalforth. I know it is coming this time but it doesn't stop my stomach from dropping out when the hovercraft drops out of the floor. It isn't a freefall Magnus explains, but it is fast and it takes some getting used to. When we are nearing the property, he puts his hand on my knee to get my attention.

"I don't want you to say anything, I also don't want you to judge all Edits by this one man alone. I can't guarantee that he won't be up to something unsavory when he invites us in."

"Unsavory?" I ask, my mind flying around, wondering what

in the world that could mean. Magnus pauses and purses his lips like he is considering his next words carefully.

"He has particular tastes and he is a bit of an exhibitionist."

The hovercraft pulls into a similar garage as Magnus's and the doors open. He takes my hand before I get out.

"Don't say anything." He is adamant I keep my mouth shut. I don't like being told to be quiet but I have to trust that this is his business. He's looking at me intensely and I realize he is waiting for an answer.

"Okay, I promise," I say and I pull my hand free and climb out. He rounds the hovercraft and pulls me close to him, one arm wraps around my waist as he leads me into the house. The garage is similar to Faust's but nothing else is. The walls instead of being bright and open are made from a kind of black stone and there is soft lighting in the hallway. We walk in without any guidance. It is clear Magnus has been here before. The hallway ends in a large archway that leads into a room, a throne room. It is a large nearly empty space with a dais at the far end and on the dais is a single large chair that is no less ornate than a throne. I almost laugh out loud at the sight, the absurdity, until I see who occupies the chair and who he has next to him on a chain. By his feet sits a young man, with a collar around his neck. He is seated on his knees and the man on the throne holds the chain with his hand, while one of his legs drapes lazily over the armrest. He sits up when he sees us come in and pulls roughly on the chain so the naked boy clutches at the collar and sits up more. Henrik Dalforth, I realize, is also naked and I cast my eyes down, unable to look at the scene without revulsion. Magnus tightens his grip on my waist, either in reassurance or to remind me to keep my mouth shut.

"Faust!" the raspy voice of Henrik rings out as we get closer. "To what do I owe this unexpected visit?"

"I think you know the answer to that," Magnus says and we stop a few feet short of the dais.

"Oh?" he says, sounding disingenuously skeptical.

"You've tried to hack the filters again." Faust accuses without preamble and instead of being offended Henrik bursts out laughing, his raspy metallic voice echoing off the walls of the nearly empty room.

"You're so uptight, Faust." he pulls on the chains again, the jangling sound unmistakable and I keep my eyes down.

"Why don't you try my new toy? He might help you loosen up." It forces my eyes up and I can't help but look up at the scene. Henrik is a large man, with long black hair hanging loosely at his sides. Like all Edits, he seems to be in excellent shape without a single blemish on his dark tan skin. The young man who doesn't look much older than me is smaller in stature. His hair is also black, his face is unnaturally beautiful, high cheekbones, and big eyes with lashes for days, but he looks broken. He won't even look up from the floor, completely subservient to his master. Henrik stands up from his throne and that's when I realize he has zeroed in on me.

"What do you have there?" he asks and he descends the dais and Faust's grip on me gets even tighter. Henrik's eyes are black, pitch black, but they still glow like Faust's eyes. It makes him look like a beast or a demon.

"Don't worry about her," Faust says smoothly.

"Is it a host gift?" he queries and ignores Magnus altogether. Henrik gets closer and all I want to do is hide behind Magnus.

"No, she's my fiancé." he announces clearly and Henrik stops and laughs another bone-chilling metallic laugh.

"You're kidding." he laughs out the words and he looks around the room like there is a punchline or an audience that will reveal the joke. I wonder why Magnus isn't hiding me behind him but I stand still and refuse to look down and be submissive like the poor boy. He stops in front of me and he bends his knees slightly to get a better look at me. His large phallus is dangling between his muscular legs and he is entirely unconcerned with his nudity.

"I admit she's appealing, but marriage Faust, really?"

"I'd appreciate it if you'd stop trying to mess with the filters, they are there for a reason."

"I don't think you're doing a good job relaxing him." he is speaking to me and Magnus squeezes me, a reminder to stay silent.

"Magnus, she is ignoring me, that's not polite." I look up at Magnus for guidance but he is looking at Henrik with a calm expression, like what he said didn't bother him at all.

"I'll tell you what I'll do, I'll take her for a couple of weeks, train her up for you, she will be as docile as a kitten and I'll teach her how to please you, for *your* particular proclivities." he waves his hand around as if to illustrate that Magnus has some particular proclivities that I know nothing about that I am somehow failing to meet.

"Thanks for the offer, Henrik, but I assure you she is quite well-behaved and pleases me immensely." Faust is smiling at this monster and I feel the bile rising in my throat.

"Really?" Henrik doesn't seem to believe Faust and he throws up his arms like he is at his wits end. He saunters back over to the boy who is still sitting by the throne with his eyes cast down. He takes the boy's chin and tilts his face up. The boy keeps his eyes cast down, "look at me" Henrik commands and the boy brings his eyes upwards, his big eyelashes landing on his eyelids, nearly reaching his eyebrows.

"Tell Faust how much you love being my pet," he commands. The boy doesn't take his eyes off Henrik.

"I love being his pet," he says and I have to admit he sounds genuine.

Henrik shifts the boy's face toward us. "Look at him when you say it."

"I love being his pet." he reaffirms and he looks straight at me with his brown eyes instead of Faust. I swallow the lump in my throat.

"See Faust, look how well-behaved he is." Henrik's member starts swelling. He forces the boy's face back toward him and squeezes the soft spots of the boy's cheeks until his mouth opens. He feeds his dick to him while we are still standing there. Henrik strokes the boy's face like he is proud of him and the boy begins sucking him in earnest. Magnus makes a noise in his throat like he is trying to regain Henrik's short attention span.

"What?" Henrik sounds annoyed now.

"I need your word that you will leave the filters alone," Magnus says again, he doesn't seem to be penetrating Henrik's resolve at all.

"Yeah yeah, you can keep your damn filters," Henrik says and waves us off. Magnus turns us around and we are nearly out of the room when Henrik speaks again.

"Dalton is your real problem" and Magnus pauses mid-stride. It is almost unnoticeable but since he is gripping me so tightly it is hard not to miss.

As soon as we are back in the hovercraft I turn to Magnus and yell at him.

"What the fuck was that?!"

"You shouldn't have come; it was a mistake," he says and reaches to touch my arm. I shrug him away.

"Magnus, what the fuck was that?"

"I told you, he is an exhibitionist, with unsavory tastes."

"You didn't seem at all concerned with anything he was doing or saying." I lash out at him and the hovercraft drops us and I am not prepared and scream.

"Fuck! I hate that!" I yell angrily.

"You never used to swear this much. I think I'm a bad influence on you."

"Shut up!" Magnus sighs loudly, rests his head back on his seat, and closes his eyes.

"I'm sorry that I brought you, but if it makes you feel any better, he was relatively tame today. He must be happy with his, uh, companion." That doesn't make me feel better at all.

"That doesn't make me feel better at all. Was that boy hand-picked like me?" I almost don't want to know the answer to that question.

"Probably." is Magnus's answer and he is so unconcerned, for a moment I just stare at him like he is a complete stranger.

"What the fuck is wrong with all of you?" He takes the question rhetorically and just throws up his arms and shrugs.

"No, I want to know, what the fuck is wrong with you Edits?"

"I told you not to judge us all because of this one guy. There are bad Edits, just like there are bad people."

"Well, can't you do something about him?"

"Technically, he hasn't done anything illegal. He probably adopted the boy and put him in the school, and since the boy seems willing, there is nothing I can do about it."

"Wait, hold on!" adopted? "Adopted, did you adopt me?"

"Technically, yes, it was the only legal way to acquire you."

"Fuck, fuck, fuck, that's fucking fucked. FUCK!" I yell, I am angry and I can't believe what I am hearing. I thought I had gotten used to this bizarre situation and accepted the unusual way we were brought together. Brought together as if it was an act of God, except in this case, Faust was the one playing God. The fact that he is legally my adoptive parent is more than I can handle. It occurs to me, is this why he wanted me to change my name? Because you can't marry your legal children? I throw my hands over my face and take a deep breath.

"Kira Tracer is the daughter of Magnus Faust, but Zoriya Faust isn't," I say out loud and look over at Magnus whose eyes are focused on me with guilt written all over his face. He looks like he is completely at a loss for words from my outburst. His mouth is slightly parted and his eyes are wide.

"I thought you knew," he says abruptly.

"Take me home. I don't want to look at you right now." he drags a hand over his face, drawing out his lips at the end.

"We can't go home yet; I have to go see Dalton. It's important, Spark."

"Don't call me that right now." I snap at him. "Fine, but I'm staying in the hovercraft this time."

"You can't, it will look like you're hiding from him. It's a sign of weakness."

"I don't give a fuck what he thinks or any Edit for that matter." I am including Magnus in that statement and he knows it.

"Well, you should, because this is your life now and the last thing you want is to look weak in front of these guys. Okay, we can discuss it when we get home, until then, behave and keep your mouth shut." Of all the things he could have said to me in that moment that was the absolutely worst thing possible. Behave? Keep my mouth shut? He is acting an awful lot like he is the master of me and right now I don't like it one bit. Now that I have some idea what that meant to some Edits. A lightning bolt of clarity hits me, the school, the discipline, having no autonomy. It had nothing to do with a good education. It had nothing to do with being good students or some other greater purpose. It was all designed to ensure we were used to being subservient. Epiphanies are those rare things that occur unexpectedly, they always reveal something new about us or a situation. Sometimes they are good, and sometimes they make you see things about yourself and your life that you wish you didn't know. I am addicted to Faust's praise. I love it when he rewards me with kind words and petting, it is like a drug. It isn't something intrinsic about me, it is trained into me. I always need gratification, abused children often do, and the school did a marvelous job of reinforcing it. Here I thought that Faust had failed to mold me, but in truth, he did such a good job that I couldn't see it myself. I see myself through that boy's eyes, so ready to please, so happy to be rewarded and praised. It could be me on that floor in chains, it is only a matter of circumstances and luck that made it Faust who found me and not Henrik. My cage is gilded and it is hard to see past the bars.

Chapter 26

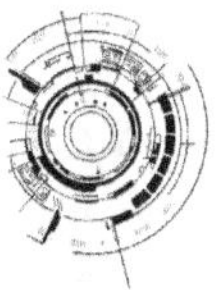

Due to their long lifespans, Edits have developed a system
that allows them to find new companions among humans.
— **Magnus Compendium, Section 11.2**

Magnus

What was I to do, I ask you? There was no other way,
I had to deal with Henrik and she couldn't be left
alone. She thought it was because I was trying to
prevent her from running away. I admit it is partially true, but it
isn't the entire reason for my decision. Now that people know
about her, I can't leave her up there alone. Dalton is up to something and I wouldn't put it past him to snatch up Zori to get his
way. Did I want Henrik to be the first Edit I introduced her to?
No, of course not. He's insane but showing weakness to other
Edit's is like offering yourself up to vultures. They trade in
power and novelty. Those two things are often the only things
that drive them on. I did let slip that Zori was my adoptive
daughter, but it's a technicality. I didn't raise her, I had nothing

to do with it. I mean yes, I paid her tuition, but I was uninvolved beyond that. I've paid for thousands of students' tuition over the last few hundred years. A piece of paper does not a father make. She looks livid next to me, she has had many angry outbursts at me, but this is by far the worst one. Now she won't even look at me or let me touch her. I can see why it is upsetting to her, she has had a cloistered life, but it could have been worse. I mean that quite literally. The last time I was forced to visit Henrik I walked in an orgy. It wasn't the cute kind either where people are just having vanilla sex in the same room. No, there were floggings, spreaders, chains, whips, you name it. Did I think there was a chance that he was going to do that with Zori as a witness? No, he usually sends invites to everyone, and he has been unusually quiet recently. He might even have some sort of love for his new companion. Hard to believe I know, but he did look unusually fond of his sub. I almost told Zoriya that he wasn't even that bad, but I think she thinks he is the worst of the worst. Henrik is mostly harmless, he's twisted and he's into domination, but he would never do anything to someone unwilling. He treats his subs fairly, in the scope of what a dominant sub relationship is.

"Zoriya, I'm sorry." I reach my hand over to stroke her knee and she shifts her legs over to the far side of the hovercraft.

"Spark," I plead with her, I don't need this right now. I have Dalton next and I need my head in the game.

"Don't you mean daughter?" If you live as long as I do, you stop seeing things the same way as a regular person. For example, if everyone you know dies, it's not unreasonable to date someone much younger, yes even almost four hundred years younger. It is within that scope that I justified dating someone so young because finding the right person has been an impossible task. It might seem absurd; I've had four hundred years to search and surely someone in that long time would have fit the bill. Even Zoriya and how perfect she is has failed me in some regard. She is still adamant about dying one day. I love her and

I've loved her since I first saw her. As a little girl, she was beautiful, shy, scared but brilliant. As a woman she is even more so, her fear is evaporating but it is having the unintended consequence of challenging the life I have laid out for us.

"No, you're not my daughter."

"Tell it to the judge."

"What do you mean by that?"

"I mean as far as the law is concerned, I am. Which makes you an incestuous pervert."

"A paper does not make this incestuous, Zori, nor am I perverted. You're an adult, I may have picked you as a child, but I never would have touched you back then."

"Really, you didn't look at me as a child, with my doll-like features, and think, one day, I'm gonna fuck that?"

"That's enough!" I don't like how she is twisting this; it wasn't like that at all. Yes, she was a beautiful child. But more to the point she was brilliant. It was never about finding a child bride.

"It is, I agree." She agrees bitterly and she crosses her arms and moves even further away from me. This is spiraling out of control and I don't know how to stop it. I know I am in a lot of trouble because the minute a woman starts agreeing with you during an argument you've lost. It is time to grovel, and if I didn't have to visit Dalton, I'd do it right away. There are things I didn't know about Zoriya as a child, of course, like the fact that Zori has a big heart, with lots of compassion. Her compassion is one of her most admirable traits. I believe strongly in the ability to understand and care about others, I didn't used to, but life has a way of teaching you lessons, even when you're an unwilling student. Dalton is waiting for us when we arrive, leaning against the door to the hanger. I don't particularly like the expression on his face. Zori gets out but keeps her arms crossed and doesn't let me hold her by the waist. It is not a good start to this exchange.

"Trouble in paradise, already?" Dalton says with a smirk. It has been my experience that sometimes it's best to just ignore Dalton and his snide comments whenever possible.

"Dalton, you've been a bad boy," I say and go up to shake his hand.

"Does she no longer want to play house?" he asks, ignoring my comment, and looking past my shoulder at Zori who is avoiding eye contact with both of us.

"Just a misunderstanding," I say hoping he will drop the subject. "What are you up to?"

"Oh, I'm just hanging out. Why don't you come in for some drinks?" Dalton says and moves out of the way, stretches out his arm, and directs us in. He knew I didn't mean what he was doing as in, what his day was looking like. He always was incorrigible. I ushered Zori in ahead of me and walked down the hallway to Dalton's living room. Dalton sidesteps us and saunters over to his expansive bar; the man always did enjoy his substances. He hands me an amber glass of whiskey and looks at Zori and back at me for guidance.

"She's never had alcohol, better give her juice," I say, Daltons raises both his eyebrows and fails to suppress a grin of amusement.

"I would actually love to have what he is having," Zori says pointing toward my glass. She was supposed to stay quiet, and now she just contradicted me in front of D. I have no choice but to pretend like I don't care. Dalton looks between the two of us to see if I am going to argue, but when I keep my expression neutral, he shrugs and fills a glass up for Zori too. Dalton leans down on his elbows and puts his hands under his chin and looks at both of us like we are the entertainment of the week. Which we might be. Zori takes the glass tumbler and brings it up to her mouth. She gives it a quick sniff and she looks momentarily repulsed but she quickly hides it and takes a large sip. She starts sputtering and coughing. I pat her on the back and she shrugs me away. Fuck, in front of Dalton too.

"Ohhh Magny, what did you do?" Dalton tsks before his grin is ear-splitting.

"Listen, princess, my offer stands, you can always come stay here if Magnus isn't cutting it for you anymore." Zori glares at him like she wants to take the ice pick in the ice bucket and stab him in the eye with it.

Dalton only smiles bigger. "In fact Magny, you could come to stay too, we could all have a little fun, it might help." he gestures between the two of us. "Whatever this is."

"Dalton, I need to know what your plans are, why did Henrik tell me you were getting into the filters?" It is time for the pleasantries to come to an end.

"It could be like old times Magny." He ignores me of course because while there was a time, I considered him a friend; he was always a cheeky bastard. Unreliable and could never take things seriously. He is brilliant but unfocused and undisciplined.

"Just answer the question." I am getting tired of all the sexual innuendos. His face has been looking at me with longing but it shifts to indifference, but I know it is his annoyed and hurt expression.

"I don't know what Henrik told you," he says fills himself with a glass of whiskey, and knocks it back in one gulp. He refills his glass and walks around the bar and flops down in one of the low-back leather lounge chairs. He stretches out his legs in front of him and he cradles his drink to his chest and glares at me. Everyone is mad at me at the moment and from my perspective, I haven't done anything to deserve it. Dalton always was good-looking, even now when he is glaring at me with contempt, he looks like a male model in an ad for whiskey. He has a 5 o'clock shadow, but his 5 o'clock shadow doesn't take a whole day to show up, with his dark coloring it only takes a couple of hours after shaving before he looks like he needs to shave again. His lilac eyes are piercing, even before replacing them with the interface eyes. Yes, his eyes have always been that color. His thick eyebrows are drawn in and he looks utterly sullen. I wish Zori wasn't here, because there are things I have to say to Dalton that I don't need her to hear. I make the choice to stop using words. I dial Dalton in my head and he arches an eyebrow at me before answering.

"D, what is this?" I ask him silently. "I thought we had moved past this."

"You moved past it," he responds and looks out the window. Zoriya is still standing by the bar cradling her drink and so far, hasn't noticed any change.

"We agreed a long time ago."

"No, you decided for us." I play back the memory of us coming to the agreement and he gets up from the seat and gets in my face.

"Low blow," he says in my face and he doesn't use the interface. "You remember it that way, but I don't." he is seething now. "You can't play back my inner thoughts!" he shouts at me.

"Calm down," I ask him in my head and his eyes flick back and forth between me and Zori.

"She doesn't know?"

"There is nothing to know," I reply automatically.

"What don't I know?" Zori asks, her drink forgotten. Dalton starts laughing maniacally as he has finally landed on something juicy.

"Don't" I plead with him and he looks ready to burst, like a balloon of information.

"Little bird, what is your name?" he asks Zoriya all of a sudden. She is looking back and forth between the two of us and lands on Dalton.

"I don't have one right now," she says and arches an eyebrow at me in challenge.

"Interesting, after all these weeks, no name?" Dalton shrugs his shoulders and he leans an elbow on the bar and faces Zori.

"Little bird, did you know that Magny here made me an Edit?"

"No."

"Little bird, did he offer to make you an Edit too?"

"Yes, but I'm not going to do it."

That bit of information is supposed to be private.

"Really?!" Dalton shouts with fascination. He smiles at me. "She is smarter than she looks."

"I think that's enough, Zori, we are going home," I say I reach out for her hand, which she shrugs off once more. I drag a frustrated hand through my hair.

"No, I'd like to hear what he has to say," she says and widens her stance, she is holding her ground.

"She's curious too, an admirable trait," Dalton says and he drinks the rest of his whiskey before slamming it down on the bar. He slides up to Zori and is closer to her than I like. She doesn't shrug away from him and it stings.

"You and I have a lot in common, little bird. Once upon a time, Magny here found a little boy with violet eyes. His home life was less than ideal. He convinced mommy and daddy dearest to relinquish their claim on him." Zori's eyes are wide and her brain is starting to draw conclusions, unfortunately, they are probably the right ones.

"Yes, it's true, Magny here picked me out of the slums. Put me into school, only to be taken out when I was of age. It sounds familiar doesn't it."

She looks livid and confused and I thought I was in a hole earlier, but now I don't even know if I can dig myself out.

"Yes, it's similar, and just like you, I was his lover for many years." her eyes flash over to me, trying to gauge my reaction to see if Dalton is lying. He isn't.

"How many years was it? Oh, that's right one hundred and five, four months, seven hours, Eighteen minutes, give or take 10 seconds to be exact."

"Okay, it's not what it sounds like. We had a relationship until it no longer worked."

"Yes, that's true, one day Magny decided that he simply didn't love me anymore. It was time to move on. I believe, were his words. Despite the promise of eternity together and undying love."

"You make it sound one-sided, but it was a mutual decision. You were bored, remember? You said that you needed some new experiences, variety."

"I never said I didn't want you still," he says and his voice cracks and he looks close to tears.

"You seemed happy to go off and play at Henrik's. We didn't want the same things in life, you moved on, and I moved on." Dalton's face contorts into a mix of anger and hurt. He swallows a lump and his breathing becomes labored.

"And now I'm moving on!" Zori says and she starts running toward the hanger.

"Fuck, why couldn't you just keep your fucking mouth shut?" I yell at Dalton before sprinting after Zori. I catch her easily enough and wrap my arms around her waist.

"Let me go!" she shouts angrily.

"Listen to me first." I plead and pull her to the ground, holding her in my lap.

Chapter 27

Nameless

He was with Dalton? It wasn't just that he had another lover; it was that he was repeating history with me. I thought I was a special case, that I was the only one. What hubris, what idiocy, what a gullible fool."

"Let me go, Faust," I demand, but he keeps a vise-like band around my waist and holds me firmly in his lap.

"Baby, I know it sounds bad."

"How many?" I demand to know, my voice trembling with a mix of anger and hurt.

"How many, what?" he asks and takes a deep breath. "Oh, you think I've done this several times?"

I nod my head and keep my spine stiff, trying to put some distance between us.

"Dalton and you, that's it. Dalton made it seem like I

dropped him and broke promises. That's not how it happened." I'm not sure it matters, because to me it speaks volumes that this is his Modus Operandi. Snatching up children to turn into lovers when they are old enough and claiming an undying love for them is repulsive.

"Let me go. I don't want you to touch me," I say and try to move off him again. Touching him feels wrong all of a sudden. I don't want to feel the heat of his body on mine. His warmth used to feel like the sun dappling on my skin and warming me. Now he feels like a furnace, and if I am not careful, I'll get burned.

"Baby, stop this," he begs, keeping me still with a gentle but unyielding grip.

"Dalton and I had a long relationship, but it was fraught with difficulty. I didn't pick him out as a lover at the outset. He was picked because of his test scores and his gene type. I needed someone to help me with my work. He was brilliant and helped me develop the chip in my brain. The team that I had worked with originally all died, and I needed someone I could trust. The world was still oblivious to what I was doing." I go still in his arms, my curiosity piqued despite my anger.

"There was one more reason my wife refused to become an Edit; I was the only one who initially survived regeneration. We didn't understand why, and after several people died, the project got shut down. The company scrubbed the project and washed their hands of it. I took on the project alone and in secret. It was difficult because I only specialized in biomolecular engineering. It wasn't enough to figure out why it worked on me and only me. I went back to school, and I got degrees in every pertinent field. It took me many years, and I had to change my name repeatedly, so no one would question why I was still young. It turned out that I had a special protein in my genome that allowed me to go through the process without dying. Dalton has the same one, so I recruited him and put him through school, not the one you went to. That didn't start until a hundred years ago. Dalton was a part of my life before my wife died. We were friends for a long time before we became lovers. You see, darling, I was lonely. I was sad. My family died, and he was the one constant in my life."

"So what happened?"

"First off, he became an Edit long before he was my lover. I never made undying promises of eternity. There was love between us, but it was always a little skewed; he felt more strongly about us until he didn't. He started going to Henrik's for orgies, and I didn't want to be a part of that life. When we decided to split ways, I did something to the emotional filter. I didn't want to be distracted by these human emotions. I wanted to make progress on my life's work. I turned them off, and for a long time, I was not a nice person. I experimented on people, willing participants, but the experiments were painful and dangerous, and some of them died. I had meaningless sex with multiple partners. In short, I was lost and functioning from a purely logical brain with a heavy dose of sexual need. Dalton sometimes ended up in my bed, along with others, but I was incapable of showing him any kind of affection or love, and I think he took it too hard."

Dalton is standing at the entrance of the hangar, looking angry and hurt as he gazes at us on the floor. When Faust finishes, Dalton comes over to us, falls to his knees, and hugs Faust while he is still holding me.

"I'm sorry." I hear him whisper, and Faust releases one hand around me to pat Dalton on the shoulder.

"It's okay," he tells him, but Dalton wails.

"No, you don't understand." Faust stills completely.

"What has happened?" he asks Dalton, and I can hear some fear in his voice.

"I've given the access codes to Penigran," Dalton confesses and slumps back on the ground, looking at Faust with wide, pleading eyes.

Faust moves me off him and stands up. The air around us sizzles with rage, a rage I didn't know Faust was capable of.

"You did what?" Faust is speaking through his teeth, looking on the verge of reaching some kind of breaking point. I slide far away from both of them as Faust looms over a frightened Dalton. Faust picks Dalton up by the collar and brings him to his face.

"When?" Dalton holds on to Faust's forearms but doesn't fight back.

"This morning," Dalton admits, and Faust throws him and screams, "Why?!" Dalton lands a few feet away, but he pulls himself up off the ground, not seeming hurt at all.

"I was so angry at you; I wanted your attention. I thought after you got your emotions back, you would come back to me, but you didn't. What's worse, you didn't even come to my bed anymore; it was like I was dead to you. To make matters worse, you replaced me with her!" He looks over at me, pointing an accusing finger. I am pressed against one of the hovercrafts, trying to stay far away from both of them.

"I still love you!" he cries out and gets on his knees, stretching out his hands in contrition. "You wouldn't do the hard thing, Magnus; you've never been willing to use your power." Magnus doesn't move; he is preternaturally still, and it feels like a moment of calm before a storm hits. I press myself further into the hovercraft. I can feel the metal digging into my back, and I still feel too close to them.

"Forgive me, Magnus, please." He crawls over to Magnus, who watches him with laser focus. He is a radiator of anger; you can almost see heat waves coming off him. Dalton takes the hem of Faust's pants, kisses them with reverence, and nuzzles his face against Faust's leg. It's an eerie reminder of what I had seen at Henrik's. Except, Faust doesn't look proud of his pet at all; he looks disappointed and ready to kill someone.

"Get off," he says under his breath, but with such force, there is no chance of missing it. Dalton slinks back, his eyes streaming with tears as he looks up at his master with deep longing and sorrow. Dalton's body crumples on the spot, going slack, and his limbs splay out as gravity pulls him down. His body is completely still, and his eyes are now dim.

"Get in the hovercraft, Zori." Faust commands, but I am too stupefied to move. He strolls over to me, picks me up, opens the door, and shoves me inside. The hovercraft starts going without Faust, and I try to open the door to ask him what the hell just happened. He stands there staring at me and follows me with his eyes as I leave. Faust looks alien to me; his eyes are hard, and I don't even recognize the man I love. The door doesn't budge, and the seatbelt locks around me before I drop out of the hangar, all the while I'm screaming after Faust.

THE HOVERCRAFT finally levels out after it drops out of Dalton's hangar. I shout at the damn thing to reroute, but it doesn't respond to my commands. I have no control over this machine. My body feels hot, and my mind is unfocused. Is Dalton dead? I've never seen anyone fall so quickly; his eyes going dim was surreal. I've seen Magnus's eyes flicker, a telltale sign that he isn't human, and as unsettling as that is, Dalton's eyes shutting off is far worse. It was as if his entire existence was erased in an instant. I shout at the hovercraft computer again.

"Return to Dalton's!" I yell, but it doesn't acknowledge that I've spoken. The landscape changes quickly beneath me as I move at a brisk pace. The vast hills and meadows below the Edit floating islands disappear behind me, and I turn to watch them vanish into the horizon. The Edit city is right below, and before I can take in its strange architecture and empty streets, it too passes, and I enter unfamiliar territory. If Magnus is controlling this thing, where is he sending me? Why is he sending me away? Questions flood my mind faster than I can find answers.

Ahead of me is a thick forest, and I pause my thoughts to stare at it. I've never seen a forest before, not a real one. No one

I know has. The tall canopied trees stretch as far as the eye can see, and I'm mesmerized by the sight. Towering conifers and evergreens, lush with life, create an emerald tapestry. The forest looks like a living, breathing carpet, rich with varied shades of green. I thought the world was full; I thought we lived in back-to-back walled cities, but the truth is starkly before me. I can't see any cities at all in any direction. The world looks empty.

I feel this weight in my stomach because it's another lie. It's another thing about my life that has been false. My life has been nothing but a weaving of untruths, every stitch dyed with deception.

I hear scratching and look down at my thigh. I'm still wearing that buttery silk dress, and I've torn up my leg. For the first time in my life, I've made myself bleed. Streaks of red blood paint my thigh and coat the undersides of my fingernails. I stretch out my fingers, overextending them. A moan escapes my lips, and I force myself to keep my hand still to avoid destroying my thigh. I take a deep breath as I feel the pain in my leg, I feel myself floating and even the pain doesn't drag me down into my body. I am untethered, floating away into an abyss. The world is a lie, my life is a lie and Magnus might be a killer. The man I gave my heart to probably didn't deserve it. He excavated my heart with a pickaxe and I let him. I let him carve me out and bleed all over him, desperate for love, desperate to have a place in the world. To belong.

The hovercraft jerks violently, throwing my head into the dashboard. Blackness peppers my vision, and I feel myself blacking out. I hear my inner voice shouting at me to stay awake, and I force myself back into consciousness. I swim to the surface of my awareness and emerge, but instead of a lungful of air, I'm met with throbbing pain.

The hovercraft is crashing. The ground is getting closer, and I frantically look around for anything to stop the descent. I shout at the computer, but it remains unresponsive. If it continues descending at this pace, I'll certainly die on impact.

My brain pounds and I feel a sticky warmth coating my hairline. I glance at my fingers and see more blood. My ears are clogged, and my vision is blurry. There's no time to think, no time to find a way out. I'm about to die. Even knowing this my survival instinct isn't strong enough because the last thing I see is the forest canopy rushing up before everything goes dark.

Chapter 28

"In this age of the Great Scourge, we live behind towering walls to ensure our safety. Every citizen is equally confined in our vast cities, and we must be grateful for our safety. We live in peace, and we thrive in our metropolises. The deadly infection outside would inevitably claim our lives if we ventured beyond these barriers. Therefore, we remain confined but secure within the walls that are our only sanctuary."

-Provisional Government Edict, 2102, from "The Chronicles of Survival"

My eyes flutter open, everything is a blur. My head throbs with a dull persistent ache, a relentless drumbeat echoing in my skull. Thump thump thump. I try to move but my limbs feel heavy, disconnected, I'm swimming through a vat of molasses. I try to open my eyes again but the world spins and I'm forced to close them to stop the nauseating dizziness. My mouth is dry, a harsh metallic taste on my tongue, blood. I need to wake up, I need to move. I peel open my eyes, there is a crust around my lashes and I bring up my heavy arm and wipe at the crust, clearing it. I blink a few times trying to clear my murky vision. I'm not in the hovercraft. I'm not even outside. I'm in a room, unfamiliar, with gray concrete walls. I gingerly move my head to take in the unfamiliar space. I'm lying in a narrow bed, a hospital bed, but this is not a hospital. Tubes and wires snake around me: an IV drip feeding fluids into my arm, EKG leads monitoring my heart, and various other devices. I pull them out, one by one, ignoring the sting as I pull out the needle from my arm. A little blood comes along with it. I blot at it with the blanket and look around at my alien surroundings. The room is dim, there are no windows, and there is nothing to tell me what time it is. The room is devoid of anything, except for me and the bed that I'm on. I sit up, ignoring the consistent ache that pounds at my head, worsening with each movement. I take a deep breath, inhaling the air, but it is stale. There is a persistent mustiness suggesting a limited ventilation system. The scent of concrete and metal is pervasive, mingling with an underlying dampness that seems to cling to the walls. Each breath feels heavy, lacking the crispness of the open air. The atmosphere is thick and oppressive, it's cold, but it's not refreshing. It clings to my bones, clammy and chilling, and my skin tingles as goosebumps spread out over all my exposed skin. I try to take stock of everything, I feel my clothing, I'm no longer in my silk dress, instead, I'm in some kind of itchy hospital gown. I touch my aching head and discover a bandage has been wrapped around my skull. I gingerly touch and I feel a deep pain at my hairline. A pain shoots through my body as I touch and I drop my hand quickly and groan. My leg is bandaged, but nothing feels broken, that is something at least. I have a concussion, but I'm not dead. I try to enjoy my small victory, but a new panic sets in as I start to wonder where I am, and who brought me here. I plant my bare feet on the cold ground and I pull myself up to stand. I sway and hold on to the bed for balance, my head swims and I breathe in through my nose until my head clears. I take a tentative step toward the door. It's a heavy metal door and I slowly move toward the door until I reach the other side of the room. The steps become easier, despite my throbbing head. I pull at the cold door handle but it doesn't budge. I'm locked inside. I'm suppressing my panic when the handle moves and I jump back. The door swings open, and a figure steps into the dim light, he is both startling and unsettling. At first, I can't quite see what is wrong, but as he moves closer, the details become disturbingly clear. His skin is an unsettling patchwork of textures and colors, some areas unnaturally pale and almost translucent, while others are rough and discolored. The stark contrast between these patches makes his appearance almost otherworldly. His face is a jarring mix of human and something else. One eye seems organic yet artificial, its surface too smooth, its color too vivid. It glows faintly, its light flickering as if struggling to stay on. The skin around it is scarred and inflamed, giving the impression that the organic implant is not fully integrated. His other eye is human, bloodshot and tired, contrasting sharply with the unsettling glare of its counterpart. His hair is thin and uneven, with patches missing entirely. What remains is streaked with gray, adding to his haggard and worn appearance. His forehead is marked with deep lines, a sign of both age and the stress of his condition. As my gaze travels down, I notice the irregularity of his body. Organic-looking joints jut out awkwardly at his shoulders and elbows, surrounded by raw, irritated flesh. His hands are an eerie blend of natural and synthetic flesh, with fingers that sometimes move with an unsettling precision and other times tremble uncontrollably. His movements are jerky and uneven, suggesting both pain and mechanical malfunction. His pristine coat does little to hide the veins and sinew that occasionally peek out, giving the impression that his body is barely holding together. The combination of human and organic bionic parts makes him look like a grotesque assemblage of a man. Despite his unnerving appearance, there is a fierce intensity in his gaze. His human eye burns with a mixture of defiance and desperation as if he is constantly fighting an internal battle. It is clear to me that whatever he has become, it is the result of a failed and tragic attempt to transcend his humanity. I back away from him completely until I'm almost against the wall. He enters the room, his good eye locked onto me.

"What have we here?" he says, straightening his spine as he takes another step toward me. "I was very surprised to find out there was a girl in that hovercraft," he continues, and I scan the room for a weapon, but there is nothing—just the bed and the sheets on it. I wonder if he is strong. Perhaps his deformed body will make it easy to overtake him and escape. I watch him carefully; his skin sags at the hollows of his cheeks. If I weren't so terrified, I'd stop looking because his appearance is hard to swallow.

"What do you want?" I ask. He tilts his head to look at me, his broken eye flickering and dimming before reigniting to glow fully.

"Where is Magnus Faust?" he asks, ignoring my question.

"I don't know. Who are you? What is this place?" I look at the door; he is still blocking the door, his hulking frame filling the whole thing. If I ran at him, could I knock him on his ass and scramble past him? Probably not—he's big, bigger than Faust. He's almost a distorted version of Faust. I now see that part of his patchy hair is blonde, the gray streaks punctuating his age. His bionic eye is green, like Faust's, but his human eye is dark blue.

"Why were you in his vehicle?" he asks, his bionic eye scanning me. There is a strange movement in the pupil; it's changing shape, jagged with splintering edges before it becomes round again. Faust's eyes never did that. He is different, and I don't know what happened to him, but he reeks of danger. My reptilian brain tries to think of an answer, one that won't get me killed.

"He wanted me gone," I reply vaguely. I am not sure what to say to him. He obviously doesn't have my trust, and I get the sense that he is not a friend of Faust's. Maybe I should distance myself from Magnus as an act of self-preservation.

"What is your relationship to Faust?" he asks. He licks the top of his teeth before coughing into a cloth napkin. I see a sprinkling of blood on it. This man is dying.

"I was his captive," I tell him. He takes another step toward me. He is no longer blocking the door, but I'd still have to be fast enough to get around him. The truth is I'm not sure how agile I am right now. My concussion is severe, and I can only hope I haven't suffered any permanent brain damage.

"A pet?" he concludes, stuffing his napkin back into his pocket. I nod, confirming his assessment. His posture changes, and he slumps. The effort of standing straight seems to have drained him.

"I'm sorry," he says, then starts a coughing fit, quickly pulling out the same napkin. He holds up a finger, asking me to wait until he's done. But self-preservation is something I'm trying to become more adept at since it's become clear in recent months that I've been lacking in it. I feel ashamed of myself. I wonder what little Kira would think of me now. I dart around him and sprint for the door. He lunges for me mid-cough, but I manage to dodge him and make it past the threshold. He sputters, "Stop her," and that's when I notice the guards posted outside. They don't hesitate to grab at me, and I get three steps before one of them tackles me to the ground. I hit my head again, this time on the side. I can feel my neck spring back from the impact, and I cry out in agony.

"Don't hurt her, you idiot," the man regains his composure and follows me outside the room. I grab my head as my vision spins violently, and I start to vomit uncontrollably. I'm on my side, so the vomit pools in my mouth, and I begin to choke on it, unable to clear it with the weight of the guard on me.

"Thompson, get off!" the other guard yells. He squats at my side, turns me over, and pats my back. The vomit sprays the ground, and I spit while trying to catch my breath. "That's it, girl, breathe," he says gently, stroking my back. I'm surprised by the kindness; it's a puncture in the cloud of my precarious predicament. I gasp and sputter, and then he helps me up to a seated position, leaning me against his chest. "That's it," he repeats. My heart is racing, my head is spinning, and I feel sick beyond words.

"Grayson, carry her back to the bed," the man orders, and Grayson, the guard, scoops me up and walks me back into the room, carefully placing me on the bed. I try to protest, sitting up and pushing Grayson away, but my head spins, and I fall back onto the pillow. I close my eyes, trying to take deep breaths.

"You're safe," Grayson says. "No one here is going to hurt you." I need a moment to regain my composure.

"Thompson, get the doctor," the deformed man says. I keep my eyes closed, praying, hoping, and dreaming that I really am safe, that they don't mean me any harm. I don't believe it for a second, but at this moment, I need to believe it because I am incapacitated. If I'm not safe, there is almost nothing I can do about it, not yet. The doctor comes in sometime later. I hear murmurs from some of the men and open my eyes to look at the slight old man. His glasses cling to his nose as he nods to whatever the deformed man and Grayson are saying. He comes over to me and picks up my wrist to check my pulse. Then, he shines a penlight into my eyes, and I blink away the brightness.

"Just look at the pen, dearie," he says. I do my best to follow the harsh light.

"Grayson, lay her down flat and elevate her head slightly with a pillow," he instructs firmly. Grayson quickly follows the instructions. He has a small crease between his eyes, his blue eyes reminding me of the sky, and I focus on his calm demeanor and the gentle touch of his hands as he adjusts me on the bed. The elevation immediately alleviates some of the pressure in my head. He notices me watching him and gives me an easy smile. I know I should be terrified of him; after all, I'm captive here and he is a guard. But there is something about him that puts me at ease. I shunt the feeling away. I can't let my guard down; I can't be such an easy lamb to the slaughter, not this time. The doctor addresses the vomiting.

"We need to keep her hydrated, but carefully. Let's start with small sips of water." Thompson is sent out of the room to fetch some water, and I watch as they fuss over me. This is not the behavior of people who want me dead, but maybe they think they need me alive to get information on Magnus.

"You took quite a bump on the head, little lady," the doctor says, gently patting my hand. "Do you want to take a painkiller?" he asks. I shake my head no. I don't need to be groggy and out of it; I need to quickly find a way to clear my head and figure a way out of here. He nods, an understanding look in his eyes, and doesn't push. He notices the blood on my elbow from where I pulled out my IV and he cleans it up and puts on a small bandage.

"If she falls asleep, wake her every couple of hours to check for any signs of worsening symptoms. Ask her simple questions to ensure she's not losing consciousness. She needs to stay awake for a while now to ensure there's no immediate danger," he says, addressing Grayson. I notice the deformed man is gone; somewhere along the line, he left the room, but I didn't see him go.

"Okay, my dear, it's important you get some rest. Stay still as much as possible. Try not to move that head of yours," the doctor says to me. He squeezes my shoulder and then speaks in low tones to Grayson by the door before leaving. "I'm glad she finally woke up from the coma, but this could be a setback. Keep an eye on her." I was in a coma? How long have I been in here? Grayson dims the lights further, and I watch him as he stands by the door. He's handsome, his features more angular than Magnus's, but there is something about him. He has a serious expression on his face; he almost looks mean, but he has been nothing but gentle to me. His hair is brown with a hint of red. He looks older than Magnus; I guess that he is in his late twenties or maybe early thirties. He's got a five o'clock shadow that adds to the harshness of his expression. Sky-blue eyes peek out from under his serious thick brows, and even in the dimness of the room, I can see their light. But they aren't Edit eyes; these eyes belong to a human.

"What is this place?" I ask him, bunching the sheets in my hand.

"It's not for me to tell you," he says, but he sits at the foot of the bed. "You're safe, I can tell you that much."

"Why should I believe that? I'm being held here against my will," I retort, anger lacing my voice.

"We rescued you," he counters. I glare at him. Did they rescue me? Something hit that hovercraft; it didn't crash on its own. An explosion of some kind—my groggy brain drags the moment back into my head. I didn't crash by accident.

"You mean after you shot me down?" I say with certainty. Grayson's lips purse and he looks away, the muscles in his jaw tightening.

"Yes, we shot you down, but we thought you were someone else," he admits, his voice strained.

"Faust?" I ask though I know the answer. I want to hear him say it and understand why they are after him. Is it possible that Magnus put me in there as a decoy? Would he do that, send me into harm's way? I swallow the thought and gulp at the discomfort. It feels like a frog has jumped into my throat, kicking its way down to my stomach.

"Yes," he says softly, his shoulders slumping slightly.

"What do you want with Faust?" I press, my eyes narrowing as I study his expression.

"That's not for me to tell you either," he says, resigned, his gaze dropping to the floor. I glare at him openly, feeling a surge of frustration.

"Who then? Who is going to tell me?"

"Penigren."

"Penigren." The name rings a bell. My eidetic memory flashes to an article I read about him. He was a trillionaire who was working on an immunity booster to free the human population from their isolated Units. These units were intended to be temporary, but they became a permanent way of life. What does he have to do with this?

"When will I meet him?"

"You've already met him." I raise an eyebrow and think about the few people I've encountered so far. It can't be the guard Thompson, or the doctor. Therefore, Memphis Penigren is the deformed man. How did this world leader, this trillionaire, become so malformed?

"What happened to him?" I ask, noticing how Grayson's expression hardens, his lips pressing into a thin line, I can already tell what he's going to say. We say it at the same time: "That's not for me to tell you." He chuckles and shrugs his shoulders, a faint smile tugging at the corner of his mouth. I glare at him.

"I was in a coma, how long have I been here?" what if I've been out for years, I look down at my body but I don't look visibly aged.

"Two weeks, in a way you were lucky, you got to be unconscious for the duration of your quarantine," he says and sighs, at least it's not been years, but two weeks is a long time to be in a coma. I've been thrust into another situation out of my control. The last one had me in a gilded cage; this time, a concrete bunker. Dalton mentioned Penigren before he died. What could Magnus have done to cause this? I'm worried I know the answer, and that means I'm in a lot of trouble.

Chapter 29

Secrets had an immense attraction to him, because he never could keep one, and he enjoyed the sort of uneasy self-consciousness which he felt when other people were telling them to him."

– Kenneth Grahame, *The Wind in the Willows*

The only visitor I have is Grayson, he insists on waking me up repeatedly throughout the first night. His gentle voice rouses me from fitful sleep, again and again, leaving me groggy and irritable the next day. I often grumble and push him away, but he stays calm and affable.

"Sorry, but I have to," he says softly, his expression earnest. "We need to make sure your concussion doesn't worsen." The next morning, my head throbs with a relentless ache, and I feel even worse than the day before. Despite this, there's a small consolation: the concussion hasn't deteriorated. The doctor drops by on the third day. He scrutinizes me with a practiced eye before carefully removing the bandage from my head. The cool air stings the wound, but I bite back a wince. I need a shower, fresh clothes, fresh air, and decent food. The food they bring me is meager, stale crackers, watered-down soups, and dried fruits. I long for a fresh baby tomato, the sweet tang as it bursts into your mouth, a crisp piece of romaine lettuce, anything fresh and alive. I also crave the sun, real light. Part of me hates Grayson for being likable because it might mean there is something deeply wrong with me. After all, he works for the man who shot down my hovercraft. He helped put me in this hospital bed. He is the reason I'm damaged and trapped. I want him to act like the villain, the villain that he is. But he doesn't. When I scream at him out of boredom and frustration from being stuck here, he offers to read to me. Over time, he sits with me and reads from books. He never asks me about Magnus Faust. He has an easy smile, one that is always readily available, even when I grumble, demand to be released, or ask to see Penigren. He just tells me "not yet" and that I need to rest.

"WHAT BOOK IS THIS?" I ask when Grayson pulls up the chair he brought into the room and sets it down next to the bed. He never leaves the chair here. I wonder if it's because they worry I'll turn it into a weapon. I could. I could smash it and use the legs as a club. I can almost feel the rough wood in my hand, the grainy texture as I grip it, ready to fracture someone in the head with it. My fingers tingle at the thought. Grayson sits down on the chair, his eyebrows knitting, creating a slight furrow between them. One brow arches higher than the other, giving his face an asymmetrical look. His lips press together, forming a thin line that hints at a suppressed smile or a perplexed frown. The corners of his mouth twitch almost imperceptibly as if he's caught between a smirk and a serious question. He knows I'm thinking something, and I quickly look away, chewing on my lip.

"What's that look?" he asks, tilting his head slightly, his voice laced with gentle curiosity. I just keep chewing my lip and shrugging.

"Okay, Petal, this book is only the best book in existence." He leans back, crossing one leg over the other casually, a playful glint in his eyes.

"In existence?" I ask, doubtful but intrigued by his mischievous expression.

"The Wind in the Willows."

"I've never heard of it," I admit, shifting uncomfortably.

"What? Really, your parents never read this to you?" He leans forward, genuine surprise and a touch of sadness in his gaze.

"No, my mother sold me when I was ten," I blurt out, over-sharing. He doesn't look shocked, just sad. He nods and takes a deep breath, not asking questions or offering words of comfort. Instead, he reaches out and gently touches my hand, a simple gesture of solidarity. His hand is warm and rough, his fingers linger a moment before he leans back into his chair.

"Well, it's never too late to read this literary masterpiece." He smiles warmly at me and opens the book. "Mr. Toad's adventures always make me smile." He starts reading aloud, his voice rich and animated, bringing the characters to life. He even uses different voices for Mole, Rat, and Toad. I lean back on my pillow and listen to his rendition of Mr. Toad, and pictures form in my head. I can't help but draw parallels between me and Mr. Toad careening through life, impulsively, recklessly, pulled toward the thrill of danger. I think of Magnus and how he was always so appealing. He was this magnet, and even when I knew it was wrong, I wanted him. I wanted his words of praise, his lips on my skin, his heavy weight on my body.

"'Independence is all very well, but we animals never allow our friends to make fools of themselves beyond a certain limit; and that limit, you've reached,'" Grayson reads Ratty's line, his eyes lifting from the book to meet mine. I can't help but wish I had a friend like that. Someone to keep me from making a fool of myself.

I AWAKEN to a movement in the room. I turn, expecting to see Grayson checking on me. In the darkness, a hulking form looms. Penigren. He stands over my bed, watching me silently. His green eye flickers like a dim, eerie night light.

"You're young," he says, as if we were in the middle of a conversation. His voice is gravelly, each word slow and deliberate. "They all are, though. They tend to keep the young ones for longer." He slides a shaky finger along my cheek, his touch cold and unsettling. I flinch at the contact, but he seems unfazed by my reaction. His face is a mask of curiosity, devoid of empathy. "I have to wonder what made Faust tire of you so quickly." His finger trails down to my shoulder, slipping under the edge of my gown. I sit up abruptly, my heart thumping in my ears, and push his hand away. He stares at me with a hard, unblinking gaze, and I scoot back deeper into the bed, trying to put as much distance as possible between us.

"He could have traded you, sold you, killed you. Why would he put you in that hovercraft to merely send you away? Edits don't leave their pets alive when they are done. So tell me the truth, girl, was Faust really done with you?" He leans in closer, his breath hot and sour against my skin. They kill their pets? I shudder at the thought and wonder if this man is telling the truth. My eyes dart toward the door, wishing Grayson would walk in and check on us. I don't like being alone with Memphis Penigren.

"What do you want with him, anyway?" I ask, ignoring his question because I don't know the answer. I don't know if Magnus was done with me. I might never know if I don't leave this room if Penigren decides to kill me.

"That's none of your concern. All you need to do is answer my questions," he snaps, his voice sharp and impatient.

"I don't know. He shoved me in there without explanation," I admit, hoping the truth will keep me safe. Penigren's eye does that thing again, where the pupil becomes misshapen and strange, a grotesque morphing that sends a chill down my spine. I get out of bed and retreat, my movements slow and cautious. His eyes follow me the whole time, a predator stalking its prey. There's a strange sound coming from him, a static crackling, it's unsettling. Is he more machine than man?

"Very well," he says after a long minute, finally shifting his focus. I notice a tremor in his hand as he pulls out his napkin. He dabs at his mouth, cleaning up some drool that had escaped during his interrogation. His shoulders slump slightly, and he turns to walk to the door without looking back at me. I hear the lock click in place after he's on the other side. I slide down to the floor, my body trembling, and wrap my arms around my knees. My tears come silently, a heavy ache in my chest. I wish I was anywhere but here. To think I could have avoided all of this if I had left Magnus when he gave me the chance. If only I hadn't been so eager to please, so desperate for love.

THE NEXT MORNING, Grayson finds me on the floor, wrapped in my blanket in the corner.

"Oh, Petal," he says softly, squatting down to look at me, his voice filled with concern. "The bed too soft for you?" I ignore him and push my stiff body off the ground. The left side of my body feels bruised from laying on the cold, wet concrete all night. I just couldn't stay in that bed; every time I tried to close my eyes, it felt like Penigren was standing over me.

"Yes, the hospital bed is too soft," I grumble sarcastically, pushing him aside and walking to the bed. On the bed is a pile of clothes. I pick them up: a simple pair of jeans, a T-shirt, and a sweater. There is even a pair of cotton underwear.

"Clothes? For me?" I ask, clutching the sweater and underwear, looking back at Grayson.

"Yes." He blushes and looks away, rubbing the back of his neck awkwardly.

"Grayson, are you blushing at these simple cotton underwear?" The thought tickles me, and the icky feeling I had all night vanishes in an instant.

"No," he says adamantly, but he doesn't return his gaze to the underwear. Instead, his eyes lock with mine. Blue on blue, his pale eyes meeting my dark ones. For a moment, we stand there, the air thick with unspoken words. His expression softens, a hint of a smile playing at the corners of his mouth. I can feel the camaraderie between us. Our friendship doesn't make sense, and I worry that Grayson has begun to develop feelings for me. It's the way he looks at me, it's like he sees me, or wants to see me. He's invested in me in a way I don't understand. But Grayson is tilting at windmills. My heart still beats for Magnus, even though he might have thrown me into the deep end. He knew what a bad swimmer I was. There is a draw to Grayson, but I dispel the feeling. It's just that he has been friendly to me and my instinct is to search out allies, but the truth is, he isn't one, and I have to keep reminding myself of that fact.

"Thank you," I say quietly, breaking the silence. I hug the clothes to my chest, a small comfort; I'm definitely ready to get out of this itchy gown someone put me in. "For the clothes."

He steps closer, his gaze intense and unwavering. "You're welcome, Petal. Actually, I have some news. You're free to leave this room. I've been instructed to give you a tour. And you've been assigned another room—one with a window."

"Really? I can leave?" He smiles, the warmth in his eyes, tricking me with its sincerity. "Yes. You'll get to see more of the place and meet a few people. And your new room... well, it's much nicer than this one." He gestures towards the door, then pauses. "I'll step outside to give you some privacy to change. Just knock when you're ready." I nod, grateful for the small courtesy. "Thank you, Grayson." He leaves the room, closing the door softly behind him. I take a deep breath and quickly change into the fresh clothes. The jeans and T-shirt fit perfectly, and the sweater is warm and comforting. The simple act of dressing in clean clothes lifts my spirits.

I KNOCK ON THE DOOR, and Grayson re-enters, his eyes meeting mine with a reassuring smile.

"Ready?" I follow him out of the room. The hallway is familiar because I've been escorted to and from the bathroom. It's a long, dimly lit concrete hallway, with heavy doors identical to my room. I wonder if they have other captives behind them. I follow him down the long passageway, scanning everything I see. I plan on making my escape, and to do that, I need information. There are things to my advantage, things Grayson and the other guards don't know. One, I've been trained in hand-to-hand combat. Had it not been for my concussion, I would have been more able to defend myself. Of course, I should have factored in some guards, but I was concussed and taken by surprise. It was an impulsive act, one I can't repeat. The second thing to my advantage is that I have an eidetic memory, which means that when Grayson punches in codes for the doors, I store them all. I don't know what I'm going to encounter on the outside; therefore, I need to do more recon before I make my escape. Grayson walks by my side through the long, desolate hallway, wordlessly leading me to my new accommodations. I'm guessing it's another jail cell, but maybe it's less restrictive. I wonder if Penigren decided I wasn't a threat. It seems unlikely, but here I am being moved to a "nicer" room. He leads me to a steel stairwell and as we climb the air changes, the stale musty scent that permeated every nook and cranny dissipates, even as I huff my way up the steps, I can't help but enjoy the fresh air. I'm emerging from a certain death and I might even get to see the sun. I feel nearly giddy, if I could escape, well, I try not to think too hard about that. One step at a time. I don't want to think about where I'd go, because I have nowhere to go. I shove it all down and focus on the sole task ahead, freedom. We reach the top and Grayson pushes a heavy, rusted steel door open. I'm immediately blinded by the sunlight forcing its way in. Shielding my eyes, I follow him outside. This isn't what I expected. I was anticipating another section of the compound, but instead, we're on a city street. I pause, shocked, taking in the ruins around me. Much like the Edit city, plants grow along every building, but here it's unintentional—a sign of nature fighting back. Cracks mar the siding of the buildings, segments are missing, signs are overturned and hanging by a thread, and glass is shattered or missing from windows.

"What is this place?" I ask Grayson, who is watching me rather than the city.

"This used to be called Portland, Oregon," he replies, turning his gaze to one of the skyscrapers that once belonged to a burgeoning civilization. "Now it's nothing. Slowly turning into mulch."

"I don't understand. What happened here?" I ask as I follow him, carefully avoiding the rubble littering the ground.

"The pandemic, the AI wars, population decline, Edits—take your pick," he says vaguely. He navigates the debris with ease, his long legs stepping over and around it. His combat boots and black fatigues are perfect for this landscape, whereas I'm still wearing the flats I arrived in, which would be useless if I stepped on a nail.

"Grayson, stop," I say, unable to focus on my footing as I process his words. "Explain this to me. I thought the world was overcrowded. I thought every city was so full it was bursting at the seams, that we were walled into back-to-back cities. But I saw a forest out there, open landscape, emptiness, and this place is dead, desolate." Grayson stops and turns to look at me.

"Welcome to the truth, Petal. The truth is, it's all a lie. The few cities left are indeed bursting at the seams, but the world isn't overpopulated—it's underpopulated. We went from nine billion people to three hundred million in the last few hundred years. Humanity's numbers have been decimated, and the decline continues at a steady pace. The government spreads propaganda, convincing people that the world is overpopulated. Edits are trying to extinguish humanity. They want to keep it all for themselves, a new species, apart from their origins. The people inside don't know the truth and their entertainment is keeping them happily contained in their boxes. Distracted by their sad little lives, content to sit behind a screen and forget that there is more beyond the wall." Frustration laces his voice as he looks past me toward the horizon. I follow his line of sight to see a piece of a building tumbling down as more of the city deteriorates. He looks unconcerned and he continues, his voice growing more intense. "The distractions are carefully crafted. Endless entertainment, social media, virtual realities—people are kept in a constant state of sedation. They've been conditioned to crave the next bit of mindless content, to escape from their monotonous lives. It's all a strategy to keep them from questioning, from realizing that they are going extinct, one at a time, decade by decade. They've traded reality for convenience, and they're too numbed to see their incasement."

"Grayson!" someone shouts, and we both turn to look at the source. "Who's this?" A woman is walking in the shadow of one of the buildings, and I can't make out her features.

"This is, uh, Petal," he says. They have never asked my name, and I never gave it. Petal is a nickname Grayson gave me, and I don't know what it means. Maybe my name just doesn't matter here, but honestly, I don't even know what my name is. Is it Kira, May, Zori, Spark…? No, it's none of those. I am a woman without identity. It strikes me that I'll have to forge one for myself, not one that is handed to me. I can't let others dictate my life anymore. I need to understand the truth about this world so I can navigate it on my own. I have been pulled apart, pieces of me floating away into the abyss. I wonder how long it will take to fill in all the holes, all the petals of my soul that have floated away. Should I catch them or try to patch them with new parts of me? A patchwork soul, the internal embodiment of Penigren. The woman steps out of the shadows, and I can finally see her features. She is covered in small burn marks. As she approaches, I see one of her eyes is cloudy white, with part of her eyelid missing. Her remaining eye is a striking amber, and her head is half-shaven, with sleek, jet-black hair on one side.

"Petal, huh?" Her voice is steady and confident. There is even a hint of humor in her tone. Whatever happened to her, it hasn't broken her.

"I'm Cindy, but around here, people call me Cinder." She turns her head, and I see a simple necklace around her neck, made from a finger bone, subtly reflecting the sunlight.

"Nice to meet you," I say, trying not to stare at her burns.

"That remains to be seen," she replies and walks past us, heading back into the bunker we just came out of.

"Come on, let's go see your digs," Grayson says, squeezing my shoulder to get my attention.

"Why are you people here?" I ask him as we move further into the city, seeking the accommodations that await me.

"It's the rebellion, Petal, and we are always looking for new members, especially former Edit pets who know what the ugliness looks like." This is his campaign, I realize. They are trying to recruit me, but I don't know any real ugliness. I know Magnus, and I know his sweet touch, his loving gazes, and his addictive lips, but I don't say that. I just follow him through the ruins silently.

AS WE WALK, he tells me things he knows about this city. My eyes follow his long digit as it points to various remnants. My mind struggles to accept the reality before me and reconcile it with the world I grew up believing in. We pass a section where an electronic wall used to be. It's broken, with no scenery or the faint humming of electricity. It's just broken pylons that once powered the wall. I could run right out of here, and there would be nothing to stop me. My legs have the impulse to sprint, my nerve endings trying to convince me to go, my primary motor cortex wants to ignite. But I don't pick up my feet; I just stare at the opening. If what Grayson says is true, there is nowhere to go. A nearly empty world with a trapped populace, harsh quarantines, and delusions. If I ran, how long before I found civilization? Too far, too long. I'd get lost in the wilds. Maybe I could survive out there alone, in the woods. Except I've never seen a forest until recently, let alone been in one. I don't know the first thing about surviving in the wilderness. My incompetence is a stark reminder of the secluded and isolated life I've lived. Grayson has stopped to watch me watching the hole in the wall. "If you run, you'll be on your own. I won't stop you, but out there is a vast terrain, mountains, forests, at least a thousand miles between you and the next city." His shoulders are tense, his eyebrows furrowed. He doesn't want me to run, but his legs are relaxed, his hands hanging loosely at his sides. I believe that he'd let me go, but he's only pointing out that I'm a prisoner of my circumstances. They don't need walls or a cage; the vast wild is doing that job for them.

It makes me feel angry and helpless again. I'm so tired of feeling this way. It makes me want to scream. Before I can stop myself, I let out a bellow. It echoes off the empty buildings, a screech of agony, frustration, and anger. It's all the things I've had to hold in my whole life. It's my pain on display. He doesn't say one word to me about my meltdown, he doesn't ask me what is wrong. It's weird how he never asks me anything about myself, as if he knows my torment, my agony. Maybe Grayson was also sold, maybe he was a pet. Maybe I'm not the only one whose life has not been their own. He watches me until I'm done. Then he steps up to me and pulls me in for a hug. His body is warm and hard, he is muscled and strong underneath his black fatigues and t-shirt. A part of me wants to sink into his warmth, let him be my balm, but I pull away from him and keep walking in the direction we are headed. We step further into the city and

Grayson gestures towards a grand but dilapidated building. The sign above the entrance, now barely legible, reads "Book Store."

"This used to be an iconic bookstore, back in its heyday," Grayson says, his voice tinged with nostalgia. "I found our copy of *The Wind in the Willows* here. If you're careful, you might be able to scavenge other books. Some parts of the building have somehow managed to stay closed off, protecting the books from the elements." I look at the building, trying to imagine it as he described it. The façade is a shadow of its past, with bricks missing and large cracks snaking up the walls. Vines and moss have claimed the structure, weaving through broken windows and door frames. The once-vibrant marquee sign, reminiscent of old movie theaters, has dulled over centuries of neglect. Its lights have long since burned out, and sections of the sign are peeling away, leaving ghostly outlines of what used to be. The glass is cracked in several places, cutting the "W" into a jagged remnant. There might be a wilderness survival book. If I sneak back later, I could scour the book section until I find the books I need. I don't plan on staying captive here. I'd rather live alone as a hermit in the woods than spend another moment with another group of people who want to dictate my life.

Chapter 30

What lies behind us and what lies before us are tiny matters compared to what lies within us.

- Ralph Waldo Emerson

We approach a grand but dilapidated building that stands out even in its decay. There are faded words over the awning, and all I can make out is the word "hotel." We stop by the crumbling stone steps. I reluctantly follow him in.

"Come on," Grayson says and waves me inside. I halt abruptly as we cross the threshold. The hotel is pristine inside, with gleaming marble floors, and dark wood inlay along the walls. There are no crumbling staircases or rubble; time has stood still here. It's opulent and lush, nothing like the facade.

"Welcome to your new home. It's beautiful, isn't it?" Grayson looks up at the ceiling at the ornate crystal chandelier hanging from the coffered alabaster ceiling. It's a starburst of light, it looks original, but how could that be true? How could this hotel sit here untouched, unblemished while the rest of the city crumbles?

"How?" is all I can think of to say. "How is this possible?" I ask, and he looks at me with a glint of joy. "Penigren restored the inside for us. He left the outside as it was, to keep us hidden, safe. If an Edit flies over the city, all they will see is the destruction. But there are rules—no lights on after dark, we don't use any power at night, we can't draw attention."

"So you just sit around in the dark then?"

"No, we will give you a candle. Everyone gets candle rations, so use yours thoughtfully, and if you light your candle, close your curtains." He gestures me forward, and we start climbing the ornate staircase inside the lobby, with its curved railing and wide base.

"One day, I want to restore the outside to its former glory. Can you imagine it? A real city again, bustling with people, people who travel and stay in hotels?" It's a nice thought, freedom of movement, travel, and seeing the world. It's a dream I've never had, never thought was possible or worthwhile. Why visit another city only to sit through quarantine, just to see another rundown, overcrowded place? Yet now, Grayson paints the picture of the world as it used to be, before all the decline.

"That sounds like a dream," I say and I mean it figuratively and literally, I don't plan on sticking around to find out. I want to get out of here. I start making a list of things I'll need. The first one is a better pair of shoes, preferably a pair of sturdy boots. I'll need a bag, some rations, and a few survival guides.

"You can help make that dream a reality, if you join us, if you want to fight with us, we could forge that future." he says as he leads me down a long hallway lined with hotel rooms. I don't answer him, because I don't want to lie, I don't want to tell him that I'm going to run away. He stops when we get to 214.

"This is you." he says and opens the door. I follow him inside. It's a lovely luxurious room, the bed is covered in crisp sheets, a dark wood headboard with intricate carvings. Plush-looking pillows and a throw blanket. To the right is a sitting area with two upholstered armchairs and a small elegant coffee table. Across from the bed is an antique armoire, with a built-in mirror and brass handles.

"I bet we can find some good books to read in those chairs," Grayson says. I look back at him; he's watching me intently, hoping I'll be pleased with the room. I walk further into the room and take in all the details, then amble into the bathroom. It's equally luxurious, with a marble shower, vanity, gold fixtures, and a large mirror framed in dark wood, in keeping with the rest of the hotel's dark inlays. I see my reflection in the mirror and I look horrible. Pale, with bluish marks under my eyes. My hair is in disarray, and my head wound is nearly healed, but there is a crusting of skin along my hairline. I need a shower, I need some sun and I need Magnus. I hate myself for missing him, for aching whenever I think of him. The old me would thank Grayson, would say something to placate him, because that's who I always was—a people pleaser. But I don't want to please people anymore. I don't want to make others feel good at the expense of myself, my soul. I don't want to let more of me splinter and drift off into the current. Grayson stands in the bathroom doorway, his hands grasping the top of the frame, leaning on his arms. His biceps are on display, and his crystal blue eyes stare at me with intensity. The light in here makes the red in his hair stand out, and I have an impulse to tug at his locks, to feel his brownish-red hair between my fingers. The texture looks rougher than Magnus's silky blonde hair. Where Magnus is perfection, Grayson is real. When he smiles, there are small crinkles around his eyes; Magnus doesn't have a single wrinkle on his pristine skin. This humanity is appealing, it's something I can understand. The moment passes and I drop my gaze, breaking eye contact.

"I'll let you get settled in. If you need anything, let me know. I'll come back to get you at dinner; you can meet some new people," he says. My eyes slide back up his long body to meet his eyes again. I give him a curt nod and look down at my hand. I'm back to scratching. My leg has healed completely. I don't stop myself; I won't scrape through the jeans. It's a delicious texture for my fingertips, rough and thick. Grayson taps the door frame after he pushes off it and leaves. "Later, Petal."

WHEN HE COMES BACK a few hours later, I've showered. I scrubbed my skin pink, and I don't look quite as disheveled as I did earlier. I found a comb in the bathroom and managed to get my hair to look somewhat presentable.

"Petal, ready to eat?"

"Why petal?" I ask, annoyed at the nickname, another name that isn't mine.

"It suits you," he says, keeping his eyes on me. I arch a questioning eyebrow at him.

"You're as delicate as a petal. So graceful and pretty."

"I'm not as delicate as you think," I say, my voice edged with defiance, not ready to reveal my combat training.

"I know you're not," he replies, his gaze penetrating. "You've got a quiet strength, like a burning ember. One day, I know it's going to burst into a flame, and I hope I'm there to see it." My breath hitches in my throat at his words. It might be the loveliest thing anyone has ever said to me.

He leans in closer, "But you won't be much of a flame if you don't eat first." I look up into his eyes and feel a jolt in my body; it tingles and zings. It's a nucleus, fleeting but revelatory. His focus shifts to my lips, the intensity in his eyes unmistakable

"Let's go," I say, walking around him and out the door before something happens, something I know I'd regret. Downstairs, he leads me to the restaurant, but instead of scattered tables for patrons, there is one big table filled with people animatedly talking to each other. The table is laden with food, illuminated by candlelight, as the sun has already set. The curtains are all drawn, giving the room a cozy, intimate vibe.

The happy chatter feels overwhelming, my brain struggling to sift through their words and unable to latch on to a single conversation. As we get closer, the conversation ceases, and they all turn to look at us.

"Guys, this is Petal. She's new here. I want you all to make her feel welcome, show her the ropes, and share your stories. She needs to hear what you've all been through because I hope we can convince her to join us," Grayson says, placing a reassuring hand on my shoulder. All eyes are on me, scanning and assessing, making me want to retreat to my room to hide. Only my grumbling stomach prevents me from leaving. The food on the table looks hearty, and after my meager meals down in the bunker, I'm ready for something I can sink my teeth into. Grayson gestures to an empty seat near the center of the table, guiding me with a gentle nudge. I take a hesitant step forward, feeling the weight of their gazes. One of the women, a redhead with a friendly smile, scoots her chair aside to make room for me.

"Come on, Petal, sit here," she says, patting the seat next to her. I nod, offering a small smile in return, and slide into the chair. Grayson squeezes my shoulder before taking a seat across from me. As I settle in, someone passes me a plate, and the aroma of the food makes my stomach growl louder.

I'm about to take my first bite when I hear a shriek and the word "May" shouted by a familiar voice. I look up at the foot of the table and there stands June holding a tray of food. I'm too shocked to react. She's here? She puts the tray down on the edge of the table and rushes around to my seat, pulling me into a bear hug.

"June?" I say, hugging her back. She pulls back a little to look into my eyes, tears welling up in her own. She's June, but she's not—her hair is pixie short, her long sable hair is gone. She looks worn, but also happy.

"How are you here?" she asks at the same time I say, "What are you doing here?" She keeps smoothing my hair away and then hugs me again. We laugh. I touch her short hair; it's soft and spiky, and we laugh some more. I feel a sudden remorse at never having touched her hair when it was long. It's sad that it's all gone.

"Your hair," I say, and she steps back, touching it self-consciously. "Yeah, I know."

"You two know each other?" Grayson asks. I nod but don't take my eyes off June.

"We were roommates at Plymouth Prep," I confess, and the room starts buzzing with conversation, but I don't process the words. June asks the guy next to me to move, and she sits beside me. There is only one reason June is here, something happened with her Edit.

"Who was your Edit?" I ask, and her smile falters. She picks at her napkin, looking away from me. "You were always astute," she says. "When you were able to pay attention, that is." She looks back at me with a melancholy smile.

"His name was Dorian Hayes, oh, and he was handsome," she says wistfully. "Or so I thought at first. He came to get me after graduation. I thought, what incredible luck, this dreamy man, this Edit found me, finally… Finally, I had some of your luck." She swallows a lump, and her cheeks redden. "I was always a little envious of you, wasn't I?" she says shamefully. "I thought you were so lucky when Faust carried you out of that hallway like a caveman. It was so romantic; he was so possessive. The girls talked of nothing else for weeks. It was the biggest sensation to happen at Plymouth." The table has stopped talking; they are all listening intently to June's story.

"So what happened?" I ask, knowing that when she's done talking, I'm going to cry for my friend. She laughs, but it's filled with a shuddering air. "Well, he wasn't my knight in shining armor." She looks at her napkin again while she keeps talking.

"He was twisted. He raped me, repeatedly. He…," she takes a deep breath, "he used to like to stab when he was about to climax. He would take a shallow knife and push it into my body, anywhere, everywhere." June is covered, with almost no skin showing, hiding her scars. My throat feels tight; the more she speaks, the harder it is not to cry. I can feel my tear ducts starting to fill, threatening to spill over. "One day, he, uh, he stabbed me too deeply, hit something vital." She still can't look at me, and I place a comforting hand on her. She drops her napkin in her lap and looks up at me, a mournful expression filling her face.

"He threw me out. Literally, he thought I was going to die, and he just dumped my body." She sighs and gives me a sad smile. "That's when Penigren's team found me. I was near death, but they were able to revive me."

"Jesus, June." I pull her in for a hug, and she leans her head on my shoulder. "I'm so sorry." My words feel paltry and empty. How can I convey the depths of my despair? My tears have unleashed, streaming down, coating my cheeks, and wetting June's spiky hair.

"Nothing to be sorry about. I'm here, I'm alive, I survived, and what's more, I am free. I found my people, my place." June releases the hug, and someone asks, "Your Edit was Faust?" I look up at the guy sitting two seats down from Grayson. I wipe my face and I realize now that everyone here has heard June's story before; it's just me. They weren't listening to the story; they were all paying attention to my reaction.

"Yes," I admit, feeling my own shame, because I don't have a horror story, I have a love story.

"Did all of you belong to an Edit?" I ask, and the room fills with murmurs of yes, with heads nodding. It has the effect of others sharing their stories. Some aren't as terrible as June's, but they are all twisted in their ways. A little girl sitting at the table is the main anomaly that draws my attention, her eyes fixed on me. She looks no older than eight, her dark skin glowing faintly in the candlelight. She's been silent until now, blending into the background. Suddenly, she speaks, her voice soft but clear.

"Beyond the veil of silence, strength gathers." I look at her, confused at first.

Grayson notices my perplexed expression. "That's Elara. She only speaks in gibberish." But it isn't gibberish. It's a profound statement that cuts through the room's heaviness, a reminder that strength often comes from the most painful experiences.

"We find strength in our wounds," I say and look back at Elara, whose eyes widen with surprise.

"What lingers in the shadows is not echoes but darkness," her voice filled with a mix of sadness and appreciation. She's telling me that she has been unheard, and to be heard is a relief.

Without thinking, I respond, "Let the radiance spill in." Elara's eyes light up, a connection sparking between us. I wonder how no one here has realized what she is doing. An awkward silence fills the room and Grayson looks at me with interest, perhaps impressed that I was able to respond to Elara. Cinder is at the table, her eyes fixed on me. I have to wonder if her burns are the result of an Edit.

"What happened to you?" I finally ask, when there is a break in the conversation.

"Dorian Hayes," she admits, and I look between her and June. "Except he used to like using cigarettes to burn me." There is a glint of humor in her eye, and I have to wonder if Cinder isn't quite all there anymore.

"It's okay though, I took his finger." She lifts up the bone necklace hanging from her neck, smiling at it as a prized possession. "I remember his damn finger holding those cigarettes, pushing them into my flesh, searing me. That forefinger always pushed so hard that his last joint would over-bend, double-jointed. I'd stare at it, his fucking finger, and I promised myself I'd take it one day." She is still smiling. "One morning, he was in one of his more volatile moods, and I knew he was going to burn me, so I bit him. I locked my jaw, and even when he picked up his cigarette with his other hand to burn me here," she points at her eye, "I held on until it snapped off. His blood filled my mouth, and it was the singularly most painful and spectacular moment of my life. While he was busy screaming, I kicked him in the balls, ran for the hangar, used his fingerprint to open the door, and stole a hovercraft." The finger bone gleams in candlelight, it looks polished. I briefly wonder if she stripped the flesh herself or waited for it to rot off. I shudder at the thought of either. "You see Dorian was paranoid, he never trusted the wrist chips, he used his fingerprint for everything, ironic that it became his Achilles heel." I look away from her, trying to imagine that kind of strength, that kind of fight. If I were in her position, would I be able to do what she did? I suddenly have a deep and profound respect for her and June. I am not so sure that I'd have the same resilience.

"Your turn, what did Faust do?" Cinder demands. I look around the table, and everyone is still focused on me. What do I say? How can I tell them that he loved me and treated me well, that he was planning on making me an Edit and marrying me? At least, that's what he told me, what I believed. I still can't understand how he put me in that hovercraft and sent me away. An extreme departure from his previous character. Did something trigger him? How did I end up here among all the throwaways, the pets who survived despite all the odds?

"I, uh, I don't know what to say," I admit. June grabs my hand.

"This is a safe space. If it's too hard to talk about, you can tell us when you're ready." I nod, grateful for the out she has given me, though she mistook my hesitation. Now I'm too much of a coward not to use it.

"Come on, guys, let's eat. Then we can clean up, and if you're all good, I have dessert," June says enthusiastically. The table laughs and cheers, and the sounds of silverware clinking against plates fill the air, creating a cacophony sound mixed in with conversation, separate and lively. Grayson is looking at me from across the table, his intense gaze dances in the candlelight, the way he is looking at me makes me wonder if he knows that Faust didn't abuse me.

I HELP CLEAN up after dinner. The large kitchen designed for an entire staff is large enough to fit a large chunk of the group. There were about fifty people at the table, most of them were older, having "aged out" as they call it. Mid 30's is apparently too old for Edits. The youngest here is me, June, and Elara. Elara vanished after dinner, her black curls bouncing as she rounded a corner. I have to wonder how a girl that young ended up here and after hearing so many sad stories today, I'm not sure I'm ready to hear hers.

"June, is this the right place?" I ask putting away the dry dishes.

"Actually, I go by Beth now, and yeah that's perfect," she tells me.

"Beth?" it suits her.

"Yes, I always loved *Little Women*, you know that. Beth was always such a tragic figure, left behind, and ill, but still, she was happy. And that's how I want to be. Life has dealt me a raw deal, but I want to be happy anyway." I think June might be my hero. She runs the kitchens here; she had never shown a passion for cooking before, not that there had ever been an opportunity. She started a hydroponic garden in the hotel basement, and with the help of the others, she transformed their meager meals into feasts.

"It's perfect," I tell her, putting the last of the plates away on the shelf.

"What about you? Did you pick a new name?"

"Um, I'm still deciding," I say, and she has a look of understanding.

"There's plenty of time." She wraps her arm around my shoulder, and we walk out of the kitchen back to the dining room, on the table is a large cake topped with whipped cream piled high adorned with fresh strawberries.

"Did you make that?" I ask, impressed.

"Yeah, every bit of it," she admits, pride lacing her voice. I'd be proud too, if I came out alive, and instead of curling into a ball to die, she came into herself. She does seem happy now, and I think that maybe, just maybe, I can also find happiness here. The idea of running away still tickles my brain, but with June here, how could I leave her again?

Chapter 31

"Manipulation is the art of convincing people to act against their own interests."

-The Journal of Kira, Book 7, page 1

I stayed up all night talking to June—Beth, as she prefers now. I'm still trying to get used to calling her that. She came into my room and crawled into bed beside me. We talk about all the things we never talked about at Plymouth. She tells me about her parents and her life before Plymouth. Her mother died at her birth, and her father died running into the wall, leaving her alone. She flitted from foster home to foster home for years before she was "selected" for Plymouth Prep. She considered herself lucky, unable to stand another new home, another new fake family who didn't care about her. I tell her about my life, my mother, and the abuse. She holds my hand under the blankets, and we talk deep into the night. We share not only time but wounds. We also found ourselves thrust into this Edit world without warning.

"I'd like to think of you as my sister," she whispers in the dark after a lull in the conversation. It strikes me that we have always been the only consistent thing the other person has had.

"You've always been my sister," I whisper back and grip her hand tighter. I can hear her tears then. I let her cry as I silently listen, a sentinel supporting and unwavering but unable to extract her pain. She cries herself to sleep, and I tiptoe out of the room, unable to find my own sleep. Grayson had left me a pack of things in the room when I came back from cleaning in the kitchen. I had given him a list of needs. He got almost everything, including a sturdy pair of boots. They are a half size too large, but it's still better than the ballet flats.

I WANDER the luxurious halls of the Rebel Hotel, as I call it. People here call it Homebase, others lovingly call it Outcast Outpost. There are no lights on, just my little candle flickering in the dark, placed into an old vintage brass candle holder with a drip plate. I can pretend I've stepped back in time. I try to do the mental math—was this the time Faust was from? No, he wouldn't be born for another hundred years. I find a stairwell at the end of the hall and start climbing. Maybe I can see outside the city if I reach the top. I want to see an aerial view of the place; if I need to leave, I want to know what direction to go. I open the door when I reach the last step and go through the door, surprised to find myself on a roof. A rooftop access, a small section before the roof slants down with its weathered copper roof, green from oxidation. The moon is bright, so I blow out my candle. The stars are out, and all my thoughts vanish. It's glorious—the stars are blinking starbursts, and the Milky Way is stretching across the sky like a luminous river of light. I've always loved the idea of astronomy. I read endless books on space and the stars when I was at Plymouth, particularly when I was in class and unable to focus on the lessons. What would it have been like to be an astronaut and travel among stars? This is the first time I've seen them so bright, so endless, so magical. The city lights always diffused the stars before, but this derelict ghost town doesn't have any lights, affording me an incredible view.

"Beautiful, isn't it?" I start at the voice and see Grayson leaning against the side of the dormer, the one I just came out of.

"Be more creepy, please," I chide, and he chuckles.

"If you wish," he says, kicking off the dormer with one foot and stalking toward me. He gets inches from me and leans over, looking into my eyes. He's trying to loom, but he can't loom; he's too friendly to be a loomer.

"It's not working," I say, grinning up at him. He raises an eyebrow.

"No?" He leans in, his breath warm against my ear, sending a shiver down my spine. It's meant to be unsettling, but it just tickles, making me laugh as I push at his chest.

"No."

"Okay, Petal, I'll have to step up my game," he says with a playful smirk, his eyes twinkling with mischief.

"I don't know, nobody looms like Penigren, so if you want to step up your game, you might need to start taking notes." He doesn't laugh at the dig.

"Penigren is suffering," he chides, and I bite my lip and look away.

"You expect me to fall in line here and join your little rebellion, but you forget I'm here against my will," I snap at him, unwilling to fall into his guilt trap.

"I figured Faust didn't abuse you. There was nothing on your body. It's flawless, isn't it? Just your injuries from the crash. Too ashamed to tell the group that you're in love with an Edit?" he snaps back at me.

"How do you know what my body looks like?" I ask, my cheeks burning, ignoring his damn insight. I don't have to justify myself to him.

"How do you think you got into that nightgown?" he asks,

and I clench my fists, seconds away from punching him. "Don't ignore my question."

"What question?"

"You love him, don't you?"

"Why does it matter to anyone here? I was sold, like the rest of you," I poke him in the chest hard, and where Magnus would have been a solid rock, Grayson steps back to catch himself.

"What is it about him? Is it the money? Is it his perfect manufactured Edit appearance? Did he fuck you so good you couldn't think straight?" Grayson leans in, wrapping his arm around my waist and pulling me tight to his body. The proximity makes my heart race, a mix of anger and something I can't quite place. "You have no right to ask me that," I whisper fiercely, my breath coming in short bursts.

"And yet, here we are," he murmurs, his lips dangerously close to mine. His lips are tempting, his blue eyes searing into me, but it doesn't feel right. He is a picture of male beauty and strength, a real human one. I should want to let go of Magnus and slide into this human experience, but still, he's a mismatched sock. He is the same shape and color, but instead of a red stripe, he has a blue stripe. An almost match.

"Let me go," I demand. "I shouldn't have to feel bad for falling for my captor. Until I came here, I always felt sorry for myself, but it's clear here that my story is the least of it. But it's still my story, it's still my pain. I shouldn't have to justify my life to you. I owe you nothing!" I push him hard in the chest, and he releases me. Grayson's eyes soften slightly, but his jaw remains tight. "You're right, Petal, you don't owe me anything," he says quietly. "But this rebellion isn't about me or you, it's about everyone. Don't you want to be a part of the change?" he asks. "It's up to you to decide if you're a captive here or if you want to be a part of something bigger." I turn away and look up at the stars again, the vastness of the sky making me feel small and insignificant. There is nothing for me here. Maybe June has found her place, but this isn't home.

"I don't think this is my place," I tell him, and he tugs at my arm, turning me to look at him.

"It could be, Petal. You could find yourself here, you could give yourself a name, and I could help you." His eyes flick down to my lips again. I know he's asking me to join his rebellion and be with him, but my soul longs for Magnus. Maybe I'm broken because the only one I want isn't here and doesn't even want me anymore.

I sigh, because I don't have any words for him.

"Just think about it some more," he insists, and I nod.

"Good." He pulls me into him again, this time it's just a hug. I let him hug me. I'm mad at him, but it also feels nice—the warmth of his body against mine. It's comforting, even though he's an ass.

I stand there for a moment, allowing myself to feel the comfort of his embrace, even if I don't fully accept it. When he finally releases me, he looks into my eyes with a mix of hope and concern.

"Take your time, Petal. I'm here when you're ready," he says softly before stepping back, leaving me alone with my thoughts and the vast, star-filled sky.

I LEAVE THE HOTEL, the moon bright above, and the stars glinting and littering the sky, firebugs dancing in the inky black space. I wander the empty streets, the rubble a constant tripping hazard in the dark, but with my eyes adjusted and the moonlight, I manage to make my way through the city until I stop in front of an auditorium, its glass doors smashed in. The ceiling is intact, so I make my way in. It's not in good condition—nothing here is, except for the hotel. I briefly consider the folly of going into a crumbling building, but I've never been inside an auditorium. I've never seen a real stage, with its rows and rows of seats. My dream of being a dancer is almost entirely smashed to bits, but my limbs still remember the movements. If I could dance on a stage just once, maybe I could lay it to rest. Maybe I could find solace in this new life. I find my way into the orchestra section. The seats are pale mauve from age, with springs bursting out and cracked armrests. It smells strongly of mildew. Some seats are toppled over, and there is debris from the ceiling sprinkling the rows. There is a large crack in the ceiling, allowing the moon to shine into the deserted theater. I walk down the long row, toward the stage, my feet squishing into some of the old carpeting. I find my way up on the stage, testing the integrity of the wood. It creaks here and there, and in the far corner, there is a missing segment. The wood is severely compromised, with termites or other insects having eaten little burrowed holes into the once-solid beams. As I stand there, looking out at the empty seats, I can almost hear the applause of an audience that never existed for me. Magnus invades my thoughts—the way he watched me when I wore my first tutu, the way he ripped it off, the way he felt, so big and impossible, and then so good. I close my eyes, take a deep breath, and let my body remember the dance steps. My feet glide across the stage, avoiding the weak spots, and I lose myself in the movement. The air is thick with the smell of dust and decay, but for a moment, I am transported to a different world, where dreams still have a chance to come true. Instead of the moonlight wrapping me in diffused light, I pretend it's the stage lights, Giselle mourning the loss of her Albrecht, his deceptions painfully revealed, his betrayal in her heart. What would it feel like to have a full audience, applauding me, a cone of sound directed at me, praising me? I want to hear the raucous sound, the claps of thousands, filling even the holes and cracks of the walls, patching me up. It's an invigorating thought, but maybe they wouldn't be able to fill me entirely. Maybe I'd be momentarily proud, but like all things in life, the joy would dissipate and my patchwork soul would remain. Magnus made me feel that way, invigorated, beautiful, and important, but now it's diffused, sublimated into a new thing, where I'm forced to analyze every exchange. When I stop, I do a curtsy and then I hear, "Very pretty." My spine tingles because I know that voice. Penigren steps out from the side of the stage, emerging from the shadows. Does no one sleep in this town? I quickly stand up and straighten my spine. I know I should be grateful that he let me go, that he saved Beth and all the others, but he scares me. I can't help but want to shrink into myself, but I stand tall, determined not to judge him by his grotesque appearance.

"I can see why he picked you out," he says, his gravelly voice accompanied by that strange crackling sound that follows him, getting louder with each step as he nears. I can't help but wonder what he is doing here—did he follow me?

"Thank you," I try to be civil, even when my body is yelling at me to run.

"For what, Kira?" he asks me. He knows who I am. I suppose I shouldn't be surprised, but I am. I never told him, but maybe Beth did.

"For letting me go, for saving Beth and all the others." But then I remember that Beth didn't know my real name, she only knows me as May. He looks at me thoughtfully and dabs his mouth before coughing into his napkin.

"What about you? Did I save you?" he asks me. God, he's asking the thing I haven't wanted to share with this group, because the truth is, I don't know.

"I don't know," I answer truthfully because I'm still not sure I ever wanted to be rescued from Magnus.

"You're in love with him," he concludes. "But they don't know how to love. They aren't human; they lost all of their emotions, don't you know?" He rounds me, and I follow him with my eyes until I'm forced to crane my neck and spin around to face him again.

"You're just a plaything, just an oddity. You'll never be anything more." He coughs again. "Did he take from you, or did you willingly give yourself to him?" He doesn't wait for my answers. "You know he's coming for you. But it's not to save you, little pet. It's to kill you. He doesn't want you left alive so you can tell the world what you know. Yet, still, you haven't agreed to join our little rebellion. Grayson tells me you are hesitant.

"I haven't had time to think it through," I tell him, my blood is rushing through my head, and I feel sick, my stomach churns with unease. He tells me that Magnus is a threat, but Penigren feels like the real threat.

"You won't have much time left. When he comes, you'll be on your own if you don't join us."

"Did he do this to you?" I ask and his pupil sputters as he gets even closer, my personal space eradicated.

"Did what? Turn me into a monster?" he laughs, it's an incredulous laugh, it chills me to my marrow. "Yes, he did this to me, but do you know what is worse than looking like a monster?"

I shake my head, my foot sliding back, ready to move away from him.

"Being one. He killed my wife. A man without the love of his life is a shell, but still, this shell will do everything to make sure no one else suffers at his hands." The truth is a subjective splintering of personalities. The theory of relativity has nothing to do with the expression "it's all relative," yet it remains the believed foundation for everyone using it. Truth has shifted and turned; it is the way of humanity. We don't all walk around with the same viewpoint. I often think about how even the colors we see might look different to everyone. I might see green and know it's green, but only because someone told me it's green. It could explain why people have such vast differences in preferences in color appreciation. I don't want to believe Penigren, but it's hard not to hear all these horrendous things and start to doubt even the integrity and faith of my own experiences. The Faust I thought I knew was not a killer, but then Dalton, his lifeless body, springs to mind. Who is Magnus Faust, the real one? This emotionless, murdering monster, conducting experiments, and discarding human lives as one would dispose of a wrapper? Or is he the thoughtful, beautiful, smiling creature who made my body come alive, the person who seemed to see every part of me, and still loved every inch? I take a step back, and Penigren leans in, grabbing me by my collar. "You're going to have to choose, little pet, and soon." His nose is pressed against mine, and I push at his chest, but despite his malformed shape, he's strangely strong, and my efforts are meaningless. "Or you might not get a chance to choose at all." A rotting smell emanates from him, his body should be dead by all accounts, it's doing its best to complete the job, yet still he walks, lurking, plotting, and demanding. I change my center of my gravity and spin under his arm, unhooking his grip.

"Here is the problem, Memphis. I know they have emotional regulators. I know they can adjust them, but Faust is not heartless. If your wife died at his hand, I'm sure he had a reason."I turn and run for the exit.

"You're delusional!" he shouts angrily after me, and I don't stop to respond. At some point, you have to figure out why someone holds power over you. In this case, Penigren has power over me because I'm trapped here amongst his rebels. But I am not going to give him my power anymore. I will find a way out of this rubbled city, and I will find Magnus Faust. I will get my answers. Beth, Elara, and Grayson—all will benefit from the realities, whatever they are now. I know one thing, deep in the marrow of my bones, that this reality that Penigren has concocted for the survivors is not the whole truth. I know that Magnus kept things from me, either intentionally or through omission, but somewhere in between the two men, lies the truth. The why of the world. To fix this place, I need to find the why because without knowing the real problem, there can be no solution. Going to live as a hermit is a cop-out, and I'm not a sole agent anymore. There is Beth to consider, and Elara, whoever she is. One thing is certain: she is a victim, a child, and must be protected. No one was there to protect Beth or me, or all the other children still at Plymouth Prep, getting fattened for the kill. My brain clears, the fog lifting, the smoke of lies and confusion evaporates. I know now who I want to be, and it has nothing to do with a name or some self-imposed identity. I want to be a protector of the weak, a person who can stand up and face the darkness when they can't for themselves. I won't be a pawn between the powers that be, but a catalyst. There will be a crumbling and a restoration, and the world will have a rude awakening. An overdue one.

Chapter 32

Daylight is your respite, not these broken thoughts
-The Journal of Kira, Book 7 page 3

My palms are dusted, my knees are scratched, and I groan as I climb up the bookcase I knocked over to use as a ladder to get to the second level. It doesn't reach all the way to the top, I look down at the bookcase that is leaning against debris and other bookcases that I moved around to make my makeshift ladder. I hear a groan from the wood and I only pray it's going to hold. The second level is at eye level with me now that I'm at the top. I'll have to pull myself up from here. I reach up and tap around to see if there is anything to hold onto, but it is just floor, coated in dust. I grip the ledge and start doing a pull-up to see to the next level. There is nothing nearby to grab, I have to figure out a way up, without any good grips. The dust makes the floor slippery, the dust reducing friction, with its thick barrier. My grip slips and I slam my chin into the edge before dropping down onto the precarious bookcase. I scream out in pain, as the whole thing wobbles and I hold onto the sides trying to steady it. If only I had a taller bookcase. Blood fills my mouth, and I spit it out. I test my jaw, it's bruised but doesn't feel broken. The blood is from my teeth scoring my tongue. I climb down and look around the dilapidated bookstore for a solution, but my eyes lock with a pair of gleaming eyes. Elara is standing in one of the corners, she is in a little frilly pink dress. A stark contrast to her beautiful black skin, the color of charcoal. I didn't even hear her come in, she is standing there staring at me and I carefully trudge my way over to her.

"What are you doing here Elara, it is dangerous." I take her hand intending to take her out of the bookstore, but she pulls me further into the store in the opposite direction.

"Elara, the daylight is your respite, not these broken thoughts." I try to speak in her riddled way but she continues pulling me.

"Alighting in a current will make you drown." I'm struggling to understand that one, but I let her drag me along. She is obviously trying to show me something. She tries to pull me under a set of beams that lean heavily against one wall. I stop; it looks too dangerous. Water drips down the beams from somewhere, pooling at their base. She tugs hard on my hand, and I reluctantly follow her in. There's a door behind the beams. She opens it, revealing a staircase.

"Thank you, Elara," I say. She smiles at me and starts climbing the stairs. I follow her, watching my footwork. Elara bounds up the stairs, familiar with all the safe places to step. I try to copy her movements, and when I reach the top, she's gone. Then, I see her hand from around the corner, gesturing for me to follow. This part of the bookstore still looks somewhat intact. A couple of bookshelves have toppled over, and beneath them lies a pile of books. However, the rest of the shelves still have books lining them, waiting for eager readers. Faded red and black signs with white lettering hang from the ceiling. Elara has vanished again. I quickly start scanning the titles—so many interesting books, but nothing about surviving in the wild. I pull a book out on nanoparticles, wishing I had the freedom to read the whole thing. I briefly consider putting it into my backpack but decide to save space for other books. I take a step back and bump into Elara, who is creepily silent.

"Dusted tomes do not alleviate events." She grabs my hand. I carefully place the book back and follow her again as she leads me deeper into the bookstore. She brings me to the corner where the survival guides are stocked.

"Elara, you clever girl," I say, marveling at her intuition. She must spend a great amount of her time observing. A product of her isolation, it appears that many of the rebels only tolerate her, perhaps even have some pity, but feel uninterested in trying to communicate with her.

"Two in tow, is more to show," she says, and I squat down to get eye level with her.

"We are a good team," I agree, but she shakes her head, a frustrated breath escaping her nose.

"What is it you're trying to tell me?"

"We march in circles, without a leader."

"I'm trying, Elara, but I don't understand." She picks up a book titled "The Oregon Trailblazer's Survival Guide: Mastering the Wilderness Hikes of the Pacific Northwest."

"Fates entwine, two paths converge, your light and mine."

"You want to come with me?" I ask, noticing her persistent pointing at the book with the forest picture. She nods.

"Elara, I can't guarantee your safety if you travel with me. It would be irresponsible of me to take you away from safety and your home."

"Safety blends into darkness; the basement knows."

"The basement? What's in the basement?" She looks past me, and that's when I see her eyes flicker, and I fall back in surprise. Elara is an Edit. How can that be? She's a child—who would try to make an immortal child? She refocuses on me, her lips forming a word that seems hard for her to say.

"Death," she says ominously. A shudder runs through me. From what I understand Elara has difficulty saying her exact meaning, or even using one word by itself. Whatever happened to her brain, which I am now guessing has to do with her becoming an immature Edit, did something to the communication centers of her brain. But this time, I'm certain she meant death, and it was clear how difficult it was for her to say it.

"Elara, can you show me?" If there is a basement of death I need to see it, since I don't know what parts will fit into the puzzle I'm trying to solve.

"The wind breaks only when the backs are strong." She says and walks away.

"That's a no isn't it?" I ask and I lift myself off the floor, I shove books into my sack hoping some of them will come in handy, and sprint after Elara.

I EMERGE FROM THE BOOKSTORE, but Elara is already darting away toward the hotel. She's fast, probably a result of her altered genome. Magnus never did explain how they managed to do that one. I hear a whirring sound and spin my head to locate it. A garage opens up near the bunker, and a hovercraft motorcycle emerges. I've never seen one before; hovercrafts don't exist in the units. Technological advancements nearly halted after we were locked inside. The motorcycle is sleek and glistens in the sun with its polished black surface. Glowing thrusters hum softly as they lift the bike a few feet into the air. A rider wearing black fatigues and a black helmet handles it beautifully, and I wonder who it is. It takes off in the opposite direction, and I watch it glide easily over the terrain, avoiding all the rubble. The physique matched Grayson. If I could get my hands on one of those, I wonder how far it would go before running out of power. The sun is mellow in the sky. I spent too much time inside the bookstore, trying to find a way up to the next level. All the books on the first level were utterly destroyed. I plod back to the hotel. I didn't tell anyone I was leaving early in the morning and I wonder how I stand with everyone after the antagonistic encounter I had with Penigren inside the auditorium. I feel fatigued but too wired to sleep. I know I need to leave here. I wanted to stay for Beth; for a moment, I wanted to believe I could be happy here, just like she is. Even Beth from *Little Women*, had a different path from her sister. I won't be content to stay and pretend the world isn't in shambles. Besides, I'm not sure they will get to live their lives here. If they truly mean to be rebels, it implies future fighting. Where there is fighting, there is death. My pack is heavy with all the books I shoved in, and I hope some of them will come in handy. I'll try to read them tonight, maybe after a nap and some dinner. I enter the lobby, and Beth emerges from the dining room.

"May! We've been looking for you everywhere."

"Oh, sorry, I was exploring," I tell her sheepishly. I suppose I should have told her, but when I go, I'm not sure I can tell Beth because she might tell on me. Not because she isn't a loyal friend, but because I'm not sure where her loyalty is stronger. She might believe, in her misguided way, that she is trying to protect me.

"You can't just go out here alone. These ruins are unstable. Next time, take someone with you. Someone experienced and who knows where the reinforced buildings are and which to avoid. God, you're lucky you didn't get hurt." She pats my back and spins me around to check for injuries, immediately noticing my scraped knees and bruised jaw.

"You did get hurt," she exclaims, starting to pull me up the stairs.

"It's nothing, don't fuss," I tell her. Apparently since now that Beth considers herself my sister, she's decided to start acting like the older one.

"There's blood on your shirt," she points out, pulling me into my room and making me sit on the bed. "Where is the blood from?"

"Uh, I just bit my tongue," I tell her. She tells me to open my mouth, tilting my head. I push her hand away. "Beth cut it out, I'm fine." She crosses her arms, a stern look on her face. It makes me want to laugh—this once annoyed, unreliable creature now acting like a concerned mother hen.

"Stop grinning at me like that," she says, her serious expression faltering, her lips involuntarily twitching between a smile and a frown.

"Yes, mother," I say, starting to laugh. She tries her best to glare at me, but her face morphs into a comical expression until she starts laughing with me. Grayson walks into the room and leans against the doorframe. "Well, well, well, look what the cat dragged in. You know when you asked for all that stuff, I was worried you were planning on running away."

"Then why did you give it to me?" I ask, my laughter vanishing. Beth turns to face Grayson. Grayson looks mildly annoyed, but even grumpy he's nice to look at. I briefly consider trying to pair the two up, but it's not my job to play matchmaker.

"Because, I told you, I'm not going to stop you." He saunters into the room and bends at his waist, his arms crossed over his chest, and leans in to get eye level with me. "I'm glad you're not gone, or dead," he says, but adds, "But if you ever leave like that again, please let us know. We had people all over town looking for you." he has a very different vibe from last night, he's back to his easy, friendly self.

"I'm sorry, I didn't think it through. I also didn't think I'd be gone so long. I just got lost," I lie. I don't want them to know I've been at the bookstore, collecting research for my escape.

"Well, next time bring someone. How did you find your way back?" Beth asks, her focus still on Grayson even though she is speaking to me.

"Elara, actually." It's a half-truth, which is easier to tell than elaborate lies.

"Really? She found you? She normally doesn't go out of her way to seek anyone out. I didn't even know she knew you were missing," Grayson says skeptically.

"Well, she did, and she was an excellent guide. What's her story, anyway?" I ask because as much as I don't want to hear it, I need to hear it.

"Truthfully, no one knows. Her gibberish isn't a very good way to get real information from her."

"It's not gibberish at all. I understand her." Mostly. A couple of things are a little unclear, but if you take the time to listen to her, she is filled with insight.

"Really?" Beth asks, surprised. "Of course, you would understand her. You go through all of school unable to hear a single lecture, but now you have no problem understanding nonsense."

"It's not nonsense. She is an insightful little girl, struggling with some very big things—things someone her age should never have to deal with," I say in her defense, annoyed at their ignorant impression of her. It occurs to me that maybe they don't know she is an Edit; so many people don't see it. Guilt crosses both of their features and they look at each other.

"You're right, she's too young to be in this situation," Beth says remorsefully. An explosive sound penetrates the air, followed by a loud rumbling. The hotel shakes and Beth holds onto the bed frame. Grayson braces with his stance, and I'm still on the bed, so I put my hand down to steady myself.

"What the hell was that?" Beth asks as Grayson runs to the window to look outside.

"We're being attacked. Get to the basement," he orders and pulls me and Beth into the hallway, and runs ahead of us. Beth grabs my hand and we both start running down the hall. The hall is empty except for us as she pulls me down the stairs into the lobby. We are about to run toward the kitchen and the basement door when the front door smashes in. We all duck to avoid any shrapnel. A plume of smoke and dust fills the air, and I can barely make out anything. Grayson pulls a gun from his side strap.

"Are you okay?" I ask Beth, trying to see through the haze to check if she is injured.

"I'm fine, are you?"

"Fine." I cough, inhaling too much dust. As we get up to keep running, We stop because someone walks into the lobby. Grayson points his gun and fires in the direction of the door as a man steps through. The bullet bounces off something and I see a pair of haunting green eyes shine through the dust. He's in black armor, something futuristic-looking, accentuating his muscular body to a dangerously delicious degree. But what really makes me stop breathing is his face—his unbelievably gorgeous face, etched with focus and concern, his usually pristine brow furrowed. When he locks eyes with me, he stomps toward me. Grayson immediately cuts him off but Magnus shoots something out, almost like a blast of air and it has the effect of sending Grayson flying through the air and landing a foot away.

"May! Get behind me," Beth shouts and pushes me behind her. Her fear ignites my own. What if he's not here to save me? What if Penigren is right? What if he's here to kill me? What if he hurts Beth, Grayson, and everyone else here? Maybe Grayson is already hurt, he's not moving. But I'm not going to let Beth get hurt on my account. I sidestep her, and Magnus follows the movement, running the distance to me. I brace myself, my heart racing in my chest. He gets inches from me and stops. I look up at him, trying to discern his unreadable expression. I breathe him in, his citrus leathery musk and my body relaxes involuntarily. Beth is shouting something but I don't hear her, because Magnus wraps me in his arms and squeezes.

"Thank god," he murmurs, he sounds relieved and I sink

into him. He's not here to kill me, I almost let Penigren get to me, almost. Beth is beating on him, but he doesn't even try to push her off, he just holds me.

"I thought you were dead," he says and I can hardly breathe, his embrace so strong.

"Magnus, I can't breathe, please."

"You're killing her!" Beth shouts, like a maniac, pounding on him with all her might. He doesn't let me go, he doesn't even pay Beth attention, he hauls me up on his shoulder, carrying me out of the hotel. Beth is crying hysterically as she tries to chase us. Her face is streaming with tears, her eyes wide, wild with terror. I call out to her, but through all the explosions and gunfire, I don't know if she hears me.

"It's okay Beth, I want to go," I shout but she doesn't stop her pursuit. She's too slow for Magnus and the distance between us gapes until Beth trips and falls down on her knees, she looks up at me, with saucer eyes, and helpless pity and I wish I could reassure her.

"Magnus, stop, we can't just leave her."

"You want to take her?" he asks and pauses briefly.

"Yes it's June, please, we can't just leave her, and I want Elara too," I tell him.

"Who is Elara?" he puts me down and smooths away my hair, "I can't stop here too long, we have them surprised and defending. Penigren is sending reinforcements."

"I need June and Elara, or I can't go," I demand, sticking my chin up, and showing him my determination.

"Okay, Spark, let's get your friends." He pushes me into a hovercraft, this one armored and nothing like the sleek hovercrafts he had in his hangar. He gets into the hovercraft, and it takes to the air.

"I thought we were getting my friends," I ask as it drifts across the city. Before he answers, it descends to the ground a foot from Beth. Grayson emerges from the hotel, bounding toward Beth. The door opens and I reach for her. She mistakes the gesture as me trying to escape. She gets up, running to grab my hand. She tries to pull me out of the hovercraft, but Magnus holds onto me Grayson holds onto Beth on the other end and I'm forced to let her go.

"If she doesn't want to come, do you want to force her?" Magnus asks me. If Beth believes this is the place for her I don't want to steal her autonomy, I know how bad that feels. Even though I don't think this place is the best, it's not for me to decide. Grayson tries to grab me and Magnus kicks him hard in the chest sending him sprawling to the ground.

"Leave her," I say and Magnus moves the hovercraft away from the hotel. Grayson shouts out after me, a bullet whizzes past his head and he's forced to fall onto the ground. I watch to make sure he's okay. He scrambles away and gets behind cover. He looks ready to run after the hovercraft and chase us. His eyes are calculating if there is a way to get to us without getting shot. I can see when he comes to the decision and he leaves the safety of the giant building chunk he was hiding behind

"No Grayson, don't!" I shout at him, he either can't hear me or he ignores me because he runs toward us in the middle of that firestorm. The hovercraft takes off and I turn to watch him running after us, his muscles strained, determination and desperation etching his features. The hovercraft loses him, and I turn back to look at Magnus who is watching me carefully.

"Elara," I tell Magnus.

"Where is she?" he asks. I bite my lip and consider; I don't know Elara enough to have a clue.

"Can you sense other Edits?" I ask him, wondering if there is a way to track her.

"Yes, I can tell if there is an Edit on a nearby shared network," he admits but looks skeptical. "But there are no Edits named Elara," he says adamantly.

"Well, you're wrong, because she is an Edit, and she is a little girl, and she is around here somewhere."

His eyes flare with surprise. "I would never have made a child into an Edit," he says adamantly, refuting my claims.

"Well, someone did." His jaw ticks as he considers the veracity of my claim. A moment passes, then he looks off into the distance before looking back at me.

"She's two blocks away," he says. The hovercraft takes off, controlled by Magnus's internal interface, speeding through the city and avoiding explosions and gunfire. I see rebels in black fatigues firing at men in armored suits like Magnus's. One or two go down, and I have to look away.

"Don't kill anyone else," I ask Magnus, who is staring at me with intensity. He nods, and the sounds of gunfire and explosions cease. His men ascend in their various vehicles, a black plague of soldiers soaring into the sky like a swarm of locusts. It's almost as if they are connected by a kind of hive mind. It's chilling and stunning. I spot Elara standing in a doorway, looking up at the sky, watching the spectacle. The hovercraft door opens upward, and I shout at her, gesturing wildly for her to get into the hovercraft.

"Two in tow is more to show!" Without hesitation, she runs toward us and gets into the hovercraft. Elara's eyes meet mine briefly, grateful. She straps herself in, her little hands snapping the buckles in place, and she sits back with a stern expression. A loud bang goes off right next to us, nearly hitting the hovercraft as we take off, tilting us and forcing part of the craft to scrape along the ground. Magnus's eyes glaze over momentarily, his complex mind working to control the situation. The hovercraft rights itself, engines roaring as it ascends several feet into the air before wings snap out, and we soar upwards. The speed pushes me back into my seat. I'll never get used to these things.

Chapter 33

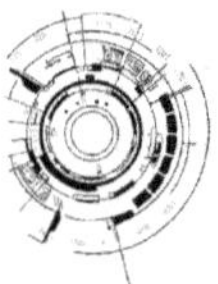

My thirty institutions are the crowning achievement of my life. Through endless efforts to restore the planet, I have also restored hope. Lives that would have wasted away behind walls were put to good use, given a new choice, and a new chance.

-Magnus Compendium, Section 11, page 4

In my dormant state, I craved her touch. I was trapped inside my body. It was hell to be locked in there without the ability to use my limbs. She awakened a part of me that I didn't know could be awake during a shutdown. I had designed a fail-safe in the event something went wrong with the chip. I knew it could happen, but all it was supposed to do was keep my autonomic functions operating. I dreamt of her the whole time, just waiting to be released from the prison that was my own body. Now she was here in front of me and she looked hesitant. She was still beautiful, but too thin. Her eyes didn't spark with the same reverence, I used to be her world. She was different and I didn't know how she had changed.

. . .

TWO WEEKS *ago*

MY DARK VOID SPARKED, and a cascade of lights flickered on in my mind. Lines of new data scrolled through my interface, a system diagnostic running through me. All my senses came online, each one reporting a status update: hormones, nerve endings, olfactory, hearing—all functioning. My eyelids flutter open as I listen to all the sounds in the lab. The humming of instruments, Kyla moving around me. With a final surge, my interface reaches operational status, and I look around. Kyla is standing over me, the glass casing of the regeneration chamber separating us.

"Magnus, can you hear me?" she asks, waiting to see if I'm functioning as I should.

"I hear you, Kyla." Her brown eyes shine, the honey-brown skin around her face crinkling into a smile.

"Good, welcome back." She disappears, and the glass cover starts to slide open, and I'm met with fresh air. My muscles feel stronger, ready to move. A surge of energy courses through my body; I feel invincible. I want to see Zoriya right away.

"Bring in Zori," I tell Kyla, who stops what she is doing to look at me. Her eyebrows draw in, confusion etching her features.

"Who?"

"My fiancée, she came in my hovercraft," I say, checking the current date. I've been unconscious for two weeks. "Three weeks ago."

"I'm sorry, Magnus, no one came in a hovercraft. I retrieved you and Dalton, but there were no new arrivals," she says, and my blood drains from my face. If she isn't here, then where is she?

"What do you mean?"

"I mean that I don't know what you're talking about," Kyla says, annoyance evident in her tone.

"Where is Dalton?" I ask, looking around the lab. I'm naked, of course, and I look around for something to wear.

"On the chair," Kyla says, points at the pile of clothes she left for me. She's done this enough times with Edits that she knows the drill.

"Dalton is still undergoing some repairs. He suffered some real damage from the virus. He had a small stroke, but he's going to be fine. "A part of his interface is damaged, and I have to make those repairs before installing the chip," she explains to me. I nod, glad that he is going to be okay. I'm still unbelievably angry at him for betraying me, but I'd never wish Dalton dead. He seems genuinely remorseful for his impulsive choice. Although, someday he is going to have to make it up to me if I can truly forgive him. We both could have died. Right now, I need to find Zori. I put on my clothes quickly and open the lab doors when Kyla stops me. "Wait, Magnus, two Edits didn't make it," she tells me, and I stop and look over at her.

"Who?"

"Gavin and Pru." I stop and take a long breath. That is a deeply unfortunate loss. I remember when I found both of them. They were young and brilliant. When I gave them scholarships to get a better education, I had no idea how far it would take them. Their parents were so proud, so happy they could afford to send them to better schools. They were my star pupils, and then they became humanitarians, some of my greatest allies. The pain of their loss hits deep. I turn down my sadness because I need to find Zori. What happened to her? She was supposed to come here before me.

"We have to consider he might try to kill others."

"I'll keep that in mind." I pat Kyla on the shoulder and squeeze. It sometimes strikes me how quickly humans age and die. It seems only yesterday that I found Kyla at an exam and put her through school. Now she is running the West Coast

Institute. She smiles sadly at me, the creases of her eyes crinkling around her intelligent brown eyes. I kiss her head, her coarse black hair tickling my nose. She squeezes my arm and looks up at me with an affectionate glint in her eyes.

"Send me the report," I tell Kyla before walking toward the hangar. If Zori isn't here, then something happened.

THE HOVERCRAFT HAS a tracker on it, but when I try to pinpoint its location, nothing comes up. I jump into the first hovercraft, one of the armored ones that line the WI hangar. I had the skimmers built after Penigren lost his mind, in case he ever acted on his threats. They are fortified with advanced armor plating and only two bulletproof windows. In case of an attack, retractable window covers can slide into place, sealing the cockpit entirely. The skimmer is controlled entirely by my neural interface, responding seamlessly to my thoughts. For human soldiers, we have developed an augmented reality device that attaches to their temples. This device is a button-shaped neural transmitter that sends signals directly into their brains, allowing them to temporarily control the hovercraft as if they had an interface. This technology is not a permanent solution for humans. Prolonged use leads to severe migraines and cognitive strain. I take a deep breath and focus my thoughts, the hovercraft coming to life at my mental command. The engines hum as I lift off, the hangar doors sliding open to reveal the sky beyond. I have to find Zori, and I have to find her now. The first place I go is my home. I search every room, every nook and cranny, but she didn't come back here. I stand in her room, staring at her things still scattered on the ground. She became a very messy person after leaving Plymouth. When she slept, I'd roam the house, working and cleaning up after her. I'd tend to my garden. She never noticed how the house always seemed to be in order. I never wanted robots in my home, but sometimes when I leave for a long time, I let them out to tend to the gardens. They are the same robots responsible for growing all the food on my land. I send the food to the Units, where it is equitably distributed based on population needs. I set aside about 200 million acres, about the size of Spain, to feed the population. This land is at the base of a volcano near Cotopaxi, in the Andes Mountains. The soil is fertile, and by restricting the growing of food to this one region, the rest of the world has had a chance to recover from over-farming. When I have to let the land lie fallow, the crops move to the Pampas in Argentina. It's worked beautifully for the last couple of hundred years. With crop rotations, I've managed to avoid soil depletion and nutritional deficiencies. With careful planning, I've utilized polyculture, growing different types of crops together to boost biodiversity and keep the soil healthy. The plants help protect each other from pests, so I don't need to use chemical pesticides. It also means better overall yields because the plants use resources more efficiently. My agricultural robots can autonomously tend the crops as well as harvest and ship them worldwide. Standing in Zori's room, I feel a pang of panic. Where could she be? She isn't here. The hovercraft tracker finally pings. I've been sending out code to try to reactivate it, and it lights up briefly before flashing away. It's enough to start.

THE FOREST IS TOO dense to land my skimmer, so I leave it at the edge and hike on foot, following the coordinates where the hovercraft was pinged. The reasons for her being in the forest can't be good, especially if she is in the center—how did she land? These forests have had a long time to become dense, returning to their wild, unmanicured state. I hear a cacophony of wildlife sounds: birds chirping, grunts from larger animals nearby, a cougar growling several miles away, an elk scraping its antlers on a tree, and the skittering of squirrels and chipmunks. I push down my panic—what if she is hurt, or worse? I can't allow myself to focus on the outcome; I just need to find her. I must remain stoic and concentrated. I usually filter out most sounds, but if Zori is out there alone, I want to hear it. It takes intense focus to scan through the noises as I navigate the forest. There are no neat hiking trails or paths, no switchbacks to make climbs easier. I scramble up boulders and even rock climb some steeper sections until the forest terrain starts to descend. I step on something that makes a metallic crunching sound and I stop and inspect it. It looks like a piece of the hovercraft. My heart starts beating in my ears. I run the rest of the distance, bounding over logs, branches crack and snap on me. My foot slips on a mossy boulder, but I catch myself by rolling into a front flip and jumping back onto my feet. A metallic scent cuts through the forest aromas—blood. My heart is racing, my palms are wet, I can feel my body begin it's panic. I stop when I see the forest floor scarred, plants mashed. Trees are broken at the tops, allowing the sun to shine through in a ring around the crash site. A light beacon highlights the debris and the spots of blood on the mossy floor. I drop to my knees, and I touch a spot of blood. I smell it and know it belongs to Kira, her unmistakable scent blends into the metallic sharpness. Despair floods my body and I start to shake. She's dead. She's dead. I can't breathe, and I drop my head to my chest, staring at my hands. "Shut it down," my brain whispers to me. "Shut down your emotions," it begs, and I want to acquiesce because this pain is burning me alive. It feels worse than regeneration; it feels like the end. I promised myself I'd never shut it off again. I scream into the void of the forest, and silence follows, the forest creatures holding their breath because of my anguished roar. My soul is bleeding out, my heart is bursting. I break my promise. I stop it all, I shut it off. My shoulder blades ease, my muscles relax, my heart regulates its beats, my vision clears, and my breathing slows. I'm left alone at the crash site. The old me is back, the one who acts but doesn't feel. It's freeing to have it all gone. I look around calmly. The pieces of wreckage are here, and there is blood. But now that I'm not panicking, I realize there is no hovercraft, and there isn't a body. If Zori is dead, someone took her body, but she could be alive. I calculate the odds of surviving a crash in a hovercraft. For a moderate impact crash, the baseline survival rate is 60%. The hovercraft's advanced safety features add 25%, and the soft forest terrain adds another 15%. Zori's condition, being properly secured and healthy, adds 15%. However, the lack of immediate medical assistance reduces the survival rate by 25%.

Total highest survival rate: 60% + 25% + 15% + 15% - 25% = 90%.

The worst-case scenario with a high-impact crash and no safety features:

Total lowest survival rate: 30% baseline - 20% for no safety features + 10% for forest terrain + 10% for being secured - 30% for no medical assistance = 0%.

I analyze the amount of blood on the ground. It isn't enough for a bleed-out, which would be around two liters. She is injured, if she's alive. Who took her? The hovercraft is damaged, which explains why the tracker stopped working here. There is a second tracker, so I analyze all the debris and confirm that it isn't among them. There are only exterior pieces, and the tracker is embedded inside the engine. I go back to the skimmer and sit down. Eventually, the sun dips low in the sky, and night-time encroaches. The cold air becomes colder with each passing hour. To save power, I leave the skimmer off. It has a long battery life, but I don't know how far I'll have to go. The second tracker on the hovercraft is set to activate as soon as someone tries to use the technology. The tracker has remained off for the duration of my repairs. If it is Penigren who took her, he will turn it on eventually. He has been scavenging my technology for years. I finally installed fail-safes, and this is the first time he's taken one with a second tracker. I should probably go back to

WI to regroup. I give up on the delusion that it will happen anytime soon. If it's been two weeks and they haven't activated it, it could be another two weeks. It's been twelve hours since I turned off my emotions. Twelve hours of searching all my surveillance drones for anything that could help me find her. The skimmer lifts, and I fly toward WI, not giving up but needing more information. I'm halfway there when I get the second tracker's ping. I immediately reroute, It's almost certainly Penigren. If my emotions were on, I'd feel panicked and worried for Zori. I am concerned but only through a clinical lens. I know Magnus with his emotions intact would want her safe, so I work toward that goal. I know Zori wouldn't want me to remain this detached. Logically there is hope for her survival. I have to honor myself and the progress I made, all these years, I can't fall back into the monstrous path I once walked. I turn back on my emotions. I feel the sadness creep in, but I let it sit there. On top of the sadness is hope, a hope where I find my spark, alive.

THE PORTLAND CITY skyline comes into view. It's been ages since I last saw the city. If Penigren is in there, then I need to be careful. I fly high above the city, away from any eyes, and land on the other side of it. I park the Skimmer far from the city and carefully trudge through the ruins of the old neighborhoods. Nature has reclaimed the area, filling in all the spaces where houses used to sit. I remember sitting on this very street corner, drinking tea and talking to friends, long before the Units, before the scourge, before the wars. It's unrecognizable now. I find myself in what used to be Forest Park. When I reach St. Johns Bridge, I stop, its green arched suspension supports still standing tall. The bridge itself is no longer usable; the road has fallen into the river below, just a skeleton of its former glory. I don't see any activity on the other side, but without going around, I'd have to swim the river. Instead, I activate recon drones. My Skimmer has five that I can deploy at will. They are miniature, and you'd have to know to look for them to spot them. They don't store data, but they can send a live feed directly to my interface. It's nighttime, making the drones less detectable. They whiz past me and scatter into the city, sending back data. They scan the numerous ruins. The city appears dead and empty, but the second tracker is still pinging its location here. I send one of the drones to the second tracker location. It hovers near an industrial-looking garage with a slatted metal door. Although it can't get inside, it gets as close to the tracker as possible. She could be inside. Drone two catches my attention when a door opens on one of the rooftops, a green copper roof that belonged to one of the old hotels. It's Zori. She's on the roof. She's here and, not only that, she is alive. She's staring up into the stars and I move the drone closer to look at her. Then Grayson steps out of the shadows. He gets very close to her and she laughs. Laughs at something Grayson said. She says something else and their playful mood shifts and they argue about something. I look at the river; how long would it take to swim across? I am considering running straight to her, but then the other drones pick up some activity: men with guns patrolling the streets, a hovercycle coming out of the garage, the tracker attached to it. They scavenged the parts from my hovercraft to make that hovercycle. I let the drones scan more before I move. A whole contingent of men is loitering at the far end of the city, a full platoon. If I went in now, would Penigren try to kill Zori? Use her against me? Grayson hugs Zori and she doesn't push him away. I want to rip his arms off, but I have to be smart about this. I send out a coded distress signal to my soldiers, calling them to arms. They are equipped to mobilize quickly and will be here within hours. In the meantime, I watch from the edge of the city, gathering as much intel as I can and preparing for the confrontation to come.

Chapter 34

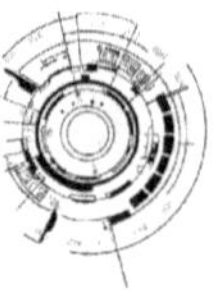

Stagnation is a mindset; if you are a tedious person, you will live a monotonous life.

-Magnus Compendium, Section 14, Page 9

Magnus

Fucking Grayson Penigren. She was worried about that asshole. Still, She's alive. When I found the wrecked hovercraft, I feared the worst. I had seconds to react before Penigrens virus tried to take over my system. I shut down after her hovercraft fell out. Thankfully Kyla got my distress signal and found both me and Dalton. It took weeks for Western Institute to install a new chip and rewrite codes to remove all access from Penigren. If he had been successful, he could have given us strokes, heart attacks, or programmed our bodies to shut down. Dalton suffered some damage and had to do more extensive repairs and the regeneration process. He looks even younger than he did. She finally emerges from the extra bedroom where she has put Elara to sleep. I brought them to the

Western Institute, which is safer than my home. Standing in the penthouse, I gaze out through the large windows overlooking the majestic Redwood forest beyond. Their large, reddish trunks tower over the WI, their presence both comforting and humbling. I've always loved these towering giants, the eternal redwoods that outlive the fleeting span of human lives. Now they grow alongside me as I stay young, and the young saplings I replanted have grown into hulking giants. I turn away from them to look at Spark as she approaches. She has a bruise on her chin, and her knees are scraped up. I drop my drink and I scope her up into my arms and I breathe her in.

"Zoriya," I whisper into her hair. "Thank god." I find her lips and I drag them into mine, it's been too long since I've held her, touched her. She is skinnier than she was, she clings to me and returns my kiss. Her breathy little sounds hardening me. My cock demands attention. I squeeze her ass through the little shorts she put on after her shower. The thin cotton does very little to conceal her perfect body. I slide my hand underneath the fabric and I find her little pussy. It's so wet for me already and I groan as I skim my finger through her labia. She whimpers as I slide a finger inside her tight center. I pump my finger into her, I'm about to add another when she stops my hand.

"Wait, Magnus, stop." She asks me and I stop my ministrations. She pushes at my chest and steps back. She crosses her arms and looks out the window. I go up behind her and wrap my arms around her waist. She closes her eyes and leans her head back.

"What's wrong my Spark?" I ask her and her eyes open and she steps out of my arms again.

"I can't do this with you." She says and her lips quiver but she holds up her chin stiffly in the air.

"What can't you do?"

"Be with you. Touch you." My heart plummets, my skin prickles. I try to breathe through her rejection.

"What's happened, why are you pulling away from me?"

"You ditched me! You threw me into that damn hovercraft, what as a decoy?" she accuses.

"I'd never use you as a decoy. I was trying to get you to safety. I was trying to ensure you'd get to WI, but Penigren must have mistook you for me."

"No kidding!" she shouts and her eyes begin producing a steady stream of tears.

"Baby, I was about to get hacked, if he had succeeded, I'd be dead. I had seconds to make a decision before I shut down." All the progress we made, all the trust seems to have vanished, because how could she believe me capable of that?

"What?" she sniffles, her eyes gleaming as she looks up at me.

"Dalton gave him access codes to our interface, he was trying to kill me and Dalton and all the Edits. Dalton got infected and he dropped, all I could think to do was send you to WI, away from me." I tell her everything that happened. How we were out of commission for weeks, how I searched for her the minute I woke up. How I found the crash hovercraft and nearly lost my mind. I turned off my emotions for twelve hours. Her tears stop, but she scratches her thigh.

"Okay, so you didn't throw me away. But there are still a million other things you've done wrong," she insists, and I run a frustrated hand through my hair.

"What other things?"

"I'd say you're responsible for the greatest suffering this earth has ever encountered," she states, and I stare at her, dumbfounded.

"You'll have to elaborate a little."

"Okay, first you made Edits." She pulls up her hand and starts counting off digits as she lists my long list of crimes. "You let them buy and abuse children, women, and men. Murder them when they are done. You have lied to me about the state of the world, lied to all of us." She stares me down, daring me to refute any of it. "There aren't back-to-back cities, there isn't overpopulation. There is vast emptiness; I've seen it with my own damn eyes. Explain that away, Faust." I hate when she calls me Faust; it's the verbal equivalent of holding me at arm's length.

"Edits don't go around murdering anyone. Abuse? No, we rescue abused children and give them another life. Yes, I did make Edits, but with a purpose." I pause and take a deep breath. "The earth being vast and empty, and thriving, I'll take full credit for that. Proudly. Restoring this planet is the shining beacon of my life's work. Edits were only a means to an end. I brought this planet back from the brink of destruction, and every decision I've had to make, every deal I've had to strike, was worth it. What is the point of immortality if there is no planet left to live on?"

She scoffs at me and walks away. "Okay."

I quickly move to block her path. "What does that mean, okay?"

"Are you serious? You can't be that ignorant. Or are you a megalomaniac? Which is it?"

"Is this what Penigren told you?"

"Penigren is an entirely different thing. I don't know what his goal is. But I do know what I saw out there. I saw the empty crumbling city, the vast empty forests, and rolling hills. I know what Beth went through. I know all of the people there, Grayson, Elara, Cinder—all suffered at the hands of an Edit."

"Fucking Grayson Penigren isn't a victim here," I say, irritated. How could she believe anything that asshole told her?

"Grayson Penigren?" she asks. "You mean Memphis Penigren?"

"No, I mean Grayson Penigren, Memphis Penigren's son. Don't think I didn't see your concern for him when he was trying to steal you back from me." I step close to her, and it's hard not to reach out for her, but her body is completely closed off to me. "Are you really going to believe that scavenger over me? That fucking heir to the Penigren fortune?" She stares at my chest, her eyes moving around rapidly, working something out.

"Penigren?" she says again, incredulously. "Scavenger?"

"Yes, scavenger, pirate, butcher, take your pick. I saw your little tête-à-tête on the roof. Is this what this is really about? Do you want Grayson?"

"You killed his mother," she says.

"Gloria Penigren?" I sigh. "That one is true." She looks at me, finally. Her beautiful ocean eyes staring up at mine. Whenever I see her eyes, I feel this sense of belonging, breath enters my body, fresh and clean. Even now, when she looks at me with contempt, estranging me, my body recognizes her as home. She still hasn't answered my question about Grayson.

"Why?" she demands an answer.

"She didn't survive the gene therapy to become an Edit."

"That's not murder, though," she concludes.

"No, it's not, but it still weighs on me, every life I've been responsible for. Memphis couldn't let it go; he's been trying to get his revenge ever since."

"Okay, you get a pass for that one, but the rest?" she rubs her temples, sighing.

"You first, Grayson, what happened between you? Do you want him?"

"Nothing happened, he's my friend. He took care of me."

"Friend? Penigrens can't be trusted. How did he take care of you?" It itches my skin that another man was there for her when I couldn't be.

"He helped me get better after my coma, my concussion. He read to me, he was kind. I wouldn't have survived in that basement for so long without a friendly face." I grind my teeth and look away, I can't exactly kill the man for saving her life, although she wouldn't have been there at all if his father hadn't attacked me.

"And you don't love him?"

"No. Now answer me, why keep us in the dark?"

"What do you want me to say? Yes, I've been complicit in the lie that humanity is overpopulated."

"Why? Why leave us to fester in squalor?"

"It's hard for you to understand because this is all you've ever known. But I was there in the beginning. I was there when the world was dying, its last breaths over the horizon. You don't know how close we came to the end."

"So, what is your goal? Are you going to replace all of humanity with Edits? Is this an extinction-level event? Is this where you tell me again that humans make shitty choices, and therefore we aren't worthwhile?"

"No, I'm not trying to make them go extinct. I want them to thrive and be happy, but not at the cost of our planet. It is our only home. There aren't enough Edits to take over. I made sure to keep immortality numbers low. I've only made Edits when the benefits outweigh the risks."

"What kind of benefits justify the way they take on people as 'pets' and then torture and kill them?"

"What are you talking about?" I ask, genuinely perplexed. I know there is kink involved and some morally gray situations, but I've never heard of anyone getting murdered or tortured. Lies intended to turn her against me.

"I need to understand what you've gotten out of this."

"I've had to make deals with some of the most powerful people to secure land, resources, advanced technology, medical breakthroughs, scientific discoveries, raw materials, military and political influence, water rights, and diplomatic agreements. All to ensure the world remains untouched, preventing further mining and scavenging of the planet. Edit contracts are intricate. They operate on a quid pro quo basis: to gain the rights I need, I must grant them eternal life. I provide upgrades, gene editing, and regeneration. If I cease these services, my contracts become void, and I lose access to those critical resources. Your turn."

"I'm talking about Beth, Cinder, and the rest of the rebels."

"And what other lie did Penigren tell you about them?" I ask, trying to keep my frustration in check, trying to remember that she has been with them for weeks, being brainwashed.

"Penigren didn't say anything to me about them. They told me themselves. They have the scars to prove it. Beth is covered in scars from stab wounds. Cinder had her whole body burned by cigarettes, including her eye. She's fully blind in one eye."

"Who did they say did this?" I try to process what she is saying. Whatever she's been told, she believes it with conviction.

"Dorian Hayes, for one," she says, and I swallow hard. I knew Dorian Hayes had a reputation for being unconventional, but I didn't think anything like this was going on.

"Do they have proof?"

"Beth has been my friend since I was a little girl. She wouldn't lie about something like this!" she exclaims, her voice filled with emotion. I take a deep breath, feeling the weight of her words.

"I swear, I had no idea. If Dorian or any other Edit is doing this, they are acting against everything I stand for. I created them to help rebuild, not to destroy." Her eyes lock onto mine, a mixture of anger and desperation.

"Then you need to fix this. You need to stop them."

"It's not that simple. There are contracts in place. If I violate them, I lose rights to everything I've built here. I've explained this to you." She searches my face for a moment.

"If you don't stop them, I will." My spark has become a fire since I last saw her. Her eyes are brimming with determination. I believe she will try, but she would die trying.

"I'll get to the bottom of this, but don't do anything reckless," I say, my voice softening. If what she says is true, Dorian Hayes will have to be punished. Of course, that means I'll lose the rights to the Atacama Basin and all its rich minerals.

"But you have to do one thing for me." She gestures with her hand for me to continue but raises a skeptical eyebrow. "I want you to go to a ball and meet some Edits. You've only seen the bad ones, but I promise you there are good ones too."

"Fine," she agrees.

"Good, now can we please go back to where we left off? I need to feel you wrapped around me."

"No, until you fix this, we aren't an item," she declares and stomps into my bedroom, locking the door behind her.

Shit.

Chapter 35

I am wearing a luxurious midnight blue gown that perfectly matches my eyes. The bodice is tightly fitted, and encrusted in black gems. The skirt is an overflowing tulle skirt, it swishes on the floor as I walk. No doubt the reason Faust picked this out for me, it's designed to resemble a ballet tutu. It exudes elegance and glamor, a far cry from the torn jeans and worn-out sweater I came here in. I emerge from the bedroom when I'm finally done doing my hair and makeup. Magnus is waiting for me in an onyx black tuxedo. His shirt is black, and his vest is black, the only thing that isn't his midnight blue bowtie. He looks delicious the way it's cut, showing off all the best parts of his body. He is adjusting his cufflinks when he looks up at me and his green eyes lock onto me. I want to slide my hands underneath his tuxedo jacket and feel the warmth of his body. I want to touch him freely, just like when I was ignorant and his obedient sex monster. I was so eager and willing and I didn't question my situation as much as I should have. He embodies seduction, he is tempting and perilous. I need to hold my ground, I need to keep him at arm's length, to ensure he complies.

"Spark, you look…" he hesitates, "sparkling," he says with a small, cheeky grin before he drops it and approaches me. I take a step back, unsure if I can keep my promise to myself if he gets too close. He notices but doesn't cease his steps. Instead of trying to pull me into his arms, he picks up my hand and gives it a delicate peck. He slides a black diamond tennis bracelet onto my wrist seamlessly and I almost don't notice, because I am so focused on the way his plump lips feel depressing the skin on my hands. I want those lips to travel up the length of my arm, up to my neck, and down my body. I want them all over me, my cheeks redden and he looks up at me.

"I'm trying very hard to be a good boy, but I can smell how much you want me," he says, and I groan and stomp away.

"Wanting you has never been the problem."

"That's a relief," he says, following me to the front door. "It's just my character in question, isn't it? Can't quite decide if I'm evil, or what was the word you used? Megalomaniac?" It's hard to ignore the hurt in his voice, and it's even harder not to want to retract my stance and make him feel better. But this isn't for me or about me; this is about the world. This is about Beth and the rest, I remind myself. "You know there would be a very easy way to resolve all of this," he says as he opens the door for me.

"Oh?"

"Yes, darling, if you would become an Edit, you could see my entire life and then you would know everything about me. I would give you full access to me, and then you could decide for yourself."

"That doesn't sound very easy. Didn't you say becoming an Edit feels like burning alive?" I retort and walk past him, my dress swishing against his thighs as I pass. It feels too intimate. I want to wrap myself around his thick thighs, climb his body, and tear off that tuxedo.

"Yes, it does, but afterward you feel like a god. It is unlike anything a human being has ever experienced."

"You know I don't want to live forever," I say, trying to end the discussion. "Plus, I think that maybe that's part of the problem. You Edits seem to forget that you're not gods at all, merely men with money." Faust pushes me against the wall, his hard body pressing into mine as he breathes into my neck, enlivening me. God, I want him to push up my dress and and… but I force myself to focus.

"Men with money? Don't you know that most mythological gods were created? If I am not Odin, Anu or Vishnu, what am I? I have made men into immortal beings and endowed them with powers, strength, and gifts beyond human reach. And you think God is unfair?" His breathy chuckle reminds me that he knows how eager I am for him.

"I am not a peasant who believes the sun rises because Sól drags it across the sky. I am a modern being, and I know magic isn't real. Science is the explanation, and science is not omnipotence," I utter breathily, his masculine scent enveloping me, reminding me of how he smells during sex—sweat, citrus, and cum.

"No, it's not, but it is something different. It is a future that you can't comprehend because you won't look," He pushes away from the wall leaving me flustered and grasping for my self-control.

"Sometimes, when you stare at the horizon too long, you can't see the sun has already risen." He doesn't say anything, just follows me into the elevator. He is in close proximity again, my skirt brushing against him with every movement.

"Your brain is maybe the most attractive thing about you," he announces, standing next to me, his hand brushing against mine. His comment about my brain reminding me of how we met—how he plucked me out of obscurity for his needs. I still don't know if I am just a toy, a precious one, but still a toy. If Dalton could be replaced after so long, am I just a part of a series? Will there be a succession of people after me? The elevator doors open and he steps out, leading us to the WI hangar. We walk through the long hangar, lined with armored hovercrafts. This isn't a personal collection; it looks like a military installation. Even though I hate the term god, he certainly exudes power. How the man has acquired a military is another burning question. Who fights with him, for him? Why are they willing to put their lives on the line for this Edit? But he isn't just any Edit, is he? He is the creator, the progenitor of immortality. A group of soldiers who were leaning against an armored Skimmer stand to attention when they notice us. They salute Faust and then one of them gestures at the open Skimmer. Faust takes my hand and helps me in, my dress fills up the interior; a sea of tulle and chiffon. Faust takes the seat next to me, gently pushing my skirt aside, but it springs back as soon as he takes his seat.

"Where are we going?" I ask as the hovercraft drifts out of the hanger.

"The Citadel," he answers, and we fly into the sky with a platoon of soldiers surrounding us. I watch as WI vanishes below us. The Western Institute isn't just a building; it's a Unit in itself. There are enough buildings that you can't see them all from up here. Redwood trees block out the view. It is one of Magnus's thirty-two institutes, which he told me he has all over the world. The center building is polygon-shaped. Each building is white and pristine, untouched by the decay the rest of the world is experiencing.

THE BALLROOM IS A GLEAMING golden spectacle, filled with beautiful Edits in their finery. The tiered crystal chandeliers illuminate the golden walls with their elaborate boiserie and intricate embellishments. The paneling is punctuated by metallic golden wallpaper, adorned with swirling, intricate designs that snake up the wall in a gradient of gold. It's an abundance of gold, too much for any room, yet it manages to be magical rather than garish. An orchestra of humans plays a waltz, and the Edits swirl through the ballroom like a mesmerizing swarm of color and glitter. We stand on the stairwell landing that leads down to the ball. The citadel is as grand as one could imagine a fortified palace: towering walls, polished stone, intricate carvings, complete with a drawbridge and battlements. Each step deeper into the Citadel has been more ornate and opulent than the last. A herald announces us, and the dancers cease. The tinkling of crystal and the sounds of chatter stop. They all turn to look up at us, at Faust. He is a magnet for attention. I've known Magnus on a deeply personal level; when I met him, I had no idea who he was. It is slowly becoming clear that I've fallen in love with a world player, a man who, if not respected by his peers, is at the very least revered for what he's done, for what he has accomplished. Faust offers me his arm, and I rest my hand on his. His strong hand steadies me, and I feel a prickling sensation from being observed. I want to scrape my leg, to float away, but he is there next to me, so I breathe. We descend the staircase, and I feel like I've stepped into a fairytale, one from ages past. I've never worn a ballgown before, danced a waltz, or been in a citadel. Yet the people below, watching us, all look bored, uninterested. They don't appreciate the grandeur, the privilege they possess. People greet us as we reach the bottom and I shrink behind Faust. I hear cadences and exclamations but the words blur. Magnus hasn't looked at me for a while but he grabs my hand and squeezes it, reminding me that he's always aware of me.

"Let me introduce my fiancée, Zoriya," he says, and a woman of striking beauty steps forward and clasps my hand. Her black hair, flecked with brown streaks, cascades down her back, contrasting against her almond skin, which exudes a warm, exotic glow. Her lips are painted a deep red, and even though she doesn't look much older than me, there is wisdom in her brown eyes. Her exquisite red gown perfectly accentuates her curvy figure, with chiffon flowing effortlessly around her, and a slit that glides all the way up to her hip, revealing her long leg.

"Oh Faust, she's lovely, like a beautiful little ballet figurine. I'd love to put her into a music box and keep her forever," she says in a deep, sensuous voice. "Welcome to my home, Zoriya. Don't mind me, I only jest. I'd never keep you in a box; I'd be too tempted to play with you." She laughs heartily at her own joke, and I press myself closer to Faust.

"Constance, be nice, this is her first time in Edit society," Faust chastises, smiling at Constance.

"Oh Magnus, you can't bring a jewel like that to Edit society without a little competition. What do you think, my little ballerina? Would you like to come live here with me? I'd be much more generous than Faust." She laughs again, her long neck stretching as her head falls back, her white teeth gleaming in the chandelier lighting.

Magnus tuts at her, and she laughs some more.

"Come, come, a little Edit humor. Let's have a drink, and I'll tell you all the Edits to avoid and who you positively must eschew." We follow her to a table laden with food and drink. She hands me a champagne glass and one to Magnus. She picks one up herself and takes a sip.

"So tell me, is she really a ballerina?"

"She is, a talented one," Magnus says, glancing at the room of partygoers who have returned to their previous frivolities.

"Oh, it would be lovely if she could dance for us. We seldom encounter talent these days," Constance says, staring at me with renewed interest.

"I'm not here to discuss Zoriya, or pleasant things, I'm afraid," Magnus says, changing the tone of the conversation. "Penigren has escalated things. He has tried to hack several Edits and has killed two."

"Oh my, who did we lose?" she asks genuine surprise in her voice.

"Pru and Gavin," he says, sorrow evident in his voice.

"No!" Constance exclaims, her hand flying up to cover her mouth in shock. "I saw Pru last month. We were planning to collaborate on a fundraiser for the Units," she laments, draining her champagne in one big gulp.

"I saw Gavin a few weeks ago. He was about to announce a breakthrough in his research on boosting human immunity," Magnus adds, his tone heavy with regret. "His new treatment showed promise in early trials and could have potentially eliminated the need for the embryo booster, making it readily available for even adults. It could have been a turning point for the human population."

Constance's eyes widen. "It's truly a devastating loss," she says, taking up another champagne glass and draining it. Magnus nods, sipping his champagne. "Penigren's actions have far-reaching consequences. His insanity and desperation could set us back decades in our work." I am surprised by their conversation. It certainly paints a different picture than the one told in The Rebel City.

"You know you have my support, of course," Constance says, placing her hand on his forearm and leaning in.

"I knew I could count on you." Magnus squeezes her hand with his free one. I feel forgotten as they stare at each other, a kind of understanding passing between them. There is a shared history there, and I have to wonder if Constance and Magnus were ever lovers. Magnus looks up from his moment with Constance out at the crowd and his lips form a thin line. I follow his line of sight. Walking toward us is a man.

"Speaking of eschewing, Dorian Hayes is a man I insist you stay away from," Constance says leaning toward me conspiratorially. My eyes flash back to the man and I stare at him. He is tall and attractive, but there is an obnoxious air about him. I thought Dalton was self-inflated but it is nothing compared to

Dorian Hayes. He saunters through the ballroom as if he is the most important person here. Dorian Hayes has pale skin, red lips, and gray eyes. He stops at the refreshment table and picks up a flute of champagne before turning to us.

"Constance, habitual creature, aren't you? Same theme, same ballroom. Aren't you tired of your little balls yet?"

"Dorian, if you find my balls so dull, I'm surprised you come at all," Constance says with a forced smile, her teeth on full display.

"Well, despite your lack of creativity, it seems that this is the event to be at, and as such, I'm forced to attend." He looks over at Magnus, who is staring at him with a passive expression.

"Magnus," he says, raising his champagne and drinking. "Looks like Constance finally dragged you away from your lab."

"Constance always throws the best parties," Magnus responds, his face remaining impassive. Dorian ignores Magnus's counter-dig, and his eyes land on me.

"And what do we have here? A human?" he says, stooping a little to inspect. My skin blisters with anger, and I want to take one of the cheese knives and stab him in his bionic eye. I imagine Beth falling for this monster, letting him touch her, then, when she finally let him in, he violated her, stabbed her, and threw her in the dumpster when he thought he'd killed her. Anger floods my brain, centered in my amygdala, like a dam breaking. It's primal and deep, my vision blurring and tinting red. It takes all my willpower to stand still, to not try and kill him. I've never been a violent person; even during the days of sparring at Plymouth, I was fair and only participated as part of the required curriculum. Yet now, I'd happily kill a man.

"I've heard the rumors that Magnus finally picked up a pet," he says, reaching out a hand to stroke my arm. I stand still, unwilling to cower before this monster. Magnus snaps his hand out and grabs Dorian's wrist before his fingertips land on my skin.

"Don't touch her," he says firmly. Dorian's gray eyes narrow, a flash of irritation crossing his face as he straightens up, pulling his hand back. Magnus's grip tightens momentarily before he releases Dorian.

"Well, well, protective, aren't we?" Dorian sneers, taking another sip of his champagne. "How very unlike you, Magnus."

"Some boundaries should never be crossed, Dorian. Remember that."Dorian chuckles, a low, mocking sound.

"Always so dramatic. Enjoy your evening, both of you." He turns on his heel and saunters off, leaving an air of disdain in his wake.

"That's it?" I say, and Constance and Magnus both turn to look at me. It's the first words I've spoken all night. "You're just going to let him walk off?" I glare up at Magnus, whose face shows anger—towards what, I don't know. Maybe me, for having the audacity to speak around his friends.

"There is a time and place, and this is not the time or the place," he insists, shutting down the conversation. I pick up a knife and start after Dorian. Magnus grabs my wrist and stops me.

"You are a good fighter, but only against humans. Dorian would turn you into minced meat," he warns. I pull my arm free from his grip, and he lets me.

"I'm not going to just stand here and let that, that…" I point in the direction of Dorian with my knife-hand. "Sadist, leave here alive."

"You're not a killer. Don't let his polluted soul pollute yours."

"Soul? You don't believe in souls. If you did, you wouldn't be this immortal bionic, fighting against death," I retort, anger lacing my voice, emanating from my being. Constance stands to the side, watching us silently, her face passive, her eyes scanning us.

"But you do," he says, stretching out his hand asking me to give him the knife.

"Maybe, but I know leaving him unpunished is not a choice.

If I believe in souls, then I believe he has violated an endless line of them. Think of all the souls we don't even know about, yet. How long has he been roaming the earth, a blight, killing, demeaning, destroying? You would know, you gave him that gift, didn't you?" I poke Magnus in the chest with the knife's edge. He doesn't move, he doesn't try to push my hand away, he just watches me.

"You two are starting to draw a crowd," Constance announces from our side. Magnus pulls my free hand and stomps out of the ballroom with me in tow.

"You're acting recklessly," he says to me when we are in the hallway.

"You're acting heartlessly," I spit back, still gripping my knife, my knuckles turning white, my palm reddening.

"You have a lot of opinions for someone with so little information," he snaps. It's the first time he's lost his temper with me. I've seen him angry, angry with Dalton. But never with me, he has borne all my anger with calm.

"Enlighten me," I demand.

"I will, I promise. Just put the knife down and take a deep breath. Maybe go to the ladies' room and freshen up. It's down that way. When you're calm again, we will go back in," he tells me, and my grip tightens. I glare at him, and walk toward the bathroom, seething with anger.

Chapter 36

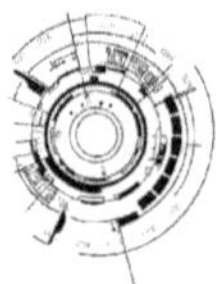

In the Edit society, a traditional court of law is unnecessary. When all memories are shared, everyone is a witness.
-Magnus Compendium, Section 9.11

Magnus

Zori walks away from me, she is stiff with rage and I look at her bunched shoulder blades as she vanishes around the corner. Her long gown disappearing last. I don't know why Dorian Hayes had to make an appearance, he rarely comes to these things. I was hoping to introduce her to people like Constance who have a heart of gold. She is always working with charities to help humanity. She has also been an invaluable partner in my efforts to change the world. A true humanitarian. Dorian Hayes walks toward me, emerging from the ballroom.

"Magnus. Your little pet looked pretty angry. You might reconsider your interest, the difficult ones aren't worth the trouble."

"Let me guess, this is the part where you offer to take her off my hands." I drawl annoyed by the consistency of Edits and their desire to poach Zoriya.

"Heavens no, I prefer my females a little more compliant," he replies quickly. "I suppose you could always send her to Henrik for a few weeks, he'd train her up for you. She would be an eager little cum kitty after that."

"That's my fiance you're talking about," I say calmly, unwilling to get dragged into Dorian Hayes and his toxic mouth.

"I heard that rumor too. Do you think calling her your fiancée will make a lick of difference to these people? Or do you plan on making that orphan trash an Edit?" he laughs, an incredulous chuckle escaping his lips. My patience has withered.

"Dorian, I wasn't going to do this here, out of respect for Constance, but fate seems to be forcing my hand. Give me access to your memories."

"You're mad. Those are private."

"Give them to me, or you'll be cut off. No regeneration, no upgrades—you'll be out in the cold."

"You can't do that!" he protests.

"Watch me," I say, unfalteringly.

"You'll lose the Atacama basin rights, you know this."

"I'm sure I'll figure it out." His eyes search my face, checking my sincerity. I can see the minute he surrenders, his eyes dim, and looks down. I connect to his interface and I begin searching through his memory log. A barrage of images floods me of women being mutilated, burnt, and stabbed. I see Beth crying begging for mercy, I see a girl named Cindy biting his finger off. I replaced that finger for him, he told me he lost it in an accident. Each one fought hard until they didn't. Until the fight left them and that's when he would kill them.

· · ·

SUDDENLY I'M BACK in my body, I didn't sever the connection. Dorian is spitting up blood, with a knife sticking out of his neck. A spurt of blood sprays out of his neck and hits me in the chest. He drops to his knees and I see Zoriya standing behind him, a determined glint in her eyes as she watches him fall. I quickly grab the knife from his neck and push Zoriya away. A group of partygoers enter the hallway and stop their chatter when they encounter the scene. I'm standing over Dorian bleeding out on the floor with a knife in my hand. One girl screams and a large crowd quickly follows them into the hallway. I wipe at my chin, his crimson blood speckling my neck and chin. I look at the blood and silently thank the universe he sprayed me with it when he died. Otherwise, there would be no way I could save Zori. It's one thing for an Edit to kill another Edit. As a human, viewed as a toy, she would be ostracized, and they would demand her death. Edits see their lives as more valuable because they can potentially live forever, barring accidents or murder. Disease and age are not fears, but we are still human enough to be susceptible to violent death. Constance pushes through the crowd and stops when she sees me.

"Magnus, what have you done?" she asks shocked.

"Justice," I say loudly so everyone can hear me admit guilt. No one is even looking at Zoriya, who is standing by the wall, her blood-soaked hand in her skirts. I want her to go to the bathroom and wash her hand. I put my hand behind my back momentarily, keeping my face passive as I look at the crowd. She quickly understands and puts her hand behind her back. Thankfully she is cooperating.

"Explain this," Constance says, and the crowd murmurs in agreement.

"He gave me access to his memory logs. He has murdered countless girls," I tell them, and they all look at his corpse.

"Do you have evidence?" one of them asks.

"Yes, if you all allow a connection, I can show you his memories," I offer.

· · ·

MY INTERFACE SHOWS several connections being opened, to receive only. I send them the images, and they flood through the ballroom of Edits, a wave of information. The feed stops, and some Edits throw up while others look white as sheets. There are a few who look unperturbed, and I make a mental note to check on their activities. A vote goes up to see if they should convict me of a crime. I wait for the results; they are a resounding no. No one wants justice for Dorian.

"Someone have this cleaned up," Constance says and ushers me and Zoriya out of the hallway, upstairs toward the apartments. She leads us into a bathroom in one of her guest apartments. I take Zori's hand and quickly wash off the blood. Blood flows into the porcelain sink, disappearing down the drain.

"Why did you do it?" I ask her quietly. Constance said she would get us some spare clothing but she could be right outside.

"It needed to be done," she answers flatly. She isn't rattled or shaking. I'm worried I've destroyed my sweet Spark. She wouldn't be here if not for me. She would be in a Unit festering away, my mind argues. Still, she wouldn't be a killer.

"You didn't know if he was guilty or not." I point out and she looks up from the sink into my eyes through the mirror.

"Yes, I did. I've seen Beth's and Cinder's scars," she says adamantly. I sigh and scrub underneath her fingernails. "Why did you take the fall?" she asks me, I focus on cleaning the last of the blood off her dainty fingers. Her forever-stained digits.

"Because they would have killed you for killing one of their own," I answer truthfully.

"And that bothers you?" she asks, insecurity lacing her voice. I look back at her and turn to face her.

"I love you, of course, it bothers me." She wipes at my chin with a washcloth.

"This won't come off" She undoes my bowtie and I watch her, waiting and hoping she will look me in the eye. Why does she doubt my sincerity? I've always been clear about how I've felt about her. I should be the insecure one. She is the one who pushes me away at every opportunity. "What about Dalton?" she asks, focusing on my vest buttons.

"What about him? I thought I explained that to you."

"I just want to know if I'm just going to be another long line of lovers. Is it possible that you have a pattern?" she pushes off my jacket and it falls to the bathroom floor.

"I can't speak for the future, it's possible that in fifty years, a hundred years, or two hundred years from now, we won't feel this way anymore. I do know that I want you now. I love you." I breathe deeply, "I don't think I have a pattern, I've never wholly given myself to anyone, the way I want to give myself to you." My vest comes off next, she still isn't looking up at me. She undoes the buttons of my shirt, each one undone carefully.

"You assume that I'll be around in a hundred years, still convinced I'll choose eternal life?" she asks and pushes open my shirt, revealing my chest.

"No, just hoping," I say and she rubs her hands over my chest and pushes off the shirt, her fingers skate along my shoulders. I shudder from her touch. Even now, with all this heavy weight between us, I respond to her. She steps closer and I can feel her breath on my chest and she leans in and presses a delicate kiss onto my skin. I shudder, the crown of her head still has the tiara she put on with her gown. She does look like a ballerina, tonight, her blue gown a stunning complement to her eyes. The way the bodice hugs her body shows me all the things I'm not allowed to have. The way her skirt swishes and rubs against me as she walks, is a whisper of a touch, another painful reminder. I lift her chin to force her to look into my eyes. Is this kiss a surrender, a thanks, why gift me her affection? Her face is calm but her eyes glitter, with unshed tears.

"Spark," I whisper and I lower my head a breath away from her lips. I wait for her to pull away, feeling her hot air around my lips, drawing me in. She crosses the distance and her lips skate over mine. Our lips rub together, delicately gliding. Her tongue darts out and I lose my self-control and I lock on to her. She kisses me back, frenzied and desperate. She moans into my mouth and I pull her closer to me. The jewels on her dress scratch at my chest, scraping as she writhes on me. I pick her up by her thighs and put her on the counter. There are too many layers of skirt between me and her. When I push up her skirts her whole upper body gets enveloped in a cascade of skirts. I laugh and she laughs with me and pushes it off her face. I recapture her lips and glide my hands up her strong thighs. It's a tactile dream, touching her soft skin. I skate up to her apex and I discover she isn't wearing any underwear. I don't know why but I don't care. She fumbles with my pants zipper and when I glide through her labia she breaks our kiss to catch her breath.

"Magnus." she breathes out and I slide a finger inside of her. So soft and wet, so eager. Always so desperate for me. It's the only thing I know for sure, she might not love me enough to trust me, but she always wants me on her, in her.

"I need.." she says as I pump my finger in her sweet cunt.

"What do you need?" I ask and kiss the long column of her neck.

"Slap it, please?" she asks

"It?" I say licking her delicious neck tendon.

"Slap my pussy" she begs, my finger slides out of her and I bring my fingertips up to her clit. I give her a gentle slap.

She groans. "Slap it like you mean it," she demands and I chuckle and find her lips with mine. She kisses me eagerly and then I slap her pussy harder. She spreads her legs and whimpers as I rub her clit.

"Again, harder"

She's so wet, my fingers are sticky with her sweet juice. I slap her harder and she throws her head back moaning deeply.

"Yes." she chants, happily. I circle her clit and the soft tissue underneath and I can tell she is close to cumming. I want her to cum on my fingers, my cock, and on my face. All of them, I want to drown in her orgasms. She's so lovely when she cums for me. She is present and real and all her fears vanish. Her plump pussy seeks out my hand when I move it away to slap it again. I slap it two more times. "Don't stop," she begs and I slap her cunt until she cums, I squat down quickly to lick at her juices. My tongue in her folds, on her clit, she's delicious. Her skirt falls over my head while I suckle on her clit and she cums even harder on my face.

"Fuck….." is all I hear from her when she stops quivering. I lick her thighs, dragging my tongue through all of her saccharine liquid. She tugs at my hair, pulling me up to her face. She kisses me deeply and I pull my pulsating cock out of my underwear and I slide into her in with a quick shove. It's so filthy how she licks around my lips tasting herself. Her explosive moans fill up the bathroom as I pump into her tight hole. She pushes herself closer, her bodice and tulle scraping my skin. I fuck her deeply, each thrust pushing her further into the mirror. I pull at her hair, forcing her head up so I can look into her eyes as I fuck her. Her chignon starts to come loose as blonde tendrils escape.

"Do you like it when I fuck you hard?" I ask her and she nods her head and closes her eyes. I slow my tempo.

"If you want me to fuck you hard, keep your eyes on me." she opens them up and stares into me. I push into her faster and deeper, she keeps her eyes locked on mine, and her eyes flutter as she moans. I love the way her thick eyelashes struggle to stay open as I assault her wet cunt. She moans boisterously, cresting an orgasm. Her slick walls start to clamp down on my cock, and I feel my orgasm approaching. My muscles tighten, my balls draw up and I spray into her, my body demanding that I fill her to the brim. She stops looking at me, her breathing ragged, her head lulls to the side. Lost in a deep orgasm as my balls empty themselves. My forehead is plastered onto the mirror leaning over her when she speaks.

"I'll do it."

"What?" I ask, confused, still coming down from the pure joy of cumming inside her.

"I'll become an Edit," she says and I pull my head away from the mirror so I can see her face. Does she mean it, and why now, why after everything?

"You will?"

"Yes, but I have conditions. I want you to agree to fix Edit Society. I want the world to reopen. I want the people who must be punished to face justice. There is one thing you want more from me than sex, which is for me to live forever. I can't hold sex against you because I can't stop myself from wanting you. Even now, after I've come twice, I want you to fuck me again."

She sighs deeply and leans against the mirror "And I want Plymouth shut down, no more buying kids."

Chapter 37

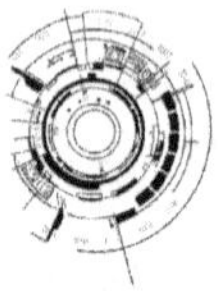

Magnus

I've been sitting, staring at my bedroom door half the night, a bourbon in my hand. It occurs to me that I'll have to get a comprehensive list of what she thinks I need to fix and damn me, I'll do it all. Even at the compromise of my goals, and my life's work. Most of her list are things I've already been trying to accomplish. Some are harder than others. Plymouth was something I started to protect the children who were adopted, ensuring they didn't leave there until they were adults.

ELARA COMES out in the middle of the night. She sits in front of me on the coffee table. She is so small, and I still can't wrap my head around the fact that there is an Edit child in front of me. I don't know who did it, but whoever is responsible for this travesty will pay.

"Dreaming of days where the sun is high and the winds are low," she says, and I stare at her honeyed eyes, trying to interpret her meaning.

"You can't express yourself properly, can you?" I say because everything that has come out of her mouth since she got into the hovercraft has been riddled. She nods in agreement, and I connect to her interface, saying hello in her head. She smiles and says hello back.

"I didn't know I could do this," she says in awe.

"There is probably much you don't know about what you are capable of."

"You can teach me, though."

"I can and I will."

"Good, it is nice to talk so easily." She sighs and smiles.

"Who did this to you, little one?"

"David and Juniper Windham," she says, and I sigh because that means someone else I'm responsible for did something awful.

"How? I'm the only one who has the technology to do this."

"Here, at WI."

"Show me."

"How?"

"Think of your memories and I'll see them."

"IT WILL BE LIKE THIS FOREVER," Juniper says as she pats me on the cheek. "Be a good girl and get into the chamber." The chamber is mostly glass, but I still feel an overwhelming panic as it slides shut over me. Kyla appears above me and smiles at me.

"Don't worry, it will be over soon," she says. She pushes a button, and I watch as all the needle tubes fill with liquids of various colors. As soon as it enters my body, I scream. My body is on fire, and I'm going to die.

. . .

SHE STOPS THE MEMORY ABRUPTLY, and my vision returns to the present. Her face is filled with tears. That experience is designed for adults who know what they are trading it for. I pull her into my lap and stroke her curly, coarse hair.

"Shh, I'm going to fix this," I promise. Kyla, all these years of trust and service, and she is making Edits behind my back. She is the only one I've ever entrusted with this process. It's fortunate my distrust in people means that she doesn't know the real formula. She must have squirreled away a vial. I wonder how much she got paid to betray me? I hope it was worth it.

"WHAT IS SHE SAYING? She doesn't make sense?" Juniper asks Kyla, who is standing next to her. They both look at me.

"Wistful winds ride on sorrowful dreams," I say, trying to tell them that I'm not okay.

"It seems that she has been damaged during the procedure," Kyla says, her mouth forming a thin line.

"Damaged? Can you fix her?" David asks, standing off to the side, his arms crossed.

"I don't know. I don't know what went wrong."

"This is what we get for paying an amateur, David. I told you we should have gone directly to Faust."

"Faust? Are you crazy? You don't know what a hardass he is. He would never have agreed to this."

"Well, she's trash now. We can't have a mistake in our home."

"We will have to try again, that's all," David says.

"Within the moon, there are hollows that need to be filled," I say, desperate to have them understand me. I'm trash? What does that mean?

"Can you deal with this?" David turns to Kyla, his question directed at her.

"What do you mean, deal?"

"Dispose of her, whatever you do with damaged products. Obviously."

"Are you implying that I should just kill her?"

"Of course, she's damaged. You said it yourself."

"You're mad. That's a little girl," Kyla says defensively.

"Forget it, we will take care of this," Juniper says and grabs me by the arm. Kyla purses her lips and watches us leave. She doesn't stop them. I look back at her, hoping she will reach out and tell David and Juniper to leave me here. I don't want to die.

ELARA'S MEMORY comes in clear, unexpectedly, and I'm crying with her when I return to the room.

"What did they do next?" I ask.

"They dropped me off in the woods, but Penigren's team found me," she says and takes her small hands to wipe at my face, drying my tears.

THE BASEMENT IS DARK; *there are other people in here crying and moaning.*

"Please just kill me," someone in the room repeats over and over. I huddle in my bed and cry my own tears. What is going to happen to me now? Is this where they send broken products? The lights turn on and blind me. When my eyes adjust, I look around the room. There are people in various states of deformity. They all look broken like me. Penigren walks into the room and squats down next to me. He pulls my arm out, and I whimper at his grip. He uses his free hand to draw blood from me.

"You might be my saving grace, little Edit."

"Please kill me," the person says again. I look over to see a woman who has a missing arm, her skin is mottled.

"Shut up," Penigren says and kicks her hed. "Useless, the lot of them. I'm told you don't make any sense." I'm too terrified to speak. "Come on, speak up!" he shouts at me, and I mutter out, "Dining in hell is a gift." His bone-chilling laugh fills the room. "Didn't quite make the cut, huh? I'm surprised. I didn't think Faust had this in him. I always knew his self-right-eousness was for show." He pulls on my hair, forcing my head up so I have

to look into his distorted eye. "You're going to help me fix this body. The rest of these experiments have been abject failures. The secret to how Faust makes Edits is inside you. I'll dig it out if I have to" I cry more, and he slaps me in the face. "Shut up, there is enough whining in here."

I DISCONNECT from her after that memory ends. I need a minute before she shows me anymore. Zori was right, I've created a world of misery. Elara paints a gruesome picture, her memories, unfortunately, are as vivid as if they were happening. One of the miracles of being an Edit, but in this case, it's torture.

"I couldn't be more sorry," I tell her and she leans on my shoulder and sinks into me. She sighs in relief. This child, this person, deserves better than this. I'll have to fix her, upgrade her, and then I'll give her the option to forget it all. Penigren has been obsessed with becoming an Edit. He failed the gene therapy himself, and without it, he can't regenerate. His body is rejecting all his implants, his foolish attempt at becoming bionic. It is the regeneration that allows all these changes, all the gene edits we've done. He will never unlock it, and in his delusional insanity, he is doing unspeakable things.

Sixteen years earlier

"Faust!" A man says my name, and I see him approach with an outstretched hand, preparing to shake my hand already from across the room. He has a pleasant face, big white teeth, and sparkling eyes. He looks to be about forty-five, a fledgling compared to me, but he looks weathered and experienced. He's the kind of man you put your faith in when it comes to serious matters. Competence is the first impression. He has an immaculately tailored suit, with a well-pressed pocket square, and I can't help but notice all the little details that were put into his appearance. His shoes are polished, his nails are clean and buffed, and his hair is neatly styled. He looks almost like what I could imagine I would have looked like if I had aged past twenty-five. There are notable differences—his hair is a darker blonde, his eyes are blue, and his nose isn't quite symmetrical. Yet, still, I could almost imagine it. Penigren made his fortune when he developed a way to instantly synthesize materials, rendering most transportation of goods obsolete. He asked me for a meeting, and after he donated a significant sum to my institutes, I felt compelled to comply. He finally reaches me, and I shake his hand firmly. He grips my hand in both hands, unfazed by my strong grip.

"Mr. Faust, what a pleasure. Truly an honor." He rambles enthusiastically, and I can't help but mildly enjoy how he strokes my ego. After all, he is no Edit, but he is a man to be reckoned with. In human circles, he's certainly on top.

"Memphis Penigren, the pleasure is mine," I say, and it relaxes him a bit as he takes the seat across from me.

"How can I help you, Memphis?" I ask, making the presumption that I can call him by his first name. He doesn't balk.

"Please call me Meph. It's what my friends call me. Mr. Faust, I like a man who gets straight to the point." He doesn't disrespectfully try to use my first name, passing my first test. He pauses briefly and steeples his fingers that hang loosely between his legs. He looks at his hands and then back at me. He doesn't balk at eye contact, something that many humans do—my eyes can be unsettling to some.

"I'm interested in immortality," he says matter-of-factly. I'm not surprised; when a wealthy man donates money and asks to meet me, this is usually the route. This is how they get my attention.

"What makes you think that you would be a good fit for eternal life?" I ask him, and he doesn't look surprised by my question. He looks prepared for it.

"Two reasons: One, I have the means; and second, I believe

the two of us could do great things together."

"Oh?"

"Yes, I have followed your work the entirety of my life. I admit, even as a boy, I was enamored by you. You've truly changed the course of humanity. You are, in essence, my idol. I don't claim to be your equal, Mr. Faust, but I've done a fair amount of great work myself. I think if I were given a chance to live as long as you, I'd be an asset to humanity. Perhaps I too could shift the course of humanity and further the cause of good."

"I'm aware of your contributions," I say, not wanting to diminish his value. But years of good men turning into bad Edits has put me on high alert. Every Edit that exists believed they would somehow be a force for good—at least that's the story they told me.

"But this is a tale as old as time. There hasn't been a man or woman who once sat in front of me who hasn't claimed the same thing. But ultimately, greed has been the underlying factor. I've created some very disappointing Edits, and it is much to my regret. As such, I'm not able to offer you immortality." His disappointment is palpable, perhaps even shocking to him. Maybe he thought he would come in here, pay me a king's ransom, and walk directly into a regeneration chamber. He is visibly surprised, and he seems to be at a loss for words. But he didn't get to where he is by being timid.

"I admit I'm disappointed. If there was anything I could do to change your mind, I'd do it. I respect you too much to push the issue. If becoming an Edit is not on the table, perhaps we could still work together. It would fulfill a lifelong dream of mine." I concede it's an intriguing offer. Memphis Penigren is considered a genius and an innovator—all qualities I value as a man of science.

"If a project comes to mind, you can send a proposal to WI, and we will review it. I'd be happy to collaborate on something in the future." As it turns out, he worked on several intriguing projects. The first one was a noble cause: developing an immunity booster for the human genome. I had toyed with the idea in my lab, but Meph had spent a fortune developing something that a typical human genome could handle. We combined our knowledge and resources to offer genetic modifications to embryos. A fully developed fetus wouldn't adapt accordingly, so it was vital to catch the pregnancies early. Many parents were hesitant, which our teams found frustrating. Still, the project was a success. The newly born babies had strengthened immunity. I didn't fully appreciate at the time how letting Memphis into my lab would lead to his current state. Scientific espionage, stealing enough data to nearly kill himself through failed upgrades and gene alterations. He had just enough information to attempt the process, but not enough to do it right.

Chapter 38

When you patch something with scavenged parts it will never be whole.

-The Journal of Kira, Book 7, page 38

Kira

When I step out into the living room, preparing to go check on Elara, I find Faust on the couch cradling Elara. They are both crying. Faust looks up at me with his tear-stained face.

"What happened?" I ask and I squat down in front of them. "Elara are you okay?"

"Sunrise bathes the world in rainbows," she says and I wipe a tear from her cheek and look at Faust for explanation.

"She's told me what happened to her," Faust tells me, his green eyes glistening.

"How?" he points to his head.

"Our interface," he tells me and Elara gets up from his lap and hugs me. I hug her small frame, and I sigh. I know it must be quite the story if Magnus is crying.

"How bad is it?" I ask him.

"Bad," he admits. "I can fix her, she will talk normally and if she wants it I will remove her memories, so she can start over."

"And the people who did this to her?"

"They will be punished," he says. Relief washes over me. I knew Magnus wasn't evil.

"We will do it together," I say and I grab his hand, and he squeezes it. His face turns neutral and tears stop. He's adjusted his emotions.

"We will do it together," he agrees.

"Three in tow is more to show," Elara says releasing me from the hug and looking between us.

"Three is more." I agree. Faust smiles broadly at her.

"Three." he agrees.

ELARA DOESN'T SLEEP, just like all Edits, but she goes back into her room to read, a pile of books that she took from WI's library stacked in a pile on the floor. When she escaped the basement, she found solace in the books from the bookstore in Portland. Which is why she found me there, I was encroaching on her space.

"If you need something, you can always come and tell me," I remind her and I stroke her coarse curls. They are up in pigtails, with pink ribbons tied neatly.

"I know," she says and she climbs into an overstuffed white chair by the large windows that face the incredible forest outside. I leave her to her books and I go back into the living room. Magnus is waiting there with two drinks, one for me.

"Spark, we need to talk about your demands."

"Ok, which demand?" I ask and I take the bourbon he hands and I sit on the sofa, my feet stretched on the sofa, and I lean back and lean my head on the armrest. He sits down next to me and he takes my legs and puts them over his lap. He rests his arm on the back of the sofa and cradles his drink with his other hand.

"All of them," he answers before taking a sip of his drink. "There are things you have to understand and consider."

"Like what?"

"You have to understand that while the humans continue to be immunologically compromised we can't open up the walls. The human-to-human contact would reinfect them and their already small numbers would dwindle further. "

"Okay, but we still have to try to fix it. How do Edits avoid the infections?"

"They have superior immune systems through gene editing."

"So can't we just edit everyone?"

"We can't, because the gene editing only works if you go through regeneration, we can't regenerate everyone. Immortality only works in small numbers."

"But you could regenerate people and then just never regenerate them again."

"Maybe, but the resources and time needed for that would require decades of support, maybe even a century. You're talking about three hundred million people."

"Ok, so let's do that then, make it happen, even if it's a hundred years from now."

"We can look into the feasibility." he concedes. "Now, you mentioned fixing Edit Society and closing Plymouth. Closing Plymouth would be a mistake." I take a long drag of my bourbon, it burns down my throat. This is disgusting, why anyone drinks bourbon is beyond me. I put it down on the coffee table.

"You want me to become an Edit, that's the deal."

"Hear me out." he requests and I gesture for him to continue, but my lips press into a thin line.

"I started Plymouth to protect the adopted children, ensuring that they wouldn't leave before they became adults. Before there were a lot more situations like Elara. No one succeeded in making a child Edit before but they were crazy about having children to groom. Some of them anyway. If we close the school they lose the smallest modicum of protection I've wanted to provide them. It was through great campaigning and effort that Constance and I were able to get approval from the majority of Edits." he finishes the rest of his drink and puts it on the coffee table next to mine. He picks up my feet and starts to massage them.

"Well, it's clearly not good enough, look at what Dorian did, look at what happened to Elara."

"You're right. I had hoped it would be enough, but that's not the case. Instead of shutting down Plymouth—which, by the way, provides a haven for orphans and offers them a very good education—I suggest we come up with a different solution." He's right, it's not enough, and maybe it's even worse. If there is no oversight they could just pick children off the street, without adopting them. They could do whatever they wanted. I bet some are already doing that. Just kidnapping whatever little human they want.

"Then do what you did with Dorian," I say. He stops rubbing my feet and looks over at me, his expression betraying his lingering thoughts about me being a murderer. He's waiting for me to snap, to break, to cry.

"What do you mean, what I did?" he asks, and I wonder if he thinks I'm also pinning the murder on him.

"Scan their memories."

"I can't do that; it would violate their contracts."

"Change the contracts."

"That's a tall order. Edits are sticklers for contracts, and they tend to be ironclad. One doesn't become an Edit without being a shark. They're heavy hitters and you have to contend with them."

"You can do whatever you want. Negotiate or stop offering them their upgrades, and their precious immortality." His jaw tightens and he looks away, the muscle in his jaw ticking. He doesn't like that suggestion.

"They could delete their memories if they knew I was going to scan them," he says, trying to find fault with my solution.

"Randomize them. If they don't know the scans are coming, they won't delete anything."

"They could do something naughty and then delete it right away."

"Is that what you would do? If you got off on suffering and control, would you delete them? If you wanted to remember how I came on your cock, would you delete it?" I ask him, and he looks over sharply at me.

"No, I wouldn't," he agrees. It's always a possibility that someone could do that, but it would increase the chances that they would behave themselves. No system is perfect, but it's a start.

"Alright, Spark, you win. I'll try. Restructuring Edit society will take time, they don't like to be told what to do."

"Well, neither do their human slaves." I counter and he sighs.

"How do you feel," he asks, changing the subject. "About what you did?" I expected to feel some kind of guilt for killing Dorian Hayes, a stain on my already tattered soul. But the truth is, I don't. Evil is not just committing acts of horror but also standing aside and doing nothing. My moral conviction wouldn't allow such a wraith to continue his reign of terror. So I've decided to live with it, accept it. I am not pure, but no one is. Purity can also be seen as naivety, and I refuse to be ignorant. I want to look into the darkness and see all the ghouls; I need to know they are there because that's the only way I know how to cope. I can't fight against evil if I close my eyes.

"I'm fine with it," I say, but I can see on his face he doesn't believe me.

"It's just the shock," he concludes.

"No, it's not. I don't feel shocked. Maybe a little surprised that I have the capability of killing someone. I don't think anyone knows exactly what they are capable of until faced with the realities of a situation. But I'm okay with it. I killed him, and I'm proud that I could end his reign of terror. I'm glad I could avenge Beth and all the girls he hurt. Plus, if even Edits felt his death was merited, then I believe that my actions were just."

"Even accidental death, and killing with justice, hurts us. It does something to our inner life; it alters us. I don't disagree that he was a blight, but I'm worried you're not giving this the credence it deserves. You don't have to decide how you feel about it now, but if you ever feel like you can't cope, or if you're confused, or if it feels like it's changed you, I'm here. I can listen to you because I know what taking a life feels like. It never sits right—it festers like an open wound."

"Okay," I say, taking his hand and kissing it. Maybe he is right—it's all very new—but right now, I can live with it. "Thank you." His eyes soften, and he leans into my hand.

"For what?" he asks, his hot breath tickling my fingers.

"For believing me, for scanning him, for taking the fall, for loving me," I say. He pulls me closer to him, so now I'm on his lap. He nuzzles his nose into my neck and breathes me in. "You've patched a piece of my tattered soul. I love you, Magnus Faust," I tell him. He pulls away and looks at me, searching my face, maybe looking for sincerity. Maybe trying to understand my meaning.

"I love you too," he says after a moment. "Your soul isn't tattered. It's the people who tried to take pieces of you that are tattered." His words settle something inside me, an unfolding of truth. I've never been broken, just surrounded by broken people who wanted to take pieces of me to repair their own broken parts. I decide that I won't let their venom turn me poisonous. I kiss Magnus with all of me and I realize that even though he isn't perfect we all exist in a moral gray place. Because the world is gray and if we lie to ourselves we will never be able to navigate the dark spaces effectively to make changes.

Epilogue

Kira

2 years later

We are celebrating a second anniversary. I'm standing on the balcony looking out at the sunset. Magnus hands me a glass of champagne and orange juice to Elara.

"Thanks, Dad," she says. He smiles at her and pats her on the cheek.

After we adopted Elara. Magnus was able to fix the damage caused to her by forcing her to become an Edit before her body had fully matured. She isn't going to go through regeneration again, at least until she is older. Her body will be allowed to age as she was intended. It turns out that when Elara went through the regeneration chamber, she was fourteen years old, and they wanted her to stay a little girl. They had lost their own child at the age of seven and had become obsessed with replacing her. They both went to prison. Elara's memories were shared through the Edit community, and they were convicted. They are serving a life sentence and will no longer receive regeneration. They still have their bionic upgrades, but Magnus has restricted their access, so they can't communicate with the outside world. Elara chose to keep all her memories. She said she wants to know what the world is really like.

"I want to know the bad, so I can appreciate all the good," she told us and I admire her wisdom.

KYLA WENT TO PRISON TOO. After thirty years of running WI for Magnus, she lost everything. She was bitter about not becoming an Edit, hoping to become rich enough to pay Magnus for the upgrade. Sadly, he had already planned on offering it to her for her years of service. She lost all her wealth and her chance at immortality. Plymouth is still standing, but Magnus is trying to negotiate a new system with the other Edits. He is walking a delicate balance, trying to keep the earth free from destruction and respecting humanity's autonomy. I am not an Edit, but someday, when I feel ready, I'll do it.

"I love you," I whisper to Magnus after he nuzzles his nose into my neck. "Really and truly."

"I love you too," he says, and I know it's true. More than two years together have proven it to me. He works tirelessly to show me his love, to make the world better, to reform Edit society. Part of my ego wants it all to be for me, but the truth is that Magnus was always after a better world. He used humanity's confinement as a chance to restore habitats, old growth forests, he cleaned up the ocean, and he let the ozone recover. The world once on the brink, is thriving, ready to give humanity another chance. Hopefully this time we will take better care of it because we are all bound by it.

"Cheers," Magnus says, clinking his champagne against mine. I take a sip, enjoying the fizzy feeling on my tongue.

Epilogue 2

Magnus

The black stage lights up with a single spotlight, and we see a folded figure in white on the stage. Her dance begins a poignant, delicate thing. Her movements are graceful and strong. Kira's debut as a prima ballerina is unfolding with a hushed audience. I see some people leaning forward in their seats, watching her with rapt attention. She was truly made to dance. She settled on Kira, not Zoriya. She said the name she was given at birth was her name, and even though her mother wasn't the person she wanted her to be, it was still who she was. She flits across the stage, the music's sorrowful melody becoming more lively, and I watch as she spins and twirls with such practiced ease. When I built the auditorium in the Edit city I did it thinking no one would come, but it would still give Kira a chance to dance on a real stage. Then the invitations went out and thanks to Constance every Edit and their human companions RSVP'd. Kira helps me in the lab sometimes when she has free time. Her big brain isn't going to waste. She is still refusing to marry me or become an Edit. Stubborn as she is.

. . .

PENIGREN IS STILL on the loose. We went back to raid Portland, but when we got there, the rebels were gone, and the bunkers were empty. One day, we will find him and punish him. Until then, we keep our ears to the ground, searching all the empty cities for any trace of them.

THE BALLET COMES to an end and she gets a standing ovation, and three curtain calls. I leave my box and quickly make my way to her dressing room. She comes in glistening from sweat, her face has a deep coat of makeup on, and glitter coats her cheeks and eyelids. She stops when she sees her dressing room, it's covered in flowers. She laughs happily and leaps into my arms.

"Magnus, you'll never stop, will you?" she asks, and it's an admonishment as much as it's a hope. A hope that I will never stop loving her.

"Never," I tell her, and I mean it more deeply than anyone could, with eternity ahead of us.

"Never." She exhales, and she kisses me with a sweetness that takes my breath away.

I used to believe that my destiny was to live forever so I could be the caretaker of the planet, but now I know that I was meant to live forever so that I could find Kira. She is the destiny of my heart.

Authors Notes

Dear Reader,

I hope you enjoyed Kira and Faust's story. Writing this book has been an immense labor of love, and I'm grateful for your support and readership. While Kira and Faust's story is concluded, if you're wondering what happens to Penigren and the rebels, my new WIP is another standalone book to continue their story, titled "The Citadel."

To stay updated on release dates and exclusive content, visit my website www.rosaliestevens.com and follow me on Instagram @rosaliestevens_author

Thank you for reading!

Warm regards,
    Rosalie Stevens

About the Author

Rosalie Stevens is an emerging author of romance novels. *Edits* is Rosalie's debut novel. Originally from Sweden, she now lives in California with her husband and two daughters. Rosalie has been passionate about writing since childhood and draws inspiration from her diverse experiences. When she is not writing, she enjoys spending quality time with her family.

Shining a Light on Human Trafficking

Human trafficking is an abhorrent crime that continues to plague our modern world, and its scale is staggering. Despite the abolition of legal slavery over a century ago, we are now faced with a grim reality: there are more slaves today than at any other point in history. It is estimated that there are about 40 million slaves at the time of this publication. Millions of men, women, and children are exploited through forced labor, sexual slavery, and coercion, trapped in circumstances from which they cannot escape.

This global crisis affects every country, and it manifests in countless ways—from young girls trafficked for prostitution to laborers forced to work in brutal conditions for little or no pay. Traffickers prey on the vulnerable, manipulating and deceiving them with promises of a better life, only to subject them to unimaginable horrors.

Human trafficking is a multifaceted problem that thrives on secrecy, corruption, and complacency. It is perpetuated by a complex network of individuals and organizations that profit from the misery of others. The impact on victims is devastating, leaving them physically and emotionally scarred, stripped of their dignity, and often devoid of hope.

The fight against human trafficking requires a concerted global effort. It demands stringent laws and effective enforcement, comprehensive support for survivors, and relentless public awareness campaigns. We must also address the root causes, such as poverty, lack of education, and gender inequality, that make individuals susceptible to traffickers.

It is imperative that we, as a society, recognize the severity of this issue and take action. Each of us has a role to play, whether by supporting organizations that combat trafficking, advocating for stronger policies, or simply educating ourselves and others about the signs of trafficking. By shining a light on this dark reality, we can work towards a world where no one lives in fear of being bought and sold.

Human trafficking is not a relic of the past; it is a pressing and urgent issue that demands our immediate attention and action. The fight to end modern slavery is far from over, and it is a battle we must all commit to winning.

Resources for Combating Human Trafficking

If you want to learn more about human trafficking or find ways to help, consider reaching out to these reputable organizations:

1. **Polaris**
   • Website: polarisproject.org
   • Polaris operates the U.S. National Human Trafficking Hotline and provides a range of services to victims and survivors.
2. **International Labour Organization (ILO)**
   • Website: ilo.org
   • The ILO works globally to combat forced labor, child labor, and human trafficking through research, advocacy, and on-the-ground programs.
3. **Walk Free Foundation**

- Website: walkfree.org
- The Walk Free Foundation produces the Global Slavery Index and works to end modern slavery through research, advocacy, and partnerships.

4. **UNICEF**

- Website: unicef.org
- UNICEF works to protect children from exploitation and trafficking through various programs and initiatives worldwide.

5. **Anti-Slavery International**

- Website: antislavery.org
- The world's oldest international human rights organization, focusing on eliminating all forms of slavery around the world.

6. **Free the Slaves**

- Website: freetheslaves.net
- Free the Slaves works to liberate people from slavery and help them rebuild their lives.

7. **International Justice Mission (IJM)**

- Website: ijm.org
- IJM works to rescue victims, bring criminals to justice, restore survivors, and strengthen justice systems.

8. **ECPAT International**

- Website: ecpat.org
- ECPAT is a global network dedicated to ending the commercial sexual exploitation of children, including trafficking.

9. **Thorn**

- Website: thorn.org
- Thorn builds technology to defend children from sexual abuse and trafficking.

10. **Not For Sale**

- Website: notforsalecampaign.org
- Not For Sale works to protect people and communities around the world from human trafficking and modern slavery.

These organizations offer various ways to get involved, whether through donations, volunteering, advocacy, or education.

www.ingramcontent.com/pod-product-compliance
Lightning Source LLC
Chambersburg PA
CBHW070611300726
48975CB00006B/1788